# The Epic of God

# The Epic of God

## Louis McCall

# The Epic of God

© Louis McCall 2017

Published by
Lighthouse Christian Publishing
SAN 257-4330
5531 Dufferin Drive
Savage, Minnesota, 55378
United States of America

www.lighthousechristianpublishing.com

## Foreword

Have you ever wondered what was in God's mind before creation? Have you ever thought of what it would be like after Christ's return? God has a story, an epic of His very own. Before everything that was created, before there were towering mountains and beaming trees, before there were animals that roamed and grazed, and before man breathed his first breath, there was God.

Genesis 1:1 states that in the beginning God created the heavens and the earth. What was the beginning like? God, who is the perfect radiance of love and unity who communes within Himself in Father, Spirit, and Son chose out of his infinite power and unending creativity to express himself in the spiritual and in the physical order through the things that he has fashioned. It is this God, who was shrouded in deep silence and mystery, that has revealed himself to his creation. God, out of his deep love, chose to go on a journey of epic proportions. This all seeing, all powerful God would choose to undergo pain, hurt, suffering, and victory!

Louis McCall wonderfully illustrates God's Epic. God's story, his epic is the story of our own. It's the story that involves all of creation! The Epic of God, although fictitious, caries the truth of the heart of God for all of us and answers questions of what things could have been like from the beginning of time before creation all the way to the very end of time itself.

Evangelist Daniel Kolenda, President
Christ for all Nations

# Contents

Chapter 1 The Beginning .................................................... 1

Chapter 2 Creation of the Universe.......................................... 6

Chapter 3 The Mystery of Iniquity............................................ 7

Chapter 4 War in Heaven and Chaos........................................ 13

Chapter 5 Earth Ruined and Put on Ice .................................. 18

Chapter 6 The Re-Creation .................................................... 20

Chapter 7 The Fall of Man, the Comeback of Satan, and the
Promise of a Messiah .............................................. 24

Chapter 8 Plots to Block Messiah .......................................... 29

Chapter 9 The Flood .............................................................. 34

Chapter 10 The Rise of False Gods ........................................ 38

Chapter 11 The Line of the Messiah........................................ 41

Chapter 12 The Exodus, the Law, and 40 Years in the
Wilderness.......................................................... 56

Chapter 13 Taking the Promised Land .................................. 83

Chapter 14 The Rise of David……………………………………………100

Chapter 15 Temple Worship ................................................ 120

Chapter 16 Breaking God's Heart........................................ 123

Chapter 17 Taken Captive .................................................. 142

Chapter 18 Enter Messiah, the Redeemer and Savior ......... 162

Chapter 19 The Quiet Years .................................................. 170

Chapter 20 The Ministry of Jesus ......................................... 175

Chapter 21 The Passion of Christ ......................................... 220

Chapter 22 The Battle in Hell and the Resurrection............. 241

Chapter 23 The Mission Continues and Broadens .............. 255

Chapter 24 The Battle for Hearts and Minds ....................... 270

Chapter 25 Darkness and Light In Conflict Over Two Millennia
.................................................................................................. 285

Chapter 26 The False Christ and the End of the Age............ 295

Chapter 27 Jesus the Messiah Returns ................................. 317

Chapter 28 One Family and a Glorious Bride ....................... 323

Endorsements................................................................331

## Acknowledgements

*The King James Version of the Holy Bible served as the source book for this fictional account. Although fictional, this book is based on what is recorded in the Bible. Where dialogue is taken from the Bible, it was paraphrased by the author into modern colloquial English. Other dialogue comes from the artistic license of the author.*

# Chapter 1 The Beginning

*In the beginning was the Word, and the Word was with God, and the Word was God. The same was in the beginning with God. All things were made by him; and without him was not anything made that was made. John 1:1-3*
This is the epic of God. Long ago, before there ever was time or any other thing, whether spirit or of physical matter, there was God.[1] God was, is, and always will be. God is from the eternal past through the eternal future. God is spirit and He is light. My name is Benelroi. I am a watcher. I was not there from the beginning because I was created later. Although I was not there from the beginning, God caused me to have knowledge and understanding of things from the beginning along with my fellow watchers.

At one point, like a cell dividing, from the great formless light that is God, a plasma-like stream of His

---

[1] Additional scriptures are presented here for context.

I was set up from everlasting, from the beginning, or ever the earth was. Proverbs 8:23

Who coverest thyself with light as with a garment: who stretchest out the heavens like a curtain: Who layeth the beams of his chambers in the waters: who maketh the clouds his chariot: who walketh upon the wings of the wind: Who maketh his angels spirits; his ministers a flaming fire. Psalm 104:2-4

glorious essence poured out until the person of the Son, who was there all the time, stood next to the Father. Fiercely beautiful, the Son phased into and out of the Father at will, for He is the same God, the same essence. Just as the Son was brought forth, so too was God the Holy Spirit. A plasma-like flow from the Father resulted in another light, like the Father. That light, the Holy Spirit, was the same as with the Father and the Son. That light, as with the Son, also phased into and out of the Father without adding too or diminishing from the Father.

The Holy Spirt, brighter than any arc welder's light, divided Himself into seven spirit lights of equal brightness. These began to circle slowly around the Father and the Son. Finally, rising up, the seven spirit lights of the Holy Spirit, still circling, came to rest upon the magnificent head of the Son. They formed, as it were, a crown of light. Such was the unity of the Godhead. There was and is and always will be one God, but He expressed Himself in these different ways and delighted in His own self-sufficient company.

**The Epic Begins with a Decision**

No one, not even me or my fellow watchers, knows how long it was before He decided to create. As one might talk to oneself, God, Elohim, the plural God of Father, Son, and Holy Spirit, decided He would make Himself a family for intimate relationship on whom He would pour out His love and goodness. God desired a family that would return His love because it wanted to do so. God and His family were to be in the love of an intimate relationship.

Knowing the end from the beginning, this all-knowing God, like a cosmic supreme master chess player, surveyed the innumerable combinations, permutations, and outcomes that would be the consequence of creating beings that would be given the power of choice. He saw that some of those beings would exercise that choice to reject His love and do works at variance with His will and nature. It would mean allowing, for a time, a great dissonance, a rebellion. That rebellion would continue until at great price on His part, those who would truly love Him would be pardoned, made perfect, and be united with Him forever. The Son thought, *This will be painful. I abhor the thought of making space for free will exercised by created beings only to see them act contrary to the perfect will of the Godhead. However, I see that what lies beyond that space will certainly make it worth what would have to be endured.*

Finally, the Son said, "I will become the price."

The Father and the Holy Spirit each said in unison, "I will go with You." Thus began the epic of God. The God who would create a family of diverse, but perfect members in perfect circumstances, and then allow members of that family to reject His love. Those that would choose to truly love Him would be made part of the eternal family of God to enjoy life and love with Him forever. God would allow His loving heart to be wounded by rejection, rebellion, and even the failures of those that, though they would love Him, would still act imperfectly.

The first thing God created was the realm of the spirit. He created the heaven of the spiritual dimension that the angel beings would inhabit. Then he created those angelic beings, including me and other watchers like me. The angels were innumerable. There was only this one-time creation of angels. Angels could not reproduce. Enough angels were created to fulfill all the need there would be for them in the eternal future.

The angels were asexual, androgynous beings. They had different appearances depending upon their functions. Some were large and some very small. Some were human-like in their appearance, but had wings. Some angels appeared as balls of light. There were seraphim and cherubim. There were four special beings that surrounded the throne of God crying out in unison, holy, holy, holy, without end. Their appearance was diverse from all of the others and diverse from each other. The watcher angels like me had many eyes. We have eyes in front of us, eyes behind us, eyes all over our bald heads, and eyes in our hands. Some angels were translucent as if they were made from crystals with sharp facets. Some angels had the appearance of controlled blue and white flames of fire. There were angels expert in musical instruments. There were angels whose specialty was singing and praising God. There was the unique angel of the Lord, who was a sort of aide de camp for the Godhead.

There were three Archangels. These three Lucifer, Michael, and Gabriel, were the highest level of angelic beings and each stood in the presence of God. Lucifer was considered the most beautiful of the angels. His chest was made of glistening precious stones and reflected the light that came from within him. He was an amazing light show all by himself. His voice was like a fine instrument. When he spoke or sang or otherwise made music, rays of colored light would beam from his jeweled chest. Lucifer was the chief musician of heaven. Lucifer led the angels in singing praises to God. Moreover, Lucifer hovered above the presence of God with his angel wings out spread. The glory of Lucifer's own light streaming from his gem encrusted chest, the reflection of the glory of God upon him, and the reflection of the emerald rainbow that surrounded the throne of God magnified the effect of this celestial light show.

The three Archangels Lucifer, Michael, and Gabriel, were close to each other and close to God. When Michael and Gabriel were conferring together, Lucifer loved to swoop in like a swift streak of light and pull up suddenly to join in and continue the conversation.

# Chapter 2 Creation of the Universe

*Through faith we understand that the worlds were framed by the word of God, so that things which are seen were not made of things which do appear. Hebrews 11:3*

After a very long interlude, God called the angels together. He said, "Children, watch this." Then he proceeded to create the physical universe. As His word went forth, there was an explosion of power. His presence filled the void that opened up beyond Heaven. Matter was created. As if painting on a celestial canvas, God spread the new heavens through the universe of physical things.

God told the angels, that he was creating a new dimension of the physical. He said, "I created you as spirits, and you live in a spiritual dimension. This new dimension of the physical is where all matter will be contained. It is a place where I will later make my greatest creation."

Like children at a fireworks show the angels watched in awe as God created the physical universe. The angels would ooh and ah saying, "How great is God our father!" "This new dimension of the physical heavens itself declares His great glory."

The physical heavens were a beautiful sight. Everything was perfect, beautiful and balanced. For the time being, there was no other intelligent life or creatures of any kind in that physical universe. Neither was it the dwelling place of angels. The angels wondered what was next. What was the purpose of this massive physical universe?

# Chapter 3 The Mystery of Iniquity

*Thou hast been in Eden the garden of God; every precious stone was thy covering, the sardius, topaz, and the diamond, the beryl, the onyx, and the jasper, the sapphire, the emerald, and the carbuncle, and gold: the workmanship of thy tabrets and of thy pipes was prepared in thee in the day that thou wast created. Thou art the anointed cherub that covereth; and I have set thee so: thou wast upon the holy mountain of God; thou hast walked up and down in the midst of the stones of fire. Thou wast perfect in thy ways from the day that thou wast created, till iniquity was found in thee. By the multitude of thy merchandise they have filled the midst of thee with violence, and thou hast sinned: therefore I will cast thee as profane out of the mountain of God: and I will destroy thee, O covering cherub, from the midst of the stones of fire. Ezekiel 28:13-16*

Of all the heavenly bodies in the massive physical universe created by God, He chose one, the earth, to populate with living things suited for the earth environment. Then he created intelligent beings to inhabit the earth. These beings were physical, not spiritual. That is when God called me and gave me my assignment as the principal watcher for the planet earth. I wasn't alone. Another senior watcher worked with me in this assignment. Other watchers were with us, but were told their individual assignments would be for a future time. Until that future time, the other watchers were to assist us two principal watchers with our duties of recording the happenings on earth and relaying that information to the Godhead. It is not that the Godhead didn't already know, but we were witnesses and kept the books on earth that were stored in Heaven.

God sent the Archangel Lucifer, one of the cherubim, to be the leader and custodian of the planet earth and its race of intelligent anthropomorphic beings.[2]

The earth beings were beautiful as well as intelligent. With their high intellects, and being under the oversight and assistance of Lucifer, these beings built great cities, inventions for travel, amusement, and for every need that they had. They knew no sickness, hunger, storms, war, or strife. Life for them was good. They lacked for nothing. They were in harmony with the plants and animals of their environment.

These physical earth beings existed before Adam and his race of humankind had their time on the earth. God was their king, Lucifer was His viceroy, and I watched and recorded the happenings on earth. All was well under the benevolent rule of Lucifer, until the change.

It was common for these pre-Adamic beings to marvel at the beauty of Lucifer. Initially, Lucifer would

---

[2] Additional scripture is presented here for context.
How art thou fallen from heaven, O Lucifer, son of the morning! How art thou cut down to the ground, which didst weaken the nations! For thou hast said in thine heart, I will ascend into heaven, I will exalt my throne above the stars of God: I will sit also upon the mount of the congregation, in the sides of the north: I will ascend above the heights of the clouds; I will be like the most High. Yet thou shalt be brought down to hell, to the sides of the pit. They that see thee shall narrowly look upon thee, and consider thee, saying, Is this the man that made the earth to tremble, that did shake kingdoms; That made the world as a wilderness, and destroyed the cities thereof; that opened not the house of his prisoners? Isaiah 14:12-17

remind them that he, like them, was created by God and that every good thing about him was a gift of God. Lucifer would lead those beings in praise of God, just as he had led the angels in Heaven. Being God's viceroy on the earth was not Lucifer's full-time assignment. He would step away from his oversight of the earth from time to time to return, beyond the stars of the universe, to move through the Heaven of God's throne and of the dimension of the spirit.

## The Birth of Iniquity

The change came gradually, and I faithfully recorded the change as it developed. As Lucifer presided over the affairs of the pre-Adamites, and they marveled at his great beauty, power, and intelligence, he began to enjoy the adulation. He thought, *I am beautiful, powerful, and possess an excellency of knowledge. I am as God to these beings.* Then he thought to himself, *But why stop here? I shall ascend to Heaven and make a place for myself above God.*

Lucifer hatched a rebellion designed to make him ruler of Heaven and earth. He began to seek the worship of the pre-Adamites. He taught them new songs that did not glorify God, but were about him and the pleasures he promised the pre-Adamites.

For their part, the pre-Adamites turned from God to Lucifer and the pleasures that he introduced to them. Over time, the paradise that had been known on earth changed. Strife began to appear among the pre-Adamites and between them and the other creatures. Eventually, that strife and division led to destructive wars and unrestrained desires for every kind of illicit pleasure.

I was disturbed by what I and the other watchers were witnessing. I returned to Heaven and presented myself in the throne room. I was full of awe and adoration every time I presented myself there. I prostrated myself before God in all of His glory until Gabriel or Michael told me to come closer to God's presence. The entire massive throne room was filled with the presence of God, but it was even stronger the closer one was allowed to come to the throne and He who was enthroned there. I reported on what we watchers were observing on earth. I knew it was not a surprise to the Godhead, since He knows everything, but it established the facts for the record books kept by the watchers. The Father said, "Well done Benelroi. Return now to earth and continue your duties as one of My watchers." This I did, but I wondered what He was thinking, because He said nothing specifically relating to the news I brought to Him.

As the change was taking place on the earth, Lucifer returned to Heaven. In Heaven he began to speak to the angels about a new order. At first he would woo them by saying, "If I were God, I would exalt you together with me. Why should you always remain at the level that you are now?"

Lucifer used his beauty and music to charm the undecided angels. The former leader of the heavenly chorus of praise to God began to introduce new music. It was music that was different from anything the angels had heard before. It was like hard rock anthems, it was syncopated. Lucifer's pristine trumpet voice, employing many grace notes and riffs fluttering through his voice, helped attract angels to his cause and they joined in his new song. At times, Lucifer led a bluesy call and response exalting himself and praising the new order that he promised to bring. Gradually, he drew a following to himself in which about a third of the angels of Heaven sided with his faction in open rebellion to the Godhead. Regretfully, the other principal watcher assigned to the earth was also carried away by Lucifer's promises. At that point, he and I stopped working together.

Thus Lucifer polluted Heaven with iniquity, the thing he fathered. In this he saw himself as a creator like God, because iniquity did not come from God. Lucifer also told lies to win adherents. In this, Lucifer was the creator or father of lies too.

The loyal watcher angels joined me and came before God as I again informed Him of what was happening on earth and we included our observations of what was also happening in Heaven. God already knew what we the watchers reported, but the Eternal One was silent. The Archangels Michael and Gabriel pleaded with God to do something to put Lucifer in check. Again, God was silent. Michael implored the Lord of the angel armies, the Son, to come forth to lead the loyalists in pushing Lucifer and his partisans from Heaven. Yet, God remained silent. The Son and Holy Spirit God remained hidden in God. Although He did not speak to us angels at the time, God thought, *"My family of created beings is divided. I am bitterly disappointed by this growing rebellion and with the loss of those I have loved. Judgment must come. My holiness requires judgment to make things right. After the rebellion and iniquity have run their courses, I will make all things new and the end will be better than the beginning."*

Lucifer was aware of the appeals of the watchers and of his fellow Archangels Michael and Gabriel to get God to actively oppose him. Lucifer took the silence of

God to the pleadings of those who would oppose him as weakness. He thought, *Heaven and the throne are mine for the taking!* Lucifer fired up his followers with his assessment and predicted that the new order would soon come into being. In this silence of God, the angels continued to align themselves either with God, as loyalists, or with Lucifer, as rebels. There was no middle ground.

Back on earth, things went from bad to worse as the blessing of God was withdrawn from the pre-Adamic rebels. Between the ravages of nature gone awry and the ravages of the pre-Adamic beings on each other, the earth and the pre-Adamic civilization with its great cities was destroyed. The spirits of those fallen beings, after their physical bodies perished, became demon spirits craving to be back in physical bodies. As demons, they still had the desires that they had in their physical bodies, but no longer had the bodies to act out those desires.

The completion of this destructive process, initiated by the iniquity Lucifer spawned, reached its apex just after Lucifer's rebellion in Heaven reached its high water mark.

# Chapter 4 War in Heaven and Chaos

*And there was war in heaven: Michael and his angels fought against the dragon; and the dragon fought and his angels, And prevailed not; neither was their place found any more in heaven. And the great dragon was cast out, that old serpent, called the Devil, and Satan, which deceiveth the whole world: he was cast out into the earth, and his angels were cast out with him. Revelation 12:7-9*

The beauty, peace, and harmony of Heaven were disrupted to the point that Michael could stand it no more. Coming before God with Gabriel, Michael said, "My Lord and God, I love You and worship You. I am jealous for You. I don't understand why You remain silent at this time. I will just say this, with Your permission; I will rally the angels that love You and cast Lucifer and his angels from heaven. If you say nothing, then I will take that as Your permission for me to proceed."

After waiting and receiving no indication from God, Michael turned to Gabriel and said, "Sound your trumpet! Call the holy, loyal angels of God together so I may address them and lead them on behalf of the Lord!"

Gabriel responded, "Now you are talking! Just stand by!" With that, the two moved from the throne room to sound the rallying call and mobilize the loyalists.

**Angels Choose Sides**

As the loyalist angels gathered around Michael and Gabriel on multiple levels, Michael stretched out his wings and slowly ascended while making his plea for the loyalists to follow him, not for his own sake, but for the Lord. He explained that he didn't understand why God was silent or why Lucifer had been allowed to go unchecked in his rebellion. Michael said, "That ends now! In the name of the Godhead, I lead you in restoring order to Heaven by pushing Lucifer and his rebels from this holy place!"

Gabriel shouted the war cry, "For God and Heaven!"

With one voice the loyalists replied, "For God and Heaven!" "Holy is the Lord and Him alone will we serve!"

With that the energized loyalists shouted, buzzed about, and blew on trumpets. Michael did not employ all of the loyalist angels as fighters. Instead he and Gabriel agreed that Gabriel should lead a major contingent to surround the throne of God to offer up unceasing praise and worship while the remainder, led by Michael, pressed the battle against Lucifer and his rebel angels.

Heaven became a war zone. Lucifer and his alliance of rebel angels against Michael and the angels that remained loyal to God. All of the angels were created as immortals. It was not possible for them to die or be extinguished in battle. However, for the first time, angels on both sides felt pain in their beings when suffering the blows of their adversaries.

Lucifer's rebel army was distinguished by black bands about the waists of their tunics. They fought by projecting a jagged lightening from their hands. The loyalist angels projected forth beams of light that appeared as golden swords with flames of holy fire seen moving along those beams. The clash of these angel weapons was like the coming together of matter and antimatter. There were loud crashing sounds and flashes of sparks at the points of contact. Whether rebel or loyalist, an angel receiving an unchecked or unparried blow felt excruciating pain. Pain was something new to angels. It was just another unpleasant thing that Lucifer had introduced.

This warfare raged on for what seemed like an interminable time. It was fought all over Heaven, individually, in small groups, and in major army scale encounters.

Lucifer and his rebels felt sure that victory was to be theirs because of the silence of God. Michael and the loyalists fought on valiantly, even though God remained silent and seemed to offer no encouragement or intervention.

At one point Lucifer and Michael faced off one-on-one as their armies pulled back to watch. Lucifer shouted, "I defy the armies of God and you Michael their field marshal. Stand aside! We are advancing on the throne room where I will exalt myself above God and sit as god on the throne. Submit to me now and it will go well with you and your misguided followers."

Michael responded, "You and your rebels have no place here! If necessary, we will resist you for all eternity, but that won't be necessary. We will defeat you and cast you and your rebels out of Heaven!" With that the battle was on. Archangel versus Archangel and rebel versus loyalist. All the while, the Godhead, surrounded by a host of worshipping, loyalist angels, led by Gabriel, remained silent.

The one-on-one battle between Lucifer and Michael was a sight to see. They were the super heavyweight gladiators in this conflict. For all of the sound, sparks, and light their encounter produced, neither prevailed against the other.

Finally, the Son came forth from the Father dressed as a warrior. Holy Spirit God also came forth and as the seven spirits of God sat as a crown on the head of the Son. The loyalist angels around the throne shouted in joy and praise. The four special angelic beings around the throne shouted holy, holy, holy even louder than usual. Trumpets sounded as the Son moved toward the main battle.

As Lucifer and his rebel angels became aware of the developments from the throne room and the approach of the Son, they were struck with fear. The Son arrived on the scene and beckoned Michael and his angels to fall in behind Him.

Lucifer and his rebels advanced on the Son shouting, "This is the decisive battle! Now Heaven and the throne will be ours and there will be a new order!"

With fire in his eyes the Son yelled a war cry. As He did, great power came from His mouth. The sound He made became an unstoppable weapon. Immediately, Lucifer and his rebels were cast out of Heaven. Lucifer, now Satan, gave the appearance of lightening as his bright angel body was speedily cast from Heaven along with his rebel angels. The rebel angels looked like falling stars in their descent.

The Son thought, *This is but the first battle. I must necessarily limit Myself in some future encounters, but victory is certain and a better future will come into being. For now it really hurts Me to have lost forever Lucifer, who was so close to me. It hurts to have lost a third of the angels I created and loved, and the souls of all on earth that were taken away in rebellion by that deceiver. I know*

*Michael, Gabriel and the other loyal angels don't
understand, but I can't reveal it all to them at this time.
They will just have to have faith and trust in Me.*
Cast out of Heaven, Satan and his angels found
themselves in the physical universe. Like a child throwing
a temper tantrum, Satan went through the universe
creating chaos. He caused galaxies to crash into one
another. Planets collided, stars exploded into nebulae.
Matter was sent flying around that eventually pock
marked planets and their satellites with craters. When
Lucifer returned to earth he found it darkened, desolate,
flooded, and frozen.

# Chapter 5 Earth Ruined and Put on Ice

*For this they willingly are ignorant of, that by the word of God the heavens were of old, and the earth standing out of the water and in the water: Whereby the world that then was, being overflowed with water, perished. 2 Peter 3:5-6*

Earth, which was where Satan's kingdom began when he, as Lucifer, became viceroy, was destroyed.[3] Whereas it had been teeming with animal and plant life, no life remained. Its cities were ruined and uninhabited. Moreover, water covered the whole earth. With the removal of God's blessing and light, the waters froze. Earth was locked up and under pressure.

Back in Heaven, the loyalists exulted in the victory of the Son. As painful as it was to the Godhead for there to be division and war in Heaven, there was good that came out of it. The loyalist angels that remained with the Godhead made a decision that would stand the rest of eternity. God thought, *These angels really love Me and stand with Me. I am so pleased with them. I can trust them to assist the Son when the time comes for the next great confrontation with Satan and his rebel forces.*

---

[3] Additional scriptures are provided here for context.
That made the world as a wilderness, and destroyed the cities thereof. Isaiah 14:7
And the earth was without form, and void; and darkness was upon the face of the deep. Genesis 1:2

The Son thanked the angels in Heaven for their loyalty. He revealed how painful it was to the heart of God for part of His creation to reject Him. The whole of the pre-Adamic race rejected Him and brought destruction on the earth. Lucifer, who was of the highest order of the angels and to whom had been given great honor and beauty, betrayed Him. Not only had Lucifer, now Satan, betrayed God, but he brought down with him the pre-Adamic beings of earth and a third of the angels of Heaven. In the process, Heaven itself was stained by the rebellion and war.

The Son explained to the loyalist angels that the Godhead took no joy in the falling away that occurred. Each angelic or earthly being lost grieved the heart of God. Then looking out on the loyalist holy angels, the Son said, "You are truly my sons and children." "You are part of the family that I have desired. You had to make the choice to be a willing part of my family. You have made that choice and the choice you have made gladdens Me. I am happy to be your God and creator." "Receive My love even as I receive your love for Me."

A heavenly lovefest broke out. The holy angels of God shouted, "Holy is the Lord!" "Blessing, and glory, and honor, and power be unto our God forever and ever!"

# Chapter 6 The Re-Creation

*For thus saith the LORD that created the heavens; God himself that formed the earth and made it; he hath established it, he created it not in vain, he formed it to be inhabited: I am the LORD; and there is none else. Isaiah 45:18*

God created the earth to be inhabited.[4] After the catastrophe that sin and rebellion brought to the world, God the Holy Spirit brooded over the dark, frozen, desolate earth. He grieved over the rejection of a loving God by the entire race of the pre-Adamic beings. This mess was the result of Lucifer's rebellion and the judgment of a holy God on the fall and turning away of the pre-Adamites.

After a gap of a very long time, God moved to bring the earth back to life. Before putting a sun in the sky, He spoke, "Light be." The light of His glory shone and there was light. Looking on this, God pronounced it good.

The next God activity was to create an atmosphere for the earth. The densest part of that atmosphere separated water on the earth from the water suspended in the sky above the earth. Again, God declared it good.

The third activity of re-creation was to separate water from land. A single great land mass rose up out of

---

[4] An additional scripture is provided here for context.
And the earth was without form, and void; and darkness was upon the face of the deep. And the Spirit of God moved upon the face of the waters. Genesis 1:2

the ocean and God made renewable vegetation of great variety to grow on the land. Again, God declared that third activity of re-creation to be good.

The forth activity of re-creation was to provide the sun, moon, planets, and galaxy to surround earth, which had been a planetary orphan. These cosmic bodies separated day from night. The planets and stars were also orderly, and not chaotic. This was so that time could be discerned, special days could be noted, and signs in the physical heavens would mark events. Again, God called this work of re-creation good.

The fifth work of re-creation was to create all types of living creatures in the seas. At the same time, birds of many kinds were created to inhabit the land mass. Once again, God called the completion of this work good.

For the sixth work of re-creation God filled the land mass with air breathing creatures both great and small. He created a great variety of animals and insects. Finally, to conclude the sixth work of re-creation, the Godhead said, "Let's make humankind and make humankind in our image and likeness. Male and female We will make him. We will give him rule over the earth, its creatures, and all nature." So God formed a man from the clay of the earth, made the man flesh and then breathed life into him so that the man became a living soul. God called the man Adam and pronounced this work, "Very good." Then God took a break from major creative works. As for me and the other watchers, we were glad to have work to do again. We watched over the re-created earth and recorded the activities of God's new creation—humankind.

The man Adam was beautiful and perfect. Adam was naked, but not unclothed. His clothing was a garment of glorious light. It was a spiritual garment covering a physical man of flesh. In this way, Adam was like God who is light. God loved Adam and liked to walk with him, only Adam did not see God. Adam only heard the voice of God walking with him.

One day God brought up from the ground a living copy of every type of creature on the earth to see what name Adam would give to them. Adam was the son of God and God delighted in him. Adam also delighted in God his Father. Adam was established as the god of the re-created world. However, Adam saw that the creatures of the animal kingdom had mates. He wondered where was one like him to be his mate. God, who is good, said, "It is not good for the man to be alone." So he caused a deep sleep to come over Adam. While Adam was asleep, God opened his side and removed part of Adam's flesh from which He made Eve, the woman that was to be Adam's mate.

When he awoke, Adam saw Eve and was glad. Knowing that Eve came forth from him of his own physical substance, Adam declared, "This is bone from my bones and flesh from my flesh." Eve, like Adam, was clothed in a garment of light.

The two representatives of humankind lived, like God, ruling over the earth that God created. They lived in an earthly paradise created by God for them and were at peace with the other creatures. The plant life was abundant, and was their food source. As the principal watcher for earth, I was happy see it inhabited again. It was my joy to confirm to God that all was well, but God loved His creation so much that He personally came down daily to talk with His human children and share each other's company. For a while, it really didn't seem like watchers were needed at all.

# Chapter 7 The Fall of Man, the Comeback of Satan, and the Promise of a Messiah

*And the LORD God said unto the woman, What is this that thou hast done? And the woman said, The serpent beguiled me, and I did eat. Genesis 3:13*

Adam and Eve experienced a blissful relationship with God until the day they fell from grace.[5] God wanted a family and Adam and Eve were the beginning of that family's human branch. God, Who is only good, gave them the freedom to love Him or to reject Him. In giving the objects of His love and generosity the freedom to reject Him, He gave them the power to hurt His heart of love. Sadly, they did just that. Afterwards, humankind hurt the heart of God many, many times.

The freedom God gave to Adam and Eve was also the freedom to create a breech in the relationship between God and mankind that would prevent God from having the close loving family relationship with humankind that He desired, because God's holiness would have to judge sin in His presence. It was not God's desire that they be lost to Him or be damned. Foreseeing that the people He

---

[5] Additional scriptures are provided here for context.

But your iniquities have separated between you and your God, and your sins have hid his face from you, that he will not hear. Isaiah 59:2

In whom the god of this world hath blinded the minds of them which believe not, lest the light of the glorious gospel of Christ, who is the image of God, should shine unto them. 2 Corinthians 4:4

created and loved would sin against Him, He had a plan, at great cost to Him, that would be revealed in due time, to restore those that would be deeply sorry for their sin and love God fully again. These would be part of His beloved family forever.

Adam and Eve enjoyed the paradise in which God had placed them. They had no unfulfilled needs. As I already mentioned, God visited with them daily and His voice spoke to them. There was nothing between them and God. God did give them one rule. There was a special tree in the garden, the tree of the knowledge of good and evil, that was devoted to God. Adam and Eve were not to eat of that one tree, but were free to eat from any other tree.

## The Fall

Satan came upon Eve one day in the form of an iridescent flying dragon. He was beautiful, multicolored, and patterned. The dragon had wings, feet, hands, and a tail. He was at home in the air, on land, in the trees, or swimming in the water. Then Satan entered the dragon and enticed Eve to eat the fruit of the forbidden tree. Satan maligned God, insisting that Eve would not die, as God had said, and told Eve that God knew she would be as a god if she ate of that tree. Eve ate. Then she offered Adam the same forbidden fruit. Unlike Eve, Adam was not deceived by Satan's words through the dragon. However, Adam loved Eve. Adam put his love for Eve above his love for God and ate, so that whatever happened, they would be together. As a watcher, it was not my role to intervene. Adam and Eve had to make their own choices.

God saw it all too, but did not intervene, because Adam and Eve had to exercise their free will and choose their own path. The Father said to the Son, "This is what we saw would happen. Now their sin separates us from them. We will get them back, but what a long and hard road lies ahead. If we judge their sin now they will be lost forever like the pre-Adamites and the rebel angels. They need a savior and redeemer to bring them back by taking on Himself the punishment for their sin and making them to have the righteousness of God so that We can have holy loving family fellowship restored."

The Son replied, "I am that savior and redeemer. I won't fail. Our word and plan in this matter won't fail or else everything in Heaven and the physical universe would be dissolved. I can't let that happen to the loyal angels, to humankind, or to all of creation."

After eating the forbidden fruit, the garments of glory light that had covered Adam and Eve faded away, and they could see that they were naked. Ashamed of themselves for their disobedience, they hid themselves from the presence of God and fashioned aprons of fig leaves to cover their naked bodies.

Satan exulted because, by listening to him, Adam and Eve had given to him the authority to be the god of the world in their place. They lost the dominion and authority that God had given to them to rule the world.

## The Promise of the Messiah

When the voice of God came at the usual time of day to speak with His children, they hid for shame. God called for Adam saying, "Where are you Adam?" Of course God could see Adam hiding in the brush and trees.

Adam responded, "I hid because I was naked."

"Who told you that you were naked" asked God. "Have you eaten from the tree that I commanded you not to eat from?"

His heart racing and ashamed of himself, Adam attempted to pass the blame to God and said, "The woman that You gave me gave it to me to eat, and I ate it."

God then asked Eve, "What have you done?"

Eve responded, "The dragon enticed me and tricked me, and I ate it."

Addressing the dragon God said, "Because you have done this you are cursed above all animals and will crawl on your belly and taste the dust." Immediately the dragon, and all other dragon creatures of that class, lost the wings, feet, and hands that had been part of its identity and became a slithering, belly crawling serpent. Further, God said there would be strife between the serpent, that is Satan, and the offspring of the woman, the Messiah to come. Although the serpent would wound that promised offspring superficially, the promised offspring of the woman would wound the serpent's head and take back control of the earth.

Turning back to Eve and Adam, God informed them of the consequences of their deed. It would be a hard life for each of them. They would die, returning to the ground from which they came. Eve would suffer pain in childbirth and be under the rule of her husband. Adam would have to scratch a living out of the ground with much effort battling weeds and thorns.

Then God killed an animal, spilling its blood, to make clothes for Adam and Eve. This was the first blood sacrifice to cover their sin. It presaged the blood sacrifice that would be made by the promised offspring, the Messiah, to forever take away their sin.

So that they would not eat of the tree of life and be forever bound in their sinful state, God had Adam and Eve driven from the garden. God placed cherubim at the entrance to the garden with a flaming sword to bar the way back for Adam and Eve or their descendants.

God's children had made a foolish mistake with lasting consequences, but they were not abandoned by God. They were not orphans. It was just that their choice to sin created a separation between them and the God that loved them. However, God had given the promise of a Messiah to restore humankind to a relationship of intimate fellowship in the family of God.

Meanwhile, Satan plotted as to how he could keep humankind in slavery to him, and, through the power of death, hold them in his kingdom forever. Thus, Satan sought to deny God the family He sought. Satan already had a major victory by getting Adam and Eve, at least temporarily, to trust and obey him rather than God. Now he was once again the god of the world. He intended to keep his captives and block the Messiah from coming to liberate his captives and spoil his plans.

# Chapter 8 Plots to Block Messiah

*And I will put enmity between thee and the woman, and between thy seed and her seed; it shall bruise thy head, and thou shalt bruise his heel. Genesis 3:15*

After being driven from the Garden of Eden, Adam and Eve began to adapt to their new environment. This meant working the land, building shelter, domesticating animals for the milk they produced and the wool that could be woven into garments and other textiles. They began to have children and erected an altar to God to point those children to God. Things were different from the days in the paradise of Eden. Their food was to be had without sweat and labor. Every day the voice of God would walk with them in the Garden and spend time with them as a loving father. As a consequence of their fall, they hungered for the close relationship with God that they had known, but now God hid Himself to see if they would seek Him with all of their hearts.

Cain was their firstborn son. After him Abel was born. Cain was a botanist and horticulturalist. He loved growing things. Abel raised cattle. The cattle performed as draft animals to plow fields, remove stones from the fields, and produce milk that could be consumed as a beverage, or made into other products for consumption like butter, cheese, and yogurt. Wool could also be taken from some of the animals to weave into textiles for clothing, wall hanging tapestries, and other uses.

Adam and Eve passed on to their sons their brief history of the world. They instilled within their sons the need to honor God and to seek Him. Both sons made offerings to God. Abel, recalling that God slew an animal and spilled its blood to cover his parents, offered up of the best available from his flocks. God showed His acceptance of Abel's offerings by opening the heavens and having fire come down from the sky to consume his offerings.

With Cain it was another story. Rather than making a sacrifice of blood, he brought some of his produce. Abel offered to give Cain animals from his flocks for sacrifice in exchange for his produce, but Cain rejected the offer. Moreover, Cain didn't honor God enough to even bring the first and best of his produce. The result was that his offerings were not consumed by fire from the skies, but lay there until they rotted and attracted flies, birds, and wild animals. Cain was not happy. God spoke to Cain to show him a better way and let him know that his own sin was in the way of the acceptance of God.

## Attempts to Thwart God's Plan of Redemption

Satan, was now back as the god of the world again. Although he was no longer God's viceroy, he saw an opportunity. Satan thought to himself, *Perhaps Abel is the Messiah that was promised. I will kill him then so that my kingdom will continue to rule in the earth without end or interference.*

So Satan put the idea of murder in the heart of the pouting, angry Cain. *Kill him and be done with him!* Cain meditated on those thoughts and finally decided to act them out. As Cain spoke with Abel out in the field, he suddenly turned on his brother and killed him. Cain then hastily attempted to cover up his foul deed by burying

Abel in a shallow grave, and then went about as though nothing had happened.

As the watcher, I dutifully reported Abel's murder to God. God said, "I shed the blood of an animal to cover the nakedness of Adam and Eve after they rejected My word and sinned. Until now, it has only been for an offering to Me that the life of an animal was taken and blood was shed. It was an anticipation of the day when humankind would be redeemed by the sacrifice of divine blood. The murder of Abel was the work of Satan. He will cause many other lives to be taken before he is judged. I am saddened by every death. I am life. I have a plan to overturn the deadly work of Satan. My plan will be revealed in its time."

When God confronted Cain, Cain responded to the voice of the unseen God by feigning not to know the whereabouts of Abel. "Am I my brother's keeper!" he responded in lying disrespect.

God exposed Cain's sin. He told Cain that the blood of Abel cried out to Him from the ground. For his sin Cain would be cast out.

Adam and Eve grieved the loss of their son Abel and the banishment of their first born, Cain. Nevertheless, they continued over centuries to have children in both single and multiple births. The first of these children, after Cain and Abel, was Seth. Eve saw Seth as the replacement for Abel. Indeed, she thought Seth was the Messiah promised by God. Seth was not that Messiah, but it was through his descendants that the Messiah would come. Indeed, Seth taught his descendants to call on God. Meanwhile, the rest of the global population turned from God and sin increased.

Having failed to prevent the coming forth of the Messiah by encouraging the murder of Abel, Satan came up with another plot to block the Messiah promised by God. Satan directed some of his evil angels to change into humans and to have sexual intercourse with as many childbearing women as possible to block a path for the Messiah to be born into the world.

The fallen angels that took on this assignment became handsome men. They set themselves up in Temples of pleasure where women lined up for the opportunity to have sex with them. They were treated as gods. The women were carried away with the ecstasy of the experience. For them the pleasure was incomparable. None of them wanted to leave the arms of their special lover, but these beings were on a mission and were greedy to have all of the women they could get. They were sex addicts themselves and enjoyed the pleasure of unlimited sexual intercourse in their new physical bodies by dent of their unlimited sexual stamina.

From this interaction of genetic pools came mutated beings. Some were giants, also known as the Nephilim. Some became revered as heroes, warriors, or idols, and were superlative in their abilities. As the principal watcher for earth, I regularly presented myself before the throne in Heaven with the sad report of what was transpiring on earth. Often God would say nothing apart from thanking me and the other watchers for our service and sending me back to resume my duties. At other times, I just wondered what my God was thinking.

To bring an end to Satan's plot to pollute the gene pool and block the pathway for a pure lineage to introduce the Messiah, God sent angels to round up those fallen angels that participated in the plot, bind them in chains, and imprison them in hell.

# Chapter 9 The Flood

*And GOD saw that the wickedness of man was great in the earth, and that every imagination of the thoughts of his heart was only evil continually. And it repented the LORD that he had made man on the earth, and it grieved him at his heart. And the LORD said, I will destroy man whom I have created from the face of the earth; both man, and beast, and the creeping thing, and the fowls of the air; for it repenteth me that I have made them. But Noah found grace in the eyes of the LORD. Genesis 6:5-8*

Because Satan's efforts to turn humankind from God and his plot to corrupt human genetics to eliminate any pure Adamic blood line through which the Messiah could come had spread widely, God decided to destroy the world as it was and its inhabitants. The people had become corrupted in their bodies and souls. Their minds were on unholy things and they mocked God. As the watcher, I continued to come before the throne of God to report on the corruption on earth due to the activity of Satan and those that fell for his lies and illegitimate pleasures. Nevertheless, God was patient and provided a long space of time for people to repent, but they rejected that opportunity.

The only thing that stood between God and a second watery destruction of every living being on earth, as had happened with the pre-Adamites, was God's promise to Adam and Eve of a Messiah, Who would be a descendant of Eve.

God found one man, Noah, who had grace in His eyes. God would destroy the world by water, but would preserve the lives of Noah, Noah's wife, and Noah's three sons Shem, Japeth, and Ham, along with their wives. Humanity would begin again through them and their descendants. Most importantly, there would be an uncorrupted lineage through which the Messiah could eventually come. To execute this plan, God commissioned Noah to both build a sea worthy, multilevel, vessel or ark.

During the construction of this great project Noah preached repentance and warning. God gave many years for people to repent. The ark itself was a great spectacle that drew crowds of construction gawkers. Noah used that as a platform to preach and urge people to turn to God and be spared from the judgment that was to come. However, there were no converts, only mockers of Noah, the ark project, and of God. After all, it had never rained before, there had never been a flood. Besides all that, Noah's huge ark wasn't even located near a body of water.

Noah and his family went into the ark a week before the flood waters arrived. Together with them were two of every creature and insect, male and female, along with fodder and drinking water. The exception was the ceremonially clean animals suitable for sacrifice to God. Those animals came seven to a group. The people on the outside took note. It was quite a spectacle, but pointless in their eyes. They continued to mock Noah and God. The whole situation made no sense to them, so they continued as they always had until the moment that judgment and destruction came.

Noah and his family were safe within the ark together with the creatures that would preserve the genetics of the animal, bird, and insect creation. All other people and air breathing creatures that lived on land perished.

Once the hatch on the vessel was closed and the one window shut, there was no way for anyone else to get into the ark for safety. Angels sent by God saw to it that the panicked mob of terrified people could not breach the ark. The rains came and geysers of water burst from the ground as the underground sources of water were forced above the surface of the ground. The ground became super saturated with moisture. With no place else to go, the waters rose as unrelenting rain for 40 days and nights combined with the water from the geysers that spewed non-stop.

Within hours, Noah and his family no longer heard the pleas of those who had rejected God. They no longer heard the sound of wild and domesticated animals bellowing in fear and bewilderment as they struggled to stay above water. It was quiet, but for the steady beating of rain and the waves slapping against the ark. The ark itself had been lifted up from its dry dock by the flood waters and was carried along to a new location. After several months, the waters receded and dried up. The ark came to rest in a stable elevated place in the mountains of South Central Asia.

Noah and his family came out of the ark after some tests to see if there was dry land again. They disembarked, along with the animals, birds, and insects that had been in the ark with them, and began life anew as the only surviving humans on earth.

Noah's first act was to build an altar to God. On that altar he sacrificed one of every kind of animal considered to be clean. That was why the clean animals boarded in groups of seven. The seventh animal was devoted to God from the time it entered the ark with the plan that it would eventually be sacrificed. That left three pairs of breeding animals of every clean type.

# Chapter 10 The Rise of False Gods

*For thou shalt worship no other god: for the LORD,*
*whose name is Jealous, is a jealous God. Exodus 34:14*

After the flood, God's judgment on a sinful world,
the only living humans were Noah and his family. They
all knew the truth of God. They all also knew that they
had been spared from becoming victims of the global
disaster. Yet, in a brief time, their descendants began to
turn their backs on God and made up their own gods as
well as pretending to be gods themselves.[6] Thus Nimrod,
a descendant of Noah's son Ham, began this first revolt
after the flood. He gained renown as a great hunter who
subdued the wild beasts that threatened the people. Most
importantly, he created a kingdom with cities and began a
massive project for the building of a tower at Babel. This
project organized and kept the people together and also
served as a platform for their worship of their gods. This
was in opposition to the will of God that the people
should spread throughout the earth and that they should
only serve Him.

---

[6] An additional scripture is provided here for context.
Because that, when they knew God, they glorified him not as
God, neither were thankful; but became vain in their imaginations,
and their foolish heart was darkened. Professing themselves to be
wise, they became fools, And changed the glory of the uncorruptible
God into an image made like to corruptible man, and to birds, and
four-footed beasts, and creeping things. Romans 1:21-23

## Alternative Gods

Nimrod and his consort, Semiramis, were treated as gods. As such, they were the first people to claim divinity as living gods or people in whom a god resided. After Nimrod died a violent death, Semiramis gave birth to a son named Tammuz, which she asserted was from a supernatural pregnancy. Satan put it into the mind of Semiramis to say that this "resurrected" Tammuz was the Messiah that had been promised by God. She claimed that Nimrod was the sun god, of which fire was one of his manifestations, and that Tammuz was the reincarnated Nimrod. As for herself, she presented herself as the queen of heaven, that is, as queen of the gods. The pair of Semiramis and her young son was worshipped together as the great mother and her son. Tammuz was seen as the deliverer. He was also represented by a golden bull calf. Tammuz became the incestuous lover of his mother Semiramis. Like his father Nimrod, he too was a hunter and also died a violent death. Tammuz was torn to pieces by a wild boar.

A cult developed around them and spread around the world. People rejected God, and instead, worshipped gods associated with bodies in the solar system or the stars beyond. They attributed to gods they made up, phases of life, death, and crop production, or of fire, wind, and the sea. Instead of worshipping God, they worshipped images of men and women, of part men - part beasts, of men who were also seen as beasts, or of animals alone. This was the beginning of the global religion that excluded the true God. In different countries they became known by names peculiar to a particular country, but they were the same or very similar gods. Behind those gods were fallen angels. It was part of Satan's plan to trap people into the worship of the profane rather than the worship of the true God.

I reported all of this to God on my visits to the throne room in Heaven. At times the anger of God against what Satan was doing on earth was such that His holiness would have destroyed all life on earth again, but for the word of His promise to bring a Messiah that would be a descendant of Eve. God's holy presence is overwhelming. When His anger was stirred up I and the other angels reverently backed away. We backed away not from fear, but because the intensity of His holy anger was more than even angelic beings could stand.

After God confused the common language, to bring an end to the tower of Babel project, it prompted people to separate by language and seek out territories for their particular common language group. As they scattered, they carried with them the religion developed around Nimrod, Semiramis, and Tammuz. In those days, a few generations from the language confusion that ended the Babel project, God separated the great landmass into separate continents. This acted to ensure that the people could not soon come back together again to reinstate the Babel project and further their rebellion against God.

# Chapter 11 The Line of the Messiah

*And the scripture, foreseeing that God would justify the heathen through faith, preached before the gospel unto Abraham, saying, In thee shall all nations be blessed. Galatians 3:8*

Humankind seemed to be an easy mark for the lures of Satan and the iniquity he had unleashed. Because all humankind was given to sin, which displeased God, it seemed there would not be a family line available through which the Messiah could come. In God's plan, the Messiah had to be born as a human and be capable of dying. In order to bring about the perfect, God had to work through imperfect ordinary people. By His grace and power He would enable such people to step into the roles He had ordained for them to fill.

God intervened and spoke to Abram, an idol worshipper living in Ur in Chaldea. This Abram and his wife Sarai were childless. God spoke. Abram listened and obeyed. Based on his personal encounter with the voice of God, Abram left his family and family idols to begin his journey of faith.[7]

Abram, whose name God changed to Abraham, which meant father of nations, did not obey completely as he took his father Terah and nephew Lot with him. His father died along the way, after a delay of several years, but his nephew Lot continued with him.

---

[7] Additional scriptures are provided here for context.

And Abraham said, My son, God will provide himself a lamb for a burnt offering: so they went both of them together. Genesis 22:8

And there shall come forth a rod out of the stem of Jesse, and a Branch shall grow out of his roots. Isaiah 11:1

As Abraham continued his journey in faith to dwell in a land he had not known, God the Son came down with His two loyal Archangels, Michael and Gabriel, to visit with Abraham and to take His pact with Abraham, and his descendants to come, to a new level. Prior to coming down to earth, the Son emptied Himself of much of His glory. This was necessary because sinful human flesh cannot stand or live in the holy glory of His full presence.

Standing beside God the Father, the golden flux of the essence and glory of God flowed from the Son back to the Father until a very human looking Jesus stood beside the Father. Jesus, the Son, called Michael and Gabriel to Him and said "Come with me. Let's go down to Abraham because he and his descendants are chosen by me." "Each of you will have a special role regarding his descendants."

With the speed of thought, the three traversed the great gap between the highest Heaven and earth. Appearing as an epiphany, God greeted the man Abraham. In his heart Abraham somehow knew this was God. Abraham bowed before Him and bid Him and His companions to come and receive his hospitality. God outlined His plan to Abraham. Abraham was to become the father of nations. Through the lineage of Abraham all of the earth would be blessed because of Messiah to come and the revelations God would give through Abraham's descendants.

Abraham questioned how this would be so seeing he was old and so was his wife. Besides, the two of them were childless. Nevertheless, God made a pact with Abraham and promised to return to him within a year. As a sign of this pact or covenant promise, Abraham and his male descendants were to be circumcised as a sign that they were part of the pact. God also promised him and his descendants the land now occupied by others. These other people would be removed in time because of their sin.

When God returned to Abraham a year later, He did not leave again before letting His friend Abraham know that Sodom and Gomorrah would be destroyed. Those cities would be destroyed because their sin had been so great. Knowing his nephew Lot resided in Sodom, Abraham began to bargain with God to spare the city for the people in it that were in a relationship of right standing with God. God went along with the intercession of Abraham until Abraham became too ashamed to ask God to lower the bar any further for the number of godly people in the cities it would take for God to spare them.

In the end, God returned to Heaven and left two angels, in the guise of men, to extract Lot and his family before destruction was allowed to rain down on the two sinful cities. Those angels entered the house of Lot and explained the urgency of his departure. Meanwhile, a mob of Sodom's inhabitants pressed on the house to demand that Lot surrender his guests so that they could have sex with them.

When Lot was unable to dissuade the men of Sodom or to even appease them by offering them his virgin daughters instead, the angels literally took matters into their own hands. They blinded the mob and pulled Lot back inside the house. Lot was then instructed to gather his family and leave at once. When Lot proved unsuccessful in getting the men engaged to his daughters to join him, he dawdled. Finally, the angels grabbed Lot, his wife, and his two daughters by the hands and pulled them out of the house and out of town. Lot was warned by them to head for the mountains and to not look back.

When Lot begged for permission to take refuge in a tiny hamlet instead the angels relented. However, when fire came down from the skies to destroy Sodom and Gomorrah, the fearful Lot decided it would be safer after all to head for the mountains.

## An Only Son Must Be Sacrificed

Abraham was 100 years old when his son Isaac was born, fulfilling God's promise to him and to his wife Sarah. Abraham and Sarah doted on their son, whose birth was a miracle. So it was a great shock, some years later, when the voice of God spoke to Abraham with a stunning demand. God's voice called, "Abraham!"

By now Abraham could recognize the voice of God. "I'm right here," responded Abraham.

Then God said, "Take your son Isaac, whom you love, go to the region of Moriah and offer him up as a burnt sacrifice on a mountain I will tell you is the one when you arrive there."

That night, Abraham pondered God's command. He knew he had heard the voice of God clearly, but it was a very hard instruction. Abraham chose to obey God. The next morning, Abraham set out with his young son, some servants, and a load of wood for the sacrifice. Although Abraham was wealthy and had servants, he split the wood for the sacrifice himself, despite his advanced age. For Abraham, splitting the wood himself was another sign to God of his obedience. He looked at each piece knowing that the wood that he prepared would burn the body of his son. On the third day of their trek to Moriah, Abraham sensed that he had arrived at the mountain that God had selected for the sacrifice. So he had Isaac carry the bundle of wood on his back while he carried the knife he would use to kill his own son.

Abraham told his servants, "Wait back here while we go to worship, and then we will come back to you."

On the three days of their journey to that point, Abraham considered both the promise of God that he would be a father of nations and the command that he sacrifice the son through whom the promise was to come. He reaffirmed to himself that he would obey this God he had come to know and trust. He also believed that, if he obeyed and sacrificed Isaac, the son he loved, God would have to bring Isaac back to life in order to keep his promise to him.

As Abraham and Isaac climbed the hill Isaac spoke, "Daddy."

"I am right here son," replied Abraham.

Isaac noted the obvious, "We have the fire and the wood, but where is the lamb for the burnt offering?"

Abraham responded, "Son, God Himself will provide the lamb for the burnt offering."

When the two arrived at the place that God had showed Abraham, Abraham gathered stones and piled them together to make an altar. Then Abraham laid out the wood on the altar for the sacrifice. Finally, Abraham tied up Isaac and laid him down on the wood on the altar.

There was no struggle between the old Abraham and the young Isaac. Isaac honored and trusted his father whom he knew loved him. Isaac recalled the stories Abraham had told him of his interactions with God. He recalled how his birth was a miraculous fulfillment of God's promise to his father. Isaac did not want to die, but he submitted to his father's will, believing, as Abraham also believed, that if he were killed and sacrificed, God would have to bring him back to life in order to make good on His promises to Abraham.

Isaac not only did not struggle with Abraham, but he did not scream out for the servants to come and save him either. As Abraham raised the knife to kill his son Isaac, the Angel of the Lord, the pre-incarnate Son of God, spoke from heaven arresting Abraham. "Abraham! Abraham!"

The voice of the Son of God went on to say, "Don't harm the boy or lay a hand on him to take his life. Now I know that you reverence God because you have not kept your only son from Me." Abraham was drained by the emotion of the moment. When he raised his head to thank God and untie Isaac, he saw a ram that had been caught by its horns in a thicket. Abraham rushed to take that ram and offered it up as a burnt sacrifice in the place of his son Isaac.

Watching from a safe distance and breathing heavily with anxiety, Isaac thought, *That was far too close for my liking, but God did indeed supply the sacrifice in my place.* That lesson stayed with Isaac for the rest of his life.

As the smoke went up from the ram that had been sacrificed, the unseen pre-incarnate Son of God spoke to Abraham a second time. He said, "I have sworn by Myself that because you have done this and have not held back your only son, I will certainly bless you and make your descendants as numerous as the stars in space and the grains of sand on the seashore. Your descendants will take over from their enemies and every nation on earth will be blessed by one that will come from you because you were obedient to what I commanded."

In this pivotal exchange, Abraham and Isaac acted out what was to presage God the Father's own plan with the Son of God to offer the Son of God as a sacrifice for the sin of the world. As Isaac carried the wood up the hill, one day centuries later, Jesus would carry His wooden cross up a hill to give Himself as a sacrifice. The judgment of God the Father would extract the penalty of sin by taking the life of His loved and only Son Jesus as a sacrifice. Just as the young Isaac did not struggle or cry out for help, when the Son of God would enter the world in a flesh and blood body, He would go to His death without crying out against God the Father or calling to His servants the loyalist holy angels to deliver Him. On that day on the mountain in Moriah, God provided an adult ram to Abraham, but He was also providing His Son as the lamb of God for a date in the future.

Just as Abraham and Isaac believed God would raise Isaac up from the dead, the Son of God would go to His death believing that He would be raised from the dead. This sacrifice, yet to come, would make it possible for humankind to be reconciled to God and spend eternity with Him in a relationship of love. Having seen that Abraham and Isaac were obedient, the Son of God reaffirmed the decision made by the Godhead, before creation, that God Himself would provide the sacrifice to satisfy the holy judgment of God against sin.

Ninety years passed from the time that God first called Abraham until the birth of his grandson Jacob. Jacob and his twin brother Esau were the only sons of Abraham's son Isaac. When Esau took wives from the local Canaanite people, with whom they were not supposed to intermarry, it left Jacob, whose name meant deceiver, to carry the line of the Messiah.

First, Satan put it in the heart of Esau to kill his brother Jacob. That was yet another plot to block Messiah. The unseen Satan whispered into the mind of Esau. *He has stolen the right of the firstborn and now has stolen the blessing intended for me. I'll kill him after my father passes away!*

Rebecca, the mother of the two, learned of Esau's plans and had Jacob flee back to Chaldea to find his relatives and take a wife from them until his brother's anger subsided.

While fleeing from his brother with only the clothes on his back, Jacob made a deal with God. He prayed saying that he would serve God if God would protect him and bless him. As Jacob slept, he saw the sky over him opened. He saw a ladder from Heaven to earth with angels ascending to God and descending from God who stood at the top of the ladder. Upon awakening, he realized that the place he was at was a portal to Heaven.

After the death of Isaac and a long sojourn in Chaldea, Jacob returned with his wives, children, servants, and cattle. His was a rich man by this time, but was afraid his brother Esau still desired to take his life.

The Son of God, as on other occasions that he went to earth to interact directly with particular humans, set aside much of His glory so that the object of His affection would not die when sinful humanity came near the holiness of God and the requirement for judgment of sin. The Son is love and ultimately He would be the sacrifice that would satisfy the demands of justice for those that would believe Him and accept His provision of His own righteousness for them.

As the Son came down to deal with Jacob, Satan intercepted Him. "So you intend to bring a deliver through him? Through Jacob, the deceiver? Ha! Why he is more like me than he is like You!"

Jesus told Satan, "Even you can speak a half-truth on occasion. Know this, I am greater than his sin and My will cannot be defeated. My plans for him are sure."

Satan replied, "Tell me, what are these plans of yours?"

The Son ignored Satan and proceeded to deal with Jacob as Satan backed away hastened by Michael who advanced on him warning him away or to suffer the consequences.

Jacob and the Son wrestled with each other all night. It was God's effort to get Jacob onto the path of his destiny as the next step in the lineage through which Messiah the Son would come into the world. The Son told Jacob to let Him go before the dawn, so that His face, the face of Jesus, would not be seen. Jacob demanded a blessing and to know the name of the one who wrestled with him. The Son touched Jacob's hip joint to disable him. Although the Son did not reveal his identity, He did bless Jacob and changed his name from Jacob to Israel.

When it was all over, Jacob realized that he had wrestled with no mere man or angel. He said, "I have seen God face to face, yet I am still alive!" It was not a statement of pride, but of wonderment. Jacob knew his own flaws and wondered how it was that he was not burned to death and instantly destroyed in the presence of God whom he actually looked upon in the partial light that came just before the dawn. Certainly, he had somehow benefited from the mercy and grace of God— the God who blessed him and told him that he had power with God.

Jacob's self-exile lasted over fourteen years. When he returned he was able to reconcile with his twin brother Esau and settled in the land with his wives and children. After living in the land again, his wife Rebecca died in childbirth when she produced her second son, Benjamin. Her first son was Joseph. Jacob had a total of twelve sons plus a number of daughters. Because Rebecca had been his first and favorite love, Jacob favored Joseph over his brothers.

God granted Joseph the gift of interpreting dreams and gave him dreams with meaning for his future. Lacking wisdom and discretion, the young Joseph offended both his brothers and his father when he related the dreams that he had, because they all understood the meaning of the dreams being that they would all bow before Joseph one day.

Jacob gifted Joseph with a beautiful multi-colored coat. It was a gift that set him apart from his jealous brothers. It was also not a working garment. So while his brothers labored in the field tending the livestock, Joseph rested comfortably in the shade of his tent. Jacob then asked Joseph to go check on his brothers and report back to him.

When the brothers saw Joseph coming they thought to kill him, but the oldest brother, Reuben counseled that they should not kill him. They threw Joseph into a pit where he pleaded with his brothers for his life. While Reuben was temporarily away, the other brothers sold Joseph to a trading caravan headed to Egypt. They had taken Joseph's special coat, ripped it up, and poured the blood of a kid goat on it so that when they presented it to their father, they would give the lie they concocted that he had been devoured by wild beasts, with only the bloodied and torn coat left behind.

The traders that bought Joseph sold him as a slave to one of the officers of Egypt's Pharaoh. Joseph rose up to be appointed major domo of that officer's household. But the wife of his master continually tried to seduce Joseph. Joseph did his best to avoid her, but she entrapped him one day.

He refused her advances and fled, but she grabbed his garment and ripped it off of him before he could get away. She then cried out, "Help! That Hebrew, Joseph, tried to rape me!" When the master of the house came home she repeated the charge. Joseph was put in Pharaoh's prison.

There in the prison, Joseph was favored and became the prison trustee. Yet, he was an innocent man imprisoned wrongfully. In time, two of Pharaoh's staff, the head butler and the head baker were imprisoned with Joseph. They each had dreams that disturbed them. Joseph interpreted those dreams for them and his interpretation was accurate. The baker was executed, but the cupbearer was restored to his position. Joseph begged the head butler not to forget him, but he did anyway.

Two years later, Pharaoh had two similar dreams that disturbed him. He had his staff of diviners and magicians attempt to interpret the dreams, but they could not. At that time the chief butler realized his fault in not remembering Joseph and told Pharaoh, "There is a Hebrew in my lord's prison that can interpret dreams."

## From Prisoner to Prime Minister

Based on the recommendation of his royal butler, Pharaoh sent for Joseph, since he was troubled by his dreams and the diviners and magicians of the royal court were not able to interpret the dreams. Messengers from the palace saw to it that Joseph was shaved, cleaned up, and dressed well in order to be presented to Pharaoh. After Pharaoh related his two dreams, Joseph made it clear that it was God that gives the interpretation of dreams and that God had shown Pharaoh that there would be seven years of bumper crops followed by seven years of famine. So Joseph advised Pharaoh to appoint someone to manage the food stocks, storing up grain from the good years so that there would be food in the lean years. Pharaoh was so pleased with the interpretation and the strategic advice that he made Joseph the Prime Minister to oversee this grand project.

It happened just as Joseph said. During the seven lean years, everyone had to come to Joseph to buy food. In the process, total wealth was transferred into the hands of the Pharaoh including money, land, cattle, and labor. Since the famine was regional, it impacted Joseph's family in the neighboring country. Jacob sent his sons, minus Benjamin, to Egypt to buy food. They didn't know they were dealing with their brother Joseph, who spoke with them gruffly and through an interpreter.

Joseph sold them grain and secretly had his officers return his brothers' money into their bags, but held back his brother Simeon as a prisoner until they would bring their youngest brother Benjamin, his only full brother, back to him to prove their story of why they came and who they had left behind.

In time the food brought from Egypt was consumed and the brothers begged their father Jacob to allow them to return with Benjamin to Egypt. Jacob resisted initially, but eventually relented. In Egypt, Joseph honored his returned brothers with a banquet. At the banquet Joseph had them seated in order by age without asking them their ages. He also had his servants put a much larger portion of food before his brother Benjamin than any of the others.

When they purchased their grain, Joseph again secretly had their money put back in their bags, but he also secretly had his silver chalice placed in Benjamin's bag. Not long after they loaded their donkeys and left the city on their return home, Joseph sent officials after them charging them with stealing his chalice. Although they denied wrongdoing, the chalice was found in Benjamin's bag, so they all went back to face Joseph. Joseph indicated he was willing to let them go, but would keep Benjamin as his slave. Judah prostrated himself before Joseph and begged that he be kept as a slave rather than Benjamin for fear that it would otherwise cause the death of their father Jacob.

Finally, Joseph was no longer able to contain his emotions or to continue with the charade. He yelled out for all of the Egyptians to leave. Then alone with his brothers, he identified himself. Sobbing uncontrollably, he said, "I am Joseph!  Is my father still alive?"

This troubled the ten brothers who had sold Joseph into slavery. If this was indeed Joseph, they feared retribution. They thought, *God has judged our sin regarding our brother Joseph, and now we will pay with our lives.*

Again Joseph spoke saying, "I'm your brother Joseph that you sold into Egypt! Come close to me please." As they drew near, Joseph, the Prime Minister of Egypt, unwrapped the linen shendyt skirt worn by Egyptian men and uncovered his genitals so they could see he was circumcised as they were.

When the brothers saw the tribal marking that was also the sign of the pact their great grandfather Abraham made with God, they knew this really was Joseph. However, they tempered their joy with fear realizing their lives were in the hands of the man they once thought to kill out of hatred and jealousy, but sold into the hard life of a slave in a foreign land.

As he covered himself and re-tied his shendyt, Joseph sought to assuage the fears of his brothers. He said, "Don't despair or be hard on yourselves because you sold me here, because God sent me here ahead of you in order to keep you all alive. We have just had two years of famine and there are still five more years of famine yet to come. Crops will not produce and there will be no harvest in that time. God sent me here ahead of you so that your generations would not perish from the earth. So, it really wasn't you that sent me here, but God. God has made me like a father to the Pharaoh and put me over all of his palace and given me rule over all of Egypt. Now go to my father quickly and tell him that I, Joseph, said that God had made me the ruler of all Egypt, so come down to me quickly. I will see that you and your children, your flocks and herds are all provided for in the region of Goshen near me. I will take care of you all, otherwise, you will be ruined and impoverished because there are still five more years of famine to come."

Joseph's Egyptian servants heard him when he wept and told Pharaoh that Joseph's family had come. Pharaoh put wagons at the disposal of Joseph to bring his extended family to Egypt to settle in Goshen.

What happened to Joseph was an indication of what would happen when the Messiah would come. Like Joseph, the Messiah would be rejected by his own people and abused. Messiah, like Joseph, would be falsely accused. At God's timing, the Messiah would come and suffer to the end that through him there would be salvation and deliverance for many. As his family and the people of Egypt literally bowed down to Joseph, the day would arrive when everyone would bow down to the Messiah who was yet to come in God's plan to restore a relationship of intimate fellowship between the Godhead and humanity.

# Chapter 12 The Exodus, the Law, and 40 Years in the Wilderness

*Behold, I send an Angel before thee, to keep thee in the way, and to bring thee into the place which I have prepared. Beware of him, and obey his voice, provoke him not; for he will not pardon your transgressions: for my name is in him. But if thou shalt indeed obey his voice, and do all that I speak; then I will be an enemy unto thine enemies, and an adversary unto thine adversaries. Exodus 23:20-22*

After centuries in Egypt, the descendants of Israel, who was originally named Jacob, went from being honored guests under a Pharaoh that had made Joseph his Prime Minister, to becoming slaves under a series of Pharaohs that did not remember or care for the history of how Joseph saved Egypt and concentrated wealth in the hands of Pharaoh.[8] Instead, Egypt's leaders feared this people that had grown to number in the millions. They so feared them that they implemented a policy to subjugate them. As the principal watcher for the earth, I, Benelroi, presented myself often before the throne of God to report on what was happening to the people with whom He had made a pact. God not only knew all of the details before I ever spoke, but He also heard the pleas of the Hebrew

---

[8] Additional scriptures are provided here for context.

And Joseph said unto his brethren, I die: and God will surely visit you, and bring you out of this land unto the land which he swore to Abraham, to Isaac, and to Jacob. Genesis 50:24

Now there arose up a new king over Egypt, which knew not Joseph. Exodus 1:8

people. God told me that He had compassion for the suffering of His people. He also told me that He was very jealous that His special people were gradually turning their backs on Him and beginning more and more to worship the gods of Egypt. The Egyptian gods were not really gods at all. This made it all the more an insult to God that the people were turning from Him to these false Gods.

In Pharaoh, Satan once again found an ally he could use as a tool in attempting to block the coming of the Messiah. One scheme was to kill all newborn male children of these immigrant slaves. Pharaoh secretly instructed Egyptian midwives to kill the male Hebrew children at childbirth, but the midwives did not carry out that policy. When questioned by the Pharaoh as to why the plan of infanticide was not working, the midwives made up the story that the Hebrew women delivered before they arrived on the scene and could intervene. Nevertheless, it was uncertain that even these newborn males would be allowed to live. For that reason, the parents of Moses put baby Moses in the waters of the Nile River in a floating basket while his big sister Mariam watched from a distance.

In the providence of God, the Pharaoh's daughter spotted the child and had him brought to her. Falling in love with the beautiful child, she decided to raise him. The princess needed a wet nurse to breast feed the baby. The quick thinking Mariam offered to find someone for the job. So Moses was raised until the time of his weaning with his own mother and family under the protection of the state as the adopted son of a princess of Egypt.

The adult Moses, a prince of Egypt, was both of the Egyptian culture and ethnically Hebrew. When he decided, at age 40, to liberate his people by his own devices, it was an unmitigated failure involving him killing an Egyptian slave overlord. This lead to the exile of Moses for 40 years in Midian as a fugitive from justice.

At 80 years of age, Moses was tending sheep in Midian when he saw a bush on fire on a mountainside. When the bush continued to burn without burning itself out, Moses went up to take a closer look at the curiosity. To his surprise, God spoke to him out of the burning bush calling his name, "Moses, Moses."

Moses responded, "I'm here."

Before going further, God warned Moses to not approach any closer and to remove his shoes, because the ground he was on was holy. Then God continued speaking, "I am the God of your ancestor Abraham, the God of Isaac, and the God of Jacob."

With that Moses prostrated himself in the dirt and covered his face out of fear that he might see God and die. God continued to speak audibly and informed Moses of His plan to extract the Hebrew nation from their slavery in Egypt and lead them to the land promised to their ancestors by having Moses go to Pharaoh to demand their release.

Feeling overwhelmed and inadequate, Moses said, "Who am I to go to Pharaoh and to lead the Hebrew people out of Egypt?"

God replied, "I will certainly be with you."

Seeking further clarification, Moses asked, "When I go to the Hebrews and tell them that the God of their ancestors has sent me to them and they ask for Your name, what shall I tell them?"

God made the statement, "I AM THAT I AM. Tell them I AM has sent you to them." Then God gave Moses additional details on how he was to call the leaders of the people together to give them this news and then go to the Pharaoh to inform him that he had met with God and demand that the people be released to go and sacrifice to God.

Moses protested, "But they won't believe me or listen to me. They will say God did not appear to him!"

So God asked Moses, "What is that in your hand?"

"A staff," replied Moses.

God said, "Throw it down on the ground." When Moses did so the staff changed into a snake, and Moses ran away from it out of fear.

But God told Moses, "Go take it by the tail." By this time the snake had coiled and rose up. So Moses came near and circled the creature until he had the opportunity to grab it by the tail. When he did so, the snake changed back into a straight staff again. Then God said, "Put your hand into your tunic on your chest." Moses complied, but when he withdrew his hand it was stricken with leprosy, much to his dismay. Then God said, "Put your hand inside again." Moses did so. When he pulled his hand out again it was the same as his other hand. So God told Moses, "If they don't believe the first sign, then show them the second sign. If they still don't believe, take some water from the river, pour it on the ground, and it will become blood."

This was all heady stuff. Moses was conversing with God and supernatural things were taking place. However, Moses didn't feel up to the task. Moses said, "I am not eloquent and it is difficult for me to get the words out of my mouth."

But God told Moses, "Who made a man's mouth? Isn't it Me, the LORD? Now go and I will be with your mouth and give you the words to say."

Instead of being encouraged by this, Moses tried to tell God that He had the wrong man and should select someone else for the job. This angered the Lord. Suddenly, the flame from the bush flared up to a raging fire and the voice of God spoke with some irritation with Moses. "Isn't Aaron of the tribe of Levi your brother? He speaks well. He is coming to see you now and will be glad to see you. You will speak to him and put words in his mouth. I will be with both your mouths. He will be your spokesperson and function in place of your mouth and you will be to him in the place of God. Now go and tell Pharaoh everything that I tell you."

Moses then said to the Lord, "If the Israelis don't listen to me then why would Pharaoh listen to me since I stutter when I speak?" The Lord answered Moses, "I have made you like God to Pharaoh and your brother Aaron will be your prophet. Go and say everything that I command you. But I will harden the heart of Pharaoh. He won't listen to you even though I multiply my signs and wonders in Egypt. Then I will lay My hand on Egypt and with mighty acts of judgment I will bring my people out of Egypt. Then the Egyptians will know that I Am the Lord."

When Aaron reached Moses, it was a joyous reunion. Moses told him all the things that God had said and shown him. With the blessing of his father-in-law Jethro, Moses took his wife Zipporah and their two sons and went to Egypt.

God spoke to Moses, "Don't be afraid, because the men that wanted to kill you are themselves dead."

When Moses and Aaron returned to Egypt they called together the Hebrew leadership. Aaron told them all that Moses had told him. Then he and Moses demonstrated the signs that God had given Moses. The people believed them and the signs.

Emboldened by their success with the Hebrew leadership, Moses and Aaron went to Pharaoh. There Aaron spoke on behalf of Moses and said, "The Lord God of Israel says let my people go!"

The Pharaoh was neither amused nor intimidated. "Who is the Lord? I don't know the Lord and I won't let Israel go." The Pharaoh added, "Moses and Aaron, you are diverting the people from their work. Get back to work!" As Moses and Aaron departed, Pharaoh called overlords of the Hebrews to himself and told them to see to it that straw was no longer provided to the Hebrews to make bricks for his projects, yet they were to keep the daily tally of bricks that they must produce at the same level. So the overlords and their subordinate officers passed the news to the Hebrew leaders. When the tally of bricks was not fulfilled, because the Hebrew slaves now had to gather straw for brickmaking as well as make the bricks, the Egyptian overlords beat the Hebrew leaders. Those leaders in turn complained to Moses and Aaron that all they had managed to do was to make life more difficult for them.

## Battle of the Gods

God told Moses "I have made you a God to Pharaoh. Just speak the words that I give you to say." Then the Lord spoke to Moses and told him to go back to Pharaoh and, when Pharaoh asks for a sign, thrown down the staff. So Moses and Aaron returned to Pharaoh as the Lord instructed them.

When Pharaoh demanded a sign of their authority, Moses gave his staff to Aaron and told him to throw it down. When Aaron threw down the staff of Moses, it changed into a snake. It caused a stir in the palace around Pharaoh as Pharaoh's officers moved back out of the way.

But Pharaoh beckoned to his head magicians Jannes and Jambres, who were expert in the dark knowledge of the Egyptians. Each magician, empowered by unseen evil angels, mumbled spells and threw down their staffs, which also became snakes. However, the smug looks on their faces soon melted away when Aaron's snake swallowed all of their snakes before Aaron took his snake by the tail and it became a staff again. Pharaoh was not impressed and still refused to let the people go.

After Moses and Aaron left the audience with Pharaoh, God spoke to Moses telling him, "Go tomorrow morning to Pharaoh while he is out in the water of the river. Strike the river water with your staff and it, the streams, and ponds will be turned to blood."

So Moses and Aaron encountered Pharaoh out in the water down from the steps of his palace. On either side of the steps leading into the water were large images of Egyptian gods of the Nile. With his priests nearby, Pharaoh praised the Egyptian gods and goddess of the Nile, Apis and the goddess Isis along with Osiris. The Egyptians believed the Nile was the blood flowing in the veins of Osiris. In the sight of Pharaoh, Aaron took Moses' staff and struck the water, which then turned to blood.

Pharaoh, his family, priests and attendants all scurried out of the Nile and up the stairs all bloodied. Their white linen tunics and skirts were all bloody on their lower portions. Not to be outdone, Pharaoh's magicians took containers of water and turned them into blood. Pharaoh remained steadfast in refusing to let the Hebrews go. So for seven days there was no water to drink in Egypt. Unable to breathe, the fish in the Nile died, floated to the surface, and washed up on the banks, creating a horrible stench. God, through Moses, had demonstrated His superiority over the gods of Egypt's Nile River.

Then God told Moses, "Go back to Pharaoh and tell him the Lord says to let me people go so that they may worship Me. If you refuse, I will send a plague of frogs throughout the entire country."

Moses did as God instructed. He and Aaron confronted Pharaoh with the words that God had commanded. When Pharaoh laughed and refused to let the people go, Moses handed his staff to Aaron and told him to stretch it out over the waters of the Nile, it's tributary streams, and ponds and command frogs to come forth. Suddenly, an army of frogs came leaping out of the Nile. In the meantime, Moses and Aaron departed to leave the Egyptians with the plague of frogs.

Frogs were everywhere and the royal palace was no exception. The frogs got into everything. They were in the bedrooms and beds so that the Egyptians couldn't sleep. Frogs got into the kitchens and the dough being made into bread. There was no place that was without the plague of frogs.

Now frogs held a special place among the Egyptians. They were treated as sacred and one was not supposed to kill them. They were a reminder of the goddess Heket, who was represented with a frog-like head and bulging eyes. To the Egyptians, Heket was the goddess of fertility and birth. Pharaoh's magicians showed him that they too could call up frogs from the Nile by calling on the goddess Heket, but more frogs was not the thing that was needed.

Finally, Pharaoh sent for Moses and Aaron. When they arrived, Pharaoh said to Moses, "Pray to the Lord to take away the frogs and I will let your people go to sacrifice to the Lord."

Moses agreed and said, "I will leave to you the honor of setting the time for me to pray so that you will be rid of the frogs, except for those that remain in the Nile."

For some inexplicable reason, Pharaoh said, "Tomorrow!" rather than, "Immediately!" When Moses did pray, the frogs died everywhere outside of the Nile. The dead frogs were everywhere, in homes, streets, and fields. They were swept out, shoveled up, carted away and dumped into huge stinking mounds.

Once Pharaoh saw that the menace of the frogs was past, he reneged on his word and refused to let the Hebrews go and would not listen to Moses and Aaron. So God told Moses, "Tell Aaron to stretch out your staff and strike the ground. The dust will become gnats throughout the land." Moses did so.

With Pharaoh and his magicians watching, Aaron stretched out the staff of Moses and struck the ground. Immediately, the dust of the ground became alive with gnats that rose up and afflicted people and animals. Animals were bucking and biting and rolling in the dirt for relief or running into the Nile and thrashing around.

People were waving, scratching, and swatting. They covered their mouths and nostrils to keep the gnats out. They squinted and rubbed their eyes to keep the gnats from sucking up the moisture of their eyes. Once again, it was impossible to prepare meals without the gnats being in the food.

When the magicians Jannes and Jambres tried to duplicate calling up gnats from the dust, they could not. They called on Set, the Egyptian god of the desert who was represented by gnats. But it was to no avail. Turning to Pharaoh, they said, "This is the finger of God!"

Then the Lord spoke to Moses saying, "Get up early in the morning and go confront Pharaoh when he is in the water of the Nile. Tell him the Lord says let My people go so that they may worship me, but if you will not let My people go then I will send swarms of flies. So that you will know that I am God, I will make a distinction between your people and My people in the land of Goshen. This sign will occur tomorrow. While you have flies, there will be no flies in Goshen where My people are living."

So Moses did as instructed and a plague of flies came over Egypt. The Egyptian god Uatchit was the fly god, but no one was happy with the plague of flies. They were in everything. The flies fouled the food for meals and would bite. Children cried, herds of animals stampeded, people swatted and beat themselves with whatever thing would temporarily cause the flies to get off of them.

Finally, once again Pharaoh summoned Moses and Aaron. He said, "Go ahead and sacrifice to your God, but don't go far. Stay nearby."

Moses responded, "That won't work. We have to go out three-day's journey into the wilderness. Besides, you Egyptians find our sacrifices to be detestable to you." So Pharaoh, agreed to the stipulation of Moses. Turning to leave, Moses said, "I will pray to the Lord to remove the flies tomorrow, but you must not go back on your word this time and refuse to let the people go."

However, once the flies were gone, Pharaoh gave orders to the overlords and army not to let the Hebrews go.

So God again sent Moses and Aaron to confront Pharaoh. He told Moses, "Tell Pharaoh that the God of the Hebrews says let My people go, so that they may worship me. But if you refuse to let them go I will send a plague on all of your livestock in the country that they all die. However, I will make a distinction for My people in Goshen. Not one of the animals that they own will die."

Again, Moses did as he was instructed, but Pharaoh refused to relent and let the people go. As the animals of Egypt were stricken, Pharaoh had his priests and magicians appeal to the god Apis and the goddess Hathor, the images of both of whom were of cattle. But it was to no avail. So all of the cattle, camels, sheep, and goats in Egypt died. Pharaoh sent people to observe the situation in Goshen and they reported back that none of the cattle belonging to the Hebrews had died. In the meantime, the Egyptians had to bury all of the dead cattle. As a consequence, there was no milk available for drinking, cheese making, or other dairy products. Neither was there fresh meat to eat, or draft oxen to plow fields, or oxen to pull carts. Even so, Pharaoh refused to let the Hebrews go.

Then the Lord instructed Moses to go before Pharaoh to pronounce a plague of boils. Standing before Pharaoh, Moses took some ashes that he brought, as instructed by God, and tossed them into the air. The ashes spread through Egypt and became painful boils. The magicians of Pharaoh were so stricken that they ran from Moses shrieking in pain. Even as Pharaoh and his family and officials struggled with the painful boils, Pharaoh continued to refuse to let the Hebrews go.

Later, God told Moses to get up in the morning and go to confront Pharaoh again. This time, the message was that there would be a plague of hail and fire if the Hebrews were not allowed to leave. Moses did as he was instructed. He warned Pharaoh that any who did not seek shelter would be killed by the plague. So Pharaoh was given time to put out the word for people to get into their homes. However, Pharaoh and his priests prayed to Set the storm god and to Nut the sky goddess to block the threat coming from Moses and the God of the Hebrews. It was a vain attempt.

When God gave the word to Moses to stretch out his staff the hail came down from the sky amid loud thundering and a strange fire ran along the ground everywhere, except in Goshen where the Hebrews resided. Any person or animal out in the open died from the plague. In addition, the crops in the field that had come up were severely damaged or burned. As Egypt was being brought to its knees by the plague of hail, Pharaoh and his priests continued to cry out to Set and Nut. They put offerings of food before their statues in the palace and bowed before them. But the hail, thunder, and fired continued unabated. Chastened, Pharaoh sent for Moses and Aaron. Pharaoh said, "I have sinned. Your God is just, but I and my people are wicked. Pray to the Lord to stop the hail and thunderings, and I will let you go."

Moses agreed to do so after he was outside of the city. However, once the hail and thunder stopped Pharaoh went back on his word yet again and instructed his officers to prevent the Hebrews from leaving.

So the next day Moses and Aaron returned to Pharaoh, as directed by God. Moses said, "The Lord says how long will you refuse to bow down to Me? Let my people go so that they may worship Me or else tomorrow I will bring locusts throughout your borders. They will cover the land and eat whatever remained after the hail." With that, Moses and Aaron left the palace grounds.

Pharaoh's officials immediately begged him to let the Hebrews go. "Egypt is being broken! How much more devastation can we endure! Let them go to serve their God! Haven't you yet figured out that Egypt has been destroyed by all of these plagues?"

So Pharaoh relented and ordered that Moses and Aaron be brought back to him. When Moses and Aaron arrived for their audience with Pharaoh, the Pharaoh at first seemed conciliatory. Pharaoh said, "You may go, but who actually will be going?"

Moses responded, "Everyone of course, our wives and children with us and our cattle."

But Pharaoh said, "No! Only the men may go!" Then turning to his guards and officials Pharaoh said, "Now get them out of here!" With that they were pushed and hustled out of Pharaoh's presence.

Once outside the palace grounds God instructed Moses to stretch his staff out over Egypt to summon the plague of locusts. So Moses raised his staff. A stiff steady wind began to blow, but there were no locusts as yet.

However, after the wind blew all night, in the morning such a horde of locusts had blown in that they covered the ground everywhere, except in Goshen. There had been locust swarms before, but nothing of this magnitude. There were so many that they almost blocked out the sun. The locusts ate everything in the fields and on the trees left from the plague of hail. Not one green thing was left.

Pharaoh and his priests made appeals to a statue of the god Osiris, the Egyptian god responsible for the fertility of crops. All the while, all green plant life was being munched away by the plague of locusts. Finally, Pharaoh urgently sent for Moses and Aaron. When they arrived he came down from his throne in the great hall and said to Moses, "I have sinned against your God and against you. Once again, please ask your God to take away this plague."

Moses and Aaron left without a word. Once outside, Moses asked God to remove the locusts. God heard Moses and granted his request. A strong wind began to blow. This time, rather than bringing in more locusts, it swept the locusts out of the country so that by morning there was not one locust to be seen, but the devastation from them was everywhere. Yet, after this supernatural display, Pharaoh still refused to let the Hebrews go.

So God told Moses, "Lift your staff to heaven and there will come darkness over Egypt so thick that it can be felt."

Moses did so and for three days there was no light, except in Goshen where the Hebrews lived. The thick darkness lasted for three days.

No Egyptian dared leave the confines of his home. In vain, Pharaoh and his priests made entreaties inside the palace to statues of the sun god Ra and of the falcon-headed god Horus and his all Seeing Eye. But for three days there was no sun and no one could see.

After three days of total darkness, Pharaoh again called for Moses and Aaron. After Moses and Aaron arrived, Pharaoh, wishing to seem generous, but still in control, said, "Go ahead and worship your God together with your wives and children, but you have to leave your cattle behind."

Moses disputed with Pharaoh saying, "That is unacceptable! We need our livestock to offer sacrifices to God. We won't leave one animal behind!"

Pharaoh's face turned dark and hard. Looking at Moses, he said, "Get out of here and don't come back, because the next time you see me you will die!"

In departing, Moses said, "Very well. It will be as you say. I will not see your face again. This is what the Lord says, about midnight I will go through the land and the firstborn son of everyone in Egypt will die from Pharaoh's family to that of the lowest servant girl. The same fate will be for the cattle." Moses was angry and let it show. "When this happens, then your officials will bow down to me and beg me to go and the people with me. Then I will go."

Pharaoh and his priests went to a statue of the goddess Isis, the goddess that Egyptians believed protected children. They prayed that she would show herself to be mightier that the Hebrew God.

When he returned to Goshen, Moses told the people to borrow silver, gold, and nice clothing from their Egyptian neighbors. The Egyptians, now terrified, gave them everything they asked for and held nothing back. Then Moses warned the people to prepare for that evening by killing a lamb for every family. They were to mark their doorposts and lintels with the blood of the lamb, and stay inside to eat the prepared lamb along with bread free of yeast, and bitter-tasting vegetables. Those that did not obey in offering this sacrifice, sprinkling the blood of the sacrifice, and seeking refuge under that blood covering, would experience the death of their firstborn sons just as the Egyptians would. This Passover meal, to be eaten that night, was to be a memorial that would be remembered every year in the future.

The next day Moses left with all of the Hebrew people and their herds. They took with them the precious things they had borrowed from the Egyptians. A few Egyptians, fearing God, aligned themselves with the Hebrews and went with them. When the Pharaoh and his army finally mustered the courage to go after their Hebrew slaves, God destroyed them in a mighty miracle of deliverance. They were drowned trying to chase down the Hebrews when God split the waters of the Red Sea to let the people of Israel go through on dry land. When the Egyptians tried to do the same, the waters returned in force and drowned them.

God used Moses to bring His chosen people out of Egypt and lead them to the land that was promised to Abraham, Isaac, and Jacob. It was His plan to have a people different from any other. God wanted a people on whom He could show His love as their Father. He wanted a people that would cause the other nations to acknowledge that there is a God and to seek Him. He wanted a people through whom He could send Messiah to redeem the world.

However, the Israelis picked up a lot of baggage from their four centuries in Egypt. God had to reacquaint them with Himself. Because of their wayward sinful nature, He spoke directly to Moses establishing laws and a detailed system of ritual cleansing and sacrifice, pointing to the future sacrifice of the Messiah. In this way, God would be able to visit His people, His human family, within limits, without having to destroy them due to their sin coming close to His holiness.

The blood of animals would not take away the sin of His people, but their obedience in following this system would cause God to look to the future when the Son of God as the lamb of God would sacrifice His life and blood to take away the sin of as many as would acknowledge Him, repent of their sin, and decide to serve God. God, in His grace, would make them sinless and give them the righteousness of the Son so that their sins would no longer be a barrier between them and their loving heavenly Father.

God promised Moses that He would send an angel before him to lead them and fight against their enemies. However, God warned Moses not to provoke the angel, because the angel would not pardon their sins. Indeed, no angel can pardon sins. The grace to pardon sins is the work of God and it is paid for by the blood of the Messiah. No angel died for mankind, nor would the sacrifice of an angel have been acceptable to God for the sins of mankind. Thus angels can seem strict and short tempered when dealing with humans. The angel God sent did indeed punish the sin of the Israelis from time to time, leading to the death of many in the desert, but he never pardoned their sins.

On the third month of leaving Egypt, God told Moses to have the people sanctify themselves, including bathing, washing their clothes, and abstaining from marital relations, because He was going to come down in three days and manifest Himself, speaking in an audible voice. God wanted the people to be unique to Him and promised Moses that if they would obey, God would make them a holy nation and a kingdom of priests. Moses was to come up into the mountain with Him, but no others could or even touch the mountain, or else they would die. So Moses relayed all that God had said to the people and the priests.

For their part, the people, as one, told Moses, "We will do everything the Lord says."

Moses carried their message back to God. On the appointed day, as Moses prepared to go up into the mountain, the glory of God came down upon the summit of the mountain. The effect was awe inspiring and frightening. The summit of the mountain began to smoke and melt into molten rock at the intense heat of the presence of God. The earth quaked so that it was difficult for people to stand. It thundered and fierce lightening cracked. Loud trumpet blasts from angels were heard.

Then Moses spoke and the voice of God replied telling him to come up into the mountain. Once on the mountain God told Moses to go back and warn the people to keep their distance. If they should come out of curiosity to attempt to gaze upon God they would force God to unleash judgment upon them and they would immediately die. Moses did as instructed and the people backed off, some tripping and getting trampled by the others as they beat a hasty retreat.

God spoke His laws in the hearing of all of the people. When this display was over, the people begged Moses, "From now on you speak to the Lord and then tell us what He said so that we don't die."

Then God called Moses to come to the summit of the mountain, into the thick darkness. While in the mountain with the presence of God, the Lord spoke to Moses alone and gave additional precepts and judgments for Moses to give to the people. When Moses finally returned he relayed to the people what God had said.

Once again the people said, "We will do everything the Lord says."

That evening, Moses wrote out on a scroll the things that God had said. On the next day, Moses offered sacrifices to God. Moses then read the scroll containing God's words to the people.

The people said, "We will do everything that the Lord has said and we will be obedient."

Moses took the blood of the sacrifices, which had been collected in basins, and sprinkled the people with the blood. Then holding the scroll up in one hand and the bloody bunch of straw-like herbs in the other that he had used to sprinkle them, Moses said, "This is the blood of the pact that the Lord has made with you concerning all of these words."

Then Moses, Aaron, Aaron's sons, and 70 of the elders were suddenly lifted up to Heaven. They were stunned by the beauty and the polished blue translucent sapphire pavement that was under them. They all saw God, but God did not touch them. The angels brought them food and drink that they ate and drank in the presence of God. When they finished eating and gazing on God they found themselves back in the encampment.

God then told Moses to return to the mountain so that God could present him with stone tablets on which would be inscribed the laws of God to be taught to the people. So Moses returned to the mountain accompanied by his aide, Joshua, and the elders. Moses told them to remain at a certain point while he would be up in the mountain. In the meantime, Aaron would be in charge. Moses climbed up alone into the thick cloud surrounding the mountain. After seven days, God called him. Moses then went toward the voice of God and remained with God for 40 days and 40 nights as God gave detailed instructions to Moses on the system of His worship to be implemented. This included the portable tent that would be a Temple, an ark or sacred chest to contain the tablets of stone, utensils, priestly clothing, an altar, and many other details. The purpose of this system of sacrifice and worship was so that God would come and dwell among them and be their God, without having to release judgement on them because of their guilt and sinfulness.

The ark of the pact made between the nation of Israel and God was made of wood overlaid with gold. Inside were placed the stone tablets on which God had written 10 commandments that were the basis of laws to govern the relationship of the people to Him as God and between them and their neighbors. Once completed and consecrated, it was not to be touched by human hands. Gold rings were on its sides so that wooden staves could be inserted through the rings and used by the priests to transport the ark. When the people of Israel were not on the move, the ark was kept in a holy place inside a tent were Moses could come and meet with the presence of God. The lid of the ark had two cherubim angels on top facing each other with their wings bent toward the center point of the ark. God's Spirit would dwell above this seat of mercy.

## An Intercessor Between God and Sinful People

In the camp, the people assumed that Moses had died up in the mountain. They then demanded that Aaron make them gods. Aaron complied by asking them all to donate their golden ear rings. From the ear rings Aaron made a golden calf from a cast. The image was of the Egyptian god Apis. Aaron told the people that this was of the gods that brought them out of Egypt.

As the people worshipped the image they also celebrated in an orgy of sensual dancing and revelry. As the principal watcher, I went to the throne room in Heaven to report to God on what was happening with His people. This situation infuriated God. God was both angry with the people and with Aaron. God was also emotionally grieved that the people He had just delivered had so soon turned on Him and rejected Him for images of their own craftsmanship that were not real gods. God told Moses to get back down to the people he had brought out of Egypt, because they had corrupted themselves.

God also instructed Moses, "Don't interfere with what I am about to do." God said that because His holy wrath was about to be unleashed on the people to kill them all and start all over again with a new nation that He would build up starting with Moses and a new family Moses would have.

Moses, at the risk of his own life, pleaded with God not to wipe out the nation that He had just brought out of Egyptian slavery. Because of the intercession of Moses, God did not kill the nation of Israel, but eventually, that adult generation, including Aaron, all died without entering into the land that had been promised.

The intercession of Moses for God to hold back His wrath against a sinful people was a preview of the greater intercession that the Messiah would make. In centuries yet to come the Messiah would let His own blood be sacrificed to cover the sins of all who would come to God for grace and pardon on the basis of His blood.

On another occasion, Korah, of the tribe of Levi, some others of that tribe and some men of the tribe of Ruben took it upon themselves to challenge Moses and Aaron for leadership in an attempted coup d'etat. There were 250 of them in all and they were tribal leaders. They argued that they were just as holy as Moses. And who did Moses think he was to set himself up as a prince over this people? After all they said, Moses had promised to take them to a land of milk and honey, but instead, they were in the desert.

Moses told them to come out the next day in front of their tents to see who belonged to the Lord and who was holy. That morning, Moses walked to their area.

God was not happy with the rebellion and told Moses and Aaron to stand aside so He could destroy the whole multitude of millions in a moment. But Moses and Aaron fell on their faces before God and interceded for the people that all would not die for the sin of one man. Moses then got up and gave the people nearby the warning he had received from God for them to separate themselves from the rebels or be destroyed with them.

Then Moses said, "If you die a normal death then I haven't been sent by God or done things by the hand of God. Let a new thing happen here. Let the ground open up and swallow up Korah and all them that side with him! Then all will know that these men have provoked God."

Immediately, the earth opened and swallowed Korah, his co-conspirators, and their tents. A fire then burned them and the earth closed back up again.

Not long after leaving Egypt, the people began to complain against Moses and Aaron over food. They said they wished they were back in Egypt where they ate their fill. They told Moses, "You brought us out here to die of starvation!"

God was displeased with their complaints, but He spoke to Moses telling him that He would rain bread from heaven. This substance was called manna. God gave Moses rules for how much and how many days a week the people were to gather the small round wafers called manna. Millions of people ate the manna for the entire 40 years of their wandering in the wilderness.

Not long after the beginning of the miracle of the manna, the people were ready to kill Moses and Aaron by stoning because of their thirst. They said, "Why did you bring us out here for us, our children, and our cattle to die of thirst? Is the Lord among us or not?"

When Moses went to God over the matter, God directed him to take three leaders with him and in their presence strike a certain rock with his staff. Out of the rock would flow enough water to meet the needs of the multitude of people and their herds of animals.

God gave Moses detailed instructions for a portable place for His presence to reside called the tent of meeting and the tabernacle of the congregation. It was a place where God's presence would reside and where Moses could come to be in God's presence and hear from Him. Explicit instructions were given for everything in this special structure and for the system of worship. When the project was completed and the tent for the tabernacle set up, the manifest presence of God came in. A cloud of God's glory covered it in the day time and flames of fire were over it at night. It was a supernatural spectacle that was present for everyday of their 40-year sojourn in the wilderness. The people would gaze at this manifestation and worship the God that lived among them. As caravans plying trade between countries came near the encampment, they saw this supernatural sight and reported it wherever they traveled. So surrounding nations began to fear this multi-million-person mass of people with the God who revealed Himself in a supernatural way that could be seen.

Although God had supernaturally provided the people with daily food, the manna, the people began to complain to Moses that they detested the manna and wanted some meat. In turn, Moses complained to God that dealing with the people was more than he could bear.

God instructed Moses to gather 70 of the elders and leaders to come with him to the tabernacle of the congregation. When they gathered, God came down in a cloud of His glory and spoke to Moses. God took the spirit that was on Moses and put it on them too so that they could share with Moses the burden of dealing with the people.

Then God told Moses what to say to the people concerning meat. They had angered God by talking against the manna God had provided and wishing they were back in Egypt. "Tell the people," God said to Moses "you will get meat to eat. It won't be for just one, two, five, ten, or twenty days, but for a whole month. You will come to detest it and begin to vomit it up through your nostrils."

Moses replied to God, "Just where am I supposed to get the meat to feed them? There are over 600,000 military eligible men among them plus their families. Shall I kill every animal in our herds to give them meat or shall we take all of the fish in the sea to satisfy their hunger?"

God answered Moses, "You will see whether my words prove true or not."

Moses relayed God's words to the people. God then sent in a strong wind that blew in a massive flock of quail from the direction of the sea. The quail were all around the encampment and were between the ground and two meters high off the ground so that they were easy to catch. However, the complaining of the people had angered God. So that when people began to actually eat the quail, the greediest among them died instantly while the quail meat was still between their teeth before they could even chew or swallow the quail meat.

Some years later, as they were going around the kingdom of Edom, which had refused them passage, the people again complained against God. They complained that there was no water to drink and said they were sick and tired of eating manna and wanted real bread instead. So God sent poisonous snakes among them that began to bite the people. Everyone that was bitten died. A large number of people died from the snake bites.

Realizing they had done wrong and displeased God, the people came to Moses. They said, "We have sinned against God and against you. Please pray that these snakes be taken away." So Moses prayed to God for the people.

The Lord answered Moses telling him, "Make a snake of brass and mount it on a pole. Everyone that gets bitten will live when he looks on the brass snake."

## The Plot to Provoke God's Wrath on His Own People

While the Israelis were encamped in the territory of Moab near the Jordan River they were tested by a satanic plot. A prophet named Balaam was hired by Balak the king of Moab to put a curse on the Israelis. Twice Balak sent a high-level delegation to Balaam to entice him to come and curse the Israelis. Balak had seen what the Israelis had done in vanquishing other kingdoms in the region that had come out against them. Fearing that his kingdom would suffer the same fate, Balak consulted with the leaders of Midian to get them to join with him or face the fate of other nations in the way of the Israelis. They sent a delegation to bring Balaam to curse the Israelis.

Three times in three different locations Balaam had Balak offer up sacrifices, but instead of cursing the Israelis, each time Balaam spoke only the blessing and prophesy which God gave him. Balak was angered to the point of doing harm to Balaam. Not wanting to miss out on a big pay day, Balaam received in his mind a scheme from Satan to bring a curse on the Israelis and he counseled Balak to implement the plan. Satan again thought to block the Messiah from coming by using the young women of Moab to seduce the Israeli men in the hope that God would become angry with them and disown them.

The plan of Satan, as passed on to Balak by Balaam appeared to work. The young women of Moab slipped into the Israeli encampment and seduced the men to have sex with them and to worship Baal-Peor, the lord of the hole or vagina. This involved the god Baal and the goddess Asherah. Temple prostitutes, fornication, and sexual perversion were all part of that system of idolatrous worship. Moses instructed the leaders to kill everyman that was taken away by this scheme. God also sent a plague among them that killed 24,000 people.

God relented and the plague was halted when Aaron's grandson Phineas saw a senior leader from the tribe of Simeon take a foreign woman into his tent to have sex with her. Taking a javelin in hand, Phineas went into that tent. He found the two in the act of intercourse and with one thrust put the javelin through both of them. Moreover, God instructed Moses to have the military age men assemble and go to war with the kingdom of Moab. In the course of events, Balaam was killed together with the royals of Moab.

# Chapter 13 Taking the Promised Land

*And I will send an angel before thee; and I will drive out the Canaanite, the Amorite, and the Hittite, and the Perizzite, the Hivite, and the Jebusite. Exodus 33:2*

Before his death, Moses gave a farewell address as recorded in the book of Deuteronomy.[9] The key portion of that farewell address was that God was going to send someone like him and that the people should listen to that man. Moses was referring to the Messiah to come who, like Moses, would have a relationship with God the Father unequalled by any other person. Like Moses, the Messiah to come would do great miracles. Most importantly, the Messiah to come would speak to the people what He heard from God, just as Moses did.

At the age of 120 years Moses was still strong and had his eyesight. He directed the people of Israel as their fighting forces defeated the Amorites to the east of the Jordan River. However, God would not allow Moses on the other side of the Jordan River because of his disobedience to instructions at Meribah, when Moses caused water to come from a rock by striking it twice in anger, rather than speaking to it as God had told him to do. Nevertheless, God led Moses to the top of a mountain

---

[9] An additional scripture is provided here for context.

And Joshua said, Hereby ye shall know that the living God is among you, and that he will without fail drive out from before you the Canaanites, and the Hittites, and the Hivites, and the Perizzites, and the Girgashites, and the Amorites, and the Jebusites. Joshua 3:10

from which He caused Moses to see all of the land that was promised on the other side of the Jordan. It was as if Moses flew over the land in that he saw every detail from north, south, east, and west. However, Moses never left the mountain during this visual excursion. Afterward, Moses died and God Himself buried Moses. There was no monument and no one knew where Moses was buried. Satan wanted access to the body of Moses, knowing how the people revered him, so that he could deceive them into rebelling against God.

The people went through a traditional period of forty days of mourning the death of Moses. God had already prepared Joshua, the closest aide of Moses, to assume leadership and take the people across the Jordan River into the land that had been promised.

God spoke to the eighty-year-old Joshua, following the mourning period, and give him his orders for the next phase in the life of the nation. God said, "My servant Moses is dead, so get up and cross this Jordan River, you and all of these people, into the land that I have given them as descendants of Israel. Just as I said to Moses, I have given you every place your feet walk on. Your boundaries shall be from the wilderness of the Negev to Lebanon, over to the Euphrates River, the territory of the Hittites, and back over to the Great Sea (Mediterranean Sea) to the west. No one will be able to successfully resist you your entire life. I will be with you just like I was with Moses. I will neither fail you nor desert you. So be strong and take courage, because you will divide up the land I swore to your ancestors as an inheritance. Just be resolute and very courageous observing all of the law that My servant Moses commanded. Don't waiver to the right hand or to the left so that you succeed wherever you go. This Torah of the law shall always be in your mouth. Meditate on it night and day so that you live according to what is written in it. Then you will overcome every obstacle in your way and have good success. Haven't I given you the command? Be stout hearted and encouraged. Don't be afraid of anything and don't let yourself get terrified and lose heart, because Yahweh your God is with you wherever you go."

Joshua gathered the leaders of the tribes and told them to tell the people to get ready, because in three days they would cross over the Jordan River and begin to take the land that God had promised. He had a special instruction for the fighting men of the tribes of Reuben, Gad, and half of the tribe of Manasseh. They liked the land on the west bank of the Jordan River and decided to take that as their inheritance. However, Joshua required their fighting men to cross over and assist the other tribes in subduing the lands that were to be allotted to them, while leaving their families and cattle behind.

The tribal leaders then swore an oath of fealty to Joshua. They said, "We will do everything you have commanded us to do and we will go to every place that you send us. Just like we listened to Moses, we will listen to you. Yahweh your God will certainly be with you as He was with Moses. Any man that challenges your orders and refuses to listen to you regarding all the things that you command will be put to death. Just see to it that you are stout hearted and courageous."

**Invade, Cleanse, and Possess the Land**

The land of Canaan was populated by wicked people. They were engaged in human sacrifice to Baal,

Molech, and Ashtoreth and worshipped other gods along with those. They were involved in sexual perversion, promiscuity, and bestiality. For that reason, God instructed that some of them were to be totally annihilated including men, women, children, and animals.

The same obstacles that their fathers saw forty years earlier were still in place. Cities had defensive walls and there were a number of giants of super-sized stature in the land. They had never had giants among them before. The giants were genetic mutations resulting from a second round of activity by some of Satan's fallen angels. In addition, the Jordan River was at flood stage and had flowed over its banks. The people that Joshua lead did not have ferries, boats, or bridges to get across the river as an expeditionary force, not to mention their women, children, and cattle.

Following God's orders, on the day of the crossing Joshua had the priests carry the ark, the most holy symbol of the pact between God and His special people, the descendants of Abraham, Isaac, and Jacob. The priests carried the ark in front of the nation and halted in the river's water once they got ankle deep. Then God did something miraculous.

Angels were sent to divide the flood waters. The angels cut off the waters flowing south so that there was no backwash. Instead, those waters continued to move south toward the Dead Sea. At the same time, other angels caused the waters above that spot to the north to reverse flow and pile up miles to the north as if contained by giant glass walls. In this way the people were able to cross on the dry river bed and the areas to the north did not flood on either side of the river. Although no one saw the angels, the effect was dramatic.

That day God caused the people to fear Joshua just as they had feared Moses. Once everyone crossed over, God told Joshua, "Command the priests carrying the ark to come up out of the river bed with the ark."

Joshua was learning to wait and act on God's instructions rather than to presume what action to take. So when he gave the command to the priests, as instructed by God, they were the last ones to cross over and come up out of the river bed. Once their feet touched the higher ground on the other side of the Jordan River, the waters that had piled up to the north came crashing down stream and the waters to the south backwashed to meet them until the Jordan River resumed its normal seasonal overflowing of its banks.

When the kings of the Canaanites and the Amorites learned from their spies what had happened, they were filled with fear. Even before that, Joshua had sent two spies into Jericho prior to the crossing. Those two spies took lodging in a bed and board house on the city walls.

The establishment also doubled as a house of prostitution. The innkeeper - prostitute that ran the place hid them from the authorities that came looking for them and assisted their escape over the city wall. But before she did, she told them that the people of Jericho were aware of what miracles God had done in bringing the Hebrews out of Egypt by drying up the Red Sea before them and giving them victories over the Amorite kings on the eastern side of the Jordan River. Because of that her people were terrified. So she bargained to assist the two spies if they would promise to spare her and her extended family when they returned to conquer the land. The spies agreed to that deal and kept their word. That woman,

Rahab, ultimately became one of the ancestors of the Messiah in what was a powerful demonstration of the grace of God and His willingness to adopt people into His family.

After the miraculous crossing of the Jordan, Joshua had all of the men circumcised, because their fathers, who died in the wilderness, did not keep up the rite of circumcision for forty years. This would have put the Hebrew warriors at a decided disadvantage to defend themselves for a few days except for the fact that the people they were invading were terrified of them because of the miracles they had seen God do for them.

Once on the other side of the Jordan River the miracle of the daily manna ceased. They would now be able to eat what they took from the people they conquered until they could plant and harvest their own crops.

One day, as Joshua walked near Jericho, he came upon what appeared to be a man with his sword drawn. Joshua asked, "Are you with us or with our enemies?"

The man answered, "Neither. I am here as the field marshal of the angelic armies of Yahweh." The man with the drawn sword was the Son of God in human guise and with most of his glory restrained so as not to unintentionally destroy Joshua in the encounter. Even so, He commanded Joshua to remove his shoes because he was on holy ground in His presence. Joshua immediately removed his shoes, prostrated himself before the man and worshipped Him as the God that he was.

God then gave Joshua explicit instructions on how to take Jericho. For six days Joshua's warriors were to march around Jericho once each day in complete silence, with the priests carrying the ark and seven other priests going before the ark with trumpets. On the seventh day they were to walk silently around Jericho seven times at the end of which the priests were to blow the trumpets and the people shout. At that sound, God said the walls would fall down and Joshua's fighting men could go straight up and take the city.

Joshua followed those instructions and it happened just as God said that it would. When the priests blew on the trumpets and the people shouted God's angels appeared, unseen to Joshua and his warriors, and pulled the walls of Jericho out flat and away from the city, leaving the city unprotected and its inhabitants paralyzed by fear as Joshua's warriors advanced and killed every living thing, except for Rahab and her family.

Not long afterwards, Joshua was tricked into making a treaty with the people of a large city called Gibeon, because he neglected to inquire of God in the matter. Nevertheless, the treaty was honored and the people of Gibeon became willing slaves once their deception was eventually exposed.

A confederation of five Amorite kings decided to teach Gibeon a lesson for their collaboration with Joshua and attacked them. The people of Gibeon then begged Joshua to honor their treaty and save them from the army of the confederation that came against them. With God's blessing and encouragement, Joshua made a forced march under darkness to Gibeon, surprised the Amorite confederation at dawn and began to slaughter them. The army of the Amorite confederation scattered and ran for their lives. Unseen angels of God also fought for Joshua. They caused large hailstones to pound the Amorite armies killing more that way than Joshua's warriors killed with their swords.

When Joshua realized that there would not be enough daylight available to chase down and kill the Amorites, he spoke to God. It was God who then put it into Joshua what to decree next. Joshua then looked up into the sky and commanded, "Sun, you stand still where you are over Gibeon, and Moon you stay right where you are over the valley of Ajalon!" Joshua shouted this command out loud so that even in the din of war his troops heard him. The sun and moon remained fixed in their locations for about an additional day's time. This kept an army of God's angels busy as they worked in concert to make the words God had given Joshua happen. They performed a notable miracle that defied the natural laws of motion, physics, gravity, and the relationships of all of the bodies in the universe. This enabled Joshua's warriors to eliminate all of the warriors of the Amorite armies.

As God had promised Moses, the campaign of taking the promised land of Canaan did not take just one year, but occurred in stages so that the people of God could take possession in an orderly fashion and wild animals wouldn't multiply against them due to an absence of human occupation. In addition, as God had promised Moses, God sent swarms of hornets against some of the nations they would be fighting against to cause them to retreat before them. Before Joshua died, he completed the process of dividing up the land among the tribes and released the warriors of the tribes of Reuben, Gad, and the half tribe of Manasseh to return to their chosen lot on the east side of the Jordan River.

The wars of possession of Canaan went on for years. In some instances, the warriors of the tribes of Israel did as they were instructed by God and killed the inhabitants. In the process they also killed the giants there. The giants were the offspring of a fallen angel that schemed with Satan to keep the land from being turned over to the descendants of Abraham, Isaac, and Jacob by giving up his angelic status to co-habit with the local women and pollute the gene pool. This was one of the reasons that God directed that the inhabitants be exterminated.

Joshua was 110 years old when he died. He lived for 30 years after taking command from Moses. Before he died he gave a farewell address that was mostly delivering to the people a prophetic word that he had received from God for them. The people swore once again that they would worship God only and not the gods of the people of Canaan that they were displacing.

## Spurning God's Love for Other Lovers

In time, all of the generation that had come out of Egypt and seen the great miracles of God on their behalf died off. They were replaced by another generation that lacked firsthand encounters with God. In addition, instead of clearing the land completely of the various nations that lived in Canaan, they put some that they did not easily defeat under taxation in the form of annual tribute. In that way, some of the people of Canaan continued to live among them. Worse still, the people of Israel, began to intermarry with the people of Canaan. They had been forbidden to intermarry with the people of Canaan. Once again, they began to worship the gods of the nations of Canaan, that is, Baal and the gods associated with him. This included the seductive goddess Ashtoreth, also known as Ashera. This turn of events once again threatened to eliminate a pure line through which the Messiah could come.

It was my sad duty as the principal watcher to go to the throne room of God in Heaven to report to Him on how quickly His people had turned aside from Him and begun to do the very things for which He had judged the inhabitants of Canaan and the surrounding nations. God was so angry and emotionally hurt that He said nothing. I felt bad for God and wondered why He put up with these ungrateful and unfaithful people. He told me to return to earth and to continue keeping my books along with the other watchers under my command.

To demonstrate His displeasure with the path the people had taken, God had an angel go up from where the ark and tent of Moses were located, appear to the people and address them as a representative of the voice of God. Speaking for God, he said, "I brought you up out of Egypt and into the land that I swore to your ancestors that I would give you. I said to them that I would never break my pact with you. I also said, for your part, you were not to make treaties with the nations that you found in this land. Instead, you were to destroy their altars, but you didn't listen to My voice. Why did you do that? Because of that, I said I will not drive them out as you advance. They will be like thorns in your side and their gods will trip you up and ensnare you." So the nations that were still in Canaan when Joshua died, were never fully conquered and driven out.

So began a cycle of the people of Israel forgetting their pact with God and engaging in all of the idol worship of the local people that they did not drive out of the land. When they did this, God allowed them to be subjugated and abused by those other nations of Canaan as well as by neighboring nations. That persisted until people called out to God and He established a judge. The judge would break the subjugation and people would live as God intended until that judge died. Once the judge died, they resumed the cycle again of worshipping Baal, and his cohort of gods and goddesses. They then fell back into subjugation to their enemies. These were the same enemies that they did not drive out of Canaan in the first place as they were instructed to do. This situation continued until God raised up another judge. During this period, the tribes of Israel also descended into bloody civil war.

In one of these cycles of the nation of Israel turning its back on God and turning instead to Baal and the goddess Ashtoreth, God showed His displeasure by allowing them to be subjugated by the nation of Midian. For seven years the people of Israel hid in caves to save themselves from the hordes of Midian that would descend on them at harvest time like a plague of locusts to take their harvest and impoverish them. Out of this dire situation the people of Israel cried out to God in prayer.

God had pity on them and sent Yahweh's special messenger to Gideon. This messenger was the pre-incarnate Son of God, Jesus, the promised Messiah, in the guise of an angel. Gideon was meekly trying to thresh his grain harvest out of sight, to keep it from the armies of Midian, when the angel appeared to him and spoke with him. The angel said, "Yahweh is with you, you mighty man of valor!"

Gideon certainly didn't feel like he met that description. So he said to the angel, "Sir, if Yahweh is with us, then why are we on such hard times? And where are all of the miracles of deliverance that our ancestors told us about like how God brought us up out of Egypt? The way I see it, Yahweh has given up on us and allowed us to come under the cruel fist of the people of Midian."

The unrevealed Son of God looked at Gideon and said, "Go in the strength that you have and you will save Israel from the fist of Midian. After all, haven't I sent you?"

Gideon asked the special angel to stay while he quickly brought back the elements of an offering that included loaves of unleavened bread, a killed and dressed kid, and a pot of broth. The angel instructed Gideon to set it on a nearby rock and pour the broth over it all. Once Gideon did so the angel, who was really the Son of God, touched it with the staff he was holding. Immediately, fire came up from the rock to completely incinerate it so that smoke from it went up. Then the angel disappeared. Gideon then realized that he had just seen Yahweh's special angel face to face and he feared he would die because of it.

But the voice of God spoke to him and said, "Peace be on you. Don't be afraid. You won't die." Then Gideon built an altar to God there and called it Yahweh is peace.

That same night the voice of God spoke to Gideon and told him to destroy the altar that his father had set up to the god Baal and cut down the wooden carved poles to the goddess Ashtoreth that were in the same place. Finally, Gideon was instructed to return to the place where he met the angel, erect an altar to God, and offer up a young bull as a sacrifice using the wood from the poles devoted to the goddess Ashtoreth as fuel. Gideon did all of this at night with the assistance of ten of his servants.

The next day when the men of the city saw what had happened to the altar of Baal and the wooden poles of the goddess Ashtoreth, and realized Gideon was behind it all, they demanded that Gideon's father produce him so that they could kill him.

However, Gideon's father said, "Let Baal defend himself if he is a god! We will kill right now whoever wants to side with Baal in this matter."

Then the armies of Midian and Amalek joined together against Israel and set themselves in battle array in the valley of Jezreel. When God's Spirit came on Gideon he called the men of Israel to arms. Thirty-two thousand fighting men of Israel responded to Gideon's call to arms.

However, the voice of God spoke to Gideon and told him that he had too many men. God did not want them to say that they beat the army of Midian themselves and thus not honor God. So God told Gideon to put out the message, "Whoever is fearful and afraid may leave." After that was done only ten thousand remained, but God told Gideon that there were still too many.

The Lord then devised a test. He had Gideon take the ten thousand brave volunteer warriors down to the waterside to drink. Those that cupped their hands to scoop up water and then slurped that water from their hand with their tongues, like a dog licks up water were set aside. Those who got down and put their faces in the water to suck up the water were put to the other side. There were only 300 in the group that vigilantly scooped up the water with one hand and maintained their vigilance while licking that water out of their hand.

God told Gideon, "I will save you with the three hundred that licked the water from their hand and give the army of Midian into your hands. Let everyone else go home."

Although the army of Midian and its ally covered the valley, Gideon and his three hundred were not afraid. That night Gideon made a raid on the opposing army. He divided his men into three companies of one hundred each with torches hidden inside clay jars and each having a horn. When signaled, they all smashed their jars. The exploding noise echoed through the valley causing confusion and fear among the enemy. They held up their torches, blew their horns, and shouted, "The sword of Yahweh and of Gideon!"

As they stood their ground, unseen angels of God swooped over the valley and spread confusion over the enemy army so that in the confusion they killed each other. As dawn broke, the remainder of the invading army fled in one direction. Although they numbered only three hundred, Gideon's men pursued them and cut them down over the course of a day. The people of the region were elated by the victory and asked Gideon to be their king. But Gideon said, "Neither I nor my son will rule over you; Yahweh will rule over you!"

The last great judge was Samuel. Samuel was born in answer to the prayer of his mother who was previously childless. Out of gratitude, she turned him over to Eli the high priest to be raised in his household. As a child, God began to speak to Samuel. It was during his childhood that God's judgment came on Eli and his two sons so that all died in the same day. The sinful and presumptuous sons of Eli thought to use the ark as a magic charm and took it into battle against the army of Philistia. However, Israel was defeated, Eli's sons were killed, and the ark was captured by Philistia. When the news came to Eli, he was so stunned that he fell over, breaking his neck in the fall, and died.

The ark brought death and disease to the cities of Philistia that tried to host it. In addition, the idol of the god of Philistia, Dagon, was supernaturally smashed before the ark when the princes of Philistia tried to put the ark in the Temple of Dagon to show the superiority of Dagon. In the end, they let the ark be returned to Israel via a driverless ox cart using unbroken oxen.

Mishandling the ark by towns in Israel resulted in massive death in those towns of Israel. The ark was then held in obscurity and away from Jerusalem and the priesthood for over twenty years. During that time, it was in the custody of one man's household.

Under the adult Samuel, whom God established as a prophet and judge, God delivered the people of Israel from the people of Philistia. When Samuel, in his old age tried to set his sons up as judges, the people rejected that and demanded a king like all of the other nations. Besides, Samuel's sons were corrupt and accepted bribes to render the judgment that was bought, and not the honest and fair judgment that was required.

**The People Demand a King, Not a Theocracy**

Samuel was offended and hurt that the people wanted a king. So he prayed to God about it. Yahweh spoke to Samuel in reply and said, "Do what the people have asked you to do in all that they have requested. They haven't rejected you, but they have rejected Me from being their king and ruling them. This is the same thing they have done from the day I brought them up out of Egypt until now. During the whole time they left Me and served other gods. So now they are giving you the same treatment. Give them what they are asking for, but at the same time don't do it gladly and warn them sternly what it will be like to be under a king."

Samuel did as God had directed him and anointed Saul of the tribe of Benjamin to be Israel's first king. At the coronation, Samuel was still nursing personal hurt over being rejected by the people. To clear the record, Samuel demanded of the people saying, "Look everybody, I am right here. So in the sight of Yahweh and your newly crowned king, step up and testify against me. Did I take anyone's ox or donkey? Give the name of anyone that I cheated or used my power to abuse their rights. Name, if you can, anyone from whom I took a bribe to close my eyes to their wrongdoing and deny justice? If I wronged anyone I will pay you back right now!"

The people responded to Samuel's sour words by saying, "You haven't stolen from us, abused your power over us, or taken anything from anyone by force."

Samuel then recounted how God had dealt with the nation from the time that He used Moses and Aaron to bring them out of Egypt. Samuel summed up by warning them, "If you don't obey Yahweh, but rebel against His commandments instead, then the hand of Yahweh will come against you as it did when your ancestors went astray. Just so you know for sure that I am speaking for Yahweh, watch this! It's harvest time isn't it? It doesn't rain in harvest time, but I am going to call on Yahweh to send thunder and rain so you will know you haven't done the right thing by demanding a king."

Samuel called out to God. Immediately, thick dark clouds rolled in and strong winds whipped up the dust.

Lightning flashed directly overhead followed by loud peals of thunder and an extremely heavy rain pelted the crowd. People screamed and cringed. Fearing God and the wrath of Samuel, the people asked Samuel, "Pray to Yahweh your God for us so He doesn't kill us! Yes, we admit that we sinned and did wrong to ask for a king."

Samuel's anger abated and he agreed to pray to God. When he did, the rain, lightning, thunder, and wind stopped as suddenly as it all began. People were left soaked and shivering. As the sun came back out through the clouds, they were just glad to be alive. So ended the grand coronation of Saul, Israel's first king.

# Chapter 14 The Rise of David

*And when he had removed him, he raised up unto them
David to be their king; to whom also he gave testimony,
and said, I have found David the son of Jesse, a man after
mine own heart, which shall fulfil all my will. Acts 13:22*

As Saul organized his kingdom he built up a small
army and took on the neighboring nation of Philistia.
Philistia had better technology and equipment. They had
many times more war chariots than Saul had soldiers in
his army. Philistia also had a mobile large swift cavalry.
In addition, it had weapons of steel that were far superior
to the bronze weapons that the army of Israel used. Worse
still, only Saul and his son Jonathan had proper weapons
and body armor. Moreover, Philistia had a secret weapon
at its disposal. They had among them the progeny of a
giant who were themselves giants. These giants had been
trained from childhood to be warriors and be the vanguard
of their army in battle. The sight of the giant super
warriors alone would melt the hearts of their opponents.

When the army of Philistia came out in battle
array, Saul's much smaller and underequipped army lost
heart and many slipped away and deserted. Samuel sent
word to Saul to wait seven days for him. After seven
days, and with his army down to only a few hundred men
due to desertions, Saul panicked and decided to usurp the
role of a prophet and priest by making a burnt offering
himself, thinking it would appease God and protect him.

As soon as Saul finished offering up his burnt
offering, Samuel showed up. Samuel was dumbfounded.
He said to Saul, "What have you done! You have been
very foolish. If you had just done what Yahweh your God

commanded, Yahweh would have given you a royal dynasty. But that won't happen now. Yahweh has already selected a man after His own heart and has decreed that he will be the leader of His people, all because you didn't stick to what Yahweh commanded."

However, Saul's end did not come immediately. While still at the battlefront, Saul summoned the ark of God's pact with the nation of Israel. As the priests brought it they heard an uproar from within the army of Philistia. Angels of God went among the army of Philistia and confused them and filled them with terror so that they turned on each other, hacking one another to death. Saul's small army then chased the remainder of the army of Philistia and killed more of them until that army withdrew and returned to walled cities in Philistia. But when Saul tried to hear from God on next steps, God was silent and would not speak to him.

Saul then rebuilt his army and began to have military successes fighting both against the neighboring kingdoms of Moab, Ammon, Amalek, and Edom, and those still in the promised land that Israel had not fully conquered; in particular, Philistia. Saul's wars with Philistia were incessant and difficult.

When God gave King Saul instructions through Samuel to attack and exterminate every living thing in the nation of Amalek, both human and animal, Saul amassed an army of over 200,000 infantrymen. Saul proceeded with the extermination of the nation of Amalek, but captured its king alive, and took the best of the cattle as booty and to offer sacrifices.

## God Rejects Saul as King

Although Samuel was in another location, the voice of God came to him at night and said, "I am sorry that I set up Saul as king because he has turned his back on me and hasn't done what I commanded."

Samuel was heartbroken upon hearing that and cried out to God on Saul's behalf all night, but God did not change His mind in the matter. So Samuel got up very early in the morning and traveled to Gilgal, where King Saul was with his army.

Saul greeted Samuel warmly saying, "God bless you! I have done what Yahweh commanded."

But Samuel responded, "Then what is the explanation for all of this noise in my ears from sheep bleating and the lowing of oxen?"

King Saul said, "The men brought the best of the sheep and oxen from Amalek to sacrifice to Yahweh your God, but we completely destroyed all the rest."

Samuel then said, "I am going to tell you what Yahweh said to me last night."

"Tell me then," said Saul.

Samuel then laid out for King Saul what God had spoken. "When you weren't much in your own eyes, weren't you made the head of all of the tribes of Israel? Yahweh sent you on a mission and said 'Go and completely destroy the people of Amalek by fighting against them until they are exterminated.' Why didn't you obey what Yahweh said to do? Instead you greedily seized the livestock doing what was evil in Yahweh's eyes."

Saul responded by saying, "But I have obeyed Yahweh's instructions! I did what Yahweh sent me to do and brought back as a prisoner Agag, the king of Amalek, and exterminated all of the other people of Amalek. However, the men took the booty, the best of the sheep and oxen, the rest of which we destroyed, to sacrifice them to Yahweh your God in Gilgal."

Samuel issued a stern rebuke to King Saul. He said, "Do you think Yahweh is as pleased with burnt offerings and sacrifices as He is with someone obeying His voice? Listen, it is better to obey than to offer a sacrifice, and to listen than to have the fat of rams on the burnt offering. I tell you that rebellion is no different than the sin of witchcraft and stubbornness is the same as sin and idol worship. Because you rejected Yahweh's word, He has rejected you from continuing as king."

Saul began to beg, blame his troops, and try to get Samuel to allow him to save face before his army. Saul said to Samuel, "I have sinned. I have disregarded Yahweh's instructions and your words, but I did so because I feared the troops and listened to them. Now please, pardon my sin and go back with me before the rest of the men so that I might worship Yahweh with you."

Samuel would not go with the king. Instead, he said, "I won't go back there with you because you rejected Yahweh's word and Yahweh has rejected your kingship over Israel." As Samuel turned to leave Saul and go home, Saul forcefully grabbed Samuel's mantle to jerk him back, but it ripped. Samuel looked at the torn mantle and then looked at Saul. Samuel then said, "Yahweh has ripped the kingdom of Israel from you today and has given it to a neighbor of yours who is better than you." Before he left, Samuel asked that King Agag of Amalek be brought to him whereupon he personally took a sword and hacked Agag into pieces to demonstrate total obedience to God's instructions. After that, Samuel chose not to see Saul again for the rest of his life.

God finally spoke to Samuel and said, "Just how long are you going to mourn over Saul since you know I have rejected his reign over Israel? Fill up you horn with oil and go. I am sending you to Jesse who lives in Bethlehem, because I have provided for Myself one of his sons to be king."

Samuel was a bit hesitant to follow through because he feared Saul would kill him if he knew what he was up to. When Samuel went to Bethlehem, the town leaders were fearful as to the meaning of his appearance there. "Do you come in peace," they asked?

"Yes, I have come in peace," said Samuel. "I am here to sacrifice to Yahweh. Sanctify yourselves and come along." Samuel specifically invited and sanctified Jesse and his sons that were present. Then Samuel had Jesse present each of his sons to him. Samuel was impressed with each one, but each time the Lord spoke into Samuel's mind that the one before him was not the one. So Samuel turned to Jesse, after reviewing seven of Jesse's sons, and said, "Yahweh hasn't chosen any of these. Are all your children here?"

Jesse said, "Only the youngest one is left and he is out watching the sheep."

Samuel said, "Send someone to fetch him here. We are not going to sit down until he is here."

When David was brought before Samuel, God spoke to Samuel, "Anoint him, because this is him." So Samuel poured his horn of oil over David's head in front of his relatives. From that day, the Spirit of the Lord came on David. At the same time, the Spirit of the Lord left

Saul. The Spirit left Saul and moved to David, although He could not be seen with human eyes.

With the Spirit of the Lord gone from Saul, an evil spirit entered into Saul and he became a disturbed and driven man. Although the evil spirit was not seen as it entered into Saul, the face of Saul immediately changed, along with his disposition as that spirit settled into its host. Saul's men in the royal court approached him about his change. They told him that an evil spirit had come to him and counseled him to have someone find and bring to him a skillful musician with the harp to help put him in a better mood. Saul agreed and eventually one of his staff recommended to him David the son of Jesse of Bethlehem.

Soon David was brought to the palace. Saul grew very fond of him and asked Jesse to let his son remain in his service. Whenever the evil spirit, which appeared as an invisible angry monster, perched on Saul's shoulders and head, agitated Saul, David would play on his harp. When David played his harp the evil spirit would relent and temporarily remove itself because it could not stand the sweet atmosphere of godly worship. Saul would then return to his right mind.

When the army of Philistia came out once again to confront Israel, King Saul led his army out against them. Three of Jesse's oldest sons were part of that army. David took the opportunity to return to his father and resume tending the sheep.

For 40 days the two armies faced off against each other, separated by a valley. The champion of the army of Philistia was a giant out of Gath named Goliath. Goliath was a super warrior and also had four other brothers who were also giants like him. Every morning and evening for

40 days Goliath would come out and taunt the army of Israel daring them to send out a man to fight him, with the loser's army to surrender. The morale of the army of Israel was rock bottom. No one had the courage to face Goliath, so they endured his taunts and disrespect of God each day.

## God's Young Champion Versus the Giant

About that time Jesse sent David to the battlefront with provisions for his brothers and the officers under whom they served. While he was there, David heard the soldiers of Israel's army speaking of Goliath. "Have you seen this man? They have put him out there to defy Israel, but the king will make a wealthy man out of whoever can kill him and will also give that man his daughter the princess and make his family tax free."

So David went around asking, "What will be done for the man that kills this Philistine that is daring Israel. Who is he anyway but an uncircumcised Philistine? He thinks he can defy the armies of the living God?"

When David's oldest brother Eliab heard of it he angrily confronted David and tried to put him down. Eliab was still jealous that the prophet Samuel had passed him over to anoint his despised little brother. "Why did you come down here? And with whom did you leave with those few sheep in the wilderness? I know your prideful self and your useless heart. You have come down here so that you could see the battle," said Eliab.

But David wouldn't stand for a tongue lashing from his oldest brother. David said, "What have I done now? Isn't there a cause to fight for?" With that David spun away from Eliab and continued to demand what would be done for the man who kills Goliath.

When men told Saul what David was saying the king sent for him. Saul was familiar with David, but he said what seemed obvious, "You can't go up against this Philistine and fight with him. You are just a skinny young teenager and he was trained to be a warrior since he was a boy."

But David didn't flinch. He told Saul, "Your subject kept my father's sheep and when a lion came, and then a bear, snatching a lamb out of the flock, I went after them, struck them, and they dropped the lamb. And when they turned to attack me, I caught them by the beard and smashed their skulls, killing them. I, your subject, killed the lion and the bear and this uncircumcised Philistine will go down just like they did, since he has challenged the armies of the living God. Besides that, Yahweh saved me from the claws of the lion and the bear and He will save me from this Philistine."

So Saul said, "Go, and may Yahweh be with you."

David took the battle to Goliath. He went after him with his shepherd's staff and a sling. Stopping at the brook in the valley, David picked up five smooth stones and put them in his pouch, then proceeded to his encounter with the giant. The giant, accompanied by a soldier carrying his shield and extra weapons, looked at David dismissively when he saw David was a mere kid and not a warrior.

Goliath said to David, "Am I a dog that you come at me with a stick?" Then the giant cussed at David in the name of the gods of Philistia. Goliath then told David, "Come here and I will feed your flesh to the birds and the wild animals."

But David, running toward the giant, said, "You take me on with a sword, spear, and a shield, but I come to you in the name of Yahweh Sabaoth, the God of the Armies of Israel whom you have dared. Before this day is over Yahweh will turn you over to me. I will strike you and take off your head. Then I will have the birds and wild animals eat the corpses of the army of Philistia so that the whole world will know that there is a God in Israel. Everyone here will know that Yahweh doesn't save based on swords and spears. This is Yahweh's battle and He will give us victory over you and your army."

David ran toward the giant, swinging his sling around faster and faster to increase the exit velocity of the stone, and killed the giant Goliath with a single stone making a penetrating blow to the giant's forehead. The giant fell face down like the toppling a tall tree. David then ran up, took the giant's own sword, and cut off his head. When the army of Philistia saw what David did to their champion they ran. The army of Israel, now encouraged by David's success against the giant, pursued them and cut them down all the way back to Ekron in Philistia.

When David returned to Jerusalem with the army of Israel he was holding the severed bloody head of the giant by the hair of its head. But when the women came out and celebrated in song that David killed tens of thousands and Saul killed thousands, Saul became enraged with jealousy and saw David as a threat to his kingship.

The next day, when the evil spirit stirred Saul, David came and played his harp for him as he had done before, but Saul took a javelin and hurled it at David, intending to kill him, pinning him to the wall with the javelin, if possible. So David avoided King Saul. In the meantime, Saul's son Jonathan had become close to David and the two pledged their lives to each other. Jonathan even told David that he knew that David would become king one day rather than himself.

## The Fugitive

Saul hatched a scheme to have David killed in war by sending him out to fight Israel's enemies, but God gave David success and only increased the admiration that the people had for him. This angered Saul even more, so he gave David his daughter Michal as a wife in the hope that this would enable him to kill David. Saul even tried to get his son Jonathan to betray David and kill him. However, Jonathan mediated between Saul and David and was successful in restoring their relationship, at least temporarily, and having David return to the royal court in peace and safety. It did not last.

Since David was anointed by God to become king of Israel in place of Saul, I, Benelroi, as the principal watcher for earth and for God's chosen people, visited the throne room of God in Heaven to report on the schemes of King Saul to take David's life. God told me that David was very dear to Him because of his tender heart toward God. He assured me that He had a plan for David and his descendants. Therefore, God sent troops of angels to surround David to protect and to preserve both David and the promise that would come through David. It pleased me to see the joy that God had over David. David certainly had won God's heart like few men before him.

When war with Philistia broke out again, David continued to make a name for himself fighting to defend

Israel. Once again, Saul became envious of the honor and adulation David received because of his victories. When the evil spirit again provoked Saul he tried once more to kill David in the palace by again throwing a javelin at him. That began an extended time of David having to survive as a fugitive from the wrath of Saul. Because David stopped at a small priestly town and was seen by a spy of Saul receiving holy bread, Saul had 85 priests there murdered by the spy, who was a foreigner from Edom. That spy also killed the families of the priests in that town.

As David continued his life as a fugitive, his extended family rallied to him. In addition, David attracted a group of men, and their families, that were on hard times, in debt, and discontented with their situations. This group of about 400 men and their families made David their leader and moved with him from caves, the wilderness, and mountains to escape from Saul and his men.

One time, Saul and his expeditionary force searched for David in Engedi. At that time Saul took a nap inside a nearby cave, not realizing that David and his men were inside the same cave with him. David cut off the end of Saul's robe while he slept, but restrained his men from killing Saul. In fact, David was even sorry that he had taken a cutting from Saul's robe, out of respect for Saul having been anointed of God.

Afterward, when Saul went away, David came out the cave and yelled for Saul's attention. David showed Saul the missing part of his robe and made it clear that he could have easily killed him, but did not. Saul was struck by David's restraint when all the while he was attempting to kill David. In the end, Saul said, "I know full well that you will become king and that the kingdom of Israel will be yours. Just swear to me by Yahweh that you won't wipe out my children and grandchildren." David swore that he wouldn't and Saul returned to his palace in Jerusalem.

On another occasion Saul went after David with a force of three thousand men. As Saul slept in a trench, surrounded by his personal guards, David went down with one aide and took Saul's spear and water jug, while passing up on the opportunity to kill him. David was able to do this daring feat because an angel assigned to protect David caused Saul and his men to fall into a deep sleep. Once David was safely a good distance away on a hilltop he shouted to Saul and his men. David taunted Saul's general Abner that he was worthy of execution because he failed to protect the king. By brandishing Saul's spear and water jug, David made it clear that he could have taken Saul's life, but chose not to do so. Saul replied, "I have sinned. Come back David my son. I won't hurt you anymore because you valued my life today. I have been acting like a fool and have made a huge mistake." Afterwards, Saul and David went separate ways.

Later, while David pursued and destroyed raiders from Amalek that had taken his garrison village and captured the women and children, Saul faced off against the armies of Philistia that had invaded once again. Since God would not speak to Saul, Saul went to a witch the night before his fateful battle to try and seek counsel from the spirit of the deceased prophet Samuel. Although the witch had no power to communicate with the spirit of Samuel, God allowed Samuel's spirit to appear and speak with Saul.

Samuel told Saul God had rejected him because of his disobedience, had chosen David to be king, and that Saul and his three sons closest in the line of succession would die in battle the following day. The next day the army of Israel was routed, Saul's three sons were killed in battle and a wounded Saul committed suicide with his own sword. When the news of the death of Saul and his sons came to David he wept for them, especially for his friend Jonathan.

David then went to Hebron, in Judah, after asking God what his next steps should be. There the men of the tribe of Judah made David king. However, Saul's general, Abner, took one of Saul's sons, made him king over the rest of Israel, and precipitated a national division for seven and a half years with a long civil war. In the end, the puppet king of Israel was assassinated after he offended general Abner. Abner himself was killed by David's general Joab to avenge a blood feud. This happened after Abner tried to broker a peaceful transfer of power to David and was given safe passage. The result was that resistance from the rest of Israel crumbled and the men of Israel made David king over a united Israel and Judah. So David reigned over a united kingdom from age 30 until he abdicated on behalf of his son Solomon 40 years later.

During David's reign, Israel reached its zenith in terms of territory as David conquered enemies, subjugated some nations as vassals, and made some alliances. David then assayed to bring the ark from where it was in a private home back to Jerusalem, but his first attempt failed and he left it in yet another person's private home until he had clear direction on how to treat something as holy as the ark. Besides, David became fearful of God's wrath. After three months he tried again to bring the ark to Jerusalem, this time transporting it in the way that God had told Moses and Aaron the ark should be moved. King David was so unrestrained in his joy at successfully bringing the ark to Jerusalem that he danced out of most of his clothes and refused to be shamed over it by his wife Michal, the daughter of Saul.

David housed the ark in a tent. Unlike the tent that Moses made, it was an open plan so that those that entered could see the ark. David also instituted non-stop praise and worship at the tent by the priests of the tribe of Levi, which he organized so that each subdivision would have a pre-determined opportunity to lead in the praise and worship. David's tender heart toward God and his habitual public worship set an example to the nation. The people loved him greatly and God gave him great success in all of his undertakings. David made it his process to go to God for instruction before doing anything of importance.

When David wanted to build a permanent Temple of stone and cedar beams for God to house the ark, the prophet Nathan told him that, although it was a good intention on his part, the Lord reserved that project for David's son. Nevertheless, over time, David donated, from his own wealth, great riches to be used by his son for the construction and beautification of the Temple. In fact, extravagant provision for the Temple was his life's work from that point on.

## Grave Sins Bring Consequences

Regrettably, David made a grave error in one season of warfare when he stayed at the palace, rather than lead his army in the field. During that time he had Bathsheba, the wife of Uriah, one of his most loyal military officers, brought to the palace. This was after he saw her, from his palace roof, bathing nude on her roof near his palace. David then had sex with her and she became pregnant. When David unsuccessfully schemed to have her husband Uriah called from the front so he could sleep with Bathsheba and think the child was his own, David then arranged for Uriah to be set up to be killed by the enemy in battle.

After the death of Uriah, David brought Bathsheba into the palace and married her as if he were being magnanimous to a widow. As the principal watcher for the earth and the nation of Israel, I, Benelroi, went to the throne room in Heaven to apprise Him of the actions of the man He anointed to be king over His people Israel. I was not an accuser, simply the bearer of unpleasant news. David's deeds hurt God's heart.

God thought, *The man I love and intend to be a key part of the line through which the Messiah will come has just committed two grave sins. He has not admitted his errors, expressed sorrow, or sought My face. He has even stopped coming to the place where My presence can be found above the seat of mercy on the ark. I miss him. It hurts that he has turned his back on Me for now. Notwithstanding these things, I will preserve him, because I still love him and My promise of the Messiah will come through his line. However, there will be consequences from My holy judgment. He will live and yet serve Me because I know he will turn back to Me. His sin will be included in those sins that the Messiah will bear when He gives Himself up as a perfect offering for sins past and sins yet to be committed by those that look to Him and accept His great gift of salvation and redemption.*

Rather than confessing his sins and being sorry for them, David engaged in a cover up. During that time, he refrained from going to God's house, where the ark was kept, to worship. David stopped speaking to God. Worse still, God was silent and stopped speaking to him as long as David was engaged in a cover up. However, after the child was born God had the prophet Nathan expose David's sins of adultery, deception, and murder.

David was undone and ashamed. Most of all, he deeply regretted having failed God and grown cold to God who was the light of his life. David was sorry for his sin and cried out in prayer "God have mercy on me. In line with Your lovingkindness toward me and in line with Your innumerable tender mercies, please blot out my sin. Wash me completely from my wrong doing and cleanse away my sin. I admit and own up to my sin. I can't get away from my sin in this matter.

It was against You, You only, that I sinned, and did this evil thing. Don't look on or consider my sins. Blot out all of my wrongdoing. Create a clean heart in me, oh God; and renew once again a right spirit within me. Please don't toss me away from Your presence. Please don't take back Your Holy Spirit from me. Deliver me from condemnation.

You don't want a sacrifice. If You did, I would have made one. You take no pleasure in burnt offerings. The sacrifice You long for is a heart broken over its sin. You won't despise a broken and contrite heart."

Although David was then sorry for what he had done and was forgiven by God, the Lord decreed, through Nathan, that the child would die and that there would always be bloodshed in David's reign and dynasty. It was a judgment that continued through the centuries. It resulted in civil wars, and ultimately, was part of the reason that the Messiah, coming from David's lineage, would be killed.

An early manifestation of that decree of judgment for the consequences of David's sin, was a violent attempted coup d'état by Absalom, one of David's own sons. David fled the palace and Jerusalem for his life, but grieved heavily when Absalom was killed, much to the consternation of General Joab and the soldiers that fought to preserve him.

After David had built up his kingdom Satan whispered into David's mind, *We should conduct a census to see how great the kingdom is that has been given to me.* David succumbed to the temptation. He did not inquire of God before doing it and refused to listen to the counsel of his general Joab not to require the census. This displeased God because of the spirit of pride from Satan that David had allowed to influence him. David later recognized his sin and confessed it, but it was too late to avoid the consequences of his pride and of listening to the spirit of pride rather than inquiring of God.

God sent the royal spiritual advisor Gad to King David with the word that he could pick the punishment for his folly from among three alternatives. The choices were either three years of famine; three months of being slaughtered by enemies; or three days of pestilence from God.

David told Gad, "Those are difficult choices, but I would rather come under Yahweh's hand of discipline than be subject to the whims of other men, because God's mercies are great."

So God released a plague on Israel that killed 70,000 people. Specifically, God sent an angel to Jerusalem to take lives in judgment. As the killing angel went about his grim work, the mercy that David relied upon came into play. God told the angel to stop killing. At that point, the angel of judgment was poised in the air by the smooth flat place where Ornan, a Jebusite, was threshing the grain from his harvest. David looked and saw the menacing angel. The angel had an unsheathed sword in his hand outstretched over Jerusalem. Then, for fear of the angel, David and the other national leaders, who were all wearing the rough plain clothing of repentance and mourning, fell on their faces. With his face in the dust and tears streaming down in anguish for his people, David said to God, "Wasn't it me that ordered the census? It was me that sinned and did evil, but as for these sheep (the people), what have they done? Please, I pray, oh Yahweh my God, take it out on me and on my father's clan, but not on Your people who shouldn't have to suffer from this plague."

Thus David offered his own life to spare the people of God. That was just one way in which David was a man after God's own heart. But it would not be David, but his descendant, the Messiah, who would give his life in exchange for the lives of the people of God. Besides, David was not without sin and as a man of war David had a lot of blood on his hands. The Messiah would be born sinless and live sinless as a man of peace to offer His life as a perfect sacrifice acceptable to God the Father to pay the penalty of the sin of the world and restore the relationship of fellowship between God and humankind.

The angel ordered Gad to tell David to set up an altar on Ornan's threshing floor. Upon hearing that from Gad, as a message from God, David quickly went to the threshing floor. When Ornan, the owner, turned to see the king, he saw the angel in the air with the outstretched sword. Upon seeing the angel Ornan and his four sons ran and hid themselves out of fear. But David came to him on the threshing floor. Ornan came out from hiding and bowed in obeisance to the king, doubling over so that his face nearly touched the ground. David asked Ornan to sell him the threshing floor at the full market price so that he could build an altar there to Yahweh and halt the devastating plague.

Ornan said, "Take it as a gift from me. I will even throw in the oxen for the burnt offering, you can use the threshing instruments as wood for the fire and the wheat here for part of the offering. I'm giving it all to you."

David protested, "No. I will buy it at the full market price because I won't take what belongs to you to make a burnt offering to Yahweh at no cost to myself." So David did not bargain the price down, but paid a high price to Ornan. Then David built an altar to Yahweh on the spot and called out to Yahweh. God answered him by sending down fire from the sky on the altar. Once that happened, God ordered the angel to put away his sword and stop the death plague.

Just as David chose not to offer something to God that did not personally cost him, it was God's plan to send His Son as the Messiah, at great personal cost to the Godhead, in the centuries to come, to halt the judgment of sin on humanity, just as David's offering halted the wrath of the angel of judgment. The offering of the life of the Messiah, God's Son, would satisfy the wrath of almighty

God against sin for as many as would believe God and accept the provision made through His Son.

# Chapter 15 Temple Worship

*If my people, which are called by my name, shall humble themselves, and pray, and seek my face, and turn from their wicked ways; then will I hear from heaven, and will forgive their sin, and will heal their land. Now mine eyes shall be open, and mine ears attent unto the prayer that is made in this place. For now have I chosen and sanctified this house, that my name may be there forever: and mine eyes and mine heart shall be there perpetually. 2 Chronicles 7:14-16*

Toward the end of King David's life, he was bedridden. One of his sons at that time made a move to take over the kingdom. Alerted to this by Bathsheba, Solomon's mother, David decided to abdicate in favor of Solomon and thus bring an end to the intrigue.[10]

After David's death, Solomon built a Temple for the worship of God and to house the ark. Because of the richness of the preparations made by David and the skill

---

[10] Additional scriptures are provided here for context.

And David said, Solomon my son is young and tender, and the house that is to be builded for the LORD must be exceeding magnifical, of fame and of glory throughout all countries: I will therefore now make preparation for it. So David prepared abundantly before his death. 1 Chronicles 22:5

And the priests could not enter into the house of the LORD, because the glory of the LORD had filled the LORD'S house. 2 Chronicles 7:2

For the life of the flesh is in the blood: and I have given it to you upon the altar to make an atonement for your souls: for it is the blood that maketh an atonement for the soul. Leviticus 17:11

And almost all things are by the law purged with blood; and without shedding of blood is no remission. Hebrews 9:22

the artisans, the Temple was magnificent. To inaugurate the Temple, King Solomon had the priests transfer the ark from the tent that David had established to the Temple. When the priests came out of the Temple the presence of God was so heavy and thick that the priests themselves collapsed to the ground unable to stand in the glory of God.

King Solomon mounted a special platform of brass that he had instructed be made for the occasion. There he lifted up his arms in prayer. As all the nation watched, Solomon gave a dedicatory prayer that was a restatement of the pact between God and the nation of Israel. Twenty-two thousand animal blood sacrifices had been prepared. As Solomon concluded his prayer dedicating the Temple and rededicating the people to worship God only, God sent fire from the sky that burned up the sacrifices. In addition, a visible shining cloud of God's glory filled the Temple and also rested upon it. Although they were unseen by the crowd at the Temple dedication, the air of the Temple grounds was filled by an unseen multitude of holy angels that were drawn to the presence of God. The angels wanted to witness what God was doing with humankind, beginning with the chosen people of Israel, and they wanted to worship and honor God who came down in His glory to sanctify the Temple.

When the people saw the supernatural display of God's presence and approval they all bowed themselves down with their faces to the ground and worshipped God. Later that night, God appeared to Solomon and told him that his prayer had been heard. In speaking to Solomon that night, God promised great things for the nation of Israel, Solomon, and Solomon's continuation of David's dynasty, if they would be true to God. But if not, the people would be scattered into foreign lands and the magnificent, opulent Temple just dedicated would cease to exist.

Solomon saw to it that the sacrifices prescribed by Moses were offered as Moses had instructed in this new era of Temple worship. He also continued the non-stop praise instituted by his father King David. Solomon reigned for forty years with a fame that spread worldwide.

# Chapter 16 Breaking God's Heart

*They kept not the covenant of God, and refused to walk in his law; And forgat his works, and his wonders that he had shewed them. Marvellous things did he in the sight of their fathers, in the land of Egypt, in the field of Zoan. Psalm 78:10-12*

David's son, King Solomon, began with a glorious reign that was world renowned. His was the high water mark of the nation of Israel as built and expanded by his father King David. However, in making alliances with surrounding nations, Solomon entered into marriages of convenience with the royal families of those kingdoms. In doing so, Solomon allowed those foreign princesses that he married to worship their own gods and built places of pagan worship for them. This displeased God. Moreover, in his old age, Solomon himself began to worship the idol gods of his foreign wives, including Ashtoreth, the goddess of the Zidonians. As the principal watcher of the earth and Israel, it was not my role to intervene. My role was to watch, record, and report to God. It was with great reluctance that I did my duty before the throne.

Solomon's actions broke God's heart.[11] After all, God had loved Solomon's father David and made him

---

[11] An additional scripture is provided here for context.

Go and proclaim these words toward the north, and say, Return, thou backsliding Israel, saith the LORD; and I will not cause mine anger to fall upon you: for I am merciful, saith the LORD, and I will not keep anger forever. Only acknowledge thine iniquity, that thou hast transgressed against the LORD thy God, and hast scattered thy ways to the strangers under every green tree, and ye have not obeyed my voice, saith the LORD. Turn, O backsliding children, saith the LORD; for I am married unto you: and I will take you one of

great. God had also appeared to Solomon twice and made a pact with Solomon as he had with David. God also gave Solomon wealth, intellect, wisdom, and renown. To be shunted aside for gods that were not God, after all of this, pierced God's heart.

God spoke to Solomon to make His displeasure plain and pronounced that the kingdom would be split, but not in his lifetime because of the regard that God had for Solomon's late father King David. As a result, God sent the prophet Ahijah to a trusted official of Solomon. That official was Jeroboam. Jeroboam administered the northern territories for Solomon. Ahijah confronted Jeroboam on the road one day and, symbolically ripping a new garment into 12 pieces, told Jeroboam to take 10 pieces because God was going to rip the kingdom out of the control of the royal line of Solomon and give ten tribes to Jeroboam. The reason given was because Israel had left God and worshipped the goddess Ashtoreth and other gods. Ahijah then offered God's bargain to Jeroboam. If Jeroboam would serve God, as King David had done, then God would be with him.

When Solomon heard of this he tried to kill Jeroboam. Jeroboam fled the country until Solomon died and Solomon's son Rehoboam began to reign. Rehoboam was young and foolish. He took poor advice from his young brash friends rather than listening to the wise diplomatic advice of more mature advisors, and he provoked the northern tribes. Those tribes decided to break away from the House of David and make Jeroboam their king. A bloody civil war was averted when the prophet Shemaiah told King Rehoboam on the battlefield

---

a city, and two of a family, and I will bring you to Zion. Jeremiah 3:12-14

that this split was God's doing and that he was not to fight against his brothers of the northern 10 tribes. Rehoboam listened and all withdrew from the field of battle peacefully and went to their own areas.

## God's People Cheat on Him with Other Gods

Although God had warned the Israelis not to worship the false gods of the inhabitants of Canaan, once they came into the land out of their period of slavery in Egypt, the people still dabbled in the worship of those gods. Behind each of those gods was one of Satan's fallen angels. They would stand with the idol images people made and soak up the worship that was offered. They also used their supernatural angelic powers to make things happen in the natural world so as to further encourage people to worship them.

The god Baal was considered to be the most powerful among those gods. He was called the Lord. He was also depicted as the sun god, the lord of fire, and the storm god. Baal was also considered the god of fruitfulness in agriculture and of human reproduction. His consorts were the goddess Asherah, also known as Ashtoreth and Astarte, and another goddess. These goddesses were goddesses of erotic love. Asherah was portrayed by a stout post or pole. Although it was the symbol of the erotic goddess, it was also a phallic symbol. It was the pagan origin of the May pole of a later era. Often, a whole group of these poles would be together on a hill. Those places were places to act out the perverted erotic practices of the worship of the goddess. This system of worship involved Temple prostitutes and the casting off of normal taboos and societal restraints.

Baal was also known in Canaan by the name Moloch. Moloch was also known as Molech. He was represented as a man with the head of a bull. A huge brass image of a sitting Moloch was forged with arms outstretched. The belly of the image had an opening in which a fire could be stoked. This heated the entire image. Flames from the belly would also lick up to the hands of the image. As part of his worship, people would offer up human sacrifices. It was infanticide. Those sacrificed were live babies placed in the menacing hands of the image. In times of national duress even a king would sacrifice one of his royal children to Moloch. The poor babies were shocked on contact with the hot metal hands and fire and died a painful death. It was because of this system of worship that God warned His people not to follow after the gods of the people of Canaan. It was also one of the reasons why the Israelis were instructed to annihilate certain of the inhabitants of Canaan and were forbidden to intermarry with them.

Fearing that the people of his new kingdom would eventually reconcile with the Kingdom of Judah, because Jerusalem and the Temple were there, Jeroboam mulled over the situation. He thought to himself, *They have been used to going to the Temple in Jerusalem to offer sacrifices. If they continue to do this they may have a change of heart and seek to make peace with Rehoboam by killing me and reuniting with him.* So Jeroboam made two young bulls of gold, the representation of the Egyptian god Apis. He set one up in the city of Dan in the north and the other in the city of Bethel in the south. Jeroboam had been introduced to the worship of Apis during his exile in Egypt. This was the very idol god that Aaron had made for the people when it was feared that

Moses had died while up on the mountain talking to God and receiving the 10 commandments. Its image is of a young bull with a disk representing the sun between its horns as an indication of the worship of the sun as well as of fertility.

Jeroboam told the people of his new kingdom that it was too much for them to go to Jerusalem to offer sacrifices. Instead, they should worship the golden images of the god Apis that he set up in Dan and Bethel. Moreover, Jeroboam created his own priesthood for this religion by appointing common and base men as priests rather than the Levites so as to further institutionalize the break with the Kingdom of Judah. Thus Jeroboam immediately broke the bargain that was offered to him by God through the prophet Ahijah.

Jeroboam took the path of evil and all of the successive kings of the Kingdom of Israel of the northern 10 tribes were also evil and did not serve God either. As the principal watcher, I reported on these developments in my periodic audiences with God before His throne. It wounded God's heart to see His people delve so completely into sin and rebellion. In His patience, God did not immediately destroy those rebels. However, God was greatly grieved that the people of the northern kingdom had left Him so quickly, thoroughly, and permanently.

God not only desired a human family, but it was His desire to be intimately related to that family as a husband is married to a wife. Out of His goodness and love, His plan was to have this wife share rulership with Him. However, time and again, God was jilted and cheated on by the wife He loved. His chosen nation of the descendants of Abraham, Isaac, and Jacob would repeatedly prostitute its affections to false gods and with nations with whom they were instructed not to mingle. This deeply hurt God. Yet, again and again, He took her back because of His great love for her.

King Ahab was the seventh king of this northern kingdom. During his reign he married a foreign woman named Jezebel, the daughter of Ethbaal, the King of Sidon (also known as Zidon), a country that bordered Israel on the north. Jezebel led the nation in the worship of these false gods to the exclusion of the true God. The true prophets of God were killed or hounded into hiding. Queen Jezebel played a major role in having the prophets of God hunted down and killed so as to not compete with her cult of the erotic goddesses. At God's direction, the prophet Elijah confronted Ahab and pronounced, "As the Lord God of Israel lives, before whom I stand, there will be neither rain nor dew in the land for three years, until I say so."

For over three years it was just as Elijah had said. Quite naturally, crops did not grow and there was a terrible famine. This outcome was a direct challenge to Baal. Pray and worship as the priests of Baal might, their storm god could bring no rain. Their god of fruitfulness could bring no crops to sustain the people. No amount of human sacrifice brought about a change in the situation.

Ahab and Jezebel put the blame on Elijah for the drought. Accordingly, Ahab sent out soldiers to find Elijah so that he could be brought to the king to be put to death. It was a mission that the soldiers could not complete because God was with Elijah.

God often spoke to Elijah in an audible voice. When the time came, God told Elijah, "Go and present yourself to Ahab because I am about to make it rain." As

Elijah was on his way he came across a senior official of the king's court, Obadiah. Obadiah had been sent by the King to search for forage for the remaining animals.

Obadiah recognized Elijah and became afraid. "Aren't you Elijah?" Obadiah said.

Elijah replied, "Yes, I am. Now go tell your master that Elijah is here."

But Obadiah resisted. "Are you trying to get me killed?" he said. "Everyone knows that when they hear you are in a certain place and the king's soldiers seek you out, the Spirit of God whisks you away to where you can't be found. If I go back and tell the king that you are here, and they don't find you here, it is likely to be at the cost of my life. Didn't anyone tell you that when Queen Jezebel was killing the prophets of God that I gathered 100 of them and hid them in a cave and saw to it that they had food and water? So why do you want to do this to me?"

Elijah responded, "Just tell him that I will be here and I will present myself to him today."

Obadiah swiftly carried the message to Ahab. So King Ahab together with his queen Jezebel and the prophets of Baal and of the goddesses went to Mount Carmel where Elijah was waiting.

Ahab thundered, "Are you the troublemaker that has troubled Israel?"

Elijah shot back, "I haven't troubled Israel. It is you that have troubled Israel by turning your back on the commandments of the Lord and following after the gods of Baal. Now call the whole nation here to Mount Carmel together with all the prophets of Baal and the prophetesses of Asherah."

## The God that Manifests Himself by Fire

Ahab sent word to call everyone there. With Ahab were 450 prophets of Baal and another 400 prophetesses of the goddesses that were kept by Queen Jezebel. When everyone was gathered together Elijah spoke addressing the throng.

"How long are you going to vacillate between the Lord and Baal? If the Lord is God, then follow Him. If Baal is god, then follow him. Now there is just one of me representing the Lord and there are 450 prophets of Baal gathered here. Give us two young bulls to offer as sacrifices. One for the prophets of Baal and one for me to sacrifice to the Lord. I propose that we each take one young bull, dress it and put wood under it, but no fire. Then let the God that answers by fire be the God that you serve."

The people agreed that Elijah's proposal was well said, after all, Baal was supposed to be the lord of fire. Elijah told the prophets of Baal to go first since there were so many of them. Baal's prophets called on him all day long. They danced around, shouted, cut themselves until the blood gushed everywhere, and even jumped up and down on the altar they had built.

Elijah began to mock them openly. "Yell a little louder! Maybe he is asleep or away on a trip, or talking to someone. After all, he is supposed to be a god." Stung by Elijah's taunts the prophets of Baal went all out until they were exhausted and so hoarse that they lost their voices.

As dusk was approaching, Elijah stepped forward to take his turn. As he did so he motioned for all of the people to come near to witness that there was no trickery involved. After making an altar from 12 stones and laying the young bull on it over a pile of wood, after slitting the bull's throat, he dug a trench around the altar. Elijah then requested that four barrels of water be poured over the sacrifice. He requested that it be repeated a second time. Then Elijah requested four more barrels of water to be poured over his sacrifice. After 12 barrels of water were poured over the sacrifice the altar was soaked, the wood on the altar was too wet to burn, and the trench he dug was overflowing with water. At that point, it was clear that no trickery was involved. There were no hidden coals or fire to set the sacrifice ablaze.

Elijah then approached the altar he had built and said a simple prayer in a loud voice that echoed around the throng on the mountain. "LORD God of Abraham, Isaac, and of Israel, let everyone know today that You are the only God in Israel, and that I am Your servant, and that the things I have done I have done in response to Your word to me. Hear me Yahweh. Hear me, that these people may know that You are Yahweh, and that You have turned their hearts back to You again."

Before the last echo of Elijah's words faded away, fire from God came down out of the sky onto the altar. It was so intense and sustained that the young bull and the wood were quickly turned to ashes. Moreover, the stones of the altar melted into molten lava and ran down causing the water in the trench to be vaporized until there was no water or mud left.

The people were astonished and chanted "Yahweh is God! Yahweh is God!"

Elijah then took over and commanded that the people capture the prophets of Baal and bring them to him. Elijah had them taken to a brook at the base of the mountain and beheaded them all there by himself. Then he approached King Ahab and said, "Get ready. It is going to rain."

When Ahab got back to his palace he told Jezebel what had happened and how Elijah had killed all of the prophets of Baal. Jezebel, the one responsible for the deaths of so many of the prophets of God, then sent a message to Elijah that she was going to take his life. With that news Elijah fled for his life. Despite having just achieved a great victory, Elijah became very depressed and asked God to allow him to die.

God ignored Elijah's request. Instead, He saw that Elijah rested and was cared for supernaturally, until he came out of his depression and fear for his life. An angel appeared and, between Elijah's naps, twice provided a fresh-baked loaf of bread and a jug of water to Elijah, admonishing him to eat so as to have strength for the journey ahead of him.

Elijah then walked on nothing more than those two supernatural meals for 40 days until he came to a certain mountain and entered a cave to take refuge there. Then God spoke to him.

"What are you doing here Elijah?"

Elijah responded, "I have stood up for You Lord God of the angelic armies. However, the people of Israel have broken the pact that was made with you. They have destroyed your altars and put your prophets to death by the sword. I am the only prophet left and now they want to kill me too!"

Rather than answer right away, God told Elijah to go and stand before Him on the mountain. Elijah left the darkness and shelter of the cave and stood outside on the mountain where he waited to encounter God. A fierce tornado came through. It lifted huge boulders and smashed them to bits against the mountain while Elijah held on as best he could.

After the dust settled, Elijah listened for the voice of God, but there was no booming voice of God. Then an earthquake came. The mountain shook and rocks fell as Elijah again held on so as to not fall down the mountain. But God was not in the earthquake either. There was only silence after the earthquake passed. Then a fire swept through causing the vegetation to burst into flame. Elijah ran back into the cave to avoid being burned by the fire, but God did not speak majestically out of the fire either.

Finally, in the stillness, God spoke to Elijah in a faint voice. Once Elijah recognized the voice of the Lord, even though it was faint, he covered his head and eyes with his mantel and stepped out beyond the entrance of the cave. God spoke to Elijah and repeated the question, "What are you doing here Elijah?"

Elijah responded as before saying, "I have stood up for You Lord God of the angelic armies. However, the people of Israel have broken the pact that was made with you. They have destroyed your altars and put your prophets to death by the sword. I am the only prophet left and now they want to kill me too!"

God responded to Elijah by giving him three assignments. "Go and anoint Hazael to be king of Syria, anoint Jehu to be king of Israel, and anoint Elisha to be the prophet that takes your place. By the way," said God, "I still have 7,000 in Israel that have not knelt down in worship of Baal."

In the following years, both Jezebel and Ahab met untimely deaths fulfilling the judgment of God. Ahab's son Ahaziah ascended to the throne of Israel in place of his father during the time that King Jehosephat was king over the southern kingdom of Judah. Although Jehosephat served God, Ahaziah did the same as his father King Ahab in worshipping Baal.

One day, Ahaziah had an accident in his palace falling through an upper floor and injuring himself so that he took to his sick bed. He then sent messengers to the Kingdom of Ekon to enquire of the god Baalzebub whether he would get well or die from his injuries. But an angel of God told Elijah to intercept the messengers on the road and give them the message to return to their king with the news that he would die because he sought help from the god Baalzebub when God was the God of Israel.

Elijah stopped the king's delegation, without identifying himself, and delivered the angel's message. When the delegation returned to the palace the king was astonished that they had returned so quickly. As they explained to the king why they had returned and relayed the message they had been given that the king would die and not recover because he sought help from Baalzebub, rather than from God, the king was furious. The king demanded to know who it was that sent them back with that message. As the men described a hairy man with a wide leather belt, the king interrupted, "It is Elijah!"

In his anger, King Ahaziah sent a troop of 50 soldiers and their officer to arrest Elijah and bring him back to be dealt with. When the troop arrived at the hill where they found Elijah, their officer yelled out in a brusque commanding voice, "Hey man of God! The king says you are to come with us!"

Elijah responded, "If I am a man of God fire will come down from the sky and burn you all up!" Immediately, fire came down from the sky as happened at

Mount Carmel when Elijah faced off with the prophets of
Baal. The troop of 50 and their officer were incinerated in
seconds leaving only a blackened smoldering patch of
ground at the base of the hill where they had stood.

The king sent a second troop of 50 soldiers and
their officer on the same mission. Upon approaching the
hill where Elijah was the second officer shouted to Elijah,
"Hey man of God! The king says come down now and be
quick about it!"

Once again, Elijah responded by saying, "If I am a
man of God fire will come down from the sky and burn
you all up!" The second troop met the same fate at the
first group. Fire immediately came down from the sky and
incinerated them in a matter of seconds. Undeterred, the
king sent a third troop of 50 soldiers and their officer on
the same mission to arrest and bring back Elijah.

This time there were no gruff commands for Elijah
to surrender. Instead, leaving his men at the base of the
hill, the officer slowly walked up, leaving his weapons
behind and with his helmet tucked under his arm. When
he came near to Elijah he fell on his knees and begged for
his life and the lives of his men. "Man of God," he
pleaded, "I beg you to let my life and the lives of my men
be worth something to you. Fire came down from the sky
and killed the two previous troops of 50 and their officers.
Please spare my life!"

An angel, unseen by the soldiers, spoke to Elijah
and said, "Go with him. Don't be afraid of him." So
Elijah went with the soldiers to see the king. Instead of
being arrested, Elijah was escorted, with honor, by the
officer. As the two walked along, the officer's helmet still
under his arms, the troop of 50 soldiers kept their distance
well behind them. As Elijah entered the palace, other

guards backed away in fear and knelt down with their spears laid on the ground so as not to anger the prophet. They were all aware of what had happened to the two troops of soldiers that angered the prophet with their arrogance.

Elijah addressed the king who was still on his sickbed. "This is what the Lord says," said Elijah. "Is it because there wasn't a God in Israel that you sent a delegation to inquire of Baalzebub the god of Ekon? Because of that you will most certainly die and not get out of your sick bed." And it happened just as Elijah said it would.

When Elijah's work as a prophet was done he walked with Elisha from the town of Gilgal. Elijah said to Elisha, "Stay here because the Lord wants me to go to Bethel."

But Elisha refused saying, "By the living God and by your soul I won't leave you." So they went on together to Bethel.

At Bethel the prophets there pulled Elisha aside and said, "Don't you know that the Lord is going to take your mentor from you today?"

Elisha responded, "Yes I know that! Just be quiet and hold your peace!"

Elijah called Elisha to him and said, "Stay here in Bethel because the Lord is sending me to Jericho."

But Elisha again refused. He said, "By the living God and by your soul I won't leave you." So the two of then went on the Jericho.

When they arrived, the prophets at Jericho pulled Elisha aside and said, "Don't you know that the Lord is going to take your mentor from you today?" Elisha responded, "Yes I know that! Just be quiet and hold your peace!"

Now Elijah told Elisha, "Stay here because the Lord is sending me to the Jordan."

But Elisha again refused and said, "By the living God and by your soul I won't leave you."

This time, as the two went on together, the other prophets followed and observed from a distance. When they arrived at the Jordan River, Elijah took off his mantel, twisted it, and using it like a club, swung it and hit the water. Immediately, the river parted and the two of them walked over dry ground to the opposite bank. Once on the other side Elijah said, "Ask me what you want me to do for you because I am about to be taken away from you."

Elisha responded, "I want a double portion of your spirit to come on me."

To this Elijah said, "You've asked for a hard thing. Nevertheless, if you see me when I am taken away from you then you will have it, but if not then it won't happen."

As they walked along, a chariot and horses of fire came out of the sky, split them apart, and took Elijah up to Heaven in a whirlwind with Elijah's mantel floating to the ground and coming to rest at Elisha's feet. Elisha saw it all, as did the prophets on the other side of the river did from a high place.

As he watched Elijah be whisked off into the sky and through the clouds, Elisha cried out, "My father, my father! The chariot of Israel and its horsemen!" In grief, Elisha tore his clothes at the chest and wept. His friend and mentor, one of the greatest prophets in the history of Israel, had just been taken from him and gone alive to

Heaven. Not since Enoch had someone been taken up alive to Heaven without having to die.

Looking down at Elijah's mantel now lying at his feet, Elisha picked it up, walked over to the river, and twisted it in the same way that Elijah had done. As he raised the twisted mantel he yelled, "Where is the God of Elijah!" and struck the water. As with Elijah, the waters of the river immediately parted and Elisha crossed over to the other side again on dry ground.

Having seen this all from afar, the prophets from Jericho said, "The spirit that was on Elijah is on Elisha." When they ran down to Elisha they bowed to him in submission. Elisha was now the master and first among the prophets of that time.

Over the years and through the rule of several subsequent kings of the 10 northern tribes of Israel, the people continued to secretly worship Baal and the goddesses. They gave in to that erotic form of worship that included human sacrifice of children. They turned their backs on the pact with God and ignored His commandments. Although God sent prophets to warn them to turn away from the path they had chosen and come back to Him and His commandments, they would not listen. For this reason, God allowed the Assyrian emperor to take them away as captives so that only the southern kingdom of Judah remained.

## Demonstrating the Broken Heart of God

During the reign of Jeroboam II, the 13th king of the northern kingdom of Israel, God sought to use the prophet Hosea to demonstrate how grieved and emotionally hurt He was by the waywardness of the northern kingdom. God instructed Hosea to marry a prostitute because the people of the northern kingdom had been like a whore in leaving God. This set Hosea up for heartbreak. No matter how loving and kind Hosea was to his wife Gomer, she would wander away and give herself over to prostitution.

Even while she was with Hosea, and gave birth three times, the third child was given a name that means "not mine" to indicate that Gomer had crept out and been unfaithful while still living with Hosea. Yet Hosea, still loved Gomer and tried to keep her at home and preserve their marriage. However, Gomer's insatiable desire for other lovers led her to leave her husband and sink to the depths of sexual immorality and unfaithfulness. Ultimately, Gomer lost everything, including her freedom.

Hosea could have simply given up on his unfaithful wife, but he did not. God told him to go and love that prostitute even as God Himself still loved Israel even though the nation left Him and went after other gods.

Hosea obeyed God's instruction and went out searching for Gomer until he found her being trafficked as a sexual slave. Hosea then bought her from the slave auction block and brought her back home. In doing so, Hosea told Gomer, "You are going to stay with me now for a very long time. You will no longer be a prostitute or give yourself to another man, and I too will be only for you."

After this heartbreaking and emotionally draining experience, Hosea prophesied the message that God gave him for the northern kingdom. Israel had been like a whore in turning from God and turning to the worship of

Baal and of the golden bulls of the god Aphis set up in Bethel (also called Bethaven) and Dan. Because of this sin, Hosea prophesied that the people would be taken away captive by the Assyrians and would wander the world away from their land. Israel ruined itself by its willfulness in sinning and abandoning God. Yet, after a long time, when the nation would look to God and decide to have nothing to do with idols anymore, God Himself will take them back and will love them freely again and put His anger behind Him.

Decades passed and a series of other kings reigned before God's patience ran out and the judgment of Hosea's prophesy was fulfilled. After the Assyrian emperor took the people of Israel away captive, he repopulated his new possession of Samaria, the other name that area was known by, with peoples from other parts of his empire.

The southern kingdom of Judah included the tribe of Benjamin, a remnant of Levites in Jerusalem and a handful of people from the northern ten tribes of Israel that had rejected the depredations of Baal worship, left their family ancestral properties in the north, and migrated to Judah where they would be free to worship Yahweh, the true God. God was grieved that the people of Israel, for whom He had done so much, would reject Him and instead serve dumb idols made by hands. Yet He still had what was left in the kingdom of Judah. With what remained, God would be able to fulfill the promises He had given of a Messiah that would come from these people.

The Kingdom of Judah was not without blame, even though it did have a number of kings that did serve God and lead the people in ways reminiscent of their ancestor King David. In Judah, the land of the Jews, some people also secretly served Baal and the goddesses. However, King Hezekiah, the 13<sup>th</sup> king of Judah after the split into two separate kingdoms, honored God and tried to remove anything having to do with idol worship.

In time, the Assyrians came again. This time they besieged the Kingdom of Judah. In doing so, the Assyrians bragged about how no other kingdom's gods could save them and that the same fate would come to Judah. Hezekiah earnestly prayed to God about the situation. The prophet Isaiah sent word to King Hezekiah from God. Isaiah's message from God said that God had heard Hezekiah's prayer. Further, God said he would save Jerusalem for His own sake and the sake of Hezekiah's ancestor King David.

One night, while the people were huddled inside the walls of Jerusalem, the surrounding countryside was lit up by the campfires of the Assyrian troops. That night, an angel from the Lord killed 185,000 Assyrians that besieged Jerusalem. The Assyrian emperor returned to Assyria in defeat. He was then assassinated by two of his own sons.

Some years later, diplomats from the Kingdom of Babylon, bearing gifts, came on a goodwill visit to Hezekiah. Hezekiah treated them well and showed them the riches of his palace. When the prophet Isaiah heard about it he told Hezekiah that Babylon would return one day to take everything those Babylonian diplomats had seen and take the people captive too, but not in his lifetime.

# Chapter 17 Taken Captive

*And say, Hear ye the word of the LORD, O kings of Judah, and inhabitants of Jerusalem; Thus saith the LORD of hosts, the God of Israel; Behold, I will bring evil upon this place, the which whosoever heareth, his ears shall tingle. Because they have forsaken me, and have estranged this place, and have burned incense in it unto other gods, whom neither they nor their fathers have known, nor the kings of Judah, and have filled this place with the blood of innocents; They have built also the high places of Baal, to burn their sons with fire for burnt offerings unto Baal, which I commanded not, nor spake it, neither came it into my mind. Jeremiah 19:3-5*

Hezekiah's son Manasseh, who reigned after him, led the people of Judah in the worship of Baal and the goddesses. He built altars for idol gods in the Temple at Jerusalem and even sacrificed one of his sons in the fiery arms of the idol of Moloch. Prophets of God reiterated the judgment that would eventually come on Judah and Jerusalem.[12]

---

[12] Additional scriptures are provided here for context.

And he brake down the houses of the sodomites, that were by the house of the LORD, where the women wove hangings for the grove.

2 Kings 23:7

But if ye will not hear it, my soul shall weep in secret places for your pride; and mine eye shall weep sore, and run down with tears, because the LORD'S flock is carried away captive. Jeremiah 13:17

Amon, the son of Manasseh, reigned after him and was no better concerning the worship of Baal and the goddesses. He also allowed in the Temple complex the worship of Baal and the goddesses. Children born of the activity of the brothel were often sacrificed to Moloch in a valley near Jerusalem. As the principal watcher for the earth, I, Benelroi, went before the Lord in His throne room to bring the sad news from myself and the other watchers of what was transpiring among His own chosen people. Their evil activities even included infanticide, the killing of innocent babies as human sacrifices to the false gods they had chosen to worship rather than the true God. They also desecrated the Temple in multiple ways.

God, who is the God of joy, became both saddened and enflamed with jealousy and anger. He of course already knew what was happening, but it was my regretful duty to appear before Him repeatedly with the report that His people were nearly indistinguishable from the people of Canaan and their neighbors whom they had displaced.

Eventually, King Amon was assassinated in a palace coup and his young son Josiah was made king in his place. Josiah took a different path from his father and grandfather. When a forgotten copy of the scriptures was brought to him and read to him, he wept for the sins of his nation against God. Josiah launched a campaign to clear out the worship of false gods that had taken over the Temple and that had become prominent through the kingdom. Among other spiritual house cleaning he removed the brothel from the Temple complex, destroyed the image of Moloch, to whom children were sacrificed, and laid waste to ceremonial high places used in the worship of Baal and the goddesses. Josiah also instituted a policy to make the people literate once again concerning their ancient pact with God. For this reason, God had prophets speak to Josiah to let him know that, although judgment would come on Judah for the sins that had been committed under his father's and grandfather's reigns, so that it would be removed out of the land in the same way that the northern kingdom of Israel was taken away by a foreign power, it would not happen in his lifetime because of what he had done in leading the people back to God.

During the reign of King Josiah, God began to speak to the prophet Jeremiah, who was from the tribe of Benjamin, and show him visions. God asked Jeremiah, "Has any group of people that served worthless idol gods ever left those gods to serve other useless idols? But My people have exchanged their glory, Me, for something that is worthless." God went on to say, "You can't even count all of the days that My people have forgotten all about Me!"

God revealed to Jeremiah that He was going to bring judgement upon the Kingdom of Judah for the evil that the people had done when they abandoned Him and worshipped Baal and the goddesses, gods that were nothing more than statues the people crafted with their own hands. God told Jeremiah, "Get up on your feet! Get yourself ready and tell them everything that I command you to say. Don't be intimidated by them! If you allow yourself to be intimidated by them I will allow you to grovel before them. They will fight against you, but they won't be able to beat you because I am with you and will save you."

In obedience to what God instructed him to do and say, Jeremiah prophesied to the people of the judgment to come. He did so during the latter reign of Josiah and into the reign of Josiah's grandson after him, King Jehoiakim, and of King Jehoiachin, and King Zedekiah after him of the same dynasty. During the reign of King Jehoiakim, Jeremiah prophesied that the people would endure 70 years of captivity in Babylon because they had turned their backs on God.

Babylon had rebelled against the Assyrian empire, defeated it, and also subdued the Kingdom of Egypt. This made the Babylonian Empire the superpower of that part of the known world. During the reign of Jehoiakim, the Chaldeans of the Babylonian empire, led by Nebuchadnezzar, invaded and took part of the people and part of the gold of the Temple back to Babylon. A few years later they returned, during the reign of King Zedekiah, and took most of the people they did not kill, and the remaining precious items from the Temple, with them.

God had the prophet Jeremiah speak for years warning the people to turn from what they were doing and return to God. God had Jeremiah use very graphic language to make it clear how God felt about the sin of the Kingdom of Judah. Judah was described as a whore and like a wild female ass in heat looking for sexual partners because of turning its back on God and going after the idol Baal and other gods. At God's direction, Jeremiah took Judah to task for not changing its ways after seeing what had happened to the Kingdom of Israel when God judged its sin and had it taken away into captivity.

On behalf of God, Jeremiah pleaded with the nation of Judah to turn back to God and avoid judgment while there was still time. Through Jeremiah, God warned that His patience had a limit. Jeremiah continued to warn and plead, but other men who made themselves out to be prophets, when they really were not appointed by God, told the people to ignore Jeremiah, and that everything would be all right. When Jeremiah complained to God about the prophets who were working at cross purposes to him, God let him know that those lying prophets would themselves die of starvation and by the sword of the enemy.

**Unrepented Sin Will be Punished**

In a major pronouncement, one day the Lord instructed Jeremiah to assemble an elite group of witnesses to the valley just outside the east gate of Jerusalem to hear a message from God. The east gate was also known as the beautiful gate. The valley outside the gate was where those Jews who worshipped Baal and Moloch practiced infanticide by taking some of their infant children to be burned alive in sacrifice to those gods.

Jeremiah said, "This is what the LORD says you kings and people of Judah." He went on to say, "The LORD, the God of Israel says I will bring tragedy on this place such that it will grab the attention of the ears of those who hear the accounts of what happened. I am doing this because the kings and people of Judah have left Me, they have disrespected this place and burned incense to other gods that neither they nor their ancestors, nor the kings of Judah had served. They have filled this place with the blood of innocent babies offered in human sacrifice. They have built places for Baal on the hills where they burned alive their sons as offerings to Baal. That was something I did not command, speak, or even think in My mind. Because of this, the days are coming when this will be called the valley of slaughter. I will cause those of Judah and Jerusalem to be killed by the sword at the hands of their enemies. I will leave their carcasses as food for the vultures and the wild animals. I will make this city to be utterly deserted and a byword. Everyone that passes by it will be astonished because of all of the tragedy that will befall this city. Before the city falls, I will cause the siege to be so severe that the people turn to human cannibalism--eating their male and female children, and the flesh of their friends and neighbors."

Those that were gathered there were stunned. Never had a prophet of God so cursed the holy city of Jerusalem. As they returned inside the city gates the notables that heard the message passed it on, but there was no change of heart by the people or their royal leadership. The people and royals choose instead to listen to the soothing words of the lying prophets that told them what they wanted to hear.

When the high priest's son heard about what Jeremiah had said, he had Jeremiah arrested, slapped him in his face, and then had him put in stocks in prison. Jeremiah grew depressed over his situation. People didn't like his message. He wished he had never been born. He complained to God. When he decided not to speak in prophesy any more, he found he could not hold it in or contain it. It was like a fire inside him that had to get out, so he continued to prophesy the words that God gave him to say.

The Babylonian emperor Nebuchadnezzar declared war on the Kingdom of Judah and laid siege to Jerusalem. King Zedekiah, the 20th king of Judah after the split that caused the 10 northern tribes to secede and form their own Kingdom of Israel, sent to Jeremiah to see what God had to say about the situation. Jeremiah continued to speak of the tragedy that would come on Judah and Jerusalem, but he added that King Zedekiah would be taken captive and not be put to death.

Ultimately, a group of leaders and priests wanted to kill Jeremiah. They called him a traitor and said he was weakening the will of the army to fight. So they put him into a lower dungeon that was filled with muck to the point that Jeremiah began to slowly sink in it. Without food or water and gradually sinking in the muck, a slow death awaited Jeremiah.

When the king's eunuch, an Ethiopian named Ebedmelech, heard what had been done to Jeremiah he reported it to the king. The king told the eunuch to take 30 men and pull Jeremiah out of the dungeon so that he would not die. They did so by lowering old clothes and rags for Jeremiah to position under his arms so they could gently extract him without causing physical damage to him against the suction force of the muck into which he had sunk. After that, Jeremiah remained in an upper portion of the prison, but free of the dungeon.

## The Judgment of Captivity Begins

King Zedekiah secretly went to Jeremiah to see what God had to say for him. Jeremiah told him to surrender to the Babylonians and go into captivity, but the city would not be burned. However, Zedekiah feared a backlash from the Jews and would not follow that advice. When Jerusalem finally fell Zedekiah attempted to flee, but was caught outside the city. He was brought to Nebuchadnezzar who sentenced him to see his royal sons put to death before they put out Zedekiah's own eyes. As for Jeremiah, who was still in the prison, Nebuchadnezzar gave instructions for him to be treated well and to be given whatever he requested.

The Babylonians carried away all of the utensils of precious metal from the Temple, although they did not capture the ark and its contents, which had been taken away by some of the Levites and hidden. The city, its walls, and the Temple were destroyed in this second invasion.

The prophet Ezekiel was in the first group of captives that Nebuchadnezzar took to Babylon. While he was there, God opened the heavens to him and caused him to see visions of unusual spirit beings.

In one vision, I, Benelroi, took Ezekiel to see what God and the watchers were seeing. I showed Ezekiel the idolatry that was going on in Jerusalem and at the Temple itself. As Ezekiel went into a deep sleep, I grabbed his spiritual self by a lock of its hair, pulled Ezekiel's spirit away from his body, and took Ezekiel, in his spirit, with me to Jerusalem.

In Jerusalem I showed Ezekiel what the spiritual and political leaders of Israel were doing. They were engaging in idolatry. They were worshiping all kinds of animals, snakes, and insects. They thought God could not see them in their hidden rooms with their walls covered with images of idolatry, but we saw them. God saw them. I caused Ezekiel to see through the wall of the Temple and find people inside worshipping idols. I then took him outside into the Temple courtyard where a group of men, with their backs to the Temple, faced the east and worshiped the sun god Baal as the sun rose. It was because of these detestable things that God was filled with jealousy and removed His spirit from the Temple. God also gave other visions to Ezekiel.

As he had done with the prophet Hosea, God described to Ezekiel how the northern Kingdom of Israel and the southern Kingdom of Judah were like two sisters that belonged to God, but were lewd, unfaithful whores in turning from Him to idols and to the men of Assyria and of Babylon. When judgment fell on the northern kingdom and it was taken captive by the Assyrians, the southern Kingdom of Judah did not take the lesson. Instead, Judah persisted in those things that were offensive to God until it too came under judgement and was taken captive by the Babylonians.

When Nebuchadnezzar first invaded the Kingdom of Judah, which was his rebellious vassal state, among the captives he took to Babylon were princes, others of the Jewish nobility, and other refined upper-class people. It was Nebuchadnezzar's plan to take the best of those, have them trained in Babylonian culture and knowledge, and put them to work in helping to administer the empire. Among these were the young men Daniel, Hananiah, Mishael, and Azariah. Each was given a Babylonian name that represented a Babylonian god. As best they could, these four maintained their Jewish dietary habits and stayed faithful to God. At the end of their leadership and management training, their graduating class was presented to Emperor Nebuchadnezzar, and they were found to be the most brilliant of all those who had gone through the training.

One night, Nebuchadnezzar had a dream that troubled him, but which he could not remember. So he called for his chief of the magicians, astrologers, sorcerers, and Chaldeans to tell him the dream and its interpretation, without the benefit of him telling them the dream itself. When they protested that no one had ever made such a request, Nebuchadnezzar, in his fury, gave instructions for them and all of the others of their craft to be put to death.

When the emperor's military official charged with executing these men came for Daniel and his friends to take them away to be killed with the others, Daniel asked for some background to the emperor's hasty command. Upon being told, Daniel told the officer to hold off so he could speak to the emperor.

Daniel presented himself to the emperor and, after understanding more clearly the emperor's challenge, he asked for a little time, after which he would tell Nebuchadnezzar the thing he wanted to know. Daniel was granted a stay of execution for himself, his friends, and the others under the death sentence. He explained things to his friends and they sought God for the answer. The answer was revealed that night in a vision to Daniel.

Armed with the dream and the key to its interpretation, Daniel returned to the emperor. Daniel first made it clear that the empire's corps of practitioners of occultic arts couldn't do what the emperor had requested, but there was a God in Heaven who reveals secrets and had shown Nebuchadnezzar what was coming in the future. With that, Daniel revealed the emperor's dream. Daniel described a great image with a head of gold, chest and arms of silver, belly and thighs of brass, legs of iron, and feet partly of iron and partly of terra cotta. That terrifying image was itself smashed to dust by a stone, untouched by human hands. After the residue of the image was blown away the stone became a huge mountain and filled the entire earth.

Having told the emperor the dream, Daniel
proceeded to give the interpretation. The emperor was the
head of gold. His empire ruled over kings as a great world
power that was superb in its reach, power, and glory.
After Nebuchadnezzar's kingdom and dynasty would
come a second, but inferior empire, followed in turn by a
third empire even more inferior. The succeeding fourth
empire of iron would be inferior still, but strong in
subduing others. It would be followed by an alliance even
more inferior, having some strength, but also some
weakness. During the time of that fifth kingdom God
Himself will set up a kingdom that will endure forever
and rule over all subordinate kingdoms.

Nebuchadnezzar was so amazed by Daniel's
mastery they he treated him like a god and said, "Truly,
your God, is a God of gods, and Lord of kings, and the
revealer of secrets." Nebuchadnezzar then promoted
Daniel to run the empire's central province of Babylon,
and acceded to Daniel's request that his three Jewish
companions be allowed to assist him.
What Daniel saw and revealed to Nebuchadnezzar was
the sweep of world history from that point until the
Messiah would come, brush away the structures of men
and establish the Kingdom of God on earth never to be
supplanted by any other kingdom. Moreover, in the space
of a few hours, Daniel went from being a captive minor
functionary in a foreign land to being the emperor's Prime
Minister and a wealthy man.

Later, Nebuchadnezzar got it into his mind to set
up a huge statue of gold. At its dedication, he gave
instruction that whoever does not bow down and worship
the statue when they hear the orchestra play music shall
be killed by being put in a furnace. Some of the

Chaldeans saw this as an opportunity to get rid of Daniel's three companions. In their jealousy, they told Nebuchadnezzar that those Jews he had placed over the affairs of the province of Babylon weren't going along with his decree.

## The God Who Delivers

Upon hearing the charges against the Jewish officials responsible for administering the Province of Babylon, Nebuchadnezzar had Daniel's three friends brought to him and asked if the report were true. However, he gave them a way out. As long as they bowed down to the image when the music played, everything would be alright, but if they refused, they would be put in a furnace to be incinerated. Nebuchadnezzar's final words were, "What God would be able to deliver you from me then?"

Hananiah, Mishael, and Azariah weren't afraid or diplomatic. Instead, they said, "Our God whom we serve is able to deliver us from you and the furnace, but even if He doesn't, we want you to know that we will not worship your gods or the image that you set up."

The insolent answer by the three Jews infuriated Nebuchadnezzar. He commanded that the furnace be stoked seven times hotter than usual. Then, with the Jews tied up and in their full clothing, so that they would burn alive like human torches, the emperor had some stout men from his army push the Jews into the furnace. This they did, but the furnace was so hot that the soldiers fainted and died on the spot in the process. While the corpses of the soldiers burned near the mouth of the furnace, Nebuchadnezzar looked and was amazed to see that the three Jews were walking around in the furnace unharmed. In addition, he saw a fourth man who he said looked like a Son of God. Curious, Nebuchadnezzar came as near to the mouth of the furnace as he could. Using their Babylonian names, Nebuchadnezzar called for Hananiah, Mishael, and Azariah to come out. When they did, they were no longer bound. Further, neither heat nor the smell of fire was on them. Neither their clothes were burned nor was a hair of their heads singed.

Nebuchadnezzar and his officials gathered around the three in amazement examining them. Then Nebuchadnezzar spoke up saying, "I call the God of Shadrach, Meshach, and Abednego, blessed, who sent his angel, and delivered his devotees who put their trust in Him. They have changed my decree, and offered up their bodies, so that they would not have to serve or worship any god other than their own God. Therefore, I am making a new decree. Anyone, from any people, nation, or language group that says anything negative about the God of Shadrach, Meshach, and Abednego, will be cut to pieces, and their houses will be made a dumping ground: because there is no other God that can deliver people like this."

Although the Jewish people were in exile as captives because of the sins of the nation in turning their backs on God, God still blessed them in the land of their captivity, because He still loved them. Daniel continued to serve under Nebuchadnezzar until he went into semi-retirement during the reign of Nebuchadnezzar's grandson Belshazzar.

On the night that Belshazzar held a drunken feast, he sent for the golden cups from the Jerusalem Temple. He and his friends and the court courtesans drank and toasted their gods with those sacred cups. Suddenly, a disembodied hand appeared and wrote something on the wall where they were partying. Belshazzar was undone and hardly able to stand. His masters of the Chaldean dark arts could not interpret the writing. Finally, the queen mother was sent for to see what she could add. She told her grandson that Daniel, who had served his grandfather, had the ability to provide the interpretation.

Daniel was brought to the gathering. Belshazzar said, "I have heard of you. You are one of those my grandfather brought out of the land of the Jews. If you can interpret this writing I will give you gifts and make you the third ranking person in the empire.

Daniel said, "Keep your gifts and give your rewards to someone else, yet I will give you the interpretation." Daniel went on to give the account of how God had given Belshazzar's grandfather a great empire and then humbled him by having him go about naked and grazing as a wild animal and out of his mind for years before restoring him, once Nebuchadnezzar realized God controls kingdoms. Daniel went on to say, "You knew all of this yet you were not humble. You got so puffed up in your pride and arrogance before God that you had your officials, wives, and concubines drink from the holy cups from God's Temple in Jerusalem while you saluted the gods made out of gold, wood, brass, iron, and stone. Those are gods that can't see, hear, or know anything. That you did rather than giving glory to the God who has your life in His hands."

Daniel went on to interpret the writing on the wall explaining that the empire was being stripped from Belshazzar and given to the Medes and Persians. As promised, Belshazzar promoted Daniel, but Belshazzar was killed before the night was over and the armies of the Medes and Persians under Darius took over. The Medes, in later centuries, became known as Kurds.

Darius set up a new administrative structure that included three Presidents at the top. Daniel was one of the three and was the first among equals. Eventually, Darius preferred Daniel over all the others. This incited jealousy among the other officials. So they plotted as to how to remove Daniel and determined that it would have to be by something relating to his devotion to God, because Daniel was otherwise above reproach.

The plotters drafted a decree that would appeal to the emperor's pride. Coming to Darius, they said all of the officials had gotten together and written a decree that, for thirty days, if anyone makes a petition of any god or man, other than you, then he will be thrown in a lion's den. They then asked Darius to sign the decree to make it official. Once that was done the trap was set.

Daniel heard about the decree. However, he not only ignored it, he opened the shutters to his widows so that when he prayed to God three times a day, as was his custom, he would be seen. The plotters gathered near Daniel's window to witness him in prayer to God. Then they went back to Darius and testified against Daniel demanding that he be thrown into the lion's den.

Realizing he had been set up, Darius was upset with himself. For hours he looked for a way to excuse Daniel and save him. That evening, the plotters came before Darius and reminded him that the laws of the Medes and Persians, as ratified by the emperor, were irrevocable. With a heavy heart Darius sent for Daniel.

Ashamed of himself, Darius told Daniel, "The God you serve so faithfully will deliver you." With that,

Daniel was thrown into the lion's den and a stone cap moved over the opening to seal it up. In addition, a wax seal was put on the stone to which Darius and the plotters impressed their signet rings so that no one could remove the stone without breaking the seal.

After spending a sleepless night at his palace without eating or using any diversion like music to get his mind off of Daniel, Darius returned early in the morning and shouted, "Daniel! Is your God whom you serve so faithfully able to save you from the lions?"

Up from the lion's den came Daniel's voice. "Long live the king! My God sent His angel who shut the mouths of the lions so that I couldn't be hurt, because I was innocent, and I haven't done anything against you."

The emperor was hilariously happy with the news. He quickly instructed that Daniel be pulled up out of the lion's den. Examining him, they found he hadn't been hurt at all. Then Darius sent for the plotters, their wives, and their children and had them all thrown into the lion's den. The lions tossed them around in mid-air like dolls and broke their bones before they ever touched the ground in the den. Darius then made a decree throughout the empire that everyone should tremble and be in awe before the God of Daniel because He is the living God. As for Daniel, he continued to serve Darius on into the reign of Cyrus the Persian.

**The Prophesy of Kingdoms and of the Messiah**

Daniel knew from reading scrolls that the prophet Jeremiah said the Jews would be captive in Babylon for 70 years before returning to their land. Daniel fasted and prayed for greater understanding. As he prayed, he repented for his sins and for the sins of the Jewish people. God sent the Archangel Gabriel to Daniel in response to his prayers.

Gabriel explained that, in addition to the 70 years of captivity for the sins of the nation, there would be 70 groups of seven years to finish off the matter of God's dealings with the Jewish people for their rebelliousness and unfaithfulness to Him.

The first 69 groups of seven years, totaling 483 consecutive years, would begin counting from the time that the empire under which Daniel was living would give the order to rebuild Jerusalem. Nehemiah, who was cupbearer to Emperor Artaxerxes I, recorded that decree in his record of the times. The Jewish born empress too was present when Nehemiah made his request to the emperor.[13] So God's timepiece for the Jews in this matter started in 445 BCE. Ezra the priest, recorded these same events, including the rebuilding of the Temple, in his writings.

Daniel was told that the end of the 69 groups of 7 years, that is 483 consecutive years, would be marked with the presentation of the Messiah, the Son of God, as the Prince. That other bookend of the period was 32 CE, when Jesus Christ would enter Jerusalem in His triumphal entry as crowds would hail Him as King of the Jews.

That left one last sequence of seven years. However, the last seven years would not be consecutive

---

[13] Some scholars argue convincingly that Darius I (that is Darius Hystapis), Ahasuerus, and Artaxerxes are all different names of the same emperor. Is Darius, the king of Ezra 6:14-15, the same king as the Artaxerxes of Ezra 7:1?, by David Austin, Journal of Creation 22:46-52, August 2008. Kingly Chronology in the Book of Ezra, by Eric Lyons, copyright 2005 Apologetics Press, Inc. http://www.apologicticspress.org

with or adjacent to the previous 483 years. Before coming to the last seven years of God's dealing with the Jewish people, there would be a parenthetical gap in time of nearly two millennia. During that gap, the Messiah, as Gabriel explained, would be killed and not die a natural death. Gabriel also said in that gap time that Jerusalem and the Temple would be destroyed by the same people who would have a hand in killing the Messiah. This was interesting because Jerusalem and the Temple were both already in a state of destruction when Gabriel spoke with Daniel. This meant that the Temple would be rebuilt and then destroyed again. That second destruction of the Temple would take place, during the gap in time, in 70 CE under the Roman army of General Titus, the son of Emperor Vespasian, and who himself later succeeded Vespasian to become emperor of the Roman Empire in the Flavian dynasty.

Prior to departing, Gabriel told Daniel the timeclock for the Jews would resume for the final seven years of God's dealings with the Jews with the signing of a seven-year treaty with the Jews. In the middle of the term of the treaty the guarantor of the treaty would end sacrifices in the Temple. Implicit in that future was the indication that the Temple would be rebuilt yet again, after its destruction following the execution of the Messiah.

Gabriel did not tell Daniel how long the gap would be, but he did give indication that there would be a gap. Ultimately, that unrevealed gap would last two thousand years. Also, Gabriel did not tell Daniel, as God did not tell other prophets before or afterwards, that something special was to happen during that gap. That special something was the mystery of the church of Jesus

Christ, a church that would be overwhelmingly non-Jewish by ethnicity.

God gave Daniel another vision early in the reign of Cyrus the Persian. Daniel fasted and prayed for 21 days. Finally, having fought through satanic opposition, an angel appeared to Daniel. The angel appeared as no mere man, but in a glorious celestial spirit body with a face as bright as lightning, a body of a translucent precious light blue gemstone, arms and feet like polished brass, eyes like the brightest light, and clothed with linen and gold cloth. Daniel was overwhelmed by it all and had to be strengthened in order to receive the message that the angel brought.

The angel proceeded to provide a detailed panorama of kingdoms to come in the future until the cataclysmic end of the age. This panorama covered the time Daniel was in, through the entirety of the time mentioned in the previous vision with Gabriel, that is, the 490 years, plus the unspecified gap of what would prove to be nearly 2,000 more years. Near the culmination of that panorama, the Archangel Michael would come to stand with the Jewish people, indicating God will have finished with the mystery of the mostly non-Jewish church and will have resumed His final dealings with the Jewish people, to the end that His anger with them because of sinning against Him would be past. He will then take from them a people that will both receive His love toward them and will freely and faithfully love Him in return.

Just as He had shown Daniel things to come, God also revealed to other prophets before Daniel, during Daniel's lifetime, and afterward, things concerning the Messiah to come. To King David and the prophet Isaiah especially, God gave vivid understanding of the Messiah to come, and how that Messiah would be rejected, abused, and put to death as a divine provision for the sins of Israel and of the whole world.

# Chapter 18 Enter Messiah, the Redeemer and Savior

*Wherefore in all things it behoved him to be made like unto his brethren, that he might be a merciful and faithful high priest in things pertaining to God, to make reconciliation for the sins of the people. Hebrews 2:17*

For 400 years the Jews had gone without a prophet. God was silent. Then things changed.[14] God identified a young virgin girl of Nazareth named Mary, who was promised to a man named Joseph, a common carpenter. Both persons could trace their lineage to King David.

In Heaven, the Son called Gabriel to Himself and gave him instructions for special tasks being given to him to introduce the Son into the world as a human. The Son, through the agency of Holy Spirit God, would lay aside His great glory and humble Himself to be born of the young Virgin Mary. He would become a man.

God the Son had visited earth on several previous occasions in the form of a man by laying aside much of His glory so that His encounters with people would not result in their deaths. Without laying aside His glory, the holiness of God would judge and burn to ashes the body of any sinful, imperfect person that would come close to God the Son.

---

[14] An additional scripture is provided here for context.

For unto us a child is born, unto us a son is given: and the government shall be upon his shoulder: and his name shall be called Wonderful, Counsellor, The mighty God, The everlasting Father, The Prince of Peace. Isaiah 9:6

He didn't hate the people, He was just very holy, and people were the opposite. This time, the visitation of God the Son would be different. He would come as a flesh and blood child, born of a woman, and then grow into a man. His assignment would be to preach the good news of salvation through belief in Him, undo the works of the devil and the agents of Satan's kingdom, and to give His sinless body as a blood sacrifice to take away the sins of the world for as many as would believe on Him. For those who would believe on Him, His sacrificial blood would make them as holy as He is so that they would be able to have a relationship of intimate fellowship with God without rejection, guilt, condemnation, or punishment from holy judgment on human sins.

The Son needed a human body to complete this assignment. It had to be a body that entered the world through birth. As the Son of Man, He would have the legal right to wrest the keys of Satan's earthly kingdom from him. As God and as the Son of Man, He could teach and preach the good news. No angel had been given that authority. It is people that announce the good news to lead others into the path of salvation and reconciliation with God.

The Father gave instructions to Gabriel and to Michael. During the life of the Son on earth, they were to oversee regular rotations of angels to guard the Son from the time of incubation in the womb of Mary, to birth and infancy, and on into manhood.

Gabriel went to earth to begin his assignment. He appeared to the young Virgin Mary. Gabriel greeted Mary, "Hello, you highly favored woman! The Lord is with you." Mary was taken aback by the angel and his greeting. Gabriel tried to calm her by saying, "Don't be afraid. You have found grace with God. Now you are going to have a son that you will call Jesus. He will be great and will be called the Son of the Most High. The Lord God will give him the throne of His ancestor David. He will rule over the descendants of Jacob forever and His kingdom will have no end."

### Messiah, the Son of God, Comes as a Man

This was a lot to take in by Mary. She asked, "How is this going to be since I haven't had intimate relations with a man?"

Gabriel explained, "The Holy Spirit will come on you, and the power of the Most High will overshadow you. So then, the Holy One to be born will be called the Son of God." "Besides that," Gabriel added, "your cousin Elizabeth, who was childless and up in age, is in the sixth month of her pregnancy. She was considered barren, but nothing is impossible with God."

Mary took a deep breath and said, "I am God's servant girl. Let it be done to me just as you have said." With that, Gabriel disappeared.

As the Holy Spirit came upon Mary, He manifested as an unseen light of glory above her head. As she struggled not to swoon, that light moved within her and rested at her womb.

In heaven, the Son said, "It begins!" As the holy seed was united with her egg, it began to immediately subdivide and throb with divine life.

Sensing that what the angel had spoken of was occurring, Mary cried out, with her hands on her belly, "My God!"

Later, when it became obvious that Mary was pregnant. Her fiancé, Joseph, assuming the worst, decided to break off the engagement and quietly put Mary away, rather than make a spectacle of her.

But the angel of the Lord appeared to him in a dream and told him, "Don't be afraid take Mary as your wife, for what has been conceived in her is of the Holy Ghost. She will give birth to a son and you will call His name Jesus, because He will save His people from their sins." This is how the prophesy was fulfilled that a virgin would conceive and give birth to a child that would be called God with us. Joseph did as the angel instructed and took Mary in as his wife, but had no intimate relations with her until after the child was born.

Near the time that Mary was to give birth, a decree was announced from Roman Emperor Augustus that the whole empire would be taxed. For the purpose of the census and tax, each male was to return, temporarily, to his home town.

As a descendant of King David, Joseph made preparations to go to Bethlehem with Mary. Before he departed, one of the town midwives in Nazareth pulled Joseph aside and gave him some child birthing instructions. Given the advanced stage of Mary's pregnancy, it was possible that she might deliver on the way without the benefit of a midwife.

Thankfully, the two eventually reached Bethlehem, but the crowded town had no available lodging for them. Seeing that Mary had gone into labor, Joseph begged an innkeeper to make an exception and provide something. The innkeeper agreed to allow them to take shelter in the stalls with the animals. As Mary advanced in her labor, Joseph reminded himself of the instructions he had received from the midwife.

Near the time of birth, Joseph got into position as the head of the child began to position itself at the opening of the womb. But something was wrong. "I don't know what to say. Something is different from what I was told to expect. I don't know what to do."

Mary smiled and said, "I am a virgin my husband." Joseph followed Mary's instructions, happy that his last doubts about the virginity of Mary had been pushed aside by this unusual proof.

Meanwhile, out in the fields, a group of shepherds watching their flocks of sheep under the stars were startled by the appearance of the angel of the Lord in the sky and surrounded by a great light of the glory of God. They were frightened, but the angel told them, "Don't be afraid. I am bringing you a message of great joy to you and to all people. For to you is born today in the City of David a savior, Christ the Lord. And this is how you will know who He is: you will find a baby lying in a manger wrapped in swaddling clothes."

Suddenly, the sky was full of a multitude of angels shouting, "Glory to God in the highest, peace on earth and goodwill to men."

When the angels disappeared, the shepherds said, "Let's go to Bethlehem and see this thing that we have been told about!" So they went and found the holy family and the child just as the angel had said. The shepherds praised God and shared with Mary and Joseph what they had seen and been told before returning to their flocks and telling others along the way what had happened.

After the birth of Jesus, Joseph remained in Bethlehem and opened a carpentry shop there rather than return to Nazareth. He loved being close to the Temple and Jerusalem. Then one evening, a couple of years later, a caravan of notable people from Persia came to the door of their home in Bethlehem. They explained that they were trained in the wisdom of the east and after the words and writings of Daniel, the greatest wise man in their history. According to scripture and the signs in the heavens, a great king had been born. This king was to be King of the Jews and savior of the world. They insisted that all signs led them to his house. Much to the surprise of Joseph, they asked that they be permitted to see this king so that they could worship him and complete their mission. Inviting them into his humble home, Joseph called to Mary and asked her to bring the toddler Jesus out to meet their honored guests.

The child Jesus smiled at the visitors. The wise men were overjoyed and called to their servants to bring the gifts they had brought on this trip. Placing their gifts of gold, frankincense, and myrrh at the feet of Jesus, they gave glory to God for the success of their mission and worshipped Jesus. Before leaving, they told Mary and Joseph of their earlier meeting with King Herod, which was according to protocol, since they were dignitaries from another land. When the wise men made their call on Herod at his palace they had asked where they could find the one born as King of the Jews. Feigning to want to honor the child himself, Herod asked them to report back to him after they had found the child. However, God had warned them in a dream not to report back to Herod, but rather to return to their land by another route. Further, to avoid drawing attention to them and the holy child, they had to make their visit brief and be on their way.

## Kill the Son and Rightful Heir

Once Herod realized he had been duped by the wise men, since they did not return to him, Satan put it in his heart to kill the child of whom the wise men spoke. This was God's Messiah that had been promised. Satan believed the time to kill Him and be done with Him was then, while He was a helpless toddler.

Satan spoke into the mind of Herod, "I must find this child and kill this pretender! I will make my own destiny!" Provoked by Satan's whispers, Herod flew into a rage. Based on the timing that he had enquired of the wise men, he dispatched soldiers under his command to kill every male child in Bethlehem and surrounding hamlets that was two years old and younger. It was a grisly slaughter meant to ensure that the prophesied King of the Jews, confirmed by signs in the heavens, would not live to challenge the rule of Herod. Herod intended to be the only king of the Jews, whatever it might take. This slaughter fulfilled a prophesy of the weeping and wailing that would come to Bethlehem because its children would be put to death.

After the visitors from the east departed, and before Herod dispatched soldiers to slaughter the young male children in Bethlehem, the angel of the Lord came to Joseph in a dream. The angel told Joseph, "Get up! Take the child and his mother and flee to Egypt. Stay there until I bring you word, because Herod is looking for the child to kill him."

Joseph got up, and quickly taking Mary and the child Jesus, fled the same night to Egypt as fugitives from the wrath and evil designs of Herod. Unbeknownst to Joseph and Mary, a large unseen troop of angels accompanied them on their flight and encamped around them wherever they paused for rest or sleep. A troop of angels remained with them, unseen, but always present during their time in Egypt. Although fallen angels with assignments from Satan wanted to look into the matter of the child Jesus, the protective angelic detail surrounding the holy family ensured that they kept their distance and that no poisonous cobra, viper, scorpion, or wild bull, lion, bear, dog, or crocodile could pose a menace to God's Son.

# Chapter 19 The Quiet Years

*And he went down with them, and came to Nazareth, and was subject unto them: but his mother kept all these sayings in her heart. And Jesus increased in wisdom and stature, and in favour with God and man. Luke 2:51-52*

One of the standing orders given to the angels rotating to earth on assignment was to protect Jesus the Son of God. An administering angel repeated to each protective detail about to do a tour on earth in connection with the protection of the Son of God, "Not one bone of His body is to ever be broken and no harm or disfigurement to his body is to be allowed, until such time as it pleases Elohim."

Satan and his evil angels would try to send harmful snakes and insects across the path of the toddler Jesus. Those angels on guard would make short work of them. From time to time words would be exchanged between the loyal angels and the evil rebel angels. Being a regular playful young child with a human nature, Jesus would run, jump from rock to rock, or leap out of trees. However, should he misstep or stumble, an unseen angel would swoop in to prevent broken bones or any other harm.

The angels enjoyed this highly sought after duty, but were amazed that Jesus the Son of God did not normally see them or know them. Jesus had become human when He was born as a male child through the womb of the Virgin Mary by divine intervention. This was possible because he had emptied Himself of His divine glory, releasing that glory back to the Father.

Eventually, an angel returned to Joseph, as promised, and informed him that Herod was dead. The family returned to Israel, but passed up on Bethlehem to settle in Nazareth in the far north of the country.

As a young child, Jesus heard from Mary and Joseph the story of His remarkable birth. It was His favorite bedtime story. He asked many questions of His human parents. "Where did I come from?" "What will I be when I grow up?" "Why am I here?" These were difficult questions for Mary and Joseph.

Mary would say, "My son, God will reveal these answers to you in due time, but for the time being, know that You are destined to be the savior of the world. In the meantime, You are mine and I will always love You and be Your mother."

It wasn't all easy for the young Jesus. From time to time He would be taunted by older children. They cast dispersions on the purity of His mother and inferred that He was an illegitimate child born out of wedlock. These encounters stung. As He learned to read for Himself, He began to spend time in the local synagogue where He read and memorized Holy Scripture. As he grew and increased in understanding and in favor with God and the people of Nazareth, He balanced his time between helping Joseph in the carpentry business and spending as much time as possible in the synagogue reading the one copy of the scriptures in the synagogue of the small town that was Nazareth.

Jesus had a good relationship with the head of the synagogue, which was important in gaining access to the scriptures. From time to time the head of the synagogue would say things like, "That Jesus the son of Joseph is a fine young man. Who knows, one day, with training, he might become a decent scribe." "It is a shame he wasn't born a Levite. Unfortunately, he will never be able to be a rabbi."

## The Learning Process for God's Son

At age 12, Jesus went to Jerusalem with His family for Passover. They were part of an annual pilgrimage of town folk from Nazareth who traveled together for safety. Men went along with men and women with women. The young children traveled with the women. The older children moved around visiting and playing. A few months earlier, Jesus had been given a bar mitzvah, the social rite of passage for young Jewish boys to mark moving from childhood to manhood. Once in Jerusalem, Jesus assumed that, like with Samuel, He would be turned over to serve God in the Temple.

When the time came to return to Nazareth the same cavalcade moved slowly out of Jerusalem and northward toward Nazareth. Three days into the journey Joseph and Mary realized, in panic, that they didn't know where Jesus was. They rushed from relative to friend searching for Him. Finally, they concluded He was not with the traveling party. Still panicky, they returned alone to Jerusalem. Their frantic search finally took them to the Temple. There, they found their son surrounded by rabbis and teachers. The men around Him were asking Him questions and were amazed at His answers.

Shrieking the name, "Jesus," Mary and Joseph descended on Jesus scolding Him. "Son why have You done this to us? We have been worried about You and didn't know where you were!"

The young Jesus replied, "Didn't you know that I had to be about my Father's business?" Apparently, Mary and Joseph didn't have that revelation. They saw the place of Jesus as submitting to His parents and returning to Nazareth to complete His apprenticeship in the family carpentry business.

The rabbis begged Joseph and Mary to leave the boy with them. They promised to take good care of Him. Joseph and Mary would have none of that. Although disappointed that His parents were not with Him in His desire to remain in the Temple, Jesus submitted to them and obediently returned with them back to Nazareth.

One evening, as Jesus poured over the scrolls of scripture by the light of a single flame of an oil lamp, He got the revelation that the scriptures were speaking of Him. This revelation came as an unseen angel poured a vial of invisible oil over His head. Jesus smiled broadly, then lowered His head and prayed to God for even more revelation. He prayed that, as with Moses, God would speak to Him as a man speaks to his friend.

In time, Joseph died a natural death. That left Jesus as the male head of the family. One Sabbath day, as the adult Jesus and his family left a service at the synagogue, Jesus requested permission to go alone just outside of town to pray. Mary said, "Alright, but don't be late for dinner!"

As Jesus walked alone in the field, He suddenly became sleepy and laid down in the grass and wildflowers. Immediately, He dreamed that God the Father was speaking to Him. The message from God was that He loved Him and was well-pleased with Him. In addition, God, in the dream, said, "You will see in holy scriptures that I spoke to my servant Moses as a man speaks to his friend and not through dreams and visions as I have done with other prophets. From now on I will speak to You openly and clearly as the Son that You are." Thus began the intimacy between God the Father and God the Son during His time as a flesh and blood human.

# Chapter 20 The Ministry of Jesus

*And Jesus went about all Galilee, teaching in their synagogues, and preaching the gospel of the kingdom, and healing all manner of sickness and all manner of disease among the people. And his fame went throughout all Syria: and they brought unto him all sick people that were taken with divers diseases and torments, and those which were possessed with devils, and those which were lunatick, and those that had the palsy; and he healed them. And there followed him great multitudes of people from Galilee, and from Decapolis, and from Jerusalem, and from Judaea, and from beyond Jordan. Matthew 4:23-25*

At age 30, His step-father Joseph now dead, the time had come for Jesus to initiate His ministry and do what God the Father was telling Him to do.[15] So he traveled down from Nazareth to Judea. In those days, people were flocking to the Jordan River to hear the

---

[15] Additional scriptures are provided here for context.

How God anointed Jesus of Nazareth with the Holy Ghost and with power: who went about doing good, and healing all that were oppressed of the devil; for God was with him. Acts 10:38

And his brightness was as the light; he had horns coming out of his hand: and there was the hiding of his power. Habakkuk 3:4

I am the living bread which came down from heaven: if any man eat of this bread, he shall live forever: and the bread that I will give is my flesh, which I will give for the life of the world. The Jews therefore strove among themselves, saying, How can this man give us his flesh to eat? Then Jesus said unto them, Verily, verily, I say unto you, Except ye eat the flesh of the Son of man, and drink his blood, ye have no life in you.

John 6:51-53

prophet John the Baptizer and to be baptized by him. Jesus himself, although without sin, also presented himself to John to be baptized. Recognizing the Spirit of God upon Jesus, John dropped to his knees in the river and said it was he that needed to be baptized by Jesus. But Jesus pulled John back to his feet and said, "Just do it so as to do what God requires."

As John submitted and baptized Jesus, God the Holy Spirit came down alighting on Jesus in the form of a dove, and remained there, visible only to Jesus and to John. God also spoke from Heaven saying, "This is My greatly loved Son." To the others present it seemed as if there were thundering rather than a discernable voice.

**Filled with the Spirit**

Immediately after His baptism and the witness of God that He, Jesus, was the Son of God, Holy Spirit God drove Jesus into the wilderness. There Jesus fasted and prayed for 40 days. Speaking within Himself, Jesus said, *This body craves for its needs to be filled, but I am the master of this body. This body does not master me. I must commune with God and build up my spirit for the task ahead.*

While in the wilderness desert, the wild animals would approach Jesus. An unseen contingent of angels always stood at the ready. The angels were unseen to others. Most of the time they were also unseen to Jesus. Jesus had to learn to walk in faith, not just by what could be seen. Natural things recognized that Jesus was the Lord of all nature, both of plants and of all living creatures. They were at peace with Jesus and sought to do Him no harm. The animals knew that Jesus was the hope for removal of the curse that was upon all living things, as well as upon inanimate nature.

As Jesus fasted, God the Father spoke to Him. "My Son, in the past, I put my Spirit upon the prophets. The portion given to them was also limited and came in episodes. It will not be that way with You. My Spirit, Holy Spirit God, will be upon You and in You. You will also have the Spirit at all times and without limits." The Father went on to say, "What is that in Your hands?"

Jesus looked and said, "I don't see anything. Please open My eyes so that I can see what You are seeing."

The Father said, "Look again and use Your faith to see."

When Jesus looked at His hands again He saw directed beams of soft blue healing light emanating from the palms of His hands. "I see it now Father," said Jesus, "What does it mean and what am I to do with it?"

The Father responded, "I want You to use Your faith by Your words and this healing light coming from the Spirit in You as the primary ways You will heal others and undo the works of Satan. The people around you will not see this light, but they will acknowledge the work You do.

At the end of 40 days Jesus was famished. It was at that time that Satan appeared to test Him. Satan reminded God of when He had allowed him to test Job the servant of God. Satan likewise requested authority to test Jesus. That request was granted, but God told Satan, "You cannot touch His body, at least not now." As Satan approached Jesus, the unseen loyalist angels attempted to intervene, but Satan told them to stand aside because he had been given authority to test Jesus from the Most High God.

The leader of this group of angels lifted his head and called out to the Archangel Michael. "Michael, something is going on down here with Satan. Do you want to come here yourself and get some of this action?"

Over the great distance Michael replied, "Satan has been given authority to test Jesus, but no harm can come to Him. Stand aside a brief while, but see that no harm comes to Jesus." Grudgingly, the angel guard moved away.

As Satan approached Jesus he remembered how he was defeated in Heaven by the Son and cast out together with his rebel angels. Satan thought, *He is in my kingdom now. I am the god of this world once again. I will either bend and twist this Jesus to worship me or I will kill Him, rule over Him, and torment Him for eternity.* As a smile came over his face he mused, *Perhaps I will be able to hold Jesus for ransom! Yes! I can ransom Him for a deal with the Almighty to make me supreme in place of God.* Such were the machinations of the mind of Satan as he prepared for his encounter with Jesus.

In his visible form, the beautiful Satan appeared to Jesus and began to tempt him. Knowing Jesus was physically weak and driven by hunger, Satan said, "If You are the Son of God, then turn these stones into loaves of bread." As Satan said "bread" the pleasing aroma of fresh baked bread entered the nostrils of the hungry Jesus causing Him to reflexively salivate for a taste of fresh bread.

Jesus did not doubt who He was or why He had come to earth as a man, but despite His now raging hunger, the physically weakened Jesus said, "It is written that man does not live by bread alone, but by every word that proceeds from the mouth of God."

Satan then showed Jesus the mighty kingdoms of the world, past, present, and those to come. "These are mine and it is in my power to give them to whomever I will. Get down on Your knees and worship me, and I will give them to You," said Satan, thinking he could tempt Jesus to take the easy road to power and thus enable Satan to achieve his dream of being exalted over God.

However, Jesus responded, "It is written, you shall serve the Lord your God."

Finally, Satan took Jesus up to a spire of the Temple. Down below them were people milling about unaware of what was being played out above them. "If You are the Son of God," Satan said, "then throw Yourself down from here, because it is written, He shall give His angels charge concerning you so that You won't even smash your foot against a stone."

The unseen guardian angels of Jesus were on alert and sprang into preventive action in the event that Jesus would step off and gravity take Him down hard, causing injury or death should they not intervene.

Again, Jesus answered Satan with scripture and said, "It is written, You shall not tempt the Lord your God!" With that Satan departed looking for another, more convenient time to tempt or strike Jesus.

Immediately, Jesus found himself back in the wilderness, still weak and famished. The angels then revealed their presence to Him and waited on Him. The angels gave Jesus strength, food, and water. An angel motioned over Him and called for His body and clothing to be clean and fresh. One angel knelt down to gently massage His feet. Another poured oil in his hair and lovingly combed it and trimmed his beard and moustache. Another angel stepped before Jesus with a golden platter on which there was fresh fruit, nuts, dates, special nutritious wafers, cheeses and fresh water. The angel said, "Lord, please eat and drink. It will refresh you and give you strength." All the while, other angels played soothing music in the background. When all of the pampering was done and Jesus was refreshed, the angels bowed and knelt before Him in worship, then they disappeared.

Jesus then heard the audible voice of God the Father. "My Son, I am so pleased with you. I will now continue to speak with you as I spoke with my servant Moses. When you speak I will hear and will answer. Remember, You are anointed with My Spirit. He will reside in You and be with You. Holy Spirit God will be Your strength and power."

Coming out of the wilderness and flush with the power of Holy Spirit God in Him and on Him, Jesus returned to the place on the Jordan where John was baptizing. When John saw Him he pointed and said, "Look, the Lamb of God who takes away the sin of the world. God told me that on whomever I see the Spirit alighting and remaining like a dove, that person is the Messiah. I saw that sign when I baptized Him. He is the Son of God, the one I told you about who would come after me, but who existed before me." Immediately, two of John's disciples left John and followed Jesus. Jesus continued to gather His core group of disciples.

Then Jesus returned to the region of Galilee in the north accompanied by His disciples. He began to teach in the synagogues of the towns and villages of that region. As He did so His fame began to spread. When He reached Nazareth, His home town, He went to the local synagogue on the Sabbath. Being a literate person and a long-time member of that synagogue, He took the scroll from the head of the synagogue. He read from the place in Isaiah that says, "The Spirit of the Lord is on Me, because He has anointed Me to preach good news to the poor; He has sent Me to heal the brokenhearted, to preach deliverance to those held captive by their sins, restoration of sight to the blind, to free those that are bruised and beaten down, and to proclaim the Jubilee year of the Lord's mercy." Jesus stopped reading at that point, gave the scroll back to the head of the synagogue, and, instead of returning to the place where He had been seated on the floor, seated Himself in the ceremonial chair that no one ever sat in, because it was the custom to reserve it as a place for the Messiah, should He ever visit them.

**The Rejection of the Messiah Begins**

The place was completely silent. The people were stunned. All they could do was to stare at Jesus. Jesus broke the awkward silence saying, "This scripture is fulfilled in your ears today."

But those present began to speak out louder and louder saying, "Isn't this Joseph the carpenter's son?"

Jesus responded, "Prophets are not honored in their own lands." When He backed up that statement with examples from scripture in which miracles of healing and provision were done for foreigners who had the faith to believe, rather than for Jews with the same needs they had, the people got up in a mob action and ran Jesus out of the Synagogue and out of town.

The mob was responding to unseen evil angels putting into their minds the thought, *Kill Him! Kill Him!*

Surrounding Him, the frenzied mob pushed Jesus toward the edge of a high bluff, intending to toss Him over the side and kill Him.

As they got closer and closer to the bluff, the leader of the troop of unseen guardian angels with the duty to protect Jesus said, "I've seen enough. It is time to intervene."

Another angel asked, "Should we just kill them all?"

"No," said the group's leader, "The Son is on a mission of mercy, so it would not be appropriate to kill them at this time."

Still another angel said, "I can blind them."

Again their leader rejected that saying, "Then they might stumble over the bluff and die, and the Son would be blamed. Just take away their mental cognition so that they don't recognize the Son. While you are doing that the rest of us will extract the Son from this situation." So the angels, still unseen by the mob, surrounded Jesus and escorted Him safely through the mob, out of the area around Nazareth, and onward toward the city of Capernaum. Unseen also by Jesus, a changing of the guard occurred along the road. A new troop of guardian angels came down from Heaven to relieve the group that had just saved Jesus.

The new troop leader said to his counterpart, "Well done!  We all saw that. You can return to Heaven now. We've got this."

Both groups of angels shouted, "Glory to God!" Then the group that saved Jesus from death in Nazareth ascended back up into Heaven.

In Capernaum, and in surrounding towns, Jesus continued to preach in the Synagogues on the Sabbath. At times, even in the Synagogues demons would shout out from their host person, "You are the Christ, the Son of God!" But Jesus would command them to shut up and would exorcise them, freeing the people who, as the human hosts of those spirits, had been tormented by them.

There was nothing that took Jesus by surprise. Although He had voluntarily limited Himself to being a man, He did not depend on Himself to do the work of God. Jesus would pray early in the mornings, sometimes after fasting. At those times, as Jesus worshipped and prayed, His spirit would ascend to the third Heaven to the very throne room of God the Father. There in that intimate place the Father would show Him what He as the Father would do as the day progressed and spoke to Jesus what He was to say in those times, so that the two of them would be in an alignment of perfect unity. This is why Jesus would say, "I only do what I see the Father doing, and I only say what the Father speaks." It was this method that Jesus employed throughout His ministry as the Son of Man and the Son of God.

Jesus continued to minister in the northern region of Galilee. There he performed many miracles of healing and commanded demons to leave people. When He extended His hands to heal someone, they were bathed in the soft blue light of healing glory that emanated from His hands. Human eyes could not see the beams of blue light and were not aware of the light.

To the amazement of onlookers, the demons obeyed Him. Although some people gladly heard Jesus and sought Him out so that they could be healed, others, particularly of the religious faction known as the Pharisees, resented Him and could only find fault with Him and with His disciples, as if they were more perfect than Jesus. Instead, they were lacking in love and compassion. They were super religious, having encumbered themselves and those who would listen to them with a multitude of rules. They were jealous of the following Jesus was accumulating and did not identify with the message that Jesus had of love, forgiveness, and calling for people to draw near to God with humble hearts being sorry for their sins.

So the Pharisees laid a trap for Jesus. They got a man with a crippled, withered up arm to place himself in a conspicuous spot in the local Synagogue on the Sabbath. When Jesus and his disciples entered, as was their habit, the Pharisees looked on to see if Jesus would heal this man on the Sabbath and, in their hard-hearted rule-bound minds, be guilty, they incorrectly reasoned, of breaking the commandment to not work on the Sabbath.

Of course, Jesus saw the set up and told the man with the crippled arm to stand up. Jesus then looked around at the assembly. The Pharisees had come to find something to charge Jesus with, rather than to worship God. So, looking into their hard faces, Jesus asked them a rhetorical question. "Does the law permit you to do good things on the Sabbath day or evil things? Does the law of the Sabbath encourage you to save a life or to kill someone and take their life?"

But the Pharisees said nothing. They would not recognize the truth of the logic and spirit of the law presented by Jesus. Instead, they were daring Him to heal the man in the Synagogue on the Sabbath day. The irony was that they believed Jesus could heal the man. That would be a sign of the Messiah. At the same time, they knew that they, for all of their religiosity, could not heal the man on any day.

As Jesus looked around at the Pharisees, He became angry and His compassionate heart was wounded by the rigidity and unloving nature of their hearts. Then Jesus said to the cripple, "Stretch out your hand!" The man stretched out the arm and hand that had been withered by palsy and frozen in a position near his chest for all of his life. He was healed! His arm and hand were no longer emaciated and immobile but normal like his other and able to move freely.

The common people thanked God for what they had just witnessed, but the Pharisees stomped out of the Synagogue. They looked completely past the sign God had just done in their plain sight and sought to bring Jesus down. So they went to those Jews who were of the political party of Herod, a group they did not normally associate with, and made common cause with them as to how to destroy Jesus.

In a short time, the crowds around Jesus swelled. Those who used to follow John the Baptizer began to follow Jesus. John's most loyal followers were jealous for him, but John did not see a competition between himself and Jesus, even though the disciples of Jesus also began to baptize people just as John was doing. Instead, speaking of Jesus, John told his disciples, "He must become greater and greater, while I must recede."

### An Unholy Alliance Against The Messiah

The situation in Israel was that there was an unwritten tacit agreement between the Roman occupiers and the local religious authorities. The chief priest, his subordinates, the priesthood, and the council of religious elders known as the Sanhedrin would not challenge the

Roman occupation and its puppet political leaders put in place by Rome. The Romans, who were pagan polytheists, did not interfere, in general, in religious matters. The rise of Jesus was sweeping the country as a phenomenon. Both the Jewish religious establishment and the Roman occupation were wary of Jesus and His movement. Each was concerned that Jesus would mount a challenge to their power.

Nicodemus was a member of the religious faction of the Pharisees. He was also a member of the Sanhedrin. He was in awe of Jesus and wanted to look closer into the doctrine Jesus was teaching and determine for himself whether this Jesus was the Messiah that Israel had been waiting for or not. However, Nicodemus was afraid of most of the other members of the Sanhedrin and of those Jews, particularly Pharisees like himself, which were so adamantly against Jesus. Therefore, Nicodemus would quietly come to Jesus by night for private audiences with Him.

## Messiah's Mission and Eternal Life Explained

Nicodemus showed great deference to Jesus and said, "Rabbi, we know that You are a teacher from God because no one can do the miracles that You are doing unless God is with him."

Jesus ignored the flattery and got to the point with Nicodemus. Jesus said, "Most certainly I tell you that, unless a man is born again he can't see the Kingdom of God."

Thinking in the natural sense, Nicodemus responded, "How can a man be born again when he is already old?" Nicodemus had never heard of anyone re-entering his mother's womb to be born a second time. But Jesus was speaking of spiritual things.

Jesus told Nicodemus, "Flesh gives birth to flesh, but the Spirit of God gives birth to spirit. Don't try to reason it out because I said you must be born again." Jesus added, "The wind blows where it will, and you hear its noise, but you can't tell where it came from or where it is going. It is the same way for everyone born of the Spirit of God."

Nicodemus still didn't get it. He said, "I don't understand. How can this be?"

Jesus responded, "You are a senior religious leader and teacher in Israel and yet you don't understand these things? If I have told you natural things and you don't believe Me, how then will you believe if I tell you spiritual things?" Then Jesus took Nicodemus into the deep waters of spiritual things in plain words, explaining that He had descended from Heaven as the Son of Man and Son of God. Jesus went on to tell Nicodemus, "God loved the world so much that He sent His only Son, the unique Son that came directly from Him, so that whoever believes in the Son won't die, but will live forever." Then Jesus added, "God didn't send His Son into the world to condemn the world, but to save it through Him. Whoever then believes on the Son will not face condemnation, but those who refuse to believe and reject the light that God has sent will be condemned because they would not believe in the name of God's Son."

Thus Jesus explained where He came from and His mission to save the world in obedience to the will and purpose of God the Father. Jesus reminded Nicodemus that Moses lifted up the bronze serpent in the desert, when people had a death sentence on them after being bitten by the snakes there. Those that looked on the bronze serpent that was held up lived, while those who would not look died. In the same way He, the Son, would be lifted up on a wooden pole, and those who would look on Him and believe would live and not die.

## Reclaiming the Temple Complex

In Jerusalem, Jesus would go and teach and preach in the Temple. The Temple was a master work of that Herod who ruled when Jesus was a child. It was the center of worship in Israel. But it had been corrupted. The outer courtyard had been turned into a marketplace with animals for sacrifice and money changers. Both the vendors of the animals and the money changers paid a kickback to the chief priest to operate in that place. Moreover, only coin produced by the Temple was acceptable for offerings or for the purchase of animals for sacrifice. The Roman coins were considered polluted because they bore images of the emperor who claimed to be a god. Besides, it was against the culture and history of the Jews to have images of men and women. By having a monopoly on the exchange of these coins, the exchange rate was set at a level that was very unfavorable to those who were compelled to seek exchange. In addition, by rejecting some of the animals that people tried to bring in themselves, on the grounds that they did not meet the standards of the Temple, people were also coerced into buying their animals for sacrifice from the vendors in the Temple outer courtyard. It was a corrupt system set up in a place that was intended to be holy.

At Passover, early in His ministry, Jesus went to Jerusalem with His disciples to observe the Passover there. However, upon entering the outer courtyard, which had become a corrupt marketplace, Jesus was moved with anger. He demanded that the animal stalls and cages be taken out of the Temple grounds. Then, knotting some cords together into a whip, He went around, overturning the moneychangers' tables and flogging them out of the Temple grounds saying as He went, "You have made My Father's house of prayer into a common marketplace!" As He did so, His disciples recalled the scripture about being eaten up with zeal for the Lord's house.

But Jesus was challenged by some of the Jews, especially, those that profited from the corrupt monopoly. They asked, "On what authority are You doing this!"

Jesus, speaking of His body, gave them a sign saying, "Destroy this Temple and in three days I will raise it back up again!"

They responded, "This Temple was 46 years in the making and You are going to rebuild it in three days?" However, many of the common people, who witnessed the miracles that He did and heard His words, believed that He was sent by God.

**The Teaching and Miracle Ministry**

As Jesus ministered in the region of Galilee, huge crowds thronged to see Him and His disciples. He went up into a mountain, and with His disciples gathered with Him, taught the people many things. In the end, the people were astonished. Jesus didn't teach like other rabbis or the scribes who made copies of the scrolls of scripture. He spoke authoritatively and they heard Him gladly. When Jesus came down from the mountain, the crowds continued to follow Him and He worked miracles as He went.

On one trip to Jerusalem, Jesus took the 12 disciples aside and explained what was going to happen to Him there in the future. How that, as the Son of Man, He would be turned over to the chief priests and to the scribes, who would place the penalty of death on Him and then turn Him over to the Roman occupiers to carry out the death sentence. He told his disciples that He would be mocked, flogged, spit upon, and killed, but He would rise again from the dead three days later.

Later, when He overhead His disciples discussing which of them would be the greatest in the kingdom of King Jesus, Jesus took them to task. Speaking of Himself, Jesus said, "Even the Son of Man did not come to be waited on, but to serve others, and to give His life to pay the ransom for many souls." So, once again, Jesus explained his divine mission in clear, unmistakable language.

Meanwhile, John the Baptizer railed against sin regardless of where it was found, and called the people to repent. His stout words against Herod, who had taken his brother Philip's wife Herodias as his own, resulted in his arrest and imprisonment. Herodias was incensed by the tough preaching of John directed against her and Herod. She wanted John put to death, but Herod, who was part Jew, believed John was a prophet and, for the time being, was unwilling to take his life.

While John languished in Herod's prison, he sent his disciples to Jesus to ask if Jesus was the Messiah or whether they should look for someone else. John, like most others, thought the Messiah would immediately re-establish the political kingdom of the House of David and throw off the occupation of the Roman Empire and its puppet rulers. More so, John wondered why the Messiah would not get him out of prison and out from under the threat of death.

When John's disciples brought John's message to Him, Jesus did not answer immediately. Instead, He launched into a power demonstration of His bona fides as Messiah by healing a large number of sick people that were thronging Him, including the blind, and those afflicted by demons.

Afterward, Jesus told John's disciples to return to John and tell him what they had seen and heard. "That the blind had their sight restored, those stricken with leprosy were totally cleansed, the deaf had their hearing restored, dead people were raised back to life, and the good news of God's kingdom was preached to the poor." After John's disciples left, Jesus spoke to the throng about John, hailing him as the greatest of prophets up to that time.

### Execution of John the Baptizer

At his birthday party, Herod got drunk. Herodias knew his foibles well and how he often leered at her daughter. So Herodias had her daughter Salome dance a seductive strip tease before Herod and his party guests. Herod was so pleased that he offered to give Salome whatever she requested. After consulting with her mother Herodias, the young teen asked for the head of John the Baptizer on a platter. Feeling unable to renege on his promise made before so many of his friends and officials, Herod dispatched the executioner who brought back John's head on a platter and gave it to the daughter of Herodias. She promptly presented the grisly gift to her mother, who smiled with great pleasure at having silenced her accuser.

When news of John's execution was brought to Jesus by John's disciples, Jesus told them all to withdraw to a quiet place, because the crowds and the coming and going of people was overwhelming. He also wanted some time to grieve the death of his cousin John. As they slipped away by ship to get to another location along the shore of the lake, people alerted others to the movement of Jesus and His disciples. They were followed on foot by people from all of the surrounding towns.

Upon landing at another shore of the lake, Jesus came out of the ship to see the surrounding area filled with an expectant crowd of people. Taking compassion on them, Jesus began to teach them for hours. The disciples then urged Jesus to send the people away, because the location they were in was uninhabited and the people needed to go into nearby villages to find food to buy and eat.

Jesus said, "You feed them."

But the disciples protested that a year's wages wouldn't be enough to feed the crowd.

Jesus asked, "Well, what do you have?"

They replied, "Just two dried fish and five bread rolls."

Jesus instructed the disciples to have the people sit down on the grass organized into groups of hundreds and fifties. He then took the bread and fish and looked up into the sky. As He did so the heavens opened to Him and He blessed the food, broke it into pieces, and gave it to his disciples to distribute. Out of a group of 5,000 men plus their women and children, a crowd of about 20,000 people, everyone ate their fill. At the end, there were 12 baskets of food left over.

Again, Jesus sent his disciples away by ship while He remained behind to send the people away now that they had been taught and fed. Jesus Himself went up to a nearby mountain to pray. The disciples departed by ship but midway in their passage they were getting nowhere. The wind and currents were working against them. Though they rowed for hours late into the night they made no progress.

The Spirit of God caused Jesus to see his disciples supernaturally, though it was too far and the weather too obscuring to see them naturally. From the mountain top Jesus was translocated (that is, transported instantaneously) in His physical body, by the Spirit, from the mountain to the water near the disciples. There He walked along on the water. As he walked on the water, Jesus made as if He would pass them by. The disciples thought it was a ghost and were afraid.

Jesus called out to them, "It's alright. It's me. Don't be afraid!" When He climbed into the boat with them, the wind stopped blowing. Moreover, the Spirit then translocated Jesus again, together with the disciples, and the entire boat they were in so that it immediately reached the shore the disciples had been fruitlessly striving to reach through their own efforts for hours. For their part, the disciples wondered at what they had just witnessed. This was no ordinary man. He defied the laws of nature.

The people in the region of Galilee began to search for Jesus after the miracle of feeding about 20,000 people from a meal that would normally satisfy one to two people. When they went to the other side of the Sea of Galilee in ships they found Him in a Synagogue at Capernaum. Upon finding Him they were puzzled as to when and how He got there.

Jesus told them, "You most certainly were looking for me, not because of the miraculous signs that you saw, but because you ate your fill of the bread and fish." Jesus further admonished them, "Don't put your efforts into getting food that will spoil, but for food that will endure for a life lived eternally. The Son of Man will give you that food because God the Father has placed His seal of approval on Him."

## Hard Sayings Cause Desertion

The crowd grew restless and challenged Jesus. They demanded a sign from Jesus before they would be willing to believe Him. They said, "Our ancestors ate manna in the wilderness." Hoping to get Jesus to provide an endless supply of food without them having to work for it, they said the scripture says, "He gave them bread from Heaven."

Jesus responded, "Let Me make this clear to you. Moses didn't give bread from Heaven, but My Father is giving you the real bread from Heaven, because the bread of God is the one who descends from Heaven and gives life to the world."

The crowd got excited upon hearing this and said, "Give us that bread every day!"

Seeing that their minds were still on their stomachs, Jesus said, "I am the bread of life. Whoever comes to Me will neither be hungry nor thirsty again, but as I have already told you, you have seen Me and you still don't believe." As Jesus continued to teach on Himself as the source of life sent from God the Father, the crowd began to complain.

The Jews that had gathered there started to murmur and be offended because Jesus said He was the bread that came down from Heaven. Some said, "Isn't this Jesus the son of Joseph? We know his father and mother, so how can He say, 'I descended from Heaven?'"

Jesus admonished them again, "Stop your complaining. It was written by the prophets 'They will all be taught by God.' No one has seen God except the one who came from God. That one has seen the Father. Let me assure you once again, anyone who believes in Me has eternal life because I am the bread of life." Jesus added, "I am the living bread that came down from Heaven. Whoever eats this bread will live forever. The bread I am giving for the life of the world is My own flesh."

The assertions that Jesus made about His identity, His origin, and His mission from God the Father was too much for many in the crowd to accept. The crowd began to buzz with arguments among its groups. "How can He give us His own flesh to eat?" they questioned.

So Jesus said, "Let me assure you, if you don't eat the flesh of the Son of Man and drink His blood, then you won't have life inside you. However, the one who eats My flesh and drinks My blood will have eternal life and I will raise him from the dead on the last day, because My flesh is real food and My blood is real drink. For the one who eats My flesh and who drinks My blood lives in Me and I live in him." Jesus went on to clarify that, "This is the bread that came down from Heaven. It isn't at all like the manna your ancestors ate. They ate that manna and they still died, but the one who eats this bread will live forever."

Upon hearing all of this from Jesus, many of those who had attached themselves to Him as followers and disciples gave up on Jesus. They said among themselves, "This teaching is too hard to accept! Can anyone here go along with this?"

Jesus knew, internally, that His followers were complaining about the things He had said. So He asked, "Are you offended by this? What if you saw the Son of Man ascend back to the place from where He had descended? Your human flesh and reasoning won't help you with this. What I have spoken to you are words that are spirit and life. I know some of you don't believe Me. That's why I told you that no one can come to Me except those who, by the grace of God the Father, are drawn to Me."

That confrontation in Capernaum was a major turning point. From that time, many of the followers of Jesus turned away from Him and no longer traveled with Him. As the crowd filtered away from the Synagogue and toward the outskirts of town some would occasionally look back and shake their heads.

Jesus stood there outside the Synagogue watching a good part of His movement dissipate. Then Jesus turned to His 12 disciples and said, "Do you want to leave Me too?"

Peter responded, "To whom would we go Lord? You have the words of eternal life. We have come to believe and to know that You are the Holy One of God!"

**Jesus Found Guilty of Doing Good**

On one of his trips to Jerusalem, Jesus passed by the pool of Bethesda. It was a Sabbath day. Gathered there was a large crowd of sick people. They were there because in the history of the pool it was said that there was an angel that would come and stir the waters. Whoever was able to get into the pool first, after seeing the water stirred, would be healed of whatever disease he had.

There was a particular man there who had been paralyzed for 38 years. For 38 years he had been brought to the pool in hope of a miracle of healing. Jesus saw him and knew he had been around the pool for a long time. As a child and young man, Jesus had seen him before, along with many others. The man was a fixture at the pool. Without identifying Himself Jesus said to the man, "Would you like to be normal?"

The man did not answer the simple question. Instead, he complained, "Sir, I don't have anyone to help me. When the angel causes the water of the pool to move and slosh around, as I am trying to get into the pool someone else steps into the water ahead of me and they are the one that gets healed."

Jesus did not commiserate with him or say how unfair that was. Jesus simply gave the man a command. "Get up! Pick up your pallet and walk!" The man was instantly healed, rolled up his pallet, tucked it under his arm, and started to walk home without so much as turning around and thanking Jesus, praising God, or inquiring as by what power Jesus was able to do this miracle. Jesus Himself continued on His own way in another direction, blending in with the crowd.

Because it was the Sabbath, some Jews accosted the man and asked, "Do you think it is permissible for you to carry your bedding on the Sabbath?"

The man said, "The one that healed me told me to do it." When the Jews demanded that he identify the man responsible, but he could not do so.

Later, Jesus came across him in the Temple and said to him, "You have been fully healed, so don't continue to sin or something worse will come on you."

However, the man left the Temple and went to those Jews that took issue with his being healed on the Sabbath and told them that it was Jesus that had healed him and then commanded him to take up his pallet. Rather than thanking God for the notable miracle of healing that had been done, those Jews determined among themselves to kill Jesus for daring to heal someone on the Sabbath.

When they found and confronted Jesus, Jesus answered, "My Father works and I work too." That enraged those Jews all the more to determine to kill Jesus, because in their faulty excessive religiosity, Jesus had sinned by healing someone on the Sabbath. Also, by calling God His Father, they believed Jesus was only a man and was making Himself equal to God. But Jesus further said to them, "The Son can't do anything on His own, except what He sees the Father doing, and what the Father does, that is also what the Son then does." Many other things Jesus said to them, which only increased their murderous rage. Finally, Jesus told the Jews that were so set against Him and thought they were enforcing the laws of Moses, "If you had believed the things that Moses wrote you would have believed Me, because Moses wrote about Me." [16]

## Traps Set to Kill the Messiah

Being determined to kill Jesus, one day the chief priests challenged Him while Jesus was teaching in the Temple complex. The chief priests brought with them an entourage that included the scribes, who were expert in the letter of the Jewish religious laws, and the Sanhedrin council of religious elders. The plan was to ensnare Jesus in His words in the presence of many esteemed witnesses so that they could condemn Jesus to death. They felt Jesus was usurping their position, because the common people greatly admired Jesus and thronged His teaching sessions in the Temple complex. The chief priests were jealous and angry that Jesus was showing them up on their own home ground. Besides, Jesus was not one of them.

Rudely breaking into the teaching that Jesus was holding, the chief priests demanded, "Tell us by whose authority You are doing these things? Who gave you that authority?"

Seeing that it was a setup, Jesus replied, "First, I have a question for you, and I want an answer. Was the baptism that John did ordained of Heaven, or was it the invention of mere men?"

The chief priests and their entourage stepped back and huddled among themselves to determine how to

---

[16] "I will raise them up a Prophet from among their brethren, like unto thee, and will put my words in his mouth; and he shall speak unto them all that I shall command him. And it shall come to pass, that whosoever will not hearken unto my words which he shall speak in my name, I will require it of him." Deuteronomy 18:18-19 KJV.

answer the question from Jesus. They reasoned that if they say John's baptism was with the blessing of Heaven, then Jesus might say, "Then why didn't you believe him?" Of course, none of them went to be baptized by John and when they did go to observe what John was doing at the Jordan River, John would verbally attack them as unrepentant religious hypocrites. They further reasoned that if they say that what John was doing in baptizing people was just something manufactured out of his mind, then they might well be stoned to death on the spot, because the people gathered there in the Temple complex to hear Jesus believed John was a prophet.

The chief priests and those with them broke their huddle and came back to where Jesus was standing. Before them was the crowd that came to hear Jesus speak. Their answer to Jesus was a non-answer. They said, "We can't tell you whether the baptism that John did was from Heaven or the invention of a man.

Jesus responded, "Then I won't tell you by what authority I do these things either."
Although the chief priests and their entourage of scribes and Sanhedrin members were bested by Jesus in that exchange, they continued to hang around. They didn't do so to hear what Jesus was teaching so that they could serve God better, but they hoped to hear Jesus say something that they could use against Him.

Jesus turned from His questioners and resumed teaching the people, although now under the gaze of a powerful group that bore Him ill will, and in their stronghold. So Jesus presented a parable of a wealthy landowner who planted a large vineyard that he left in the hands of caretakers while he went off for a long time to a distant country. At the time when his vineyard should have produced a profitable harvest, the owner sent one of his servants to the caretakers to collect his profit. However, the caretakers gave that servant nothing but a beating. After humiliating him, he was sent away empty handed. In succession, the owner sent two other emissaries on the same mission at different times. Each was beaten, humiliated, and sent away empty handed.

Wondering what to do, the owner decided to send his son, thinking the caretakers would behave themselves and show respect to his son once they saw it was the son and heir, rather than someone on the staff of the owner. But when the owner's son showed up, the caretakers said among themselves, "This is the heir. Let's just kill him to get him out of the way and the inheritance of the vineyard will be ours!" So the caretakers threw the son of the owner out of the vineyard and killed him.

Asking a rhetorical question of the crowd gathered around Him, Jesus said, "What will the vineyard's owner do to those people?" Answering His own question, Jesus said, "He will come and destroy those caretakers and give the vineyard to others."

The chief priests and their group were shocked and said, "God forbid!"

But Jesus turned, and looking right at the chief priests and their entourage that came to find some trumped up charge on which to sentence Him to death, Jesus tied the parable to scripture. Jesus asked, "What is the scripture saying when it says the stone that the builders rejected has become the cornerstone?" Jesus added, "Whoever stumbles on that stone will be broken, and whoever that stone hits will be pulverized."

The chief priests and the scribes realized that Jesus was accusing them in the parable of the vineyard and in the scripture of the stone that was rejected by the Temple builders, but which then because the keystone. Making a quick and shameful exit as the people laughed at them, the chief priests and the scribes went immediately to their headquarters within the Temple complex and made plans to arrest and kill Jesus, but they were wary of retribution against them from the people.

On another Sabbath day, Jesus was teaching in one of the Synagogues. Among those in the audience was a woman who was physically bent completely over. She had been in that state for 18 years unable to lift herself up straight. Seeing her, Jesus called her over to Him. He said, "Woman you are freed from your condition." Then, when He put His hands on her, she immediately sprang up completely straight and began to praise God for what had been done to her.

The leader of that Synagogue was indignant. Appealing to the people gathered there he said, "People have six days in which they can work. You can come and be healed on one of those days, not on the Sabbath!"

Jesus looked at him and said, "You hypocrite! Doesn't everyone, on the Sabbath, untie his ox or donkey and lead it out of the stall to water? So shouldn't this woman, a descendant of Abraham that had been tied up by Satan for these 18 years be untied and loosed from her confinement on the Sabbath?" With that the leader of the synagogue and the legalistic Jews with him were put to shame and held their peace, while the rest of the people present celebrated the amazing things being done by Jesus.

## Revelation of the Christ and His Mission

When Jesus was with His disciples, in the area of Caesarea Philippi, He asked them, "Whom are people saying that I am?"

Several of the disciples repeated what they had been hearing. "Some say that you are John the Baptizer come back to life. Some say Elijah, others are saying You are Jeremiah or one of the prophets from the past."

Then Jesus asked, "But who do you all say I am?"

Peter then sprang up and, with conviction said, "You are the Christ, the Son of the living God!"

To which Jesus said, "You are blessed Simon Johnson, because you weren't shown that by some flesh and blood person, but from My Father in heaven. Let me add this, you are Peter, a rock, and it is on the foundation stone of the revelation that I am the Christ that I will build My church; and the very gates of hell will not be able to resist it. I will give you heavenly keys so that whatever you oppose and put a stop to on earth will be opposed and halted by Heaven; and whatever you release on earth will be released by Heaven."

Then Jesus told His disciples not to tell anyone that He was the Christ. Also, from that point onward, Jesus began to tell His disciples how it was necessary for Him to go to Jerusalem, where He would be abused and mistreated by the Sanhedrin, the chief priests, scribes, and be killed, then be raised back to life after three days.

While in the region of Galilee, Jesus commissioned 70 of his followers to fan out and carry the good news. In sending them out He gave them power over Satan's power and promised no hurt would come to them. Unseen by the 70 were angels that went with them to enforce the words that Jesus spoke when He commissioned them.

After some days, when the 70 returned, they were overwhelmed with joy and shared stories of the things that had happened in the villages and towns they had gone to with the message. They said, "Lord, even the devils obeyed us when we gave commands in Your name!"

Then Jesus told them something no mere man could say. He said, "I saw Satan fall like a lightening flash from Heaven. Now I have given you power over all of the enemy's power, but don't cheer because evil spirits must obey you, rejoice because your names are written down in Heaven."

A little later, Jesus turned to his disciples and, speaking to them privately, said, "The eyes that see what you are seeing are blessed, because there were many prophets and kings before you that wanted to see the things that you are seeing, but did not see them. They wanted to hear the things that you are hearing, but they didn't have that opportunity in their time."

## Transfigured

One day, calling the three core disciples Peter, James, and John to Him, Jesus took them on a journey alone. Finally, on Mount Tabor, Jesus was transfigured before them. As the transformation began to take place a deep sleep fell on Peter, James, and John, so that as they slept they saw, as in a dream, Jesus, together with Moses and Elijah. Jesus and His clothes began to shine to the point where it was difficult to look on Him. Moses and Elijah talked with Jesus of how all the saints who had died were waiting for their redemption by Him. They also mentioned the difficult test before Him. Then Peter, James, and John awakened to see that it was not a dream, but reality. They saw Jesus standing before them as they had never seen Him before. Overcome, but not knowing what to say, Peter offered to build three tents of memorial, one for Jesus, and one each for Moses and Elijah. At that point the glory of God appeared as a bright cloud enveloping them so that they could see nothing on account of the glory.

Out of the cloud of glory God the Father spoke. "This is my beloved Son! I am well pleased with Him. Listen to Him!"

Being fearful, they fell on their faces and shut their eyes hard. As the cloud of glory lifted Jesus touched them to get them up again. As they opened their eyes and stood, they saw the very human Jesus standing before them.

Jesus admonished them, "See that you don't tell anyone what you have seen here until the Son of Man has risen from the dead."

## Renewed Attempts to Kill the Messiah

While Jesus was in the Temple complex in Jerusalem teaching the crowds that were drawn to Him, a group of Jews from the Pharisee faction attempted to engage Him in a debate to challenge His authority. They hoped to trip Him up in His words so that they could file charges against Him with the chief priests to the end that He would be condemned to death.

The Pharisees considered themselves to be the epitome of religious practice and had nothing but animosity toward Jesus. "Who are You?" they challenged.

Jesus replied, "That is what I have been telling you from the beginning. I have a lot to say and to judge concerning you, but the One that sent Me is true. I have heard from Him and I tell those things to the world. When you lift up the Son of Man, you will know then that I am He, and that I don't do anything by My own will. Instead, I say the things that the Father teaches Me. The One who sent Me is also with Me. He doesn't abandon Me because I always do the things that please Him."

As Jesus was saying this, many there in the Temple complex who heard Him also believed Him. So Jesus turned from the Pharisees and said to those who believed Him, "If you keep My words then you really are My disciples. You will know the truth, and the truth will set you free."

The Pharisees that had gathered to confront Jesus objected. They said, "We have descended from Abraham and have never been enslaved to anyone. So then how can You say, 'You will be free'?"

Jesus replied to the Pharisees, "I assure you that everyone that sins is a slave of sin." Jesus went on to say, "I know that Abraham is your ancestor, but you are trying to kill Me because you don't accept what I have to say. I speak what I have seen in the presence of God the Father. So you go and do what you have heard from your father."

"Our father is Abraham!" the Pharisees shot back.

Jesus countered, "If you really were children of Abraham you would do what Abraham did, but you are out to kill Me, a man who has told you the truth I heard from God. That isn't what Abraham did! Instead, you are doing what your father does." Jesus said this referring to the devil as their father.

Now the Pharisees were stirred up even more and launched a personal attack accusing Jesus of being a bastard child born out of wedlock. And to add to the indignity, they inferred that His father wasn't even Jewish, but likely a Roman soldier. "We weren't born from sexual sin like You were," they said. They added, "We have one Father—God!"

Again addressing the Pharisees, Jesus said, "If God were your Father, you would love Me, because I descended from God and I am now here. I didn't come on My own. He sent Me. There is a reason you don't understand what I am saying, because you can't listen to My words. You are of your father the devil, and you want to fulfill your father's desires. He was a murderer from the beginning and has not stood for truth, because there is no truth in him. When he speaks a lie it is because that is his nature. He is a liar and the father of lies. Because I tell you the truth you don't believe Me. Which one of you can prove that I am a sinner? If I am telling you the truth, then why won't you believe Me? The person who is from God listens to God's words. That is why you don't listen to Me, because you are not from God."

After these stern words from Jesus, the Pharisees responded, "Aren't we right to say that You are a half-breed Samaritan and that You have a demon?"

Jesus replied, "On the contrary, I honor my Father, but you dishonor Me. Whoever keeps My word will never, ever experience death."

Then the Pharisees said, "Now we know you have a demon. Abraham is dead and so are the prophets. Yet, you say those who keep Your word will never taste death. Are you more important than our ancestor Abraham who is now dead? Just who do you think you are? Who are you pretending to be?"

Jesus said, "If I give glory to Myself, it is of no account, but My Father, the One that you say, 'He is our God,' He is the One who gives me glory. You have never known Him, but I know Him. If I were to say that I don't know Him, then I would be a liar just like you. But I do know Him and I keep His word. Your ancestor Abraham was bursting with joy that God would show him My day in the future. Abraham saw it and he rejoiced."

The Pharisees countered, "Why You aren't even 50 years old and You are saying that that You have seen Abraham?"

Then Jesus said to the Pharisees, "Let me assure you, before Abraham was, I Am."

With that statement, which signified that Jesus was God, the Pharisees flew into a frenzy of murderous rage. They no longer wanted to charge Him to the chief priests, rather they decided to kill Him on the spot by stoning Him to death. They didn't even want to drag Jesus outside the Temple complex, but were willing to desecrate the Temple by killing Him where He stood. As they picked up stones with which to kill Jesus, an unseen troop of angels swooped around Jesus and covered Him with their wings. The angels hid Him from the eyes of the Pharisee vigilante death squad, and translocated Him safely out of the Temple complex and on His way.

Turning to where Jesus was a moment ago, their leader shouted in amazement, "Where did He go? Spread out and find Him! Alert the Temple guards at the gate to hold Him and prevent Him from leaving the grounds until we can kill Him here and now!"

At this time, as the principal watcher for Earth and Israel, my visits to God's throne room in heaven became more frequent and urgent. I reported on the opposition to the Son and how some men's hearts not only rejected Him and His message, but drove then to try and kill Him. The loyal angels assigned to the Son were effective in giving Him space to minister, yet still protecting Him from Satan's plots to kill Him by enflaming the minds of some people against Him. God said, "Benelroi, I am sorrowful over the situation. I have sent My Son to my own chosen people with whom I have made a pact, yet many have rejected Him and My love, of which the Son is the representation in human flesh."

## The Healing of a Man Born Blind

On another day in Jerusalem, as Jesus was passing by with His disciples, he saw a man who had been born blind. His disciples asked Him, "Was this man born blind because he sinned or because his parents sinned?"

Jesus replied, "Neither this man nor his parents sinned causing him to be born blind. This has been allowed so that the works of God would be demonstrated in him." Then, stooping down, Jesus spit on the ground, stirred it into a mud paste, and applied it to the eyes of the blind man. Jesus then told the blind man, "Go and wash your eyes at the pool of Siloam."

The blind man did as he was instructed. Though blind, he knew the city and quickly made his way to the pool of Siloam. In his haste and anticipation, he jostled a number of people, some of whom had little patience with him. Others excused themselves and a few offered to assist him and lead the way. However, he needed no pity or assistance on this day. Coming to the pool, he leaned over and began to splash water into his blind eyes. As he did so he began to see light, then clear images of all that was around him for the first time in his life. Praising God for this new gift of sight, he returned to what had been his habitual begging spot where he had the encounter with Jesus. His heart overflowing with joy, he wanted to thank this man of miracles that gave him sight.

On the way, his neighbors and people who habitually gave him coins or food as he begged noticed that he was not moving with care as a blind man would, but strode confidently as a sighted person weaving his way through the crowds in the street. They said to each other, "Isn't this the man who used to sit begging for money?"

Some, hardly able to believe it said, "He is the one."

Still others, unable to believe it at all said, "No."

Yet others said, "But he sure looks like him."

Hearing the comments, the man who had been born blind would do a pirouette and point to himself with a broad smile, while briefly walking backwards so as to look at those who were questioning his identity, saying, "I'm the one!"

A crowd soon gathered around him preventing him from going on his way as they examined him closer and asked him questions. "How is it that your eyes were opened?" they asked.

He said, "The man called Jesus made some mud, rubbed it in my eyes, and told me to go to the pool of Siloam and wash my eyes there. So when I went there and washed my eyes I received sight." That a notable miracle had happened was undeniable.

The man's neighbors and habitual benefactors who knew him well wanted to see this Jesus. "Where is He?" they asked him.

Alas, he had to admit, "I don't know where He is."

The crowd took the man who was healed of blindness to the Pharisees, because this all transpired on a Sabbath day. Upon being presented to the Pharisees, the man was questioned by them too. They wanted to know how it came about that his eyes were opened on the Sabbath.

So again the man rehearsed the events of that life-changing day. "He rubbed mud into my eyes, I washed them out, and now I can see."

Instead of praising God for what was a mighty miracle of healing, some of the Pharisees piously said, "This man Jesus is not from God because He doesn't regard the Sabbath!"

But the Pharisees were divided. Some of them said, "A sinful man can't perform signs like this."

So the Pharisees turned to the man who was given sight and asked for his opinion. "What do you have to say about Him? It was your eyes that He opened."

The man replied, "He's a prophet!"

As this interrogation went on the crowd grew larger and now included people who didn't know the man. These latecomers and some of the Pharisees could not believe the man's story. They could not believe that he had been born blind and now had been given sight.

So the Pharisees sent for the man's parents and questioned them. "Is this man your son and was he born blind? If so, then how is it that he can now see?"

The man's parents were happy to see that their son could now see and embraced him giving thanks to God.

But they were afraid of the Pharisees, because they knew that those Jews had agreed among themselves that anyone who would say that Jesus was the Messiah was to be excommunicated and put out of their Synagogue. So they answered carefully in order to maintain their position in the community and in the Synagogue. "This is our son and we confirm that he was born blind, but as for how he now sees, we neither know how that happened nor who opened his eyes. He is a grown man. Ask him. He can speak for himself."

So the Pharisees brought the man before them again and said to him, "Glorify God!" "We know that this man Jesus is a sinner!"

But the man replied, "I can't say whether or not He is a sinner, however, I do know this, whereas I was blind I now can see!" With that the man laughed and danced a jig for joy.

Not satisfied, the scornful and judgmental Pharisees pressed the man for more details. "What exactly did He do to you? Just how did He open up your eyes?"

The man, still joyful, decided to have a little fun at the expense of the Pharisees. "I've already told you, but you didn't listen. Why is it that you want to hear the story again? Is it that you want to become disciples of His too? Is that it?"

The man's sarcasm did not go down well. The Pharisees said, "You're the one that is His disciple. As for us, we are disciples of Moses! We all know that God spoke to Moses, but this fellow Jesus—we have no idea as to where He comes from."

The man now was fearless, and continued to mock the Pharisees. "This is truly amazing," he said. "You say you don't know where He is from, yet this man opened my eyes! We all know that God doesn't hear sinners, but, if a person fears God and does His will, God hears him. Through all history, it has never been recorded that someone opened the eyes of a man that was born blind. If the man wasn't from God then He wouldn't be able to do anything."

At that point, the Pharisees had all of the man that they could take. In the presence of his parents they said, "You were conceived altogether in sin, and you presume to teach us about the things of God?" With that, the Pharisees threw the man out and banned him from the Synagogues.

The news came to Jesus about what had happened to the man who had been blind and how he had been thrown out of the Synagogues. So Jesus went and found the man and asked him, "Do you believe that the Son of Man is the Messiah?"

The man pleaded, "Sir, tell me who He is so that I may believe in Him."

Jesus told him, "You've seen Him already, and in fact, He is the One talking to you right now."

Falling to his knees, the man said, "Yes Lord. I believe!" Then with tears of joy and reverence in his eyes that now could see, the man prostrated himself in the dust and worshipped Jesus as the Messiah sent from God.

**Lazarus Raised from the Dead**

Outside of Jerusalem, but not far away, was a small town called Bethany. In Bethany, Jesus often stopped at the home of Lazarus and his two sisters Mary and Martha. They had become fast friends. While Jesus was in the region of Galilee, Lazarus became deathly ill.

So Mary and Martha sent a message to Jesus that their brother Lazarus, whom Jesus loved, was sick.

When Jesus got the message, He did not immediately go to Bethany in Judea and He did not send a word of healing. Instead, He remained where He was for two more days. Jesus told His disciples that the sickness that His friend Lazarus had was not going to be his death, but was to bring glory to God by bringing glory to Him as the Son of God.

After two days, Jesus said to His disciples, "Let's go back to Judea."

But His disciples were hesitant to return to Judea. They said, "Ah Master, lately the Jews there have been looking for You with the intent of stoning You to death—and You want to go back there?"

Jesus replied, "Our friend Lazarus is asleep, but I am going there so that I can wake him from his slumber."

But the disciples protested, "Lord, if he is sleeping he will be alright." They were not keen to risk their lives on an unnecessary trip into a hotbed of resistance to Jesus in and around Jerusalem. After all, they thought Jesus was talking about Lazarus recovering from his illness by natural sleep and rest.

Then Jesus told them plainly, "Lazarus is dead. For your sakes I am glad I wasn't there so that you would believe who I am. Be that as it may, let's go to Lazarus."

The disciples thought this had all the makings of a suicide mission. But Thomas was unwilling for Jesus to make the trip alone and said to the other disciples, "Let's go with Him so that we may die with him."

As the group trekked from Galilee to Bethany they were silent. In their minds, they considered the prospect of death that awaited them. Some thought, *We will be stoned to death or pushed off a cliff somewhere.* When they arrived in Bethany, they learned that Lazarus had been dead and buried for four days already. Because Bethany wasn't too far from Jerusalem, many of the family's friends came to Bethany from Jerusalem to comfort Mary and Martha in their bereavement.

As soon as the word was passed to Martha that Jesus was near their home on the way there, she jumped up and ran to meet Him, leaving Mary behind in the house with the other mourners. When Martha reached Jesus she said, "Lord, if You had only been here my brother would not have died. Yet, I know that God will still give You whatever You ask of Him."

Looking on Martha, Jesus said, "Your brother will live again."

Martha, being familiar with the teaching of Jesus on the eventual resurrection of the dead, said, "Yes, I know he will rise up again in the resurrection on the last day."

Jesus said to his friend Martha, "I am the resurrection and I am life. The one who believes on Me as the Son of God, even if he were dead, he shall still live. Whoever is alive and believes in Me will not die, ever. Do you believe this?"

Martha replied, "Yes Lord. I believe that You are the Messiah, the Son of God, that was to come into this world." After Martha made that statement of faith, she turned and ran back to her sister Mary who as inside the house with the mourners. As Martha entered the house, Mary sat there with eyes red and still teary after four days of mourning. Slipping up to Mary's ear, Martha whispered, "The Master is here and He is calling for you."

Once she heard that, Mary sprang up and went to meet Jesus.

The friends that came to mourn with Mary and Martha presumed that Mary was heading to the grave of Lazarus. So they followed her to resume their mourning at the graveside. Jesus hadn't come into Bethany yet. He remained on the road where Martha had met Him. When Mary saw Jesus, she ran to Him and threw herself down at His feet sobbing. She said to Jesus, in a sentence broken up by her sobs, "Lord,—if—only—You—had been here—my brother would not have died."

Jesus became moved in His spirit when He saw Mary and the other mourners all crying. "Where have you laid him?" asked Jesus. The family friends beckoned Jesus to the grave. As Jesus approached the grave of Lazarus He thought of how Lucifer had betrayed Him, rebelled, and introduced death to the world. For a moment, He contemplated all of the people who had died before that time and who would die in the years to come. He also thought of how He Himself, would have to soon experience death as a man. As Jesus recalled the sweet friendship He had with his friend Lazarus, who was now dead, large tears began to roll down His cheeks.

The Jews that were gathered around said, "Look, He really loved Him!"

Some of them said, "This man opened the eyes of the blind, don't you think He could have kept this man from dying?"

## I Am the Resurrection

Groaning internally with emotion and anger toward Satan and death, Jesus came to the grave, which

was a cave with a flat stone rolled over the entrance. Jesus said, "Remove the stone."
But Martha reminded Jesus that Lazarus had been dead four days. To open the grave would release the stench of death.

Jesus then turned to Martha and said, "Didn't I tell you that if you would believe you would see God be glorified?"

So the family friends removed the stone cap from the entrance of the cave where the body of Lazarus lay inside. As Martha had warned, a horrible stench of death wafted out of the cave as if to defiantly announce that there was no hope. But Jesus looked up, as He always did, to see into Heaven. The sky was clear. Those standing by saw nothing but clear blue sky. However, Jesus saw the sky part to reveal the dark sky of space speckled with stars and galaxies. Angels were ascending up from Jesus and descending down to Him as if His head and gaze were the homing beam for their transit through the portal that had opened over Him. In the process, Jesus received fresh angelic reinforcements to assist Him, working with Him to carry out the will of God the Father and God the Holy Spirit. The angels stood ready to implement the words Jesus would speak after Jesus first heard from the rest of the Godhead and saw what the rest of the Godhead wanted to be done at that moment.

The disciple Nathaniel had his eyes fixed on Jesus. Suddenly, he grabbed the clothes of Thomas standing next to him. As he did he pulled him near, his eyes still fixed on Jesus and above Him. Nathaniel whispered to his friend Thomas, "Do you see what I am seeing?"

"See what?" Thomas asked.

"The angels! The angels!" said Nathaniel.

Thomas shielded his eyes from the sun and squinted. Then Thomas said, "I still don't see a thing."

Nathaniel declared, "It is just as the Master told me when I first met Him. He told me he had seen me under a fig tree before He ever arrived. I said, 'You are the Son of God! The King of Israel.' Then He said there was a time coming when I would see the angels of God ascending and descending on the Son of Man. This is it. I see it as He said I would."

But Thomas said, "I don't see anything special, so I can't believe you are really seeing a vision. I'm a disciple too. If angels were present, wouldn't I see them too? Maybe you need to sit in the shade and have a drink of water."

Meanwhile, Jesus prayed silently. Then Jesus prayed again out loud, "Father, I thank You that You heard Me. I know that You always hear me, but for the sake of the people standing by I am saying it again out loud, so that they might believe that You have sent Me." When Jesus finished those words, He turned toward the open cave and leaning toward it He yelled the command, "Lazarus, come out!"

In a few moments, Lazarus hopped out of the entrance of the cave, constrained by the grave clothes that he had been tightly wrapped in and that covered him from head to toe, including a cloth tied about his face and head. Bystanders shrieked. Some women mourners fainted. Then Jesus said, "Turn him loose and let him go." As they did they found Lazarus was back! Freed from the restrictive grave clothes Lazarus ran to Jesus, first knelling before Him and then hugging Him and his sisters.

The Jews that came to Mary and saw what Jesus did believed at that moment that Jesus was the Messiah, the Son of God. Those that came down from Jerusalem returned there and spread around the city and Temple what Jesus had done in Bethany. Some of them went to the Pharisees in Jerusalem and let them know too what had been done.

Jesus and his disciples left Bethany, but rather than go on to Jerusalem they went to another town. But six days before the Passover they returned to Bethany where Martha and Mary prepared a feast for Jesus. Because it was near the Passover, many Jews had come by as much to see Lazarus as to see Jesus. Lazarus had become a celebrity. Because of him being raised to life after being dead for days, many Jews began to believe that Jesus was indeed the Messiah, the One that God had anointed.

# Chapter 21 The Passion of Christ

*Mercy and truth are met together; righteousness and peace have kissed each other. Psalm 85:10*

After hearing what Jesus did in raising Lazarus from the dead after four days in the grave, the chief priests and the Pharisees met to strategize. Jerusalem was buzzing over Jesus and many were ready to welcome Him as the Messiah, a descendant of King David who would take the throne and free them from the Roman occupation, or so they hoped. The Pharisees, meeting in a closed council with the chief priests said, "What are we going to do? This man is doing a lot of miracles. If we don't stop Him everyone will believe that He is the Messiah, and then the Romans will come and take away our positions and do away with this Jewish nation."

But Caiaphas, whose turn it was to be the high priest that year, said, "You don't know anything and you don't realize that it is necessary that one man should die for the people so that this nation of the Jewish people won't be wiped out."[17] From then on, the chief priests and the Pharisees schemed together on how to kill Jesus.

---

[17] Additional scriptures are provided here for context.

Looking unto Jesus the author and finisher of our faith; who for the joy that was set before him endured the cross, despising the shame, and is set down at the right hand of the throne of God. Hebrews 12:2

But he was wounded for our transgressions, he was bruised for our iniquities: the chastisement of our peace was upon him; and with his stripes we are healed. All we like sheep have gone astray; we have turned everyone to his own way; and the LORD hath laid on him the iniquity of us all. Isaiah 53:5-6

The Passover was approaching. It was an annual event that brought many devout Jews to Jerusalem from many countries as a pilgrimage they wanted to make at least once in their lives. Not only were Jews drawn to this, but interested non-Jews and those who, though not born Jews, chose to worship God according to the teachings and practices of Judaism. Many of these people had been hearing about Jesus and now they were in Jerusalem and had hoped to see Him, especially after hearing the recent news of Jesus raising Lazarus from the dead. For this reason, the chief priest decided that it would be necessary to kill Lazarus too in order to eliminate any evidence of the great miracle that had occurred and to stop people from talking about it and believing that Jesus had to be the Messiah to be able to do such things.

**Expectations and the Path Ahead**

When word got out that Jesus was coming to Jerusalem the city was charged with excitement. Jesus came into Jerusalem, escorted by His disciples and sitting atop a young donkey.

People who had been in Bethany when Jesus raised Lazarus from the dead shouted out, "Its Him! There He is! He's the one that raised a dead man back to life!

---

Awake, O sword, against my shepherd, and against the man that is my fellow, saith the LORD of hosts: smite the shepherd, and the sheep shall be scattered: and I will turn mine hand upon the little ones. Zechariah 13:7

I, even I, am he that blotteth out thy transgressions for mine own sake, and will not remember thy sins. Isaiah 43:25

Blotting out the handwriting of ordinances that was against us, which was contrary to us, and took it out of the way, nailing it to his cross. Colossians 2:14

We saw it ourselves and it is true! People took branches from palm trees and rushed to greet Jesus. As they did they waved the palm branches and laid them on the street in front Jesus for the donkey that carried Him to walk upon.

The excited crowd began to shout, "Hosanna! Blessed is Israel's King that comes bearing God's name!"

The Pharisees were beside themselves with rage and frustration. They said to each other, "Do you see how our plan to kill Him has been ruined? The whole world is flocking to Him!" In that circumstance they dared not touch Jesus for fear that the adoring crowds would stone them to death.

As Jesus sat at a feast later that day, some Greek pilgrims who had come to worship according to the Jewish faith approached Philip. Philip was one of the disciples of Jesus who had a Greek name. His name recalled the past Greek national hero Philip of Macedon, the father of Alexander the Great. They begged Philip, "Sir, we really want to see Jesus." Philip consulted with Andrew and the two went and let Jesus know of the request of the Greeks.

Jesus said, "The time has come for the Son of Man to be glorified. I tell you most assuredly, if a grain of wheat is not buried in the ground and dies, then you will just have one grain of wheat. But, if it dies, it will produce a great harvest."

Jesus continued to speak. He said, "I admit My soul is disturbed by what is to come. But what should I say? 'Father deliver me from this moment?' It is for this reason that I have come to this point." Then looking up toward heaven, a portal opened. Angels ascended up from Jesus and other angels descended down from Heaven to

Jesus through the portal, although it was seen only by Jesus. At that moment, Jesus said, "Father give glory to Your name!"

An audible reply can back from God through the portal, "I have given it glory and I will do so again."

Jesus and His disciples heard the voice, but it was unintelligible to the crowd of people near Jesus. Some of them said, "Oh, that was just thunder."

However, others said, "An angel spoke with an answer to Him!"

Jesus clarified what had just happened. He said to those gathered around Him, "This voice was heard, not for My sake, but for yours. The world is about to be judged and the ruler of the world will be thrown out of power and dominion over the world. And I, if I am hoisted up from the earth, will attract all men to Me." Jesus said this to let them know how He was going to die.

Some people were disappointed that, when Jesus entered the city, He didn't lead the crowd immediately to a confrontation with the civil and occupying authorities and take up the kingship they were proclaiming for Him. Instead, He taught openly in the Temple complex and continued to do so leading up to the Passover. This He did right under the noses of the chief priests and Pharisees that had determined to kill Him.

As Jesus was teaching in the Temple, two religious factions, the Sadducees and Pharisees, came to try and have Him say something that they could use to attack Him with in order to discredit Him. Jesus put them to such shame with His answers that they decided not to ask Him questions again. When that was over, Jesus said, "There is a curse of judgment coming on you! You scribes and Pharisees are a bunch of hypocrites! You are like graves that have been whitewashed outside to look beautiful, but inside are full of the bones of the dead and nastiness. You look like you are holy to people by the way you dress and carry yourselves, but in your hearts you are full of hypocrisy and sin. There is a curse of judgment coming on you scribes and Pharisees because you make memorials of the graves of the prophets and maintain the graves of just men now dead. You say that you wouldn't have killed the prophets if you had been living back then. Well, you have judged yourselves because you admit that you are the descendants of the ones that killed the prophets. Go ahead and finish what your ancestors started! You bunch of poisonous snakes; you think you are going to avoid damnation in hell? I will send you prophets, men of wisdom, and men of the scriptures, but you will kill and crucify some of them. Some you will flog in your Synagogues and hound them from city to city. This is so that on you will be the guilt of all of the spilled blood of holy men. Blood spilled from righteous Abel to the blood of Zachariah and Barachiah that you killed between the Temple and the altar. I tell you of a certainty that all of this will happen to this generation."

**Visions of Horrors to Come**

Jesus then turned from the religious factions that had attempted to bait Him as well as from the throng that came to hear him at the Temple. Finding a place where He could sit alone and ponder His thoughts, He began to be grieved by the history of the Jewish people in rejecting the messengers of God, and also rejecting Him, the Messiah that came from God the Father to save the world.

As He sat there, He considered the terrible visions God had given him of Israel's near future when Roman armies would massacre the people and demolish the Temple.

He thought also of the vision He had seen of a horrendous holocaust to come in a great world war centuries in the future, when millions of Jews would be murdered and treated worse than animals. As He thought on these things, the vivid pictures in His mind from the terrible visions, and the prophesies of doom in Deuteronomy and Daniel, He spoke out loud, but to Himself. He said, "Oh Jerusalem, Jerusalem, you who kills the prophets and stones to death the very ones that are sent to you. How often I longed to gather your children together, just as a hen pulls her chicks under her wings, but you just wouldn't have it! Now your place will become desolate ruins. I tell you, you won't see me after this until you as a nation say, 'Blessed is the One the comes having God's name'."

As Jesus left the Temple complex He headed for the Mount of Olives, a favorite place where He would spend time with His inner circle of the 12 disciples. On the way His disciples were pointing out the Temple buildings, with their massive stones, that had taken nearly five decades to erect and fit out. They were truly impressed. It was unique in all of Israel and was a world class complex.

So Jesus said to them, "You see all of these things? I tell you for sure that there is not one stone laid on another that will not be knocked down." The disciples wondered what could possibly cause such a calamity.

When they reached the Mount of Olives overlooking Jerusalem, Jesus sat down looking out over the city knowing what would soon happen to Him there and to the city itself. From there He could also see the place where He would soon be put to death by crucifixion. There, away from the crowds, His disciples came up to Him and asked, "When are these things going to happen? What will be the sign of Your coming and of the end of the world?"

Jesus said, "Be careful and don't let anyone trick you. A lot of people are going to come, using My name, they will say 'I am the Christ' and they will fool a lot of people. When you hear about wars and rumblings of war, don't be anxious. All of these things will happen, but that won't be the end.

Countries will rise up against other countries and kingdom against kingdom. There will be times of famine, disease, and earthquakes in different places. This is just the beginning of difficult times. Then they will turn over believers to be tortured and will kill you. Believers will be hated around the world because of My name. Then many will be angry with God for the way things will happen and will betray and hate each other. A large number of fake prophets will come along and will fool many people. Because sin will be rampant, the love of many people for God will grow cold. But the one that stands firm in his faith until the end is the one who will be saved. This good news of the kingdom of God will be preached worldwide as a witness to all nations. When that is accomplished, then the end will come."

Jesus went on to tell them of the destruction and death that would come on Jerusalem and the Jewish people, both in their lifetimes and in the distant future. Jesus described a coming time of great instability and calamity. At the same time, people would be deceived by those claiming to be the Messiah. These fakes would have the power to perform signs and supernatural acts that would seem to validate their claims. There would also be momentous signs in the solar system. And then He will come, but this time with great power and glory and with His angel armies, all of them in clouds of the glory of God. On the signal of the sound of a trumpet blast, the angels will gather those appointed for salvation from all around the world. Jesus went on to tell them that many people were going to be unprepared for what was to come.

When Jesus finished speaking to his disciples on the Mount of Olives concerning future events, including the time of the end, he said, "You know that in two days will be the feast of Passover, and they will kill Me."

Fearing the people, the chief priests and Pharisees determined that it would be necessary to arrest Jesus while He was away from the crowds that believed He was the Messiah. To do so at night when the city streets were empty and there were few witnesses would be ideal, but they needed someone close to Jesus to facilitate His arrest under these circumstances.

Judas Iscariot, one of the 12 disciples, had some connections to the faction of the Zealots. The Zealots were radicalized Jews that were religious, aggressive, and very political. They wanted the Roman occupation of Palestine to end and to throw out the family of half-Jewish collaborators with the Romans that were sons of Herod, each of whom ruled a third of Palestine as Tetrarchs. Because they were only part Jewish and thus considered the same as Samaritans, and they were secular, the Zealots wanted them removed too so that a true Jewish nation could function under strict religious rules and free of the foreign idol worshipping Romans.

Herod the Great, the father of the Tetrarchs, had built the magnificent Temple in Jerusalem as a way to buy off the religious leadership. He would allow them space to exercise leadership in religious matters as long as they supported Him as their patron and did not interfere in the civil government that he headed.

Judas was disappointed that Jesus did not immediately proceed to lead the people in a revolt against the civil authorities and the Roman occupiers when He entered Jerusalem to the acclaim of the crowds. As he moped about some of his Zealot acquaintances found him and pressed the same issue.

"Judas, why didn't your Master seize the kingdom and use His miraculous powers to take over! We were with you and would have backed Him up. A great opportunity has been missed. This is the moment to take power by force and rid ourselves of these Romans and their collaborators from Herod's family along with their quisling tax collectors. Can you get your Master to see this opportunity and take action?"

Judas responded, "I wanted an uprising as much as you did, but all He does now is talk about His death."

"You are worthless Judas!" said the Zealots, and they left Judas alone.

At this point Satan saw the opportune time he had been waiting for since tempting Jesus in the Judean wilderness three and a half years earlier. Satan began to whisper thoughts into the mind of Judas. Judas could not see Satan and believed the thoughts were his own ideas. Satan whispered, *The chief priests and Pharisees have been trying to get their hands on Jesus. If Jesus were to be turned over to them He would no doubt be forced to use His mighty powers to overthrow not only them but*

*Herod and the Romans as well. Facilitating this crisis might also earn a reward from the chief priests.*

Acting on the seed that Satan planted in his mind, Judas secretly met with the chief priests and made a bargain to lead the Temple guards to Jesus away from the crowds. For this, the chief priests paid him 30 silver coins. Taking the bag of coins, Judas left them and looked for an opportune moment to implement his plan.

As the days ticked down, Jesus arranged to have a final meal with the 12 disciples before Passover. During the event, Jesus stunned the disciples by laying aside His prayer shawl and tunic, wrapping a towel around His waist with the length of it falling below His knees. Then He, the one they had come to believe was the Messiah and Son of God, got down on His knees before them with a basin of water, and like a common servant, went from disciple to disciple and washed their feet. After getting dressed again and returning to the table set out with the Passover meal, He said, "Do you know what I have just done for you? If I, as your master, can serve you, so too you must serve each other."

## A Betrayer

As they sat down to the Passover meal, Jesus said, "I have to tell you that one of you eating with me here at this table will betray Me."

This saddened the disciples. Each was afraid that he might be the betrayer. So each began to ask, "Is it me?" Jesus said nothing.

Then Peter whispered to John, "Ask Him which of us is the betrayer!"

John leaned on Jesus, as they were seated in lounge type chairs, and asked, "Who is it?"

Jesus responded, "It is one who dips his bread in the platter with Me." Then as Jesus and Judas were dipping their morsels of bread in the platter, Jesus put His morsel in the mouth of Judas, in what was culturally a sign of favor and affection.

After Judas was dismissed by Jesus, some thought to give money to the poor, since he was the treasurer, Jesus spoke of His imminent death. He took bread and wine and blessed it and gave it to the eleven disciples remaining with Him saying, "This is the blood of My new pact which is shed to save many. I tell you I won't drink wine again until the day that I drink it with you in the Kingdom of God." Then looking up, He once again saw a portal open with a view into the heavens from there in the room where He sat with them. Angels continued to ascend up from Him and to descend down from Heaven to Him.

Jesus then prayed out loud, "Father, the time has come. Give glory to Your Son so that Your Son can give glory to You. I have completed the assignment that You gave Me. Now glorify Me with the same glory that I had with You before the creation of the world. I have made Your name known to the men You gave me. I gave them the words that You gave Me, and they both received them and believed that You sent Me. Now I will no longer be in the world, but these are in the world. Holy Father, keep these that You have given me through Your name, that they may be one even as We are one. I don't pray for them alone, but for all that will believe on Me on account of their word of testimony."

After He prayed, Jesus took the eleven remaining disciples with Him to a garden outside the city walls on the Mount of Olives where they had often gone before. There Jesus asked the three pillars among the disciples, Peter, James, and John, to go with Him a bit further to pray. He then asked the three to remain in prayer while He separated Himself from them by a distance and prayed.

As Jesus contemplated what was to come, His humanity shrank from the ordeal before Him. His spirit also cringed at the prospect of becoming sin to save a world lost in sin. Jesus was intense in His prayer and cried out to God, "Father, if you agree, please let this cup of sin and suffering go from Me. Nevertheless, let Your will be done in this matter and not mine." An angel then appeared to Jesus to strengthen Him for what was ahead. As Jesus got up from prayer, He walked over and found Peter, James, and John asleep. They awoke ashamed that they weren't able to continue in prayer with Jesus.

Judas knew the place well where Jesus had gone with the disciples and went there with a band of Temple guards and their officers provided by the chief priests and Pharisees. They tramped through the night with lanterns, torches, and assorted weaponry; spears, swords, and clubs.

The disciples all sprang to their feet at the commotion, aghast to see that their comrade, Judas was leading this band that they realized had ill intent. Judas walked up to Jesus, as if greeting an old friend, and he kissed Jesus, the signal to the Temple guards to arrest Him because there was positive confirmation in the darkness that this was Jesus.

Looking at Judas, Jesus said to him, "Judas, You betray the Son of Man with a kiss?" Jesus stepped forward and asked the armed men, "Who are you looking for?"

They answered, "Jesus of Nazareth!"

Jesus replied, "I am He." With that unseen angels swooping in and extending their wings out caused Judas and the armed party to all stumble and fly backwards as if blown off their feet by a whirlwind, and fall on the ground with a loud crash of their armor, weaponry, and shields. There was no way they were going to be able to take Jesus if He resisted and allowed the angels to defend Him. However, Jesus made a slight motion of His hand to call off the angels. As He did, and they backed away, Jesus stepped forward and again asked the armed men, "Who are you looking for?"

As the arresting party struggled back to their feet they said again, "Jesus of Nazareth." Some of them were somewhat frightened at this point as they did consider Jesus to be a prophet having miraculous powers.

One armed guard whispered to another, "Remember how the prophet Elijah called down fire on the king's soldiers sent to arrest him? I hope this doesn't end badly for us!"

Again Jesus declared, "I told you I am the one. If it is Me that you want, then let these others go on their way." Jesus did not want the disciples in whom He had invested over three years of preparation to be killed, as they would be needed to carry on His message after His death and resurrection.

But Peter took the sword he had brought and lunged toward the guards, swinging with the intent to mortally wound the first man in his way and then take on the remainder of the armed group. In the process, his first target, Malchus, an attendant to the high priest, ducked, which saved his head, but not his ear, which Peter managed to sever from his head, though he was aiming for more. But Jesus broke it up before it could become a full-scale melee and possibly end in death for the disciples. Turning to Peter, Jesus said, "Sheath your sword! My Father has given me this cup to drink, and I will drink it!"

Peter remembered how Jesus once rebuked him and even called him "Satan" for suggesting that He would not have to give up His life. Jesus knew, as He had previously told His disciples, no one could take His life, but His mission was to willingly lay down His life to pay for the sins of the world. As the disciples slinked back, and then ran away, Jesus stooped down, picked up the severed ear, and put it back in place on Malchus restoring it without even evidence of a wound or scar.

It was a miracle, but the miracle did not deter the Temple guards from their task. Their officer ordered them to take Jesus and tie him up. With that the Temple guards escorted their prisoner back to the high priest, abusing Jesus along the way. Unbeknownst to them, a troop of angels accompanied them, with thousands more on standby. They were ready to kill all of the Temple guards before they could take another step, and then whisk Jesus to Heaven. But Jesus would not give that command. In His words, He drank from the cup of suffering that was necessary in order to save the world.

Once Jesus was taken to the house of the high priest, His captors, now being directed by fallen angels that put thoughts into their minds, blindfolded Jesus and began to punch and slap Him. As they did so, they joked and amused themselves telling Jesus, "Prophesy and tell us who it was that hit you!"

Meanwhile, the loyal angels had withdrawn a distance, but were ready to intervene, if called upon. The Archangel Michael himself was with the angel army at its head. He said, "I have specially selected most of you from those angels that have previously done the duty of protecting our Lord Jesus, the Son of God. Discipline is key at this time. Regardless of what you see or feel, no one is to intervene unless the Lord Jesus requests it. No one is to break ranks and go after demons just to take out your wrath on them. This is difficult for me too. As angels we have seen Lucifer, with his beauty, lies, and pride, lead a third of the angels in revolt against the Godhead. Lord Jesus laid aside his glory and position to become the Son of Man and serve humans, even washing their feet. He has done nothing but good for these humans, but they have turned against Him, disfigured Him, and they plan to kill Him. All the while our enemies, the fallen angels, surround Lord Jesus, celebrating what they think is their victory, taunting Lord Jesus, and influencing the minds of evil men to do harm to our God. Our charge from the Father is to standby and be ready to rescue Lord Jesus if, and only if, He calls out to be saved from this situation."

When the chief priests, members of the Sanhedrin, and Pharisees all arrived, they attempted to try Jesus for breaking religious laws. They had paid some men of ill repute to testify against Jesus, but they contradicted each other.

Finally, the chief interrogator said to Jesus, "Tell us whether or not you are the Messiah, the one anointed by God!"

Jesus replied, "If I were to tell you, you would not believe Me, but after this, the Son of Man will sit on the right hand of God's power."

Then they all screamed at Jesus, "Are you then saying that You are the Son of God?"

Jesus replied, "You've said it."

So the inquisitors said, "We don't need to call any other witnesses, because we have all heard Him ourselves!"

From there they took Jesus to the residence of the Roman Governor Pontius Pilate. They wanted Jesus to be publicly executed, but the power of capital punishment had not been delegated to them. They needed the Roman authorities to condemn Jesus to death. But Pilate refused to take the bait and said he believed Jesus was innocent of a capital offense. When Pilate learned that Jesus was from Galilee he sent Him to Herod, who happened to be in Jerusalem for the Passover.

Herod was excited to see Jesus because he had heard so much about Him and wanted to be entertained by Jesus performing some miracle for him. But Jesus stood silent before Herod's questioning. All the while the chief priests and Pharisees railed against Jesus leveling many charges. Herod then allowed his soldiers to trifle with Jesus including putting a purple robe on Him to mock His kingship. Afterwards, Herod sent Jesus back to Pilate.

Pilate knew the chief priests were jealous of the following that Jesus had amassed. Pilate addressed the chief priests, members of the Sanhedrin, and the others with them. He said, "You have leveled a lot of charges against this man, but neither Herod nor I find Him guilty of a capital offense. So this is what I will do, I will have Him flogged and then release Him."

Jesus was questioned again in private by Pilate. Pilate was determined to release Him based on the pleas of his wife, who had a disturbing dream about Jesus.

Also, Pilate feared from his questioning of Jesus that Jesus just might be more than an ordinary man. Pilate reminded the people of the custom of releasing a prisoner at Passover. He offered a choice between Jesus and a notorious criminal named Barabbas. To Pilate's surprise, the crowd, stoked by the Pharisees and allies of Barabbas, called for the release of Barabbas. Pilate asked, "And what shall I do with the one called the King of the Jews?"

"Crucify Him, crucify Him!" was the chant of the crowd.

Amazed, Pilate said, "You want me to crucify your king?" Pilate said this thinking the Jewish nationalists would want to spare Jesus.

But the Jews shouted, "If you release this man then you are no friend of Caesar. If someone makes himself out to be a king then he is setting himself up against Caesar."

Then the chief priests said, "We have no king but Caesar!"

Fearing that his political career would be damaged should an unfavorable report get back to Caesar in Rome, Pilate agreed to the crucifixion of Jesus. He summoned a basin of water and towel to wash his hands. After he did so he proclaimed, "I am innocent of the blood of this innocent man."

But the crowd shouted, "Let His blood be on us and our children after us!"

As the principal watcher for earth and Israel, I made special note in my book of this last statement by the crowds and the chief priests. Indeed, out of their own mouths the Jewish nation would be judged in that generation as well as in the future.

## The Holy One Given Over to Torture and Death

Jesus was sent out to be flogged. The Roman soldiers charged with the task took a sadistic delight in their work. Two soldiers beat Him in tandem. After they laid on two lashes, unseen demons, like black bats, flew to the floggers and attached themselves to them, screaming into their minds, *Hit Him harder! Kill Him!* Instantly, the faces of the two floggers changed from the effect of the demons. With great fury they renewed the lashing and picked up the pace. Those demons stirred the soldiers to do their worst and danced around Jesus tormenting Him and mocking the loyal angels standing nearby. The Archangel Michael and the other loyal angels were disgusted at what they were witnessing, but kept their distance and did not intervene.

The sergeant of the flogging detail finally yelled at the two floggers. "Enough you morons! What good does it do to crucify someone who is already dead! Leave some life in Him or I will lay a few lashes on the two of you myself!"

After Jesus was flogged, Pilate brought out the bleeding and battered Jesus to be presented to the people. As Jesus stood there with a crown of thorns on His head and a purple robe draped over His blood soaked tunic, Pilate said, "Look, here is the man!" But there was no pity in the crowd for Jesus. Finally, Pilate said to the chief priests, "You see to it."

A tumultuous crowd escorted Jesus through the streets of Jerusalem to a place of crucifixion not far from the city walls. The demons stirred up the crowd, which taunted Jesus, as Jesus and two criminals carried the crosses on which they would soon be nailed. John, and

Mary the mother of Jesus, flowed along with the crowd.
Not all were against Jesus. Some women wept for Him as
He passed by. The loyal angels continued to standby, but
not intervene, notwithstanding unceasing provocations by
rebel angels and demons. When Jesus reached the summit
of the hill called the place of the skull, He was stretched
out on His cross. As the nails were driven into His hands
and feet by the Roman soldiers, He felt the searing pain
and gasped, but said nothing. Likewise, as the cross was
lifted and sank down with a painful jolt into the hole for
its base and wedged into place to stabilize it.

As Jesus suffered on the cross, he looked up, and
as had always happened before, He saw heaven opened
and He peered into heaven through a supernatural portal.
The clouds parted to a circle in the sky. The darkness of
the universe was revealed with its galaxies, and a stairway
to heaven was revealed. With this channel open, Jesus
said, "Father, forgive them, because they don't know
what they are doing." Jesus saw the army of angels at the
ready to rescue Him, should He call them. He would not
crumble now. He thought about His conversation with
Moses and Elijah on the mountain where He was
transfigured. He also thought of the joy He would have
when the ordeal was over and He would one day celebrate
in Heaven with those He redeemed.

Meanwhile, demons were dancing in glee around
Him tormenting Him and mocking Him and the loyal
angels with laughter. Finally, the sins of the world were
poured onto Him and He became sin. Jesus looked up
again to heaven, but the portal closed up to Him. The
army of angels disappeared from His sight. With the
exception John and His mother Mary, no other disciples
were there to support Him. Jesus was left alone with the

sin of the world and the excruciating pain of His crucifixion.

Jesus cried out, "My God! My God! Why have you left me alone and turned your back on Me!" In that moment, the unimaginable happened. The Godhead was split. The Son of God received the punishment that the holiness and judgement of God required for sin. The sky darkened like the night, though it was mid-afternoon. Then realizing that He had fulfilled His mission and the scriptures of prophesy concerning Him, Jesus said, "It's done." Jesus then bowed his blood soaked, thorn-pierced head, and breathed out His last breath as He died. His death was accompanied by a great earthquake causing havoc in Jerusalem as well as on Golgotha, the crucifixion site.

The Roman Centurion overseeing the grisly work and taking note of the earthquake and signs in the sky said, "Truly, this was the Son of God!"

The tension between God's holiness, on the one hand, with its demands for justice and judgment, and, on the other hand, the love, mercy, and grace of God, were resolved with the sacrifice of the Son of God, that holy lamb of God whose blood was shed and His human life given up so that the He could finally be united with the people he loved in a relationship of intimate fellowship. Those that accepted Him would be able to exchange their unworthiness for God's holiness. Jesus would make them His bride, in an intimate union, with no distance or thing between them. This was the mission of Jesus. It was his unswerving passion to fulfill His purpose. That purpose was to save the world and redeem those who were devoted to God and believed that He came from God, by giving His holy life as a sacrifice for sin that would be acceptable to God the Father.

# Chapter 22 The Battle in Hell and the Resurrection

*But we speak the wisdom of God in a mystery, even the hidden wisdom, which God ordained before the world unto our glory: Which none of the princes of this world knew: for had they known it, they would not have crucified the Lord of glory. 1 Corinthians 2:7-8*

Jesus literally went to hell after His death where he was confronted by Satan and the hordes of hell.[18] The fallen angels mocked Him upon His entry with the salutation, "Welcome!" dripping with sarcasm. Upon arriving in hell, Jesus, standing in a dingy, ragged robe representing the sins of the world that He had taken upon himself, was surrounded by Satan and crowds of fallen angels and demons.

Meanwhile, in Heaven, Michael the Archangel became so angry that sparks flew from his face. Addressing the armies of loyalist angels, Michael said,

---

[18] Additional scriptures are provided here for context.

If I ascend up into heaven, thou art there: if I make my bed in hell, behold, thou art there. If I take the wings of the morning, and dwell in the uttermost parts of the sea; Even there shall thy hand lead me, and thy right hand shall hold me. Psalm 139:8-10

Thou hast ascended on high, thou hast led captivity captive: thou hast received gifts for men; yea, for the rebellious also, that the LORD God might dwell among them. Psalm 68:18

Neither by the blood of goats and calves, but by his own blood he entered in once into the holy place, having obtained eternal redemption for us. Hebrews 9:12

"We could have prevented this, but it was not the Father's will that we do so. Now that it is over, let's storm hell and bring back our leader, the Son!

Gabriel, the other great Archangel said, "I am in on this one and will be in the forefront with you!"

Michael replied, "We will make Satan and the rebel angels pay dearly!"

Just then, the voice of the Father overshadowed them and said, "My loyal sons whom I love, although it was a good thought that you had, this part of the fight is not yours. Just hold steady and you will see my plan. For now, I want you to protect those people who followed My Son while He walked the earth as a man. I have assignments for them and for those who believe their testimony of My Son. They cannot be allowed to perish from the earth before they complete their mission, though many will surrender their lives for their testimony."

## Jesus in Hell

Back in hell, Satan, still appearing as an angel of light, said, "Well, well Jesus. You are in the center of my kingdom now. The earth You left behind when You died is also my kingdom, thanks to Adam surrendering it to me. No person who enters here on account of sin is ever able to leave. But since I have the keys of death, I can release you, provided you bow down now and worship me as your god. Oh, and one other important thing. I will return to Heaven with you and I will rule as the most high god, with You at my side and second to me." Jesus said nothing. Satan again spoke. "So You have nothing to say? If You thought Your flogging and crucifixion were painful and embarrassing then just wait until You taste of what is in store for you here if you don't cooperate." Satan motioned for three fierce looking fallen angels to approach with instruments of torture in their hands.

Jesus looked up and said, "Father, according to Your word, You will not leave my soul in hell."

Just then, Holy Spirit God entered hell and came to rest inside Jesus. The garments of Jesus were transformed and became bright shining light emitting clothing. Satan yelled, "Seize Him and give Him a taste of what he can expect here for eternity!" But the cohorts of Satan were unable to touch Jesus.

Instead, Jesus wheeled about with His arms outstretched toward His would be tormentors and emitted a pure bright power that caused all of the fallen angels and demons to collapse and writhe in excruciating pain. Satan shook it off and personally approached Jesus to attempt to subjugate him. However, by simply motioning with one hand, a palm rising up, flipping, and slamming down, Satan was lifted up and slammed to the ground. Quickly getting up, Satan attempted a rushing attack on Jesus. But again, without even needing to touch him, Jesus motioned as if catching an object and flung it against Satan's throne. With that motion, Satan was halted in his tracks and thrown against his throne. Screaming in pain, and with the fallen angels and demons still writhing in pain and slithering away from Jesus, Satan transformed from an angel of light to a giant muscular winged dragon with fierce teeth, a scaly skin, and smoke and fire coming from his mouth. The dragon made its move toward Jesus with sharp teeth bared, but Jesus leaped and flew swiftly over it landing with his feet on the Satan's dragon head and neck. Lifting his bare foot, Jesus slammed down His foot on Satan's dragon head, smashing it into the ground. Then He repeated it again and again and again.

The dragon appearance of Satan was exhausted and defeated, as was his entire hellish cohort. Jesus then spoke, "Who is Lord of all?" But there was silence other than the whimpering of beings in pain. Raising His hands Jesus emitted currents of raw power that struck all of the fallen angels and demons. It continued unabated, greatly increasing their torment. Again, Jesus said "Who is Lord of all?"

Satan and his cohort grudgingly said, "You are! Jesus, You are Lord of all!"

With one last stomping of the head of the dragon that was Satan, Jesus said, "Where is your sting now death? I have won and now I have the keys of death, this kingdom of hell, and the graves of the dead." Jesus then disappeared from that portion of hell and reappeared in the place called Paradise.

Paradise was a beautiful place, but it was shut off from Heaven and the presence of God. Jesus, in His Spirit, presented Himself in Paradise as the conquering Son of God and Son of Man. He did this before the righteous dead, that is, those honorable people who had worshipped the true God, offered sacrifices for their sins, and looked for the Messiah that God had promised.

Moses and Elijah, who had appeared with Him on the mountain of Transfiguration, came forward to greet Him. As they did they fell at His feet and worshipped Him. They were followed by Adam and Eve and all of the patriarchs and prophets from Able to John the Baptist. All hailed the Son as God and worshiped Him.

Then the Son beckoned to the man who had been crucified alongside Him. Falling at the feet of the Son to worship Him, the man said, "I am not worthy to be here."

The Son replied, "I told you that you would be with Me in Paradise today. Thank you for honoring me in my time of suffering on the cross. My blood that was spilled for you and the world; your repentance and confession of Me as your Savior and God; and My forgiveness of your sins are what made room for you here. However, better things are in store for all who accept the good news of the love of God the Father who sent Me, His only Son, to pay the price of the sin of humanity for all who turn from evil and confess Me as Lord and Savior."

The Son called upon all in Paradise to listen as He preached to them the good news and explained the scriptures that spoke of Him. This preaching and teaching went on continuously, because in that place, no one got tired or sleepy. Time and again the righteous dead in Paradise would burst out in shouts of praise and thanksgiving for the goodness of God and God's love that was so strong that He sent His Son to be the only acceptable offering for the sins of the world.

Finally, the Son told them that He had to leave them temporarily to fulfill scripture and His own prophesies concerning His resurrection after three earth days and nights in hell. Before departing, the Son promised to return shortly to usher them from Paradise to Heaven, where He would present them to the Father. The Son then departed Paradise to a sendoff of joyous praise.

## Death and Resurrection

While Jesus' spirit was in hell, the loyal angels watched over His battered, lifeless body. Joseph, a rich Christ follower from Arimathea, and a member of the Sanhedrin, successfully petitioned Pilate for the body of Jesus so that it could be interred before the beginning of Passover. Joseph returned to the place of crucifixion along with Nicodemus, some of his servants, and tools for extracting the spikes from the hands and feet of Jesus. John and Mary were still there mourning the brutal death of Jesus. When Joseph and Nicodemus presented the letter of authority from Governor Pilate to the Roman officer overseeing the crucifixion, they were given permission to remove the body. The chief priest and Pharisees had already asked the Romans to speed up the execution deaths, as they didn't want dying men on the crosses during the coming Passover. To comply, the legs of the two criminals crucified with Jesus were broken with strong blows from a heavy metal rod. Mary and John pleaded that there be no further mutilation of the body of Jesus seeing that He was already dead.

"Dead so soon?" said the Roman officer. Just to make sure, he directed a soldier in the execution detail to thrust a spear into the trunk of the body of Jesus. As he did so, blood and water spurted out and poured down upon the body of Jesus, covering the cross, and pooling on the ground at the base of the cross.

With evening and the Passover coming, Joseph's men and Nicodemus quickly set about bringing down the body of Jesus. Before placing the body of Jesus on a stretcher to carry Him from that place to the nearby new tomb that Joseph had commissioned for himself, Mary begged for one last moment to hold her son. As they laid the lifeless of body in her lap at the foot of the cross, Mary heaved in sighs of deep grief for her son and for what she had seen Him endure. Patiently, Joseph gently reminded Mary that the Passover was approaching and they needed to hurry.

The Passover was a high holy day and treated as a Sabbath in addition to the regular weekly Sabbath that would come later that week. They moved hastily to get the body of Jesus to the tomb prepared for Joseph. It was carved from stone and had never been used. They quickly washed the body of Jesus, applied burial ointment and spices, wrapped Him in grave clothes, placed a cloth over His face, and spread a shroud over the entire body. It wasn't as complete a job as they preferred, but it was necessary to do it in haste so that all could reach their homes before the sundown of Passover and cleanse themselves after handling the dead.

Meanwhile, the chief priests and Pharisees petitioned Governor Pilate to place a guard over the tomb. They clearly understood that Jesus spoke of Himself, and not Herod's Temple, when He said, "Destroy this Temple and in three days I will raise it up again." They advised Pilate that should the disciples of Jesus remove the body and claim He had risen from the dead, the revolt and end of the matter would be worse than had Jesus been allowed to continue without being crucified. So Pilate granted a continuous guard for the tomb and instructed that it be sealed with a Roman seal as evidence no one had entered or left.

No sooner had Mary, John, and Joseph left the tomb than a group of fallen angels came to claim the body of Jesus. However, powerful loyal angels were on guard in the tomb, with thousands more nearby in the skies above. The fallen angels said, "Stand aside! His spirit has gone to hell and we claim His body."

"That is not going to happen," said the leader of the loyal angels. "Go!" he shouted, and as he did he and the other angels with him protecting the body of Jesus unleashed a furious burst of power against the rebel angels. The rebel angels were overpowered and in great pain as they were flung away from the tomb and quickly moved further away to avoid a prolongation of the confrontation.

The Roman guards were oblivious to what had transpired in the spirit dimension. They griped about having to camp out at the tomb. "There is no good reason for us to be here," the squad leader said. "I have yet to see anyone come back to life after being crucified, and I have witnessed many crucifixions in my day."

Another soldier cautioned, "Those Jewish priests are afraid His followers will come to take His body."

The squad leader rubbed the stubble on his chin and said, "If they were so zealous, then why didn't they attack before He was crucified? And where were they when he was crucified? We don't have anything to fear from those cowards. Nevertheless, let's take turns standing on guard at regular intervals so that we are not surprised by any mischief."

## The Resurrection

At dawn on the third day, angels caused all of the Roman guards to sleep soundly. They prepared for the return of Jesus and were not going to allow these pagans to be the first human eyes to see the risen Lord. As the

Spirit of Jesus left Paradise and entered His body in the tomb His battered body was transformed as a great light from Holy Spirit God burst forth from Him. That burst of energy burned the image of His body onto the burial shroud. Under the burial wraps the eyes of Jesus blinked open and He took a full gasping breath of air like that of a free diver coming back to the surface after a deep dive in the sea. Outside the tomb, the sleeping guards did not see the bright shafts of light coming from the openings between the stone cap and the opening of the tomb. Inside, the transformed body of Jesus sat up, leaving the grave clothes to fall behind for lack of support. Jesus was clothed in the glorious light of the presence of Holy Spirit God. His face and body shone as they did on the mountain of His transfiguration.

The angels in the tomb and in the sky above began to shout, cheer, and blow trumpets. Their wings also beat and flapped in a deafening celebratory noise as they shouted, "Glory to God! Our Lord reigns!" As the glory around Him subsided, Jesus was found dressed in a beautiful white robe and His body bore no contusions, lacerations, or disfigurement from His ordeal, except that the holes in His hands, feet, and side remained as a memorial of what He had done. With joy, an angel flipped the stone aside and Jesus walked out of the tomb.

When the Roman guards finally awakened and realized the tomb was open and empty, they looked desperately for the body of Jesus. Then they looked around for evidence of the party they thought must have come to raid the tomb, but there was no evidence of that either. The other strange thing was that the heavy stone cap was some distance away from the tomb, rather than next to the opening. The guards went back to Jerusalem to their garrison to beg for their lives. They knew the price of failure in their mission. They were immediately imprisoned to await Governor Pilate's sentence. However, when the chief priests heard what had happened, they demanded to see the Roman guards that had been at the tomb. After hearing their story, the chief priests told them to say that Jesus did not rise from the dead, but that His disciples came and stole His body away to make it appear as if He had risen. Then they gave them money and promised to intervene with Governor Pilate so that they wouldn't have to fear execution.

Early the morning of the third day, while it was still dark, Mary Magdalene, together with Mary the mother of James, and Salome went to the tomb with more ointment and spices to finish the job of preparing the body of Jesus. They went by themselves and were unescorted because the disciples were too afraid to venture out for fear they too would be executed. The women had not really thought through their plan because there was no one to roll away the heavy stone that covered the entrance of the tomb.

When Mary Magdalene arrived at the tomb and found it empty, she hurried back to Peter and John with the message that the body of Jesus had been removed and they didn't know where His remains had been taken. Peter and John ran to the tomb and found it open. Although they saw the linen grave clothes they did not see the body. Also, the grave clothes had not been unwrapped. The grave clothes simply looked like the body they held had just melted away without a trace, that is, except for the image of the Lord that marked the shroud. The two went back to the other disciples pondering what they had seen, but it did not occur to them that Jesus had actually risen from the dead as He said He would and as scripture had foretold.

Mary Magdalene returned to the tomb again weeping. Alone, she looked into the tomb and saw two angels looking like men sitting at the head and at the foot of where the body of Jesus had lain. The angels asked, "Why are you crying miss?"

She responded, "Because they have taken my Lord away and I don't know where they have put Him." As she continued to cry she turned away from the tomb and through her tear-filled eyes saw a man she supposed was the gardener.

The man said, "Who are you looking for and why are you crying?"

Mary answered, "Sir, if you have taken Him away just tell me where you have put Him and I will take Him away to another place."

Then the man called her name. "Mary."

When He did she immediately knew it was Jesus. "Master!" she shrieked with joy opening her arms to embrace Him.

But Jesus said, "Don't touch Me because I haven't yet ascended to My Father. Go to My brothers and tell them I ascend to my Father, and to your Father, to My God, and to your God."

After showing Himself to Mary near the Garden tomb, Jesus returned to Paradise and from there ascended to Heaven taking with Him the souls of the righteous dead, for his blood covered them too, as well as those after His death who would believe in Him.

The righteous dead had been kept in the compartment of hell known as Paradise. Paradise was a pleasant place, but until those there had had their sins paid for by the Redeemer, they were cut off from God. They had been captives in Satan's kingdom, but were protected from being tormented. Now, thanks to the work of Jesus, they were taken to Heaven.[19]

As Jesus led this throng into Heaven, the angels shouted and praised God. The former captives of Satan sang a song of the redeemed. Since redemption by the blood of Jesus was limited to humankind, the angels could only listen to that song.

Jesus led those He freed to the throne room. He approached the Father clothed in a white robe like the redeemed, but His was stained red in the lower parts, wet with His blood. Jesus said, "Father, I bring these to You by My blood that covers them all and as many from now on that will believe in Me."

The Father responded, "Because of Your blood I see no fault in them. They are welcome to enter into our rest."

Then the Son of God poured a golden bowl of His blood on the altar of Heaven. "With My blood I consecrate Heaven and cleanse it from the traitorous deeds of Satan and his rebel angels," said the Son.[20]

Then the Son said, "Father, I have completed the assignment that You gave me. Now restore to Me the glory that I had with You from the beginning." With that, the plasma-like flow of God's glory poured from the Father back into the Son. As it did, Jesus changed into His former glory of the awesome God of white hair, fiery eyes, molten feet and a deep bronze tan. He wore a white tunic with a golden band about the chest, and a gold

---

[19] Hebrews 9:15; Psalm 68:18; Ephesians 4:8; and Romans 3:25.

[20] Colossians 1:20; Job 15:15, and 25:2; and Revelation 11:19.

trimmed deep red robe draped over all. Holy Spirit God came forth out of the Father as a bright light, and then subdivided into seven lights of equal brightness. These lights, representing the seven spirits of God, swirled around and sat on the head of the Son as a crown.

The Father then announced, "This is My beloved Son! Worship Him all you angels and redeemed ones." At that all the angels and the redeemed bowed and worshipped Jesus the glorified Son of God.

Meanwhile, back on earth, Mary returned to where the disciples where and told them exactly what she had seen and what Jesus said to her, including His instruction that they were to wait for Him in Galilee. Unfortunately, they didn't believe her. After all, Peter and John had also gone to the tomb and saw nothing except the unexplained placement of the burial linens.

But that evening, as they hunkered down in a safe room with the doors barred and braced, for fear the Jews were trying to hunt them down to kill them too, Jesus came through the closed door, stood in front of them, and said, "Peace to you all." The disciples were speechless, but when Jesus showed them His hands and side they exploded with joy realizing that Jesus was alive and had risen from the dead as He said He would.

Again, Jesus said, "Peace to you all. As I was sent by My Father, I am sending you." Then Jesus breathed on them saying, "Receive the Holy Ghost. Whoever's sins you forgive will be forgiven them, and whoever's sins you allow to remain will remain on them."

Not long after Jesus disappeared from among them, two Christ followers, including a man named Cleopas came to where the disciples were that same evening. The two were known to the disciples and had been among the seventy that Jesus sent out with them to preach the kingdom, heal, and cast out demons.

The two men were out of breath from running and explained that Jesus was alive and had risen from the dead. "We were walking with Him on the road, but we didn't know it was Him at the time. He explained to us from the scriptures how the Messiah had to die and be raised again to redeem the souls of men. When it seemed like He would continue on His way, after we reached our home, we pressed Him to lodge with us for the night and join us for a meal. Then, as He blessed our bread and broke it, we realized it was the risen Lord Jesus! When He disappeared from the table, we left and came running here to let you know that Jesus has risen as He said He would." Then the two rehearsed the scriptures that Jesus explained to them. The ten disciples there believed that Jesus was alive and risen, but Thomas was not there with them.

# Chapter 23 The Mission Continues and Broadens

*But ye shall receive power, after that the Holy Ghost is come upon you: and ye shall be witnesses unto me both in Jerusalem, and in all Judaea, and in Samaria, and unto the uttermost part of the earth. Acts 1:8*

The death and resurrection of Jesus Christ, the Son of God, not only released the souls of the righteous dead from Paradise and took them to Heaven, but it forever changed how mankind related to God. Animal sacrifices were no longer necessary, because Jesus was the only perfect sacrifice. Neither He nor any animal needed to be sacrificed again. Also, the sacrifice and blood of Jesus opened up a new channel for relationship with God. As promised, Jesus sent Holy Spirit God from the Father to live inside those that acknowledged Jesus as Lord and God and who turned from the control of sin in their lives.[21] Further, the redeemed that were still living on earth in their human bodies could, in their spirits, approach God to worship Him on a spirit to Spirit basis. These living people, and as many as would follow in the same way, were now Temples of God themselves by

---

[21] Additional scriptures are provided here for context.

I am he that liveth, and was dead; and, behold, I am alive for evermore, Amen; and have the keys of hell and of death. Revelation 1:18

And he said unto them, Go ye into all the world, and preach the gospel to every creature. Mark 16:15

But we have this treasure in earthen vessels, that the excellency of the power may be of God, and not of us. 2 Corinthians 4:7

virtue of God the Holy Spirit taking up residence in each believer.

After His resurrection, Jesus appeared to his followers over a period of 40 days. These many appearances shored up the faith of His followers. The appearances also established, by the many who witnessed these appearances, that Jesus was alive, and that what He prophesied about His death and resurrection had happened. Therefore, people could believe that what He prophesied about things to come was also true and would happen. Those things included His return for His church and to set up a kingdom on earth to be ruled by Himself.

## Transported by Translocation

Jesus not only made appearances in Israel, but He was instantaneously translocated by the Spirit, in His physical body, to a number of places in what would later be known as the Americas, across the oceans, as prophesied in Psalms. To be translocated was to have one's physical body transported instantaneously to another place on earth without untoward effects on the physical body. This enabled the risen Jesus to cover thousands of miles at a time at the speed of thought. Distance did not matter. Language was not a barrier. His purpose was to preach the good news to these indigenous peoples until other believers would reach them in the coming centuries. The good news message of salvation through the crucified and risen Christ, the Son of God, was a message to be delivered by descendants of Adam. However, since Jesus, as the second Adam, was both God and a man, He had the right to make this special intervention.

It was not the first time, nor was it to be the last time, that God would translocate the physical human bodies of His people over distances, in an instant of time, to pursue kingdom assignments on His behalf.[22] Besides, the people of the Americas, who had been isolated since God had broken up the great landmass in the generations following the rebellion of the Babel project, were His children too, even though they had turned from God to worship other things.

When Thomas finally joined up with the rest of the disciples the day after the resurrection, they very excitedly told him of how Jesus had appeared the day before to Mary, the ten other disciples, and to two Christ followers known to them all. That Jesus had died, as He had foretold, was clear. John, who observed it all with Jesus' mother Mary, retold the crucifixion, including the final breath of Jesus and how they took down His lifeless body to put it in a tomb.

They all were filled with joy that Jesus was back from the dead. However, Thomas was skeptical. He couldn't believe it was true. The other disciples had to admit that even they initially did not believe Mary who had the first sighting of Jesus and brought His instruction back to them, but the evidence from their own experience and from others of good reputation was undeniable. Still Thomas refused to believe that Jesus was alive. He said, "Unless I see where the nails pierced His hands and touch it with my finger and put my hand in His side, then I am not willing to believe."

Eight days later, as the disciples were together, including Thomas, Jesus appeared to them again. They

---

[22] See 1 Kings 18:10-12; Psalm 139:8-10; Ezekiel 3:12-15; Matthew 4:5; John 6:16-21; and Acts 8:39-40)

were still fugitives, concerned that the Jews and the Romans would come for them and put them to death too. So the doors were barred and barricaded. Yet Jesus appeared with them. As they stared at Him, Jesus said "Peace to you all." Then, pulling back His robe to reveal the open wound in his side and extending the palm of His other hand with the still open wound left by the nail spikes that had held Him to the cross, Jesus addressed Thomas. "Put your finger into My hand and stick your hand into My side. Don't continue in a state of unbelief, but believe!"

Without daring to take Jesus up on His offer, Thomas fell to his knees and proclaimed, "My Lord! And my God!"

Jesus responded, "You believe because you have seen Me. There is a bigger blessing for those who believe, but haven't seen Me."

The disciples were elated to have seen Jesus alive again. Now all of them believed without a doubt that Jesus was the Messiah, had risen from the dead as He said He would, and was truly God. However, they were still wary of the Jews and decided that the Jerusalem area was still too dangerous for them for the time being. So they went back north to more familiar and friendly surroundings.

After aimlessly spending time on the shores of the Sea of Galilee, also known as the Sea of Tiberius, Peter said, "I'm going fishing." The rest of the disciples agreed to go fishing with him that night. However, they fished the whole night without catching anything.

As day broke they saw a man on the shore who called out to them, "Have you caught any fish?"

They replied, "No."

The man then said, "Throw your net over the right side of your boat and you will catch some."

They did so, and when they did they netted such a haul of fish that they couldn't lift it up into the boat. At that point, John said to Peter, "It's the Lord!" Peter, who had been stripped down to keep his clothes dry, grabbed his tunic, tied it around his waist, and jumped into the water. The disciples weren't that far from shore, so they brought the boat in dragging the large catch of fish behind them.

When they approached Jesus they found He had already grilled fish and baked fresh bread on a fire of coals. Jesus said, "Have some breakfast and bring some of the fish that you caught."

So Peter pulled the net onto the shore with the fish. No one dared to ask if this man was Jesus, but they knew it was Him. The miraculous catch of fish, after having no success all night, was further confirmation.

Because Peter had denied Jesus three times after His arrest, Jesus challenged him before the other disciples. Jesus said to Peter, "Simon Johnson, do you love Me more than you love these fish and bread?"

It stung a little that Jesus called him Simon, rather than the nickname "Rock" that Jesus had given him over three years ago. So Peter protested, "Why yes Lord! You know I love You."

"Feed my lambs," came the command from Jesus. And again Jesus said to Peter "Simon Johnson, do you love Me?"

Peter blurted out, "Yes Lord! You know I love You."

In response, Jesus commanded, "Feed my sheep." For a third time Jesus asked, "Simon Johnson, do you love Me?"

Peter began to cry. The reality that he had denied the Lord three times weighed heavy on him. Through his tears, Peter said, "Lord You know everything. You know that I love You!"

Jesus said to Peter, "Let Me tell you something. When you were young you tied your cord about your tunic and went wherever you pleased. But when you are old you will stretch out your arms and someone else will tie you and take you to where you don't want to go. Now follow Me!" Peter remembered how Jesus had taught about taking up your cross and following Him. Peter and the other disciples realized Jesus was both reinstating him as a disciple and also indicating how Peter's life was going to end.

## The Commission and the Ascension

On the 40th day after His resurrection, some were still doubtful that Jesus was alive. Jesus appeared again one final time with 500 of his most intimate followers, including the eleven disciples, His mother Mary, His half-brother James, and others on Mount Olivet in the region of Galilee in the north. When Jesus suddenly appeared among them, they prostrated themselves at His feet and worshipped Him as God.

These were the last people to see the living, breathing Jesus Christ, the Messiah, and their God, before He returned to Heaven. Jesus instructed them not to leave Jerusalem, but to wait for the promise of Holy Spirit God, as promised by God the Father, and taught by Him while

He, Jesus, lived among them. Jesus said, "John the Baptizer baptized with water, but in a few days, you will be baptized with the Holy Spirit."

They asked Jesus, "Lord, are You going to restore dominion to the Kingdom of Israel now?" They asked this because they thought the immediate mission of Jesus was to rid them of the Roman occupation and their secular rulers that had been installed by the Roman Empire.

Jesus said, "It's not for you to know the exact time or the season for restoration of the kingdom. God the Father has put that under His prerogative and power. But, you are going to receive power, after God the Holy Spirit comes on you; and you will be My witnesses in Jerusalem, all of Judea, in Samaria, and to the very ends of the earth."

As Jesus spoke to them He affirmed, "I have been given full power in Heaven and on earth. Therefore, Go and teach all nationalities, and baptize them in the name of the Father, and of the Son, and of the Holy Ghost. Teach them to keep everything I have commanded. I will be with you all always, right up to the end of the world."

After Jesus said that, while the 500 looked at Him, He and His clothes began to shine with the bright glory of God. Slowly, a cloud of glory formed under Him and He ascended to Heaven through a portal that opened in full view of His followers. As He became fainter and more distant, two angels dressed in white, took their attention. The angels said, "You Galileans, why are you standing around gazing up into Heaven? This same Jesus, who has been taken up from you into Heaven, will come back in the same way you saw Him ascend into Heaven."

The last words that Jesus left with His followers made it clear that the good news message was to be taken throughout the world. The good news message was to go to all nationalities, beginning in Jerusalem and branching out to Samaria and beyond. This was a radical change for this revolutionary faith. The Jews didn't like the Samaritans. They considered them half-breeds, a mixture of Jewish and pagan parentage, and no better than pagans. On top of that, Jesus wanted them to go and be witnesses of who He is and what He did to the broader pagan world.

It wasn't an overnight change. Divine intervention was employed to confirm this direction for the church. These interventions included appearances of Jesus, a vision to Peter, and both seeing and hearing the gifts that would be given to them at Pentecost be given to former pagans who now believed the good news of Jesus the Christ. Holy Spirit God also enlightened their minds to recognize and understand Old Testament scriptures about God's plan for the non-Jewish nations.

### Pentecost and God the Holy Spirit

It took the disciples and followers in the region of Galilee about a week to trek from Mount Olivet to Jerusalem. Once there, they squeezed into a large second story room and waited in fasting and prayer for what Jesus had promised. In time, the 500 dwindled down to 120. The smaller group included Mary, the mother of Jesus, the half-brothers of Jesus, and the 11 disciples. On the 50th day after the Passover, known as Pentecost, as they continued in united prayer, the room in which they were all gathered was filled with the sound of a tornadic wind. As they looked around, hearing the noise of the strong wind fill the house, but not feeling the wind, they saw flames of fire appear.

The flames came to rest on the heads of each one of them. At that point the 120 were filled with the Holy Spirit and began to speak in a language unknown to them under the influence of the Holy Spirit. Moving outside, and still speaking in tongues, but without the flames of fire visible, a large crowd gathered. It was full of devout Jewish pilgrims from all over the world that had come to Jerusalem for Passover and had remained for a while longer. These observers looked at how the 120 were dressed and said, "Aren't all of these people from Galilee, yet how is that that each of us hears them speaking about the mighty acts of God in the languages of the places we have come from, from all over the world?" Some joked that they seemed to be drunk.

Peter stood up and in a loud voice spoke for the 120. "These people are not drunk as you may think. It's too early in the day for that! But you are seeing what was foretold by the prophets!" Peter went on to preach Jesus as the Messiah that was sent by God and killed by them, but who rose from the dead. As he continued to preach, Peter said, "It was not possible for death to hold Him. God resurrected Him and we are all witnesses of that. He has been exalted to the right hand of God the Father and has given to us, from the Father, the gift of the Holy Spirit, which you all see and hear. Know this; God has made this Jesus, the one you crucified, Lord and Messiah!"

The throng believed the preaching of Peter and the confirmation of the miracle of tongues. They asked, "What should we do so that we can be saved?"

Peter responded, "Be sorry for your sins and be baptized, each and every one of you in the name of Jesus Christ for the forgiveness of your sins and you will receive the gift of the Holy Spirit." Peter continued to admonish the crowd to believe. Many did and about 3,000 joined themselves to the believers. They all formed a church community that met daily, took in the teaching of the apostles, and witnessed numerous miracles being performed by the power of the Holy Spirit.

## Miracles of the Holy Spirit

The promised baptism in the Holy Spirit on Pentecost brought a major change in the disciples, now the apostles of Jesus Christ, and of the church. They were no longer afraid. With boldness they gave witness of Jesus. They also went about publicly, including in the Temple complex, where they taught as Jesus had done.

One day, as Peter and John were about to enter the Temple complex, they saw a crippled man and healed him. The man had been crippled from birth. His friends brought him to that same entrance everyday so that he could beg. The man sought some charitable gift of money from Peter and John, but rather than giving him money, they commanded him to get up in the name of Jesus as they took him by the hand and pulled him to his feet. Immediately the man was healed and began to praise God as he leaped and jumped around for the first time in his life.

A large crowd came running and gathered around. Those that frequented the neighborhood knew this was the cripple that they had seen for years and they wondered what had happened. Peter took the opportunity to explain that the miracle of healing was not brought about by their power, but Peter explained, "The God of our ancestors has done this to give glory to His Servant, Jesus, who you turned over to Pilate. You denied that He was the Messiah, the King of Israel and pressed Pilate to execute Him when Pilate was desperately seeking to set Him free. Instead, you rejected the Holy and Righteous One sent by God and demanded that a murderer by released. You killed the One who was life, but God raised Him from the dead and we all are witnesses that it really happened. It was by faith in His name that this man, whom you all see here and know well, that he has been made strong and given perfect health in your presence."

Peter went on to say that he knew they acted out of ignorance in putting Jesus to death. Peter then preached Jesus through the scriptures showing the plan of God to send His Son as the Messiah to save them from their sins and that it was the plan of God to first send Him to the Jews to fulfill the pact that God made with Abraham. About 3,000 men, plus thousands more of women and young girls and boys responded to Peter's preaching and joined the church.

Peter and John were immediately accosted by the Temple guards, priests, and members of the religious faction of the Sadducees. The Sadducees did not believe in life after death. Peter and John were remanded into prison and held overnight. On the following day they were brought before the high priest, Ananias and his family of other senior priests, as well as members of the Sanhedrin and other interested religious parties. The man who had been crippled was also present as evidence. Ananias demanded, "By what power have you been able to do this miracle?"

Emboldened by the Holy Spirit, Peter responded, "If you are asking how the crippled man was healed, let everyone here and all over Israel know that it was by the name of Jesus Christ the Nazarene. Yes, the same one whom you all crucified, but whom God raised up from the dead. It is by Him that this man stands before you healthy." Then Peter made the case for Jesus as Messiah and Savior, though He was rejected by those present, who considered themselves the judges of the faith. Finally, Peter said, "Salvation is not possible through anyone else. There is no other name given to people by Heaven by which it is possible to be saved."

The priests, Sanhedrin members, and other religious factions that came to accuse and punish Peter and John huddled to the side and debated the issue among themselves. They considered Peter and John to be uneducated working men from Galilee, untrained as they were, but they realized they spoke with authority because of the time the two had spent with Jesus. They didn't know what to do. "We can't deny this notable sign. Everyone in Jerusalem knows about this and that they did it. However, we have to stop this from spreading!"

When the session was called back to order, the priests charged Peter and John not to preach or teach any more in the name of Jesus.

Peter did not agree to that bargain. Instead, he said, "You decide if you think it is better for us to listen to you rather than to God. As for us, we can't stop speaking about what we have seen and heard." So the priests threatened them with the consequences and released them.

The disciples continued to preach Jesus and habitually met in the part of the Temple complex known as Solomon's Colonnade. Holy Spirt God was in them, as Jesus had promised, and continued to do miracles and signs through them that added to the growth of the church. Now people began to come to Jerusalem from distant towns to be part of what was happening. They began to lay sick people in the streets hoping that, at the least, Peter's shadow would touch them. As Peter walked past the sick, unseen angels specializing in healing would follow along. Those who believed on the message of Jesus and activated their faith were healed and delivered from tormenting demons.

The high priest was jealous of all the attention the apostles were getting and was concerned that the Jesus faction, now known as The Way, was growing out of control. So they had Peter and John re-arrested and held overnight for trial. However, an angel released them and told them to go back to the Temple complex the next day to keep preaching Jesus. When the high priest and the Sanhedrin convened on the next day to try them, they were told they were not in prison, although the cell was locked. Then someone came in to advise them that Peter and John were out teaching openly in the Temple complex. So the high priest had Temple guards escort them into the meeting, but without using force for fear of the crowds that accepted their message.

The high priest scolded Peter and John saying, "Didn't we severely warn you not to teach in this name? You have filled Jerusalem with your teaching and seem determined to make us accountable for His blood."

Peter replied, "We have to obey God, not men. The God of our ancestors raised Jesus from the dead, the One you murdered by hanging Him from a tree. Yet God has raised Him up to His right hand as a royal prince and Savior to provide repentance and forgiveness of sins to Israel. We were eye witnesses of these things as is the Holy Spirit whom God has given to those that obey Him."

When the religious leaders heard Peter's reply they wanted to kill Peter and John on the spot, regardless of whether it was inside the Temple complex. But Gamaliel, a revered teacher, asked that Peter and John be taken outside temporarily while they went into an executive session. After Peter and John were removed, Gamaliel counseled the religious leaders to let this movement run its course and come to naught on its own as had happened with others before them. However, if this movement was really of God, did they want to be in the position of fighting against God? So Peter and John were brought in again, flogged, ordered not to speak in the name of Jesus anymore, and released.

The Godhead was very pleased with the movement the Son started and how it was expanding empowered by newfound boldness and gifts from Holy Spirit God. God the Holy Spirit expressed to the Father and to the Son how He felt about His new and expanded role now that the Son was back in Heaven. "I have great joy in dwelling in our people made possible by the blood of the Son and the promise made to send Me from the Father to be with and in believers. At the same time I am grieved if the Christian I live in continues to sin. That makes it difficult for Me to live in that person in a growing relationship where I manifest my power, speak to their spirit, and bring them closer and closer to the full measure of the image of Christ. Some are honorable and develop friendship with Me, as some did with the Son when the Son lived among them as a human in the flesh. Others take me for granted and don't seek to grow in the relationship of intimate fellowship that is made possible by the blood of the Lamb of God. I do enjoy fellowship with the jewels among them who hunger for more of God.

In time, all who believe on the Son will learn to keep watch over their hearts and walk in greater levels of sonship and intimacy with their God."

# Chapter 24 The Battle for Hearts and Minds

*For I think that God hath set forth us the apostles last, as it were appointed to death: for we are made a spectacle unto the world, and to angels, and to men. 1 Corinthians 4:9*

God, in His divine wisdom, entrusted the work of His risen and ascended Son, into the hands of the apostles. God also entrusted this work to others who had followed Jesus, or who believed eyewitness testimony, or had their own direct encounter with the risen Savior. This small initial group spread the good news of the love of God and of salvation through belief in His Son and the efficacy of His own blood sacrifice, throughout the world. As they went about, they were empowered by the Holy Spirit. They proclaimed the healing and saving virtue of the blood of Jesus; and gave their personal testimonies, even at the cost of their lives.[23]

As the principal watcher for the earth, I took great joy in observing the growth of the church. The salvation and redemption of humankind by the blood of Jesus the

---

[23] Additional scriptures provided here for context.

And others had trial of cruel mockings and scourgings, yea, moreover of bonds and imprisonment:They were stoned, they were sawn asunder, were tempted, were slain with the sword: they wandered about in sheepskins and goatskins; being destitute, afflicted, tormented;(Of whom the world was not worthy:) they wandered in deserts, and in mountains, and in dens and caves of the earth. Hebrews 11:36-38

These that have turned the world upside down are come hither also. Acts 17:6

Son was a new thing. God loved and favored these believers so much that Holy Spirit God empowered them to do many of the same miracles that he Son did when He walked the earth as the human Son of Man. Many hearts were turned to God. This was a report that I gladly gave when I would appear before the throne of God in Heaven. But at the same time, I reported on the efforts of Satan and his kingdom to halt the work of God by persecuting and killing His witnesses and planting false doctrines and false leaders in among the faithful to pollute the pure faith and cause some to fall away back into the system of the world.

As the first Christians went about, they appealed to both Jews and pagans. Although these Christian witnesses were slaughtered at times, over the centuries since Christ ascended back to Heaven, the church grew to number in the billions. They were living letters to both the physical and spiritual dimensions. People took note of them. Holy angels were humbled by the spectacle of the seemingly weak representatives of redeemed humankind fearlessly offering up their lives time and again in loyalty and consecration to the God that loved them so much that He became one of them for a time, gave up His life to pay the price of their many sins, and restored a relationship of intimacy between the Godhead and the people He loves.

As the church grew in Jerusalem it was necessary to begin to add structure for administration. Seven deacons were selected to assist in administering benevolence and to serve tables for the faithful. Stephen was among the seven. Stephen was so full of the Holy Spirit that signs and miracles were done by him and he became a dynamic preacher of the good news of Jesus Christ. Since a large number of priests were also being persuaded to follow Christ, the chief priests, the Sanhedrin, and the Pharisees plotted to bring an end to the movement.

## Persecution of Believers

As a watcher, I and my fellow watchers continued to record and report to the throne room in Heaven. It wasn't that God didn't have the same information without us. Once the Son ascended back to Heaven and God the Holy Spirit came in His place to live inside believers, our focus as watchers became more active in watching and recording the deeds of those who rejected the true God. We also watched and recorded what Satan together with his fallen angels and demons were doing in the earth realm to blind the eyes of men to the good news of their Savior, and to hinder the work of the believers. As persecution of believers grew we watchers were kept busy. As the principal watcher for earth, I reported on these details to the Godhead ever more frequently given the war that Satan and his cohort unleashed on believers.

Stephen the deacon was arrested, based on false testimony, and dragged before the Sanhedrin as a blasphemer against the Temple and the religious traditions that came down from Moses. When asked by the high priest if those charges were true, Stephen launched into a long sermon, beginning with Abraham, showing how God had dealt with His people and how His messengers were often rejected. Then Stephen addressed them directly and said, "You prideful bunch of hard heads with hearts and ears lacking in any tenderness or receptiveness! Just name one of the prophets that your ancestors didn't persecute! They even killed the ones that foretold the coming of the Messiah, the Righteous One. Now you have become betrayers and murderers of the prophets too! The Law of Moses came to you with the assistance of angels, but you haven't kept it!"

The priests, the Sanhedrin, and members of other religious factions present became so angry they were ready to kill Stephen. But Stephen became oblivious to them as he saw a portal into Heaven open up, just as Jesus used to see portals open. He was filled with the Holy Spirit and in a state of ecstasy as he saw a vision of Jesus. With his eyes open, Stephen began to describe what he saw. Stephen said, "Look! I see Heaven opened and the Son of Man standing at the right hand of God!"

Stephen's accusers covered their ears and screamed at the top of their lungs so that they wouldn't hear any more. They then rushed Stephen, dragged him outside the city and began to kill him by stoning. As they did, they left their coats at the feet of a young Pharisee named Saul for safe keeping. Saul was in agreement with their actions and approved of this summary murder. As he reeled under the onslaught of the stones thrown full force at close quarters, Stephen shouted, "Lord Jesus receive my spirit!" But before he died, the Holy Spirit pressed Stephen to forgive his murderers, as Jesus did, because God had plans for one of those present, that is, for Saul. As Stephen crumpled to his knees, he cried out in a voice that everyone could hear, "Lord, don't hold this sin against them!" With that, Stephen fell over dead from the trauma to his head, face, and neck.

Although, just prior to His ascension, Jesus told His followers to go beyond Jerusalem to Judea, Samaria, and the ends of the earth teaching and making disciples, the movement remained in Jerusalem until the day

Stephen was martyred. That same day a persecution of those who believed in The Way that Jesus taught began to be hunted down, dragged from their homes and imprisoned. As a result of that persecution, many of those who had followed Jesus and the teaching of the apostles fled into Judea and Samaria. As they did, they preached the good news.

## Accelerated Evangelization

Philip, an evangelist and one of the original seven deacons, went to Samaria. The people of Samaria were considered foreigners by the Jews of Judea. Philip's preaching of Jesus as the Messiah, accompanied by the miraculous signs he performed under the power of the Holy Spirit, resulted in a great revival as the Samaritans took heed to his message. When word got to the apostles still in Jerusalem, they sent Peter and John to Samaria to help Philip. After Peter and John arrived in Samaria they ministered with Philip. As they laid their hands on the new believers in The Way in Samaria, they were filled with the Holy Spirit and spoke in tongues just as they and the other Jewish believers did in Jerusalem on Pentecost. On their way back to Jerusalem, Peter and John evangelized villages of Samaria along the way.

An angel spoke to Philip and told him to go south to the desert road connecting Jerusalem and Gaza. Philip immediately followed the angel's instruction and went down to that road. As a chariot from Africa approached, the Spirit told Philip to go up to it.

The chariot contained a foreign official, Queen Candace of Ethiopia's royal treasurer. The Ethiopian official had gone to Jerusalem to worship and on the way home was reading out loud the portion of Isaiah that foretold the death of the Messiah. As Philip jogged along next to the chariot he asked, "Do you understand what you are reading?"

The Ethiopian official replied, "How can I unless someone helps me and walks me through it?" So the Ethiopian invited Philip to join him in the chariot. Philip then explained how the scripture spoke of the Messiah, Jesus Christ.

As Philip explained the scriptures and showed their fulfillment in Jesus, the Ethiopian said, "Look, there is some water. Is there anything to prevent me from being baptized?"

Philip answered, "You can be baptized if you believe with your whole heart."

The Ethiopian responded with his confession of faith, "I believe that Jesus Christ is the Son of God!" He then commanded the charioteer to stop the chariot while he and Philip went to the nearby water for his baptism. As the Ethiopian came up out of the water the Spirit took Philip so that the Ethiopian couldn't see him any longer. The Ethiopian went on to Africa with a joyful heart determined to share what he had learned and experienced once he returned home to Ethiopia and the court of the queen. In the meantime, in an instant, Philip was supernaturally translocated by the Spirit, in his physical body, to Azotus, also known as Ashdod, on the Mediterranean coast. From there, Philip began to evangelize the towns from Azotus to Caesarea heading northward up the coast.

## The Conversion of Saul

While Saul was carrying out his reign of terror against followers of The Way, as the Christian faith was then called, believers fled Jerusalem for safer places such as Damascus, Syria and beyond. Saul asked for and received letters of authority from the high priest in Jerusalem to go to the Synagogues in Damascus to arrest any followers of The Way there and bring them back to Jerusalem as prisoners to face the high priest. However, as Saul and his assistants neared Damascus, he was knocked off his horse to the ground by a bright light. While on the ground he heard a voice that said to him, "Saul. Saul. Why are you attacking Me?"

The men traveling with Saul heard the sounds, but they were not discernable to them and they didn't see anyone speaking. But Saul responded, "Lord, who are you?"

The reply came, "I am Jesus, whom you have been persecuting. Now get up, go into the city, and you will be told what you have to do."

Saul's escorts saw that he was blinded and unable to see, so they led him into Damascus. There Saul remained blind and unwilling to eat or drink for three days. God then spoke to a believer in Damascus named Ananias to go and pray for Saul. Ananias was initially unwilling and tried to inform God of all of the bad news about Saul, as if God needed the information. But God sternly commanded Ananias, "Go! Because this man is a chosen instrument of Mine to take My name to pagans, kings, and to the people of Israel. I will also show him the things he will have to endure for My name."

Ananias left his home and found the place where Saul was staying on the main street in Damascus known as Straight Street. After he introduced himself, Ananias put his hand on Saul and said, "My brother Saul, the Lord Jesus, who showed Himself to you on the road as you were traveling, has sent me so that you would receive your sight and be filled with the Holy Spirit." All of a sudden, cloudy cataracts fell out of Saul's eyes and he could see again. Saul then got up and was baptized by Ananias before taking nourishment.

Saul remained in Damascus for several days with the believers there. Saul immediately began to tell people that Jesus was the Son of God, the Messiah, and proved this from the scriptures. People were astounded that the man who had come on a mission to take prisoner those who believed in The Way and haul them before the chief priests in Jerusalem was himself a believer. Saul was so effective, teaching in the Synagogues that Jesus is the Son of God that Jews in the city that rejected that message conspired to kill him.

Saul was assisted in a nighttime escape over the city wall. From there he went back to Jerusalem where the believers' initial reaction was distrustful. They thought it was a clever ruse to expose them so that they could be arrested. But Barnabas presented Saul, who later became known as Paul, to the apostles and explained what had happened in Damascus. The apostles and the church were convinced that Saul's conversion was sincere and accepted him.

As Paul debated with Jews who were steeped in the Greek culture, they decided to kill him. But other believers found out about the plot, escorted him to Caesarea, and put him on a ship out of the country.

## God's Grace Extended to Pagans That Believe

In Caesarea, an angel came in a vision to a Roman Centurion named Cornelius. Cornelius had adopted the faith of the Jews and was generous to the local community. The angel told him to send for Peter, who was temporarily staying in a house on the sea in Joppa. Cornelius sent two of his servants and a believing soldier to Joppa after he explained what happened and their mission. Prior to their arrival in Joppa, God gave Peter a vision in a trance. The vision was repeated three times because Peter found it difficult to comply with the instruction in the vision to eat animals that were considered ritually unclean to Jews. But the vision wasn't really about the animals; it was about those born outside of the Jewish heritage that God now wanted to receive the same message of salvation that Jewish believers of The Way had received.

When Peter woke up he pondered the vision he had seen and its meaning. Then the Spirit spoke to him letting him know that three men were coming for him and that he was to go with them without question. When the three men from Cornelius in Caesarea arrived Peter heard from them and invited them to lodge there for the night. The next day Peter, accompanied by some believers from Joppa, went with the men to Caesarea. When they arrived, Cornelius was waiting and ushered them into his residence where his relatives and friends were waiting.

Cornelius explained the vision he had received and the instruction the angel gave him to send for Peter. For his part, Peter realized what the vision he had was about and how he then realized that God doesn't show favoritism. He realized anyone from any nationality that reverenced God, believed in the Son of God, and lived a righteous life was acceptable to God. Peter then began to preach the good news of Jesus Christ, the Son of God and Savior of the world, and of the things pertaining to Christ to which Peter had been an eyewitness.

Before Peter could finish his message, the Holy Spirit came on Cornelius and the other Romans that were in his house that believed the message brought by Peter. They all spoke with tongues praising God as did Peter and the other Jewish believers with him on Pentecost. The Jewish followers of The Way that accompanied Peter from Joppa were amazed that these non-Jews received the same outpouring of the Spirit that they had received. Peter, turned to the Jewish believers that came with him from Joppa, and asked if anyone objected to these people being baptized. Then he commanded that the whole lot of them be baptized.

When Peter finally returned to Jerusalem, there was quite a debate over Peter fraternizing with pagans, and in their eyes, ritually defiling himself. So the apostles convened a meeting. Some people wanted to insist that it was necessary to keep the old Jewish faith, plus believe in The Way. Peter patiently explained how God intervened with visions and angels and led him, by the Spirt, to Cornelius and those Romans who were with him. In the end, as he recounted the experience, he affirmed that God gave them the same gift of the Holy Spirit as had been given to them. So Peter asked, "If God gave them the same gift that He gave us when we believed on our Lord Jesus Christ, how could I resist God?"

There was silence after Peter spoke as those present tried to process it all. Then those present began to smile and praise God as they said, "So God has allowed eternal life through repentance even to the pagans!"

Once the persecution of believers began, following the martyrdom of Stephen, believers from Jerusalem and Judea began to leave the country venturing to the northern coastal Syrian city of Antioch, the island of Cyprus, and the North African city of Cerene in Libya. However, they initially only shared the message of the good news with other Jews. That was until some of them, traveling from Cyprus and Cyrene, went to Antioch and shared the good news with pagans of the Greek culture. When people in Antioch responded and the church in Jerusalem heard about it, they sent Barnabas to Antioch.

Barnabas was encouraged by what he saw and went to Tarsus, a city to the north and across a small bay in Asia Minor in the province of Cilicia, to find Saul and bring him back to assist him. That venture had great success and the church grew. It was there that followers of The Way were first called Christians.

In the meantime, the persecution of believers continued in Jerusalem, where many of the apostles remained for the time being. However, King Herod beheaded John's brother James. When Herod saw this pleased the anti-Christian Jews, he followed up by having Peter arrested and held in prison to await his execution. But the church mounted a prayer campaign for Peter.

The night before Peter's scheduled execution, an angel came to his cell and rescued him. The angel slapped the soundly sleeping Peter on the side and said, "Get up and get your clothes on! Wrap your cloak around yourself and follow me."

For Peter, the experience was surreal. He thought he was seeing a vision in his sleep. When the angel told

Peter to get up, the chains that bound him fell off. As Peter followed the angel past guard posts they were not noticed. Then, as they reached the perimeter of the prison and the gate that led to the city, the angel caused the gate to open by itself. Once Peter passed through the now open gate and continued on past one street, the angel disappeared and Peter made his way to the home of friends.

In time, the apostles carried the message of the good news to their world and eventually left Jerusalem. It ultimately was fortuitous that the believer's left Jerusalem and sold their properties there either to fund their resettlement elsewhere or to share their wealth in common with other believers. That was because this spared them from being caught up in the massacre of Jews in Jerusalem in 70 A.D. under the Roman general Titus, who came to put down a rebellion. Gradually, they began to fulfill the worldwide mission to all nationalities that Jesus set for them just before He ascended back to Heaven.

Paul became an intrepid traveler on missionary trips. He faithfully presented the good news to local Jewish communities and then reached out, as Jesus in a vision instructed him to do, to the pagans. In the process, he set up a network of bishops and elders in different countries and cities, and helped the apostles at Jerusalem to establish the policy and doctrine that Jews and pagans are all saved the same way, by turning from sin, believing that Jesus is the Son of God, and confessing Him as savior. Some common standards were set, but adherence to Jewish traditions was not obligatory.

Although Paul was determined to go to Rome, the center of the major empire of the day, to complete what Jesus had shown him, he also had major successes elsewhere. In Athens, and other parts of Greece and Macedonia, he challenged humanistic philosophies and the ignorant serving of a system of polytheistic gods. In Asia Minor, one of his greatest challenges was in Ephesus, a major port city where the cult of the goddess Diana was a central aspect of life and commerce. Diana was just another representation of the sensual mother goddess that Satan had used over the centuries to keep people from knowing the true God and to seduce those who were weak in their commitment to God.

John, accompanied by Mary the mother of Jesus, worked as an eyewitness team. They settled in Ephesus. People from other countries came there on business or to join in the pagan worship of the goddess Diana. This meant that the team of John and Mary could reach many people without undergoing the rigors of travel. They gave witness to the locals and to the people from all over the world that passed through the city about the one true God and how He sent His only Son, born a man, to pay with His life for the sins of the world.

## Enduring Hardships for Christ

The apostles and those who accepted their message endured tremendous hardships. Paul catalogued his not yet completed suffering for the cause of Christ in a letter to the church he founded in the Greek city of Corinth. He said, "Five times I was flogged by the Jews with 39 blows. I was beaten with rods three times during my ministry in various lands. I was stoned once. I was in three shipwrecks, spending a night and a day treading water in the sea. I made frequent evangelistic trips during which I suffered the possibility of death from flash flood waters, from robbers, from Jews that were out to kill me, from the dangers of the wilderness, under threat from wild barbarians, at risk in cities, at risk on the sea, and at risk from betrayers who feigned to be friends. I was wearied and I endured pain. I often went without sleep, suffered hunger and thirst, deliberately fasted frequently, and had to deal with cold and the lack of adequate clothing."

Their mission was fraught with danger, but unlike the men who ran like cowards and left Jesus alone on the night He was taken prisoner, these men and women, were filled with the Holy Spirit promised by Jesus. This gave them boldness and a determination to stand true to the risen Savior.

With the exception of John, all of the apostles and Paul (formerly called Saul) died as martyrs. Most met their deaths in the lands they were led to by the Spirit. Peter and Paul were executed in Rome at the behest of Emperor Nero, who also began the first of the major wholesale persecutions of believers. The apostles went to Europe, Eurasia, Asia Minor, North Africa, Arabia, Southwest Asia, and India. Their blood was the seed that grew the church around the world. Some were beheaded, some were crucified, some were stoned and bludgeoned, some were stabbed with knives or spears, and one was skinned alive. John was boiled alive in oil, but God did not allow him to die a violent death.

The deaths of the apostles did not end the church. Other faithful believers gave their lives over the centuries rather than denounce Christ, recant their faith, and openly honor local deities or political leaders claiming to be gods. They were burned alive at the stake, thrown to wild animals, shot through with arrows, drawn and quartered, drowned, and tortured to death, among other means of death. None of these saints of God died alone. They received grace from God to stare death in the face and give their lives as consecrated offerings to God. Jesus promised to be with them always. As with the first Christian martyr Stephen, many had visions of Jesus or were comforted by angels at the hour of their deaths. In the process, many people that were witnesses of this persecution were convicted in their hearts and decided that they too would follow Christ.

# Chapter 25 Darkness and Light in Conflict Over Two Millennia

*Who shall separate us from the love of Christ? Shall tribulation, or distress, or persecution, or famine, or nakedness, or peril, or sword? As it is written, For thy sake we are killed all the day long; we are accounted as sheep for the slaughter. Romans 8:35-36*

Until the Son of God came to earth, born of the Virgin Mary, as Jesus, God's focus was on select people, known as the patriarchs, and then on the nation of Israel. The prophet Daniel saw into the future by revelation from the Spirit of God. What he saw involved a period of time determined by God to deal with His chosen people of Israel. What neither Daniel, nor any prophets before him, did not see was a hiatus of approximately 2,000 years before God would complete, in about seven more years, His dealings with this special people to fulfill what was revealed to the prophet Daniel.

That 2,000-year hiatus featured the introduction and growth of a largely non-Jewish church to carry God's message and to affirm that Jesus was the Christ or Messiah of God. Jesus Christ, and the apostles Paul, Peter, Jude, and John all prophesied about what that hiatus would look like and God's final judgment that would follow.

Satan, his fallen angels, and demon spirits, opposed the church, continued to persecute Jews, and authored a reign of darkness that included virtually every evil thing imaginable during that hiatus. God was troubled by the evil darkness and the suffering of His people, both Jews and the Christian believers. It did not take God by surprise. In fact, Jesus told his followers to take up their crosses and follow Him. Just as God allowed Noah to preach and warn of judgment for years before the judgment day of the great flood, He delayed judgement during the 2,000-year hiatus, while His church called people to Him.

## Satan Continues to Resist God and Wreak Havoc

Satan's plan was to overcome followers of Jesus Christ and take revenge on the Jewish people through whom the Messiah came. This began with Herod's attempt to kill the apostles. Saul's persecution of followers of The Way was also part of Satan's plan. Then came the mass persecution and martyrdom of Christians beginning with Roman emperor Nero in the first century.

In the first century, in 70 AD, the Romans killed over 1 million Jews in brutally crushing a revolt. It was then that the Temple in Jerusalem was utterly destroyed. From the 4th century to the 20th century, Jews were reviled by many Christian leaders as the assassins of the prophets and of Christ. Jews suffered repeated massacres at the hands of those who claimed to be Christians. From the 13th to the 16th century, various European countries expelled their Jewish populations or persecuted them in order to get them to give up Judaism. From 1938 through 1945, over 6 million Jews died in the holocaust. In addition, in the 19th and 20th centuries, the Russian Empire carried out a number of pogroms against Jews marked by massacres.

Two millennia passed from the time Jesus gave His life to redeem humankind and the rest of creation. Although Jesus promised He would return, people mistook God's patience for evidence, in their minds, that there was no God. As God did before He sent the Messiah, He continued to send people bearing His message of reconciliation between God and humankind through His Son. Regrettably, many people continued to reject the good news. Those rejectionists despised the messengers God sent. After sending His own Son, God sent, in the Christian era, apostles, prophets, evangelists, pastors, teachers, and ordinary witnesses. Some were killed.[24] Just as had happened with Jesus, some of these

---

[24] Additional scriptures are provided here for context.

The fool hath said in his heart, There is no God. They are corrupt, they have done abominable works, there is none that doeth good.     Psalm 14:1

For my people have committed two evils; they have forsaken me the fountain of living waters, and hewed them out cisterns, broken cisterns, that can hold no water. Jeremiah 2:13

And all things are of God, who hath reconciled us to himself by Jesus Christ, and hath given to us the ministry of reconciliation;To wit, that God was in Christ, reconciling the world unto himself, not imputing their trespasses unto them; and hath committed unto us the word of reconciliation. Now then we are ambassadors for Christ, as though God did beseech you by us: we pray you in Christ's stead, be ye reconciled to God. 2 Corinthians 5:18-20

Knowing this first, that there shall come in the last days scoffers, walking after their own lusts, And saying, Where is the promise of his coming? For since the fathers fell asleep, all things continue as they were from the beginning of the creation. 2 Peter 3:3-4

Now the works of the flesh are manifest, which are these; Adultery, fornication, uncleanness, lasciviousness, idolatry, witchcraft, hatred, variance, emulations, wrath, strife, seditions, heresies, envyings, murders, drunkenness, revellings, and such like: of the which I tell you before, as I have also told you in time past, that they which do such things shall not inherit the kingdom of God. Galatians 5:19-21

messengers met their most fierce resistance from those that held positions as religious authorities. This opposition came down not only on the messengers, but also on those that listened to them and gave heed to their message.

God, who is patient, longsuffering, and merciful, gave a space of time before the great time of His judgment. One purpose for the delay in judgment was to leave an open door for those who would respond to the good news and believe that Jesus is the Son of God. Those believers would be saved and have a place reserved for them in God's eternal kingdom.

In the meantime, in addition to the ancient religions that Satan authored to blind the minds of people and entrap them in rebellion against the true God, new religions and heresies sprang up, including the introduction of errors in parts of the church. The new religions and heresies became established and entangled billions of people in what was Satan's plan to keep people from God's light and to chain them in satanically inspired confusion and darkness.

For two millennia, men bent on conquest, domination, enrichment, power, and pleasure filled the earth with death and despair. They were barbarous. They oppressed nations and peoples. Men died on battlefields.

---

And ye shall hear of wars and rumours of wars: see that ye be not troubled: for all these things must come to pass, but the end is not yet. For nation shall rise against nation, and kingdom against kingdom: and there shall be famines, and pestilences, and earthquakes, in divers places. All these are the beginning of sorrows. Then shall they deliver you up to be afflicted, and shall kill you: and ye shall be hated of all nations for my name's sake. Matthew 24:6-9

They shall put you out of the synagogues: yea, the time cometh, that whosoever killeth you will think that he doeth God service. John 16:2

Others died from starvation and disease and plagues like that of the 14$^{th}$ century that killed 25 million people in Europe.

Beginning in the 7$^{th}$ century, as Islam was founded and grew, until the 21$^{st}$ century, rulers and nations under Islam discriminated against and even killed Christians. This was done both by direct action or by tolerating such acts. In the 20$^{th}$ century, Islamic atrocities against Christians by the Ottoman Empire included the Armenian genocide, the Assyrian genocide, and the Greek genocide. In the Armenian genocide, for example, there were instances of young Christian women being raped and then their nude bodies crucified on crosses as an act of disrespect for the Christian faith.

When Christians were not killed or forcibly converted to Islam on the threat of death, a special tax was levied on them and their men were forced to fight in the armies of Islam. Laws of apostasy and blasphemy made it easy to condemn a Christian neighbor to death for converting a Muslim to Christianity, allegedly speaking ill of Islam's prophet Mohammed, or allegedly desecrating the Koran. Violence against Christian communities, Christian leaders, and church buildings went mostly unpunished.

In its early centuries, Islam developed a caliphate combining political and religious rule. Satan used this powerful force to try and eliminate Christianity from the lands it conquered in Africa, Arabia, the Levant, South Central Asia, South Asia, and parts of Eastern Europe and the Iberian Peninsula. In the providence of God, that advance was halted and driven back from most of Christian Europe.

In the 13<sup>th</sup> century, forces of as many as 150,000 Mongols from Far East Asia, invaded Europe. The Mongols overcame Russia and parts of Eastern Europe. It was another satanic attempt to subjugate and defeat Christian Europe. In the end, the Mongols pulled back.

In both the cases of the rise of Islam and of the Mongols, Satan assigned powerful fallen angels, which were anti-Christ spirits, to influence the human leaders assigned to them. These spirits assisted their human subjects in moving from one conquest to another.

The thing that hurt the heart of God even more than the attacks on the church were the schisms in the church itself. God was also grieved by the corruption that took root in the church. Christians fought Christians in bloody religious wars in Europe from the Middle Ages until the Renaissance. Where they did not fight each other, they broke fellowship with each other and weakened the church. Satan sowed spirits of error, heresy, division, nationalism, and pride into the church. This added to the divisions in the church.

In the reformation, believers in an unalloyed faith were persecuted by the larger organized institutional church. In addition, beginning with the first crusade in the 11th century, crusades to retake and Christianize the Middle East, in the name of God, at times were responsible for hateful atrocities of mass slaughter against Jews and adherents of Islam.

Satan used spirits of nationalism and racism to do great violence against the people of Africa by Arabs, Europeans, and North Americans. From the 7<sup>th</sup> century to the 21<sup>st</sup> century, Islamic Arabs practiced enslaving the peoples of Africa. European and American slave traders took millions of people by force from Africa as slaves from the 15<sup>th</sup> century into the 19<sup>th</sup> century. Even after slavery was abolished in America, people of color in America endured lynchings, mob violence, the destruction of entire settlements, summary extra-judicial executions, and all types of injustice and discrimination.

The same spirits of nationalism and racism led to the death and subjugation, by the millions, of the indigenous Indian people of North America, South America, and the Caribbean by Europeans and Americans from the 15<sup>th</sup> century through the 19<sup>th</sup> century. The indigenous people were killed, starved, enslaved, and infected with diseases both deliberately and unintentionally. Racism and nationalism also led the Japanese people to commit horrible atrocities against the Chinese, Korean, and Filipino people in the 1930s and 1940s.

The world witnessed a frenzy of attempts to exterminate entire peoples. New weapons of mass destruction heralded a nuclear age in which mass death of civilian populations and cities was threatened. A staggering 85 million people lost their lives in what became known as the Second World War. That number included about 6 million Jews exterminated by Nazis.

Satan and his fallen angels and demons used communal and political violence, religious violence, racism, and nationalism to kill hundreds of thousands of people at a time. About 1 million people died on the Indian subcontinent in a short time during the bloody communal violence that accompanied the partition of peoples in 1947 into what became India and Pakistan. The political violence in Columbia from 1948 to 1958 killed over 300,000 people. In 1994, the world sat by during the slaughter of over 800,000 Tutsi people in 100 days by Hutus in Rwanda.

Many cases of mass death were the result of the lust for power. Over 1 million people were killed in the killing fields of Cambodia from 1974 to 1979 by the Khmer Rouge. Nearly 500,000 people were killed in the Syrian civil war of the early 21$^{st}$ century.

The history of that time since the early church was filled with more tragedy than has been recorded here. With notable exceptions, all of this devastation over the centuries did not cause people to seek consistently the true God. In that respect, human nature in this period was no different than was human nature before Jesus came. Instead, they tended to blame God, or to celebrate or attempt to appease the false gods that Satan had inspired them to worship, including men that insisted on being worshipped and obeyed as gods in fact, or as if they were gods. Of such were some of the Roman emperors, Chinese and Japanese emperors, Inca emperors, and many persons on into the modern age that claimed to be gods, possessed by a god, or to be the special messenger of their god.

Over time, technology advanced and populations increased, but rather than turn to God, some people pursued the things that were important to them, whether that was the basic necessities for existence, or the vanity of consumption and pleasurable diversions.

Strong drink had a long history of ruining lives. In the latter centuries, the addictive and, ultimately, self-destructive use of drugs such as natural and synthetic opiates, mind and mood altering drugs like LSD, methylenedioxymethamphetamine ("molly"), also known as ecstasy, plus cocaine, other methamphetamines, nicotine, and so-called "recreational" drugs such as alcohol, cannabis, and kat, became epidemic in some areas of the world.

The lust for sexual pleasure had always been a feature of the history of humanity. As time began to run out on domination of the world by men, rather than by God, the pursuit of immoral sexual pleasure took on a new look. It was no longer limited to an industry of prostitutes or forcing the captured women of enemies into becoming unwilling concubines. This pursuit led to slavery and human trafficking on massive scales, in addition to the continued oppression of minorities and the use of rape as a tool of war. As technology increased, immoral sexual pleasure was made available virtually through pornography, in media, the internet, and other means, including through the use of virtual reality devices.

The love of money and power continued unchanged. It drove many in both illicit and legitimate pursuits to heap up wealth and conspicuously consume it on themselves. At the same time, the concentration of wealth in the hands of a few left a vast majority in poverty, hunger, subsistence, and debt.

The latter centuries, with the introduction of mass media, global television, and movies, meant that seekers of fame could become de facto demi gods in the eyes and hearts of their followers. In their narcissism and pride they exceeded all societal bounds. Some entertainers and movie actors even made intentional deals with the devil in exchange for fame.

In the midst of this Satanic darkness, God still sent out His messengers. God continued to show grace to those who would hear His messengers and respond to their message. God showed grace to those who believe that Jesus is the Son of God who came in the flesh to pay the price of human sin, those who seek to honor God, and to turn from wickedness to right standing with God. To these messengers was also given grace. They received grace to persist when it seemed no one was responding. Some also received grace to work miracles and healings that helped to persuade lost souls of the truth of their message.

With or without signs and wonders, there were periods of spiritual awakenings, such as in the 18$^{th}$ century, marked by the rise of evangelistic ministries having great sway in some countries. At times, tragedy and war would increase the numbers of those who turned to God. However, when things returned to normal, many dropped their pursuit of God and returned to their old ways.

# Chapter 26 The False Christ and the End of the Age

*And then shall that Wicked be revealed, whom the Lord shall consume with the spirit of his mouth, and shall destroy with the brightness of his coming: Even him, whose coming is after the working of Satan with all power and signs and lying wonders. 2 Thessalonians 2:8-9*

The two-thousand-year hiatus in which the earth was dominated by non-Jewish kingdoms and nations drew to an end. God's time for focusing again on His chosen people, the Jews, had come. Thus began what the prophet Daniel described at the 70th week of Jacob's trouble. It was the time also spoken of by the Apostle John, among other prophets, and by Jesus Christ Himself. Some of these prophesies identified countries and national groups by name. God had been patient for centuries, but now the time had come for Him to unleash His holy wrath on those that had killed His faithful martyrs, mistreated His chosen people, the Jews, and who had steadfastly rejected His gift of the Son of God.

**The Time of the End**

The end of this age of world domination by pagan nations was marked by an increase in wars, civil wars, violence, and instability.[25] Weapons of mass destruction,

---

[25] The additional scriptures are provided here for context.

whether conventional, nuclear, or chemical and biological, were employed with increasing frequency. Once again, populations were displaced and armies were mobilized and deployed by single countries or by alliances in numbers that were breathtaking.

---

Come now, and let us reason together, saith the LORD: though your sins be as scarlet, they shall be as white as snow; though they be red like crimson, they shall be as wool. If ye be willing and obedient, ye shall eat the good of the land: But if ye refuse and rebel, ye shall be devoured with the sword: for the mouth of the LORD hath spoken it. Isaiah 1:18-20

Chapters 38 and 39 of Ezekiel, and Daniel 11:36 through 12:1.

For God hath not appointed us to wrath, but to obtain salvation by our Lord Jesus Christ. 1 Thessalonians 5:9

And when ye shall see Jerusalem compassed with armies, then know that the desolation thereof is nigh. Then let them which are in Judaea flee to the mountains; and let them which are in the midst of it depart out; and let not them that are in the countries enter thereinto. For these be the days of vengeance, that all things which are written may be fulfilled. But woe unto them that are with child, and to them that give suck, in those days! for there shall be great distress in the land, and wrath upon this people. And they shall fall by the edge of the sword, and shall be led away captive into all nations: and Jerusalem shall be trodden down of the Gentiles, until the times of the Gentiles be fulfilled. Luke 21:20-24

For then shall be great tribulation, such as was not since the beginning of the world to this time, no, nor ever shall be. Matthew 24:21

And I heard a loud voice saying in heaven, Now is come salvation, and strength, and the kingdom of our God, and the power of his Christ: for the accuser of our brethren is cast down, which accused them before our God day and night. And they overcame him by the blood of the Lamb, and by the word of their testimony; and they loved not their lives unto the death. Revelation 12:10-11

God created the earth to be inhabited and to be at peace. As the principal watcher for the earth and for Israel, I, Benelroi, made frequent visits to the throne room of God in the later days of the age of earth's rule by men. As always, God already knew what I was going to report. However, I was concerned that men would destroy God's earth or exterminate His special people, the Jews. The Father assured me that He had heard and was emotionally moved with compassion and anger by the prayers of His precious martyrs and those persecuted for their faith in the Son, Jesus. He said, "Benelroi, I will certainly avenge them, save the planet, and deliver My special chosen people from annihilation at the hands of Satan and all of his allies."

In one great regional war, near the end of the age, the Muslim Arab nations of North Africa, the Arabian Peninsula, and the Levant, united with Iran, the nations of South Central Asia, and the Russian Federation, conspired to exterminate the Jews of Israel. Israel was vastly outnumbered and in a seemingly hopeless situation.

However, as in days of old, God sent His angels, led by the Archangel Michael, among the invading throng and annihilated the allied invading army by causing them to be confused and to kill each other, on the one hand, and by unleashing a violent storm of flash flood waters, giant hailstones, and fire.

A new generation of air to ground missiles was fired by Israel and her allies such as the United States of America, at the massed, heavily armored divisions that were deployed against Israel. By far, the greater casualties were as a result of the angelic intervention. Because the United States intervened on the side of Israel, Russia unleased a limited nuclear strike on some of the cities of the United States. The United States responded in kind. Major cities in both Russia and in the United States were devastated. When the leaders of the two countries realized the absurdity of continuing with nuclear exchanges, the two nations stood down rather than unleash the totality of their respective nuclear arsenals. The people of Israel realized that it was because of divine intervention, and not its limited supply of missiles and the missiles of its allies, that the multinational army that came against their nation was defeated. Nevertheless, they did not yet recognize Jesus as their defender and Messiah.

## Enter The Antichrist

It took months to clear away all of the destroyed war material and bury the dead of the invading army. In the meantime, an ominous new leader emerged in Europe, named Christoph Lawless. Christoph Lawless succeeded in unifying the continent and also took advantage of the vacuum in the Muslim world, due to its defeat in the war against Israel, to take control of North Africa, the oil rich Arabian Peninsula, and the Levant. The great military powers of America and Russia had also been weakened by the war and were in no position to oppose Christoph.

Christoph portrayed himself as being benevolent. Over time, his power and influence grew. He promised peace and prosperity, but he cruelly crushed those nations that dared to oppose him.

One of his innovations was to eliminate transactions in hard currency by forcing movement to electronic transactions. He introduced biometric verification and tracking via microscopic sensors cosmetically implanted under the scalp in the forehead or in one's hand. This was ostensibly to eliminate fraud, to secure electronic transactions, and to provide a reliable means of identification. The implant was activated by scanners at every point of sale, and also via an application on the smart phone of the owner of the account. Because it was linked to biometric data and other records, the implant did away with the need for passports or voting registrations. In addition, a tracking feature ensured that continual global positioning system coordinates were available on every person that had taken the mark of the device.

Gradually, Christoph's united Europe and its vassals in other regions managed to control the global financial system. His spiritual advisor, Musa, was totally devoted to Christoph and took great pains to see that Christoph Lawless was honored wherever he went, either in person or where he projected himself via three dimensional holographic images communicated through telepresence technologies. In this way, Christoph Lawless seemed ubiquitous. From his headquarters in Europe, he could appear virtually, in real time, and hold meetings with other world leaders.

Under Christoph, there was a temporary reduction in wars; problems of famine were also brought under control. It was the age of Christoph, and that age promised peace and prosperity to those who accepted what was presented as his benevolent rule.

As Christoph extended his Pax Christoph to more and more countries, he turned an eye to Israel and announced that he would solve the Middle East conundrum that had baffled the world for generations.

By having subjugated the Muslim countries that surrounded Israel on every side, Christoph had the bargaining power to make and deliver a peace deal. At first, the Israeli's were skeptical. In a great national debate, one faction argued that, just as God had miraculously delivered them in the last war, they should stand pat and not deal with Christoph, who seemed to have an insatiable appetite for bringing countries under his sway. On the other hand, there were those who were mesmerized by Christoph and believed he was the man they were looking for to bring Israel lasting peace.

When Christoph came to Israel in person, he was mobbed by adoring throngs of Jewish and Arab residents of Jerusalem. He announced that his experts had discovered the true site of the last Jewish Temple. Although that site was in the old city of Jerusalem, it was not on what had been known as the Temple Mount above the Western Wall. Instead, it was in a part of Jerusalem that had been known as the City of David.

This opened up new possibilities. Israel could build its Temple in this newly discovered and identified site while Muslims could continue to have their two historic mosques, Al Aqsa and the Dome of the Rock, that were located on what had mistakenly been called the Temple Mount. Jerusalem would be undivided and under Israeli rule. The capital would be moved from Tel Aviv to modern Jerusalem and all Muslim nations would make peace with Israel, with full travel, trade, and diplomatic relations by accepting this agreement. There would be no more talk of annihilating Zionists. The caveats were that Jordanian and Palestinian authorities would manage access to the Temple Mount mosques, and for seven years Christoph's United Europe forces would be the guarantor of peace and safe borders for Israel living side by side with an independent, demilitarized, peaceful Palestinian state.

The new Palestinian state would have no standing army. Israel's neighbors would agree to demilitarize and disarm militias. Israelis in some selected West Bank settlements would remain, but, disarmed, and under the protection of Christoph's forces. No Israeli armed forces would be permitted in the territories of the new Palestinian state. Likewise, Arabs with Israeli citizenship would be guaranteed equal treatment under the law, should they choose to remain in Israel. Borders would be open, walls would come down, and Christoph's forces would guarantee the peace. There would be no rogue attacks on the people of Israel by non-state actors not in agreement with the treaty. Christoph's forces would guarantee that. Palestinians not residing in Israel would receive remuneration for lands lost, but without the right of return to those lands in Israel. The entire treaty would be recognized by the United Nations, the Arab League, and the Organization of Islamic Cooperation, as well as by Israel. At the end of the seven-year confidence building period, if all parties agreed, Christoph's forces would be gradually withdrawn as all of the nations in the region accept the new normal of peace, prosperity, freedom of religion, trade, freedom of movement, and peaceful self-governance.

Following a plebiscite in Muslim countries, and a referendum in Israel, the treaty was implemented. Within six months, Israel, working night and day, completed its new Temple and reinstituted the Mosaic sacrifices. It seemed that peace had truly arrived and all of the credit was given to Christoph.

In the immediate years that followed Christoph's diplomatic breakthrough, Christoph tightened his control over the global financial system. Organized crime began to wane as the new cashless society and the ability to monitor and freeze bank accounts meant there was no underground economy or ability to launder cash. Plaudits continued to be showered on Christoph. Besides, Musa made sure that praise flowed in steadily from around the world.

## The Great Vanishing

One day, an amazing thing happened. Hundreds of millions of people around the world vanished without a trace. What they had in common was that they were all fervent believers in God, acknowledged Jesus Christ as the Son of God, and had been looking for the second coming of Jesus. Leading up to this event, there were many reported sightings of Jesus as He moved among His people and urged them to prepare for His coming, which would be soon. Evangelists, apostles, and prophets at mass meetings not only would see thousands healed, but there would be mass visions of Jesus and of angels attending Him. Millions of people gave their lives to Jesus and were saved as the result of a great awakening that began to transpire.

All the while, there was increasing persecution of Christians. The world considered them intolerant of the faith experiences of others. Especially in the part of the world controlled by Christoph, churches were harassed, unless they extolled Christoph and were loyal to him. It was all right if the churches were social clubs or involved themselves in community projects, but spirit-filled worship and evangelization were considered disruptive and not in the spirit of the age of Christoph.

It happened suddenly and without warning. For those who were looking for Him, Jesus, the Son of God, appeared in the sky with His angels. Jesus made a mighty shout in a clear trumpet-like voice, heard only by the faithful dead and the faithful who were still alive. Within less time than it takes to wink an eye, armies of holy angels rounded up those who had died as believers. It made no difference how they had died or where their remains were scattered. The dead in Christ had already been in Heaven in their spirits, but now their physical bodies were reconstituted and brought up to be transformed and united with their spirits. Then those in Christ who were still alive were taken up to meet Jesus in the atmosphere above the earth. As they ascended, their bodies too were transformed. As quickly as they had been gathered, they were all gone. Jesus and the angels swiftly took the huge multitude to Heaven. There, Jesus presented them to the Father and began to celebrate with those He loved and died to save. It was a supreme moment of joy for the Son of God.

The disappearance of hundreds of millions was the topic of the news around the world. There were many rumors and speculation. Some scientists suggested there was an unknown virus that loosed the binding forces of the cells of those people causing them to disappear and dissipate.

Christoph announced that he had been in contact with an alien intelligence from outer space. According to Christoph, these beings had been responsible for planting life on earth and now had come to remove those that were a threat to progress. According to Christoph, intolerant Christians were that threat to progress.

## Angel Armies at War

Meanwhile, Michael led his warrior angels in a battle against Satan and his angels. Satan had long ago been put out of the Heaven where God had His throne, but was able to move about freely in the physical universe and in the atmosphere and air of the earth. Now Michael and his angels fought with Satan and His angels to restrict their freedom and limit them to the earth itself.

Michael relished the opportunity to defeat the fallen Archangel that had once been at the pinnacle of created beings with him together with Gabriel. Michael's army also liked nothing better than to put the forces Satan to flight once again and severely limit the zone of operation of the rebels. Once kicked out of the broader physical universe, Satan turned his fury on any that dared to seek after God. He plotted to exterminate the Jews and take the land God had promised them away from them as a way of dealing a defeat to God and His angels.

In the midst of this uncertainly, there were those who were Christian by church affiliation, but who had never truly given their lives to Jesus. Many of them realized what had happened. They were stunned that they were not taken along with their Christian loved ones and Christian friends who were taken. Some were bitter and cursed God over the situation. Others began to search their Bibles, Christian books, and ministry recordings to make sense of it all.

The departure of the true Christians lifted the restraint of God the Holy Spirit, who had kept the world in balance and from total destruction for the sake of believers around the world. With increasing frequency, the world began to be racked by tragedies, famine, war, and disease. Many men stood up to say that they were the Messiah and, with the assistance of demons, they performed feats that amazed crowds that believed they were indeed special.

The age of Pax Christoph began to be marred by increasing civil and cross-border warfare around the world. As transportation and communications were disrupted, famine began to be a global problem. This led to runaway inflation and epidemics that took a heavy toll on starving people. Between the uptick in war, famine, and the epidemics, the mortality rate increased, especially among the weak, sick, infants, and children.

The Holy Spirit was still operating on earth. Those not taken when Jesus came for them could still give their lives to Jesus and receive the Holy Spirit, who was still drawing them, but now they would only get to Heaven by dying the death of martyrs standing strong for their testimony of Jesus.

## A Renewed Focus on the Jewish People and Israel

Now that Christians were gone from the scene and the influence of the church greatly diminished, God turned His dealings to the Jewish people. Two mighty prophets arose. In fact, they were Enoch and Elijah. These two Old Testament men each were taken to Heaven without experiencing death. Now they were sent back to earth, without having to be reborn or reincarnated, to speak of Jesus Christ and to give their lives for that testimony.

They were not normal men. If anyone tried to harm them, they were able to call down fire from the sky and destroy them. As Elijah had done when he last walked the earth, he and Enoch commanded it not to rain in the region of Israel and surrounding countries. From their witness and preaching there were 144,000 Jews that believed that Jesus was their Messiah. That 144,000, which represented Jews from all of their tribes from around the world, began themselves to go about Israel and the world as evangelists. God assigned angels with them to protect them, although the angels were not seen. Each of the 144,000 Jewish evangelists were marked supernaturally, so that they were identified to the angels. It was after the 144,000 Jewish evangelists were identified that the troubles increased, but without an adverse effect on the 144,000.

More and more of the nominal Christians who were not taken to Heaven by Jesus made decisions to truly accept Jesus as Lord and Savior. This cost them dearly as the world grew intolerant of true Christians and blamed them for the world's misfortunes. Many were martyred and died for their faith. Still, most of the Jews of Israel did not accept the truth of the teaching that Jesus was the Messiah.

## Satan Enters Into His False Christ

Meanwhile, back in Christoph's headquarters, as Christoph sat in his office in the company of Musa, the unseen Satan entered into Christoph. As Satan entered into Christoph, his visage began to change to sharper features and a visible aura of Satanic power enveloped Christoph. Satan then spoke through Christoph. "I am god and you Christoph are my son." Turning to Musa, he continued, "You Musa will be my prophet! Stretch out your hands and receive my power!" As Musa gladly extended his open hands toward Christoph, a surge of power went from the satanically possessed Christoph to Musa.

It was three and a half years since Christoph had established peace in the Middle East. The now Satanically possessed Christoph went to Israel with Musa. Once again, Christoph was mobbed by adoring throngs, grateful for the Pax Christoph, and the restoration of Temple worship. But instead of going to the Knesset for a political speech, Christoph went to the new Temple. There he strode into the holy section and with cameras broadcasting his every move and word, Christoph sat down in a chair ceremonially intended for the Messiah and announced that he, Christoph, was their god. He was uniting all of the religions of the world to recognize him as god, and Musa as his high priest and prophet.

The Jewish priests screamed and ran from the Temple, as did the other worshippers. However, Christoph would not tolerate disobedience to him or to Musa. Not only were the new believers in Jesus hunted and killed, but the Jewish people that refused to worship Christoph were also put to death.

## A Time of Great Trouble

God began to judge the world for rejecting His gift of His Son, Jesus. He dispatched a series of angels to unleash the judgment of His wrath on a world that continued to reject Jesus. The first angel unleashed blood red hailstones that fell around the world accompanied by brush fires that destroyed crops, burned cities, and left the air heavy with smoke and soot. The grassy plains in the continents were burnt up so that there was no forage for animals. Also, a third of the trees in the world combusted and burned.

The second angel directed a comet from the frozen bodies in the Oort cloud at the edge of the solar system to hurl toward the earth. It was a new comet that had not visited the interior of the solar system before. Comet watchers determined that it was on track to strike the earth. Fearing a mass extinction event, Christoph arranged for missiles with nuclear warheads to intercept the comet. Christoph hoped to divert the comet or change its speed so that it would miss the earth. That tactic only partially succeeded. The comet broke into several pieces, some of which would indeed miss earth, but the main body of the comet was still on track to strike the earth.

When the impact finally came the comet burned brightly as it entered earth's atmosphere and hit the Atlantic Ocean with the force of many nuclear blasts. Immediately, a tsunami spread around the world causing a third of the world's ocean going shipping to be swamped and go down. The tsunami washed over low lying islands killing many, and smashed into the shores of the Americas, Europe, Africa, and the countries around the Mediterranean Sea. The frozen deep space ice from the comet turned the ocean waters toxic and caused a major bloom of a red tide that, together with the toxic water, killed a third of the fish in the sea, devastating fisheries and eliminating yet another source of food.

The third angel directed yet an additional comet toward the earth. That comet fell on the landmass of Eurasia and poisoned the water table, underground natural aquifers, and the rivers. Many people died from drinking the poisoned fresh water sources.

God summoned a fourth angel to deliver another form of God's judgment. The tectonic plates around the world shifted because of the comet impacts, prompting major volcanic eruptions. So much particulate matter of dust and gas was released into the atmosphere, and hung there, that the luminosity of the sun, moon, and stars was reduced by a third from the vantage point of people on earth. That made it colder and darker.

When the fifth angel stepped up, he heaved a fallen angel down to earth. That fallen angel opened a portal to the bottomless pit. Smoke came out that made it even darker and colder. In addition, demonic tormenting locusts with scorpion stinging tails came forth. These flying creatures covered the earth for five months, but were only able to sting and torment those who still refused to acknowledge Jesus. They did not kill, but the pain of their stings was so great that people wished they were dead. A great fallen angel also came through the portal and served as the general for the demonic creatures. There were so many of the demonic tormenting creatures that the sound of their wings was ear piercing in its loudness.

The sixth angel stepped forth and released four fallen angels of war. Those fallen angels incited the movement of an army of 200 million human soldiers. As this army moved and fired its weapons, a third of humanity was killed. However, the surviving population did not turn to God. Instead, they persisted in all of their evil ways including worshiping idols of their making that were not gods.

## The Mystery of God Finished

When the seventh angel presented himself he made a notable sound. His sounding marked a singular point in time in which the mystery of God, that hiatus that was kept from the Old Testament prophets, was finished. The Jews were now at center stage as the end of the age of the non-Jewish church and of earth's domination by pagan nations was ended.

The ministry of the two witnesses, Enoch and Elijah, came to an end when Christoph and his forces were finally able to kill them. Their bodies laid in the street of the old city of Jerusalem, uncovered and unburied for three days. There was a global celebration with 24-hour satellite TV coverage of their dead bodies and of people mocking, cheering, and celebrating. But, after three and a half days, with cameras trained on them, God sent life back into their bodies. Enoch and Elijah stood up, looked toward Heaven and, in response to a voice from above telling them, "Come up here!" the two ascended in a shining cloud of the glory of God before the now silenced revelers and the global TV audience. The ascension of Enoch and Elijah was accompanied by the simultaneous ascension of the 144,000 Jewish evangelists from Jerusalem and wherever else they were in the world.

Immediately after Enoch and Elijah ascended to Heaven, there was a great earthquake. Thousands died in Jerusalem. Only the handful of surviving new Christians remained as witnesses to Jesus's Lordship. The remainder of the Jewish people still did not recognize Jesus as their Messiah.

Christoph remained in Jerusalem holding court in the Temple, where he continued to insist on being worshipped as god. An assassination attempt was made on his life and Christoph received what appeared to be a mortal blow nearly severing his head from his shoulders. With cameras on him and the world watching by television, Musa exercised his own satanic powers over Christoph, and Christoph was healed. The world marveled at what transpired and, in unison, worshipped Christoph as god. For his part, the infuriated Christoph redoubled efforts to kill any who said Jesus was Lord and he also sought to exterminate the Jewish people.

Christoph cursed the God of the Christians and Jews and went after them. Fugitives were unable to buy food or shelter and were tracked by communications systems. Christoph succeeded in wiping out the remaining Christians. They all met a martyr's death. Without a human witness in the earth to appeal to people to turn to God, something unique happened.

Although God had chosen to use ordinary people to preach the good news, He was still unwilling to let anyone die and go to hell if by any means they could be convinced to seek God and receive Jesus. In one last effort to save any who would give heed, God sent an angel to preach the gospel message of forgiveness of sin and salvation through the blood of Jesus. The angel flew in the sky. The angel was visible and audible around the world warning that the judgment of God was coming and pleaded with people to turn to God the creator and giver of His Son for earth's salvation.

Musa began to perform ever greater miracles. Like Enoch and Elijah, he made fire seem to come down out of the sky. After healing Christoph and bringing him back to life, Musa introduced what appeared to be an inanimate, but otherwise exact copy of Christoph. It was initially as stiff as a mannequin. It had no sign of life, although it looked lifelike. Musa, by his demonstration of dark arts with demonic assistance, caused the copy of Christoph to speak, move about freely, and interact to anyone's questioning. It did this through artificial intelligence that had been engineered into it, but was also a modern tool of divination. Behind the copy of Christoph was an unseen demon spirit working in concert with Musa. People marveled at the similarity of the copy to Christoph and its abilities. Musa directed that in worshiping Christoph, when Christoph was not there himself, people were to worship the copy, and warned that Christoph's all Seeing Eye would see them and take note of who complied and who didn't.

Christoph tightened his domination over finances and food by requiring everyone to receive radio-frequency identification implants in the forehead or hand that showed they were in the system of Christoph and worshipped him as god and were entitled to the benefits of food and other commodities. The implants also enabled continuous tracking of each person through the wireless internet.[26]

At the same time, another angel appeared in the sky warning that anyone who worshipped Christoph or his copy or who took the radio-frequency identification implants of Christoph in their forehead or hand would be subject to the full wrath of God immediately, and be tormented in hell for eternity.

---

[26] The internet itself is the world wide web or www. In the Hebrew alphabet, letters double as numbers and the number for the equivalent sound of w is 6. Moreover, the name of the man of sin or antichrist will be interpreted as the number 666, or six hundred sixty-six.

After the church was taken away by Jesus, Enoch and Elijah were killed, revived, and ascended, the 144,000 Jewish evangelists ascended, and the martyrdom of late believers completed, there was nothing to prevent the full wrath of God from being unleashed on the earth. God still intended to save a portion of the Jewish people, although the Jews that were still alive did not recognize Jesus as Messiah. Nevertheless, God, through His angels, preserved a portion of them from complete extermination by Christoph.

At God's command, seven more angels stepped forth with judgments of the wrath of God on the stubborn humanity that continued to reject Jesus as Lord. The first angel caused painful sores to afflict the bodies of those who worshipped Christoph or his copy. The second angel touched the waters of the oceans and seas so that the water became like coagulated blood with no oxygen. This caused every remaining living creature in the oceans and seas to die.

The third angel executed God's judgment on the sources of fresh water in the rivers and lakes. Just as Moses had done with Egypt, the fresh waters became red like blood and coagulated. The fourth angel caused a mammoth solar flare to shoot out from the sun. The excessive heat and radiation caused painful sunburn, skin cancers, and fires. Yet people chose to curse God rather than worship Him. The fifth angel executed a judgment that had been used by Moses. He caused black out darkness to envelop the headquarters of Christoph's empire. Still people cursed God.

The sixth angel dried up the Euphrates River, clearing the way for an army of 200 million soldiers to easily come into the region and advance. Satan spoke and his words were echoed by Christoph and Musa, so that three special fallen spirits were released with the assignment of bringing the armies of the world together at Megiddo. Those three spirits spoke into the minds of world leaders and convinced them to mobilize and meet at Megiddo in Israel. Their choice to heed the allure of those evil spirts would prove to be a fateful decision causing them to mass at Megiddo, the Valley of Decision.

The 200-million-man army from the east crossed the dried-up Euphrates and entered Israel. They joined with Christoph's forces and other militaries in the valley of Megiddo as the satanically possessed Christoph dared to take on God and to complete the extermination of the Jews. Satan's intent was to negate God's promise to Abraham and his descendants that the special land known as the holy land would be theirs to inherit. Christoph was assisted by all of the fallen angels and demon spirits under the command of Satan in this effort.

God sent an angel to warn the remaining Jewish people in Rome to flee that city just prior to the great battle. Rome was the symbolic capital of Christoph's United Europe, the heart of his empire. As such, it represented the global commerce of that system. It also was the center of the persecution of the early church and of the martyrdom of the apostles Peter and Paul along with tens of thousands of other believers in the first two centuries after the death and resurrection of Jesus. Rome's emissaries carried out the execution of Jesus and massacred Jews when Rome's legions burned, looted, and totally ripped apart the Temple in Jerusalem a generation later. The devastation was so complete that not even one stone of the Temple was left standing on top of another, just as Jesus had prophesied.

The time had come for God to unleash His judgment and wrath on Rome and the rebellious world system it represented. Rome had also become the seat of the corrupted world church. It was a corruption that became complete after Jesus came for the true church. What was left was corrupted further by Christoph and used to lead an ecumenical, one world -- one god religion. When Christoph no longer needed this ecumenical religion, it was cast aside. He then presented himself as the one god and demanded that he be worshipped. The destruction of what had been known as the eternal city was swift and complete.

The seventh angel unleashed a global earthquake. The earthquake was another demonstration of the wrath of God. The ground on every continent shook causing buildings, bridges, and other structures in major cities around the world to collapse on themselves. The tectonic plates moved all over the crust of earth such that up thrust mountain ranges suddenly disappeared as they returned to plains. Islands that were the peaks of undersea mountains also disappeared under the ocean as those features also flattened out. Jerusalem itself was pulled into three parts as the earth's surface ripped apart and moved. All of this was accompanied by tremendous lightning storms as the earth's magnetic properties interacted with the electrical charges in the atmosphere, and solar ionization from the increased activity of the sun. In addition, huge hail stones fell around the world adding to the carnage. People only cursed God all the more for what was happening.

The angels and spirits of redeemed humanity in Heaven began to rejoice that God's judgment had come on the world system that had rejected the Son of God and killed His saints. The spirits and transformed bodies of those who were martyred after Jesus came for the church had ascended to Heaven where Jesus put on an elaborate celebration for all of His saints.

The saints of all the ages, who were made righteous by the blood of Jesus, the Lamb of God, were given dazzling white garments of God's glory. They all shouted, "Alleluia! The Lord God omnipotent reigns! Let's celebrate and give Him honor because the marriage of the Lamb is finally here, and we His bride have been made acceptable to Him." Jesus, as a beaming bridegroom, flowed among the hundreds of millions of the redeemed who made up the bride of Christ. There was singing and dancing, and cheers as Jesus loved them and they expressed their love in return. The angels observed, and sang their own songs out of joy for the Son whom they too loved.

# Chapter 27 Jesus the Messiah Returns

*And he shall send Jesus Christ, which before was
preached unto you: Whom the heaven must receive until
the times of restitution of all things, which God hath
spoken by the mouth of all his holy prophets since the
world began. Acts 3:20-21*

The marriage banquet of the Lamb of God and the
redeemed saints was glorious, but it was not the end of
God's work. The Son moved on to unfinished business on
the earth.[27] Suddenly, over Megiddo, a great portal

---

[27] Additional scriptures are provided here for context.

And then shall appear the sign of the Son of man in heaven:
and then shall all the tribes of the earth mourn, and they shall see the
Son of man coming in the clouds of heaven with power and great
glory. Matthew 24:30

For the Lord himself shall descend from heaven with a shout,
with the voice of the archangel, and with the trump of God: and the
dead in Christ shall rise first. 1 Thessalonians 4:16

But in the days of the voice of the seventh angel, when he
shall begin to sound, the mystery of God should be finished, as he
hath declared to his servants the prophets. Revelation 10:7

And he laid hold on the dragon, that old serpent, which is the
Devil, and Satan, and bound him a thousand years, And cast him into
the bottomless pit, and shut him up, and set a seal upon him, that he
should deceive the nations no more, till the thousand years should be
fulfilled: and after that he must be loosed a little season. Revelation
20:2-3

Why do the heathen rage, and the people imagine a vain
thing? The kings of the earth set themselves, and the rulers take
counsel together, against the LORD, and against his anointed, saying,
Let us break their bands asunder, and cast away their cords from us.
Psalm 2:1-3

opened from the physical dimension to the dimension of the spirit. Jesus appeared in a way He had not been seen before. He appeared as the Great King of Kings and head of the armies of loyal angels, and with them the redeemed saints. The saints, who were corporately the Bride of Christ, were given the honor of participating in this battle. Jesus was a fierce warrior. He wore a dazzling crown and his garment appeared as if it had been dipped in blood in its lower quarters. It was the blood of Jesus mixed with the blood of His faithful martyrs. All of the angels with Jesus were mounted on spirit steeds just like the one Jesus was mounted upon.

## The Return of the King of Glory

Jesus descended to the Mount of Olives outside of the old city of Jerusalem while the two opposing forces faced each other. As He dismounted from His steed, as soon as His feet touched the ground at the Mount of Olives, the mountain split. One portion moved toward the Mediterranean Sea and the other in the opposite direction creating a very large valley. As the mountain moved it also shirred. Half of it moved northward and the other half moved southward.

Some of the angels with King Jesus ushered the Jews that were still alive into the valley that was created, just as angels had removed Lot and his family from Sodom and Gomorrah before the destruction of those cities. It was a place of shelter for them and angels stood guard over them forming a protective canopy while King Jesus returned to take up His place at the head of His combined army of loyal angels and of the redeemed and transformed saints. Then the light changed so that it was neither bright day nor dark night.

Satan and his angels dared to attempt an attack on the Lord by massing their formidable power, but the Son spoke. Out of His mouth came judgment that instantly killed all of the armies of humankind that had been gathered and, with them, also defeated the fallen angels and demons.

Christoph and Musa were thrown alive into the lake of fire while a powerful angel took Satan prisoner and bound him with a special chain from which he could not escape. Satan no longer appeared as a beautiful Archangel, but rather as an ugly serpentine dragon. The angel then threw Satan and his fallen angels and demons into the bottomless pit and sealed it up.

## The Messiah Recognized and Worshipped

The residue of the Jewish people saw what happened. Their spiritual eyes were finally opened. They both cried and were happy at the same time. They cried because they realized that they and their ancestors had rejected the Messiah and put Him to death when He first came to visit them as a man. But they also rejoiced saying, "Blessed is He who comes in the name of Yahweh!" As their conquering king descended from the slaughter at Megiddo and moved among the remnant of remaining Jews that were alive in Israel, they looked at His hands and asked, "Why do You have these wounds in your hands?"

Jesus replied, "These are the wounds I received at the hands of My own people."

The surviving Jews cried for shame and repentance calling out, "Yeshua! Yeshua!"

The Son responded "I hear you. You are My people!"

To which the Jews responded "Yahweh Yeshua is our God!"

Jesus set up a place of judgment to deal with the people from the nations of the world that remained and were still alive. Not all that hated God and the Jews had been in Megiddo when that decisive battle was fought, so the judgment was a time of reckoning as Jesus began to rule on earth with an iron hand.

The angels assisted Jesus in transitioning the earth to His rule. The angels went through the world and separated those that were wicked and had given allegiance to Satan, Christoph, and Musa. Those who had supported the program of the ethnic cleansing of the Jews on one hand were separated from those that resisted Christoph and his mark and who tried to harbor those Jews that were in their territories.

## Judgment Before the Throne

The angels translocated the surviving people in groups to come before King Jesus. The ones considered worthy were placed to the right of Jesus and the wicked ones to His left. Jesus spoke in a voice that could be heard audibly and in the minds of all those He addressed. He said to those placed at His right hand, "Come, you who are blessed by My Father. You can take part in the kingdom that was planned by the Godhead from the very beginning of the world. You may inherit this kingdom of mine because when I was hungry, you gave Me something to eat. When I was thirsty, you gave Me something to drink. When I was a foreigner in your lands, you took Me in. When I was naked, you provided clothing for Me. When I was sick, you visited Me. When I was imprisoned, you came to see about me."

Those on the right of King Jesus were a bit puzzled and asked, "When did we ever do these things for You? When did we ever see You hungry, and fed You, or thirsty and gave You something to drink, or a foreigner and took You in, or naked and provided clothing and blankets for You, or sick or in prison and came to Your aid?"

King Jesus told them, "To the extent that you did so for the very least of My Jewish family, you did it for Me."

Then, turning to the wicked ones that the angels placed before King Jesus on His left, Jesus said, "Away from Me you evil doers! You are cursed! Take your place in the eternal fires of punishment that were prepared for the devil and his angels, because when I was hungry, you didn't give Me anything to eat. When I was thirsty, you didn't give Me anything to drink. When I was a foreigner in your lands, you wouldn't take Me in. When I was naked, you wouldn't provide clothing for Me. When I was sick or in prison, you didn't think about visiting Me."

But those on the left, which included religious leaders and nations that had considered themselves to be Christian protested and said, "But Lord, when did we ever see You hungry or thirsty, or an immigrant, or naked, or sick, or in prison, and failed to come to Your aid?"

King Jesus told them, "I tell you most certainly, to the extent that you did not do it for one of the least of these of My Jewish family, you didn't do it for Me."

Then the super religious among them, wishing to justify themselves, protested further. They said, "But Lord, Lord, hold on! This isn't fair! We were working for You! We prophesied in Your name and even cast out demons and did many humanitarian acts in Your name!"

However, King Jesus passed His judgment on them saying, "I never recognized you as one of Mine. Away with you, you pack of evil doers!" With that the angels assisting King Jesus threw the groups on His left alive into the fires of hell, but those on the right that were considered worthy by King Jesus were permitted to be part of the thousand-year rule of King Jesus on earth.

# Chapter 28 One Family and a Glorious Bride

*For this cause I bow my knees unto the Father of our Lord Jesus Christ, of whom the whole family in heaven and earth is named. Ephesians 3:14-15*

Much had been accomplished to reconcile humanity back to fellowship with God, but one final test remained.[28] Jesus set up his headquarters on earth in

---

[28] Additional scriptures are provided here for context.

That in the dispensation of the fullness of times he might gather together in one all things in Christ, both which are in heaven, and which are on earth; even in him. Ephesians 1:10

Who being the brightness of his glory, and the express image of his person, and upholding all things by the word of his power, when he had by himself purged our sins, sat down on the right hand of the Majesty on high. Hebrews 1:3

The kingdom of heaven is like unto a certain king, which made a marriage for his son. Matthew 22:2

And there came unto me one of the seven angels which had the seven vials full of the seven last plagues, and talked with me, saying, Come hither, I will shew thee the bride, the Lamb's wife. Revelation 21:9

Let us be glad and rejoice, and give honour to him: for the marriage of the Lamb is come, and his wife hath made herself ready. And to her was granted that she should be arrayed in fine linen, clean and white: for the fine linen is the righteousness of saints. Revelation 19:7-8

And he said unto him, Well, thou good servant: because thou hast been faithful in a very little, have thou authority over ten cities. Luke 19:17

And they sung a new song, saying, Thou art worthy to take the book, and to open the seals thereof: for thou wast slain, and hast redeemed us to God by thy blood out of every kindred, and tongue,

Jerusalem. The angels went about restoring the city and the earth. The redeemed saints that were the bride of Christ assisted Jesus in administering Israel and the rest of the world serving as kings and priests to God and assisted by the angels. The redeemed saints were given different levels of authority based on the lives they led while on

---

and people, and nation; And hast made us unto our God kings and priests: and we shall reign on the earth. Revelation 5:9-10

And hath raised us up together, and made us sit together in heavenly places in Christ Jesus: That in the ages to come he might shew the exceeding riches of his grace in his kindness toward us through Christ Jesus. Ephesians 2:6-7

But as it is written, Eye hath not seen, nor ear heard, neither have entered into the heart of man, the things which God hath prepared for them that love him. 1 Corinthians 2:9

Nevertheless we, according to his promise, look for new heavens and a new earth, wherein dwelleth righteousness. 2 Peter 3:13

And I John saw the holy city, new Jerusalem, coming down from God out of heaven, prepared as a bride adorned for her husband. And I heard a great voice out of heaven saying, Behold, the tabernacle of God is with men, and he will dwell with them, and they shall be his people, and God himself shall be with them, and be their God. And God shall wipe away all tears from their eyes; and there shall be no more death, neither sorrow, nor crying, neither shall there be any more pain: for the former things are passed away. Revelation 21:2-4

A new heart also will I give you, and a new spirit will I put within you: and I will take away the stony heart out of your flesh, and I will give you an heart of flesh. Ezekiel 36:26

The LORD hath taken away thy judgments, he hath cast out thine enemy: the king of Israel, even the LORD, is in the midst of thee: thou shalt not see evil any more. In that day it shall be said to Jerusalem, Fear thou not: and to Zion, Let not thine hands be slack. The LORD thy God in the midst of thee is mighty; he will save, he will rejoice over thee with joy; he will rest in his love, he will joy over thee with singing. Zephaniah 3:15-17

earth. Some were made viceroys and others were subordinate under them.

Jesus ruled as the absolute authority that He was. Not everyone had died under the judgements of God. Nations continued to exist. Because Satan and his fallen angels and demons were quarantined in the bottomless pit, they could not motivate the humans that remained on the earth to rebel or sin. Nevertheless, of their own volition, some continued to rebel against the rule of God. If a nation's representatives refused to come to Jerusalem and honor the Son of God and be at peace with Israel, then Jesus would judge that nation by withholding rain and harvests.

People continued to procreate, have children, and raise families, but there was no longer any infant mortality. People lived to be at least 100 years old. If they still persisted in stubbornness or trying to do evil, then they would die. The rest of the people continued to live without dying. In time, the earth was at peace and once again resembled the Garden of Eden, a paradise on earth.

## Satan's Last Stand

After a thousand years of the benevolent, but iron rule of the Son of God, Satan and his hordes were temporarily released from their quarantine in the bottomless pit. Satan and his cohort used their freedom to once again deceive the world. They convinced many that it was better to be self-reliant and rule themselves rather than be under the rule of the Son.

Satan marshalled a great army of the rebellious to descend on Israel to exterminate the Jews and overthrow the Son of God. But God had fire come down from the skies and destroyed those armies as they surrounded Israel. Then for a final time, Satan was thrown into the lake of fire to join Christoph and Musa in unending torment. The spirits of the unregenerate dead were then brought before the Son sitting on a great white throne. There they were judged and consigned to hell and torment for eternity together with the fallen angels and demons. Both I, Benelroi, and the other watchers, opened our books that recorded their deeds over the millennia and they were judged out of those books.

After the wicked were judged, I and the other watchers destroyed our books that recorded the deeds of the wicked. I only kept those books that recorded the greatness of God and His deeds comprising the great Epic of God. Those books included the beginning of all creation, the separation out of the loyal angels, the creation of humankind, the plan and its implementation for the redemption of humankind by the blood of the Lamb of God, the re-consecration of Heaven, the joyful marriage supper of the Lamb of God with the Bride of Christ, the final defeat and quarantine in hell of Satan and those that followed him, the new universe and earth, and the presentation of the New Jerusalem.

After the final temptation that occurred when Satan was released from the bottomless pit, people made a choice to side with Satan in his rebellion or to be true to Jesus. With Satan, fallen angels, demons, and the spirits of rebellious humanity out of the way forever, God made a supernatural change in the hearts of those people who had made Him their choice. God forever changed their hearts to confirm the choice they had made. God clothed each of them with a visible aura of the glory light of God, just as Adam and Eve had experienced before they sinned.

They and their progeny would forevermore be unwilling and unable to sin, rebel, or stray. There was no more sickness or death. Humanity continued to live as humans and multiply in numbers.

In a new creative move, God changed the earth. The earth became all landmass and everything was fertile. There were no deserts or arid land. There were no more oceans or salt water. Springs were fresh and, as in the early days of the first earth, there was no rain, storms, or floods. Plant life was nurtured by a mist that would come up from the ground providing all that was needed. This opened up a great expansion of habitable areas for the population that now continued to increase without sickness, death, or war.

As it was in the original Garden of Eden, people became vegetarians again. Nothing would ever be killed again, because death was defeated and had no place in God's kingdom. Then God remade the universe around the earth. The old universe parted and disappeared with a great noise from the transformation of all of that mass and energy. The new universe was more immense than the one it replaced. Everything in the new universe was prefect, in balance, unmarred, and non-toxic. It was created to be inhabited.

As a gift to the new Temple that the Son constructed in Jerusalem together with the angels, the ark of the covenant, with the tablets of stone inside bearing the ten commandments, was revealed and donated by its custodians in Ethiopia where it had been guarded in obscurity for centuries.

As the earth's population increased, overtime, colonies moved from earth to other star systems and planets. They had no need of space ships. They moved, en masse, and were translocated at the speed of thought, together with the things they needed to live and develop. Each new planet colonized was presided over by one of the redeemed saints who was viceroy, king, and priest. Unlike Lucifer, who corrupted the original earth and led the pre-Adamic race astray, the redeemed were faithful brides of Christ. In their love for God and in humility, they led their charges in worship of God and the enjoyment of happy lives.

Angels continued to assist humankind wherever they were located. The eyes of all people were also opened to see into the spirit realm so that the angels were no longer invisible to humans.

The colonists to the new worlds were not in exile there. They could visit colonies on other planets in other star systems. They could also visit earth and the New Jerusalem. The Son Himself, being unlimited and omnipresent, would visit with His children on each world they inhabited. He was able to do so simultaneously and in unique interactions.

Earth remained central, because it provided the seeds used on the other planets to grow what was needed. In addition, God made King David His viceroy in Jerusalem on earth. Jerusalem continued to receive visitors.

## The New Jerusalem

God created a New Jerusalem of planetary size, but of the spiritual dimension. The New Jerusalem came down from Heaven and was the place where Jesus lived with the redeemed saints when those saints were not out administering the people over whom they had been given authority. It was cubic in shape and had twelve levels. It was in fact a massive city. Although it was in the spiritual dimension, it could be seen from earth, but was suspended above earth centered above the earthly Jerusalem. Each of the redeemed saints had a grand residence there and they all worshipped the Son of God. The Son had His throne there and from it flowed a river. On the banks of that river on each side were the trees of life. The trees bore unique fruits and gave up their renewable leaves to the redeemed saints who then dispensed them to the members of humanity. The flesh and blood humans periodically needed to eat the leaves of the tree of life in order to live continuously in their constantly rejuvenated physical bodies.

Using the earthly Jerusalem as a jumping off point, people could visit in the New Jerusalem in the spirit. It was through the Son that the Godhead carried on restored fellowship with humanity.

## The Family of God with Him Forever

At last, God's kingdom of angels, redeemed transformed saints, and humans, was in fellowship with Him and would remain so forever. They all loved Him and He loved them as He had from the beginning. That blissful state would never change or be threatened again. God would no longer experience the emotions of sadness, disappointment, heartbreak, or anger. All rebel spirits were quarantined forever in hell. God would never again be rejected and have His heart broken by humankind or angels. Everyone in His kingdom, in both the spiritual and physical dimensions, had chosen God, when tested, in response to His great love.

I, Benelroi, remained in my role as principal watcher for the earth. We watchers never again had to record or report to the Godhead any unpleasant news. It was our pleasure to report that God's kingdom and family continued to grow greater and greater to the glory of God.

God shouted for joy, sang, and danced for joy over His big faithful, loving family. Finally, nothing hindered God from being able to enjoy a relationship of intimate fellowship with all in His kingdom. The angels, the redeemed transformed saints, and humankind all shouted, sang, and danced for joy along with their wonderful loving God in a mutual lovefest through eternity without end.

## Endorsements

*It is a great pleasure for me to write an endorsement for the book "The Epic of God," for my dear friend, Louis McCall. My late husband, Mark, and I came to know Louis as a friend and supporter during his time in Calcutta (now Kolkata), India in the 1980s. Although he was a Consul at the American Consulate General at that time, he was an active and faithful participant in our mission. His living testimony, including his public and private witness, was of one who was not ashamed of the gospel. His friendship and interest in our mission Calcutta Mercy has endured.*

*Louis' book, The Epic of God, provides a unique speculative view into the entire sweep of God's history and future in relation to the people He created and loved. God loved the people so much that He sent His own Son to pay the price of their sin and redeem them back to an unhindered relationship with Himself. Just as our Lord Jesus used parables to reach His audiences, Louis skillfully uses this modern parable, closely aligned with scripture, to open the eyes of the reader to the nature of God and His unfailing love toward the human race. The Epic of God helps the reader to understand the heart of God and His divine struggle to win wayward people and nations back to Himself. God persevered despite the oftentimes unfaithfulness of people and despite the efforts of the devil, and his fallen cohort of evil angels and demons, to lure them from God in order to enslave them. I believe this book will be a source of understanding, revelation, and real blessing to each reader.*

*In this modern day of imaginary super heroes and false self-proclaimed saviors, I am sure this book will reveal the true hero and lover of our souls. I am thrilled that God has chosen a committed Christian such as Louis to tell this story in a way that it has not been told before. The Epic of God is perfect for our time. I heartily recommend it for your library of inspirational Christian literature.*

Rev. (Dr.) Huldah Buntain
President, Assemblies of God Mission
Calcutta, India

*The Epic of God masterfully and creatively unfolds the history of creation and the saga of its relationship with the Creator. McCall uses creative license to draw the reader into the story, giving the opportunity to ponder well-known events with a new and fresh perspective. You won't be able to put the book down as you find yourself wondering how a story that you've heard your whole life will end. Beyond the story-telling, though, you will feel as perhaps you've never felt before, the love of a Creator, who went to painstakingly great lengths to reunite with His creation. Don't just read this book. Join the story. Reflect on it. And, let it have its eternal impact on you.*

Harrison Wilder, President
The Wilder Foundation
Author of The Honor Cycle

*The "Epic of God" is a wonderfully written story drawn from the unique well-known writings found in the Bible. A biblical story only God, the creator of time and everything drawn in it, could create. The "Epic of God" may be a fictional story but its characterization is well narrated by a fictional Godly angel who brings it to life. This fictional creature of God delivers his visual accounts of each biblical personality and his review, which is the original biblical account, is the makings of the "Epic of God." Author, Louis McCall, beautifully wrote "Epic of God" as an enjoyable easy read. Louis McCall carries your read through each biblical book from Genesis to Revelation. He glides you into the sights and sounds before creation, through creation completion, into the lives of those who followed and worshiped God. This beautiful narration introduces you to whom Lucifer was before he became Satan in Genesis, his never ending battles against God, to his final demise in Revelation. I recommend you acquire your copy of "Epic of God." You need to read for yourself how this fictional story carries you through the biblical accounts of the Bible. You'll discover the complete biblical story through this easy to understand read. The "Epic of God" just might be the read that sparks your desire to read God's book, the Holy Bible. I congratulate you, Louis McCall, your book, "Epic of God," is well done. Yes! Well done indeed!*

Cheryl L. Davis
Author of many Christian books

*Louis has, very impassionately, revealed his deep and concise understanding of Biblical norms while conscientiously challenging people to think out of the box*

*about stories which certainly allow for a bit of license.
What a masterpiece of a must-read and totally absorbing
Genesis to Revelation narrative. This should also be made
into an epic Biblical television series.*

Philip DeVries, Chairman
Life Enterprises
George, Western Cape
Republic of South Africa

*It is a great honor to have the opportunity to write
an endorsement for Dr. Louis McCall's book, "The Epic
of God." My name is Winston Broomes, Jr. I am the
son of the first Missionaries from the Caribbean to Africa,
Apostles Drs. Winston, Sr. and Gloria Broomes. They
arrived in Africa in 1976, and we all had the privilege of
meeting Dr. McCall who was at the time, the U.S. Vice
Consul to Zambia.*

*Many thanks are owed to Dr. McCall for teaching
my dad how to play lawn tennis, a sport that my dad
would later teach me and we played for many decades.
Dr. McCall not only served his country more importantly,
he served God. One of the first churches that my parents
planted was located in Ngombe, Lusaka. Dr. McCall and
Rev. Winston Siwale, gave leadership to that church
plant.*

*Dr. McCall could often be found at the altar. He
worked closely with Apostle Dr. Winston Broomes in the
Deliverance Ministry. Together they witnessed many
lives being transformed and delivered through the power
of Jesus in Zambia.*

*In his book, "The Epic of God," Dr. Louis McCall
takes us on an adventure through the Bible. This book*

*will inspire you as you take a ride through the eyes of Benelroi. You will find out who that is. Sit back and enjoy the ride. You will gain an understanding of the Epic of God from Genesis to Revelation. This book will touch your life. I pray God's blessings upon Dr. Louis McCall and this book.*

Rev. Winston Broomes, Jr., Senior Pastor
Grace Assembly of God
Atlantic City, New Jersey

*I first met Dr. Louis McCall while serving with the Pentecostal Assemblies of Canada as the Field Secretary's Representative in Zambia. We lived in the capital city, Lusaka, where Louis was employed at the American Embassy as the Vice Consul. We were introduced after a Sunday morning service at Northmead Assembly on October 24th, 1976. A bond of friendship began and grew over time.*

*Dr. McCall was a faithful servant of the Lord with a deep desire to share God's love and the truth of the Gospel in all circumstances. We enjoyed times of fellowship in both his home and ours. When a plot of land was allocated for us to build a new church at N'gombe Township, Louis was there to help. He purchased necessary materials and transported them to the building site. Whatever Dr. McCall did, he did with all his might, to extend God's Kingdom and bring glory to His Name. Dr. McCall taught a Bible Study in both his home church and one of the compound churches. His deep understanding of God's Word enabled him to teach biblical truths so they were easily understood by those* with a desire to learn, regardless of their level of education.

What I find interesting and enjoyable about "The Epic of God" is how Louis recounts Biblical stories and proposes details where scripture is silent. Though this book is speculative fiction, I appreciate that he maintains the truth of God's Word when he retells Biblical stories. Louis is a man of vision and the Word, so we know "The Epic of God" will be an exciting and thought-provoking read. We unreservedly recommend Dr. McCall as a writer and as a person, as a humble man of God.

Robert Seaboyer
London, Ontario
Canada

Dr. Louis McCall's life journey is encouraging, inspiring, and exciting. Dr. McCall takes us on an encouraging, inspiring, and exciting journey in The Epic of God. His depiction of getting to know God through lenses different than what we experience everyday challenges us to celebrate the vastness of God. In The Epic of God, Dr. McCall captures his heart for the truth and the power of the scriptures.

Marion Mason
Echostage Campus Pastor
National Community Church
Washington, D.C.

www.ingramcontent.com/pod-product-compliance
Lightning Source LLC
Chambersburg PA
CBHW071153100726
47908CB00002B/361